The
Garden
of
Martyrs

ALSO BY MICHAEL C. WHITE

Dream of Wolves

The Blind Side of the Heart

A Brother's Blood

The
Garden
of
Martyrs

Michael C. White

St. Martin's Griffin
New York

www.stmartins.com

Library of Congress Cataloging-in-Publication Data

White, Michael C.
     The garden of martyrs / Michael C. White.
          p. cm.
     ISBN 0-312-32208-9 (hc)
     ISBN 0-312-32209-7 (pbk)
     ISBN 978-0312-32209-0
     1. Daley, Dominic, d. 1806—Fiction. 2. Halligan, James—Fiction.
3. Travelers—Crimes against—Fiction. 4. Executions and executioners—
Fiction. 5. Irish Americans—Fiction. 6. Judicial error—Fiction. 7. Boston
(Mass.)—Fiction. 8. Prejudices—Fiction. 9. Immigrants—Fiction.
10. Catholics—Fiction. I. Title.

PS3573.H47447G37 2004
813'.54—dc22   2003070876

P1

To Karen,
again and always

Fear none of those things which thou shalt suffer: behold, the devil shall cast some of you into prison, that ye may be tried; and ye shall have tribulation ten days: be thou faithfull unto death, and I will give thee a crown of life.
—Revelation 2:10

PART I

The public attention in this vicinity has lately been much excited in the consequence of the great variety of contradictory reports which have been circulated respecting the horrid murder committed in this county. We have spared no pains to obtain as correct information on the subject as possible, and we believe the following statement may be relied on. On Sunday evening the 10th inst., the body of a person was discovered in the Chicopee River in Wilbraham, partly covered with stones. . . . A variety of circumstances rendering it probable that the murder was committed by two persons who were seen about 12 o'clock the preceding day, a number of persons went in pursuit of them, and on Tuesday about 10 o'clock in the morning, arrested them at Rye, about 30 miles from New York. . . . The two men who are supposed to have committed the murder were brought to the gaol in this town last Friday evening; and will probably be tried at the next Supreme Court. They declare themselves to be Irishmen.

—THE REPUBLICAN SPY, NOVEMBER 1805
NORTHAMPTON, MASSACHUSETTS

Commonwealth of Massachusetts
By his Excellency Caleb Strong, Governor

A PROCLAMATION

Whereas on the ninth day of November inst. at Wilbraham, in the county of Hampshire, a horrid MURDER was committed on one Marcus Lyon, who was there traveling on the highway and it is presumed that divers valuable articles were then and there feloniously taken from the said Lyon: I do hereby, in behalf of the Commonwealth, offer a reward of Five Hundred Dollars to any person or persons who shall apprehend him or them until he or they be convicted of the said murder. Given under my hand and seal of the said Commonwealth, this 12th day of November in the year of our Lord one thousand eight hundred and five, and in the thirtieth year of the Independence of the United States of America.

I have been long apprehensive that what we have above everything else to fear is Popery. As you value your precious civil liberty and everything you can call dear to you be on your guard against Popery. Much more is to be dreaded from the growth of Popery in America than from Stamp Acts or any other Act destructive of civil rights.

—SAMUEL ADAMS

ONE

A cold, pewter-gray rain fell like a scourge upon the city. It buffeted the ships in the harbor and swept unobstructed over Long and India wharves, strafing the recently closed business establishments on State Street and wreaking havoc in the crowded Faneuil Hall market. Winter-raw and relentless, the rain turned the cobbled thoroughfares slippery and the unpaved back lanes into dangerous quagmires. Horses lost their footing and pedestrians slogged through the mud and filth and sewage runoff. At the end of a long workday, the city hummed with weary activity. Hackney coaches conveyed well-to-do businessmen to Bowdoin Square or Beacon Hill, or to the Hancock Tavern for a late supper. Having closed their stores, shopkeepers were briskly making their way homeward. Wagons drawn by oxen carried farmers out to Dorchester after a day of selling milk or eggs or livestock at market, while now-empty carts pushed by fishmongers headed down toward the docks. Workers from the sail-duck factory or one of the many ropewalks moved with tired steps toward a home they hadn't seen since before dawn. Eager to get out of the driving rain, they pushed and jostled those they passed in the street.

Among them, a smallish figure dressed in black made his way along State Street, near the old Capitol building. He was concentrating on not losing the man he was following through the crowded streets and wasn't watching where he was going. As he made to cross the street, he very nearly stepped into the oncoming path of a large roan horse pulling a cart loaded with steaming dung.

"Hell, man, watch where you're going," the driver scolded him.

The small man looked up at the driver and mumbled an embarrassed apology.

The man swore, gave the reins a smart crack, and moved on down the street.

Little did the driver know that the darkly clad figure he had just cursed was a priest. Then again, in the gathering darkness and with the bulky capote hiding both his cassock and the large silver cross that dangled from his neck, he would not have been recognized as one. With his small stature and boyish features, he could easily have passed for a student returning to his lodgings after a day's reading at the Athenaeum. Besides, though the city could now boast some twenty-five thousand souls, its inhabitants were still unaccustomed to the sight of a priest. A papist clergyman remained a rarity even in Federalist Boston, which counted among its ministers only two Roman Catholic clerics. The small man recognized the advantage of blending in, his occupation hidden from the common view, particularly in certain questionable sections of the city, and especially of late.

The man was Jean Louis Anne Madeleine Lefebvre de Cheverus, thirty-eight years old, a French émigré who had fled the Revolution. He had come to America ten years earlier to assist Father Matignon in the founding of the Catholic mission in New England. Cheverus hardly looked like a man to found much of anything. He stood an inch under five feet tall, small-boned, as finely fashioned as a hummingbird, though in the past few years he had developed a slight paunch. He had smooth, pale skin, an unusually large head for his tiny body, and brooding, chestnut-colored eyes. His nose was long and thin, his small mouth usually pursed in an attitude of vaguely recalled regret. His once soft, delicate hands, now roughened from ceaseless physical labor, still retained the cautious poise of one used to conveying fragile things from one distant place to another.

With his short, slightly bowed legs, he had all he could do to keep pace with the larger figure he was following in the press of people and vehicles and horses. What was more, he'd recently been bedridden with an ague fever and was still feeling its effects. His body had been racked by chills and night sweats. He had lost weight, and his hands still trembled. It was only in the past day or so that he had begun to feel a slight improvement in his health and had felt well enough to sit up and take some broth. Even now, his face felt flushed and his head throbbed, and each time he took a breath of the icy evening air, the middle of his chest bloomed with bright petals of pain. *Mon Dieu*, he thought, believing it had been a mistake to come on this errand.

Earlier, they had passed Faneuil Market and were now making their way up Fish Street toward the city's North End, when he was forced to stop to catch his breath.

"A moment please, Tom," he called to the man.

Leaning against a hitching post, he thought perhaps he ought to turn back. Whatever it was Rose Daley wanted, it would simply have to wait until tomorrow, when Father Matignon would be able to go in his stead. He closed his eyes, took long, deep breaths, trying to regulate his breathing. Pain, and its attendant, fear, were merely the result of a lack of will, he liked to tell himself. A lazy mind given to distraction. Though he would be the first to admit he wasn't always able to conquer it, he firmly believed that it was only through an intimate knowledge of suffering that one truly knew God. Out of habit, he fingered the cross that hung beneath his cloak. He could feel the well-worn engraving, the delicate filigree of silver cool against his skin. "*Je suis là*," his mother's voice came to him suddenly from the darkness, "*mon petit chou*." She had called him that: her little cabbage. He was a boy once more, and they were kneeling together in the grand cathedral in his hometown of Mayenne. They were praying to a beautiful wooden statuette of the Blessed Virgin with the baby Jesus holding a bunch of grapes: Our Lady of the Miracles, it was called. He saw his mother's head bowed, the curve of her long, swan-like neck, the shapely hands holding her cross—the same one he now wore. A woman of delicate, fragile beauty.

Maman, he whispered to her.

Oui, mon petit chérubin. . . .

"Should I call for a coach, Father?" The priest opened his eyes, momentarily suspended between two worlds. The coarse countenance of

the Irishman replaced that of his mother. The man was leaning solicitously toward him, his face close. Cheverus could smell the fumes of the
raw poteen on his breath. The odor turned his stomach, and he had to
repress the urge to retch.

"No need," Cheverus replied. *Don't be sick,* he chided himself. He
knew it would be all over the parish by morning, how the little French
priest had vomited right there in the street, like some besotted wretch.

"Are ye sure, Father? I saw one just back a ways."

"No, Thomas. I can make it."

He hardly ever hired a carriage, even when he was called upon to
brave a nor'easter to make a sickbed visit up in Salem, fifteen miles away.
Father Matignon was always chastising him for endangering his ever-frail
health. To Cheverus, though, it was a matter both of frugality and of
pride. They were a poor parish, hardly able to buy votive candles or communion wine. The collection plate never provided nearly what was
needed, and every penny counted. Besides, there was his pride. Most of
his parishioners were, like this fellow Tom, newly arrived Irish immigrants, unlettered farmers and laborers and indentured servants, a hardy,
rough-hewn, peasant stock. He himself was so unlike them, coming from
such a different world, one of education and culture and refinement, a
world of certain luxuries. He knew what they thought of him, what they
said of him behind his back: that he was soft, weak, effeminate. And
worst of all, French. Once, just after he'd arrived in America, he had
overheard an Irish charwoman say to another, "Be glad I will when they
send us a real priest instead of that uppity little Frenchman." So he was
always trying hard to prove them wrong, that he wasn't weak, in body or
in spirit, that he was capable of bearing up under all the demands, all the
hardships of this wild, unforgiving land.

"I could carry you, Father," the big Irishman said to him.

Cheverus glanced at him, saw that he was serious. "Heavens, no. That
won't be necessary, Tom," he told the man, embarrassed. "Lead on. I will
follow."

The Irishman had come to the rectory behind Holy Cross Church an
hour earlier. When the parish housekeeper, Yvette, answered the knock

at the door, the man asked to speak to one of the two resident priests. Yvette was a thin, light-complected Negro from Guadeloupe, a former slave whom Father Matignon had brought north to Boston. She had a nasty, contentious disposition with everyone, except for Father Matignon. Even with Cheverus she could be brusque, impatient, sometimes rude. In her island patois, she informed the visitor that Pére Matignon was away in Quincy and not expected back until late, and that Pére Cheverus was confined to bed by illness.

"You must come back," the woman declared. "*Demain matin.*"

"But I need to see the priest," the Irishman stated emphatically.

"Father Cheverus seek. *Malade de la fièvre. Tu comprends?*"

"Please," the man begged. "It's important I speak to him."

"*Non, non.* You must come back. Now go," she commanded sternly.

They went back and forth, their voices growing heated. Cheverus could hear all this from his bedroom at the top of the stairs. He had awakened earlier from a feverish dream and had been lying in bed in the growing darkness of twilight. As a child he'd always been afraid of the dark. He would cry out in the night, and his mother would come to his room to reassure him, to sit by him and stroke his head. That's when he heard the voices below. They grew louder. When he could no longer ignore them, he got up, threw on his robe, and went downstairs.

"Go back to bed, Father," Yvette insisted in French.

"What is the matter?" he snapped at her in English. He usually spoke English with her as it tended to put her on the defensive, to give him an advantage. He was not normally a man to lose his temper, not even with Yvette, but his mind was restive, on other matters. His face was unshaven, the flesh around his eyes drawn and haggard. He had not been out of bed for days, and his skin had a sickly bluish hue to it.

"Forgive me, *mon Père*," the woman said, taken aback by his curt tone. She was closing the door on a figure standing just outside in the rain. "I handle it."

"*Who* is it? What does he want?"

"*Je ne sais pas,*" she said with a shrug. "I tell him Père Matignon is no here and you seek." Then she added contemptuously, "*Poivrot irlandais,*" and crossed herself. *Drunken Irishman.* Though a former slave, she nonetheless held the Irish in great disdain. A sentiment she had acquired since arriving in Boston.

"Well, have the poor man come in out of the rain," he said.

Yvette, reluctant to have her authority questioned, frowned but opened the door.

"Wipe you feet," she scolded the man as she showed him in. She took up a position behind the priest, arms folded sternly over her flat chest. The Irishman stood silently in the entryway, head down, nervously fingering his woolen workcap in his large hands. His greatcoat was soaked and his boots covered with mud. The rain had matted his thinning gray hair to his skull, and water dribbled down the lines in his face and fell to the floor. He was a man of impressive size, well over six feet, broad-shouldered, with a long horse-like face. A flatness between the eyes made the face seem all the more equine. It took Cheverus a moment to recognize Tom Daley.

"Good evening, Thomas," he said finally.

"Evenin', Father. Sorry for disturbin' you," he replied, wiping his face.

"Come and warm yourself by the fire."

"I think not. I'd get your floor all dirty," he said, glancing warily at the housekeeper.

"What may I do for you?"

"You didn't hear then?" he said, his face sagging with disappointment. The man looked down at the cap in his hands. "Word come today. From the attorney general."

"I see," Cheverus said. So that was why he was here. Confined to bed for the past fortnight, the priest had not read any of the city's papers, nor had he spoken to a soul save Yvette and of course the old abbé. Still, he should have guessed as soon as he saw the man here that it had something to do with his son.

"Have they set a trial date, Tom?"

He nodded. "They did, Father." The man's tongue flicked out and licked moisture from his upper lip. He didn't look the priest in the eye, almost as if he were embarrassed by all this. "It's to be on the twenty-second."

"Of April?"

"Aye."

"Why that's only . . ." but Cheverus had lost track of the day.

"Three days from tomorrow," the man replied for him.

"Three days! That is all the time they're giving them to prepare a defense?"

"That's what they tell us."

"Well," Cheverus said, running his hand over his unshaven jaw. His beard, reddish with streaks of gray in it, made him appear older, his mouth small and callous. The news, that they were at last going to try the two Irishmen after all these months, hardly came as a surprise. The case had been in all the Boston papers, the talk of the taverns and grog shops, the markets and coffee shops, even the pulpits. From everything he'd heard, Cheverus gathered the outcome of the trial, whenever it took place, would hardly be in doubt. But it surprised him that they were only being granted three days to prepare a defense. After all, the commonwealth had had months.

"How has Rose taken the news?"

"You know her, Father," the man replied. "She's a tough old bird. She's seen bad times before this."

"And Finola?"

"Ah. Not so good. She's got the little one to think about."

"Of course," the priest said. Finola Daley, whose husband, Dominic, was one of the accused, would come by the church with her baby in tow to light a candle and pray to the Blessed Virgin. Cheverus would come over and try to console her, tell her she must not lose hope, when in his heart he knew there was little cause for hope. After she left, he would find himself still thinking about her. "Please tell Finola that Dominic will be in my prayers."

"Thank you, Father," he said. "She'd like that. But you see . . . why I come is . . . well, Rose was wantin' to speak to you herself." The man looked up and his gaze met the priest's for the first time. His eyes were red, slick as glass beads soaked in lamp oil.

"Did she say what she wanted? Is it about your son's case?"

He hesitated in a way that told the priest he was about to lie. "I'm not sure, Father. She could tell you herself."

Some months previous, after she had made confession, Rose Daley had asked Cheverus if he would go out to the Northampton jail where her son was being held and hear his confession, too. He had told her that, while of course he would very much like to, he was then far too busy with his normal pastoral duties to spend the four days' coach ride out and back. Perhaps when he had a moment's free time, he'd told her. And then, just a few weeks before this, he had received a letter from the prisoners themselves asking that he come out to hear their confession. He didn't respond. Though it was certainly true that the two priests were very busy, it was more that they didn't want to involve the Church in this matter. Father Matignon had talked to him about the case, warning how it might prove damaging for the parish.

"She'd a come herself, but she's abed now with the cough," the man explained. "Got herself a bad clogher, she does."

"Father Matignon is away," the priest replied. "He's expected back tonight but with the weather who can say? And I'm afraid I, too, have been unwell."

"She was wantin' to speak to a priest."

"Could it not wait till morning? Father Matignon will be back by then." He felt guilty. Despite the fact that he was ill and should have been in bed, he knew he was foisting the responsibility of dealing with the family onto his colleague.

"It's just there's not much time before the trial," the Irishman said.

"So it *does* have to do with the trial," Cheverus said. The man, caught in his lie, nodded like a child exposed for telling a falsehood. "I would like to go, Tom. But the doctor has not permitted me to venture out of bed."

"I understand, Father. I wouldn't want you gettin' sick on our account. You've done enough for us."

What have I done for them, he thought. He'd offered some prayers. He'd consoled Dominic's wife when she'd come by the church. He'd organized a small collection to help the family out financially. A pittance, really. That's all he'd done.

"Perhaps I could come by tomorrow," he offered.

"Tomorrow it'll have to be then, Father. Sorry for wakin' you. G'night."

The tall Irishman put his soaking cap on and turned to leave. How can you deny them, Cheverus thought to himself. How can you refuse them whatever small comfort your presence might mean at a time like this? Besides, the Daleys were good Catholics. They came to Mass each week and made confession regularly. Just last October, Dominic and his young wife had had their baby baptized at Holy Cross. Cheverus could remember Daley, a great big lout of a man like his father, standing there, holding his tiny son in the crook of his arm, beaming with pride; and the mother, Finola, a thin nervous woman with wide olive-colored eyes and a doleful mouth, staring at her child with such deep love. And though the Daleys were dirt poor, they gave what little they could for the support of the parish. When they hadn't money, they gave in other ways. After Father Cheverus had said a funeral Mass for Rose and Tom's youngest child, William, who'd been carried away by the yellow fever outbreak a few years back, Rose had repaid the priest by knitting him a pair of socks. Now and then, though she could hardly feed her own large brood, she'd drop off at the rectory something she'd made, a fish pie or some potato dish. What was more, Tom and his oldest son Dominic, the very one who now waited in prison, had pitched in with the digging of the foundation of the new church several years before.

And how had the Church repaid the Daleys' loyal support? By doing absolutely nothing. It had cautiously, albeit prudently, kept its distance. Given the public outcry over the murder, Father Matignon had thought that best. And Cheverus, seeing the logic of such a course, had quietly acquiesced. Neither priest had been to visit the imprisoned son out in the western part of the state. Nor had they offered a word of support from the pulpit or used whatever little influence they had in Boston to see that the two prisoners received fair treatment, legal counsel, a timely trial. They had done nothing whatsoever to protest what was, by any reasonable standards, a gross miscarriage of justice—even if they were guilty.

"Wait, Tom," he said finally. He didn't relish the thought of venturing out on such a night feeling the way he did. And he knew that Father Matignon, when he found out, would frown on his going. Still, he decided to accompany the man and see what it was Rose wanted. That was the least he could do. "Give me a moment to get dressed."

"*Mon Père.*" the housekeeper said, taking him aside. "You must stay in bed."

"I am fine, Yvette. When Father returns, inform him where I have gone."

Upstairs in his room, he changed quickly. The fire in the fireplace had almost burned out, and the room was chilly and dark. He jabbed a piece of pine kindling into the still-live coals and used it as a taper to light a candle on his bedside table. From the drawer of the escritoire, he withdrew his cross, kissed it, and placed it around his neck. He then took up his stole and his well-worn silver pyx box containing hosts, in case Rose Daley wished to take communion, and slipped them into the deep pockets of his cassock. Before he closed the desk drawer, his eye happened to fall upon the several letters lying there. The letters from home he had not yet answered—did not know *how* to answer. They had remained there for weeks.

He blew out the candle, but for some reason he remained standing in the darkened room for a moment. He felt light-headed, his legs unsteady, a slight tremor in his hands—the residual effects of the ague fever he'd had. Yet there was another feeling, one beneath the effects of the fever, something which he recognized as an uncomfortable heaviness in the region of his heart. Like a great stone sitting on his chest. A sensation that had been growing for several weeks now, one he'd been aware of even before the sickness had come upon him, though being confined to bed had intensified the feeling, brought it to a head, like a boil to which a heated knife had been placed. Lying in bed day and night with nothing to do but think. He couldn't say exactly what caused it, though he was convinced the letters sitting in his drawer had something to do with it.

He closed his eyes for a moment and recalled the dream he'd had earlier. Distorted as images are in dreams, it was, he knew all too well, the garden attached to the Convent of the Carmes. The bright courtyard garden gleamed in his mind, brilliant, gem-like. The high, whitewashed walls, the late-summer lushness of the flowers, the trees heavy with fruit, a ripe, almost cloying odor hanging in the dull torpid air. The profound stillness of the place, so quiet he could hear the bees' low drone, flitting from flower to flower, the soft wind from the Seine in the treetops, the low murmur of prayers. And sometimes, as now, he even saw the men there, too. Dressed in their long black robes and cassocks, some kneeling in the heat, heads bent, hands folded over breviaries or rosaries, others reading letters from home or reclining on the soft grass of the convent garden. . . .

This too he thought was part of it. Part of that feeling of heaviness in his chest. He knelt by his bed and prayed. *O, Dieu de miséricorde. Me pardonnerex-vous jamais? Most merciful Lord. Can you ever forgive me?* He waited quietly in the cool darkness of his room, waited for the voice of God to come to him as it always used to in the past. Instead, there was only silence. *But your iniquities have separated between you and your god, and your sins have hid his face from you, that he will not hear.*

They kept walking, the tall Irishman in front, the small priest following along behind. He'd managed to weather the wave of nausea, though his stomach was still queasy and his head continued to throb. The rain swept in off the water, stinging his face. From Fish Street, he could make out the lantern lights and masts of a half dozen newly arrived ships anchored in the harbor. He heard the bells from the New North Church over on Hanover, a few streets away. They passed on into a squalid, run-down part of the city down near the wharves. The Daleys lived in a neighborhood of slovenly homes, of dungheaps and sewage oozing into the streets, of crime and poverty, of dirty, ragged children selling apples on the corners and working fourteen-hour days in the ropewalks. The stench of rotting fish mingled with the pungent odors of rum and molasses, pine pitch and spices. Raucous laughter and the harsh language of caulkers and carpenters and sailors slipped from the numerous taverns and public houses along the way. He was often called here, since it was where many of his parishioners lived. To a sickbed. To hear a final confession. In daylight it was an unsavory place, but as night drew on it became even more disheartening and bleak.

Mostly the area was occupied by the Irish now. When he'd first arrived in Boston a decade earlier, there were only a handful of Irish in the entire city and those were mostly the Protestants from Ulster, somber, hard-edged people, successful merchants and traders and shipping captains. Back then, the Catholics of his tiny parish were made up of the French who had moved down from Quebec after the Revolutionary War, a few prosperous Germans or Italians or Poles whose business affairs brought them to America, the family of Don Juan Stoughton, the Spanish counsel. Or Frenchmen like himself, émigrés having fled the Revolution, clergymen and aristocrats and intellectuals. For the most part, they were Catholics of education and culture and breeding. They often came from the upper classes of French society. But over time, most of those people had packed up and moved westward, to better situations out in New York or Pennsylvania, where they established orderly farms or ran successful businesses.

Now his parish was almost exclusively Irish, brutally poor, mostly illiterate. Each year more and more arrived on the ships that put into Boston harbor. Especially after the persecution and wholesale slaughter that followed on the heels of the failed Rebellion of '98 back home. They came here, Cheverus knew, to get away from the English and the landlords, pursuing the dream of freedom and opportunity, hoping for enough to feed their children, a piece of land that was their own, a place to worship as they saw fit. What they often found, though, was only more of the same—prejudice, oppression, poverty, hatred. If they didn't die of fever on the crossing, they spilled down the gangplanks with their emaciated brood, their meager possessions on their backs, and joined those already here. Entire families shared a single room in some back alley down by the docks, living in filthy, rat-infested quarters, working for wages even a freed slave would refuse, or actually becoming a slave for seven years of indentured servitude. The work no one else wanted fell to the Irish, the backbreaking or dangerous or demeaning jobs of digging canals or draining the fetid swamps that ringed the city or emptying the chamber pots of the wealthy. And when the yellow fever or typhus broke out as it did every few years, their neighborhoods were always the hardest hit. The death rolls posted around the city were filled with the O'Briens and the

O'Donnells, the Doyles and Duggans, the Mahoneys and McCarthys. Father Cheverus knew all too well, because it fell to him to utter the humble words over their graves, to make sense of their too-short, brutish lives.

As their priest, Cheverus saw firsthand the bigotry and prejudice and hatred that greeted the Irish that landed on these shores. They were considered little more than vermin, carriers of disease. They were thought to be ignorant and lazy and licentious. They were overly fond of their drink, everyone knew, and when drunk they became violent and wild, little better than animals. They had large families they couldn't feed or clothe adequately, or raise to be law-abiding citizens. Only a few years before, Harrison Gray Otis, a wealthy congressman from Boston, had given a fiery speech in congress, in which he gave voice to the unspoken fears of many Americans regarding the growing influx of Irish immigrants. Americans, he had said, no longer wished to invite "hordes of wild Irishmen" to come here with a view to disturb our domestic peace and tranquility.

And what were his own feelings for them, these poor, misunderstood Irish? Pity, certainly. Except perhaps for the Indians he ministered to up in Maine, no group was so traduced and maligned. Why even the Negroes, freed almost twenty years ago in Massachusetts, fared better. Admiration, too. The Irish were generous, often to a fault. They gave of themselves when they had nothing more to give. They offered their help when they could hardly help themselves. And despite their unlimited capacity for—and seeming enjoyment of—suffering, they loved life as no other people. Not even his beloved French peasants savored living as did these Irish. They liked to sing and dance and laugh, even through the worst of times—*especially* through the worst of times. They were like children—poorly behaved, hungry, filthy children. How many wakes had he attended which seemed more celebration than mourning, with their drinking and storytelling and laughter? And then there was their faith. The English were said to believe in God with their heads, the French with their eyes, the Italians and Spaniards with their hands and tongues. But the Irish! They believed with every ounce of themselves, with their whole being. Their faith surrounded and encompassed them, every moment of every day. Cheverus had slowly come to understand that their belief in God was like a dreadful, crushing weight, a millstone they labored to carry each day with quiet humility, yet one that sustained and nurtured them at the same time. He admired that terrible faith of theirs, longed to emulate it, and in some way he couldn't quite explain, feared it a little, too.

But in his heart of hearts, Cheverus also felt a certain uneasiness with the Irish. He felt uncomfortable when he was around them. Not with all of them. With some he'd managed to establish a close bond, a friendly rapport. There was Mr. Herlihy, one of the church wardens, with whom he would have lively but cordial discussions of politics. And Liam Broderick, who ran the bookseller's shop on Cornhill Street and who would lend him volumes for free. And of course young Máirtin, one of the altar boys, a clever and serious youth who might someday, Cheverus fervently hoped, have a calling. But with many of the Irish, especially the poor ones newly fled from the oppression back home, he felt this distance, as if he were an outsider among them: he with his education and his cultured upbringing, with his delicate French mannerisms, and they with their ignorance, their roughness and coarseness, with the odd tongue they sometimes slipped into to keep him from knowing what it was they were saying. At times he found himself annoyed by their backward and superstitious ways, frustrated by their obstinate acceptance of suffering, repulsed by the filth and squalor they often lived in, as if by choice. Though he had worked among them for ten long years now, baptizing them and hearing their confessions, marrying them and easing their passing when the time came, he couldn't say he fully understood them. Although he felt their respect, he wasn't sure he had their love—would *ever* have their love. In many ways, their hearts remained an enigma to him.

On the other side was the Protestant majority, the Yankee descendants of those grim and unyielding Puritans. They were always looking suspiciously at the two "papists" and their small, curious congregation. Watching them, waiting for trouble, for their prejudices to be confirmed. And just when it seemed the Church was making a little progress, when it was beginning to be, if not quite accepted, at least left alone, something would happen and the image of Catholics was set back years. An Irishman would be caught stealing something, and there would be the public spectacle of him being flogged or put in the stocks or losing an ear on the Boston Common. Or there would be some scathing anti-Catholic diatribe in the papers, about how they were idolaters or that Rome condoned sin by selling indulgences. Not long before, the *Columbian Centinel* published a vicious unsigned attack on the Catholic Church and its welcomed collapse under Bonaparte: "If the papacy be justly designated by the title of Antichrist," the writer had said, "what Christian can grieve on account of its extinction." Or an Irish ship would put in to port and supposedly be the cause of a fever outbreak. And once more the prevailing stereotypes and animosities were proved all too true: that Catholics, and especially *Irish* Catholics, only brought trouble with them wherever they went.

And now this latest incident—the brutal murder of a Yankee farmboy by a couple of Irishmen. It couldn't have come at a worse time, when Irish immigrants were starting to stream into the harbor, when French Catholics were again placed under suspicion because of Napoleon and the French privateers that seized American ships on the high seas. Since November, the entire commonwealth had been eagerly awaiting word about when the trial out in the western part of the state would start, or more precisely, when those two would get what was coming to them. It was said that Dominic Daley, Tom and Rose Daley's son, and another man, a drifter named Halligan, had robbed and murdered a young farmer named Marcus Lyon along the Boston Road. According to published reports, they'd shot him, pulled him from his mount, and viciously stove in his head. Then—and it was this last bit of savagery that really inflamed people—tossed his body into a nearby river and placed a large stone on it to hide their handiwork. Cheverus at first found it hard to believe that Dominic had had a hand in this. He'd known Daley to be a gentle person, a loving husband, a good Catholic. But all the evidence suggested otherwise. Supposedly, witnesses had spotted the two Irishmen near the scene of the murder, and one even said he'd seen them in possession of the dead man's horse. When apprehended, they had money on them which they couldn't explain and no plausible alibi. Everything pointed to their being guilty. They had waited in jail for five months, while public opinion mounted against them—and against all Irish Catholics for that matter.

The case had played upon the people's unstated fears, even as far away as Boston. Governor Strong, facing a tough reelection, had offered the unbelievable sum of five hundred dollars for their capture. The heinousness of the crime combined with the fact that the accused were Irish Catholics had aroused the deep-seated but always latent prejudices of the populace. Immigrants in general and Irish-Catholic immigrants in particular felt threatened. Pope's Day, November 5th, had taken place only a few days before word reached Boston about the murder, so anti-papist feelings were still running high. Though officially banned since the Revolutionary War, the celebration had continued among the lower classes, bringing out drunken packs of Catholic-hating youths from the North and South End gangs. The celebration of the old Guy Fawkes Day was more than anything an excuse for them to become inebriated and terrorize the town for a night. Carrying torches and pushing a large cart with effigies of the pope and men dressed as devils, they wandered the streets of Boston, singing and destroying property and generally causing mayhem. And this year, on hearing of the murder by a pair of Catholics, the same rabble element again took to the streets, this time, instead of fighting each other, looking to accost anyone with a brogue or wearing a crucifix or seen coming out of Holy Cross Church. Several Irish homes had had windows broken, and a few walking home from church were harassed or threatened. One man, Declan O'Brien, while returning home from his job at the sail-duck factory, had been accosted by a group of thugs and badly beaten. In the Catholic portion of the Central Burial Grounds, a number of gravestones had been overturned or vandalized. And a note had been nailed to the Daleys' door making vague threats if they didn't return to Ireland. Since November church attendance was down, as many parishioners were fearful of retribution. Even such a reasonably well liked and respected man as Cheverus was, on several occasions, called names by those he passed in the streets—filthy papist, Catholic whore.

That sort of behavior he could chalk up to ignorance, the usual prejudice against Irish and papists. Far worse was the fact that educated Bostonians, prominent citizens, even Cheverus's fellow clergy had also weighed in with incendiary comments—against the Irish and the rising tide of Catholic immigrants. There were editorials in the papers and broadsides put up here and there throughout the city, railing against the threat posed by "foreigners" and "aliens." Some writers decried the abandonment of former President Adams's Alien and Sedition laws and the leniency of the immigration policies under Jefferson, that atheistic jacobin. Even the man who was to prosecute the case, Attorney General Sullivan, well known for his hostility toward Catholics, had made inflammatory statements concerning Irish and Catholics. Indeed, the Church already had enough enemies without this latest incident.

Here we go, Father," Tom Daley said, leading him into a decrepit three-story, wood-frame building down by the waterfront. The place was unpainted, slowly rotting from the harsh salt winds and winter storms.

The priest had not been to the Daleys' since the wake for their youngest boy Willie several years before. He found himself in a smoky, low-ceilinged room. Though a charcoal fire smoldered at one end, it was cold and drafty, the sodden dampness of the night seeping right through the wooden walls. A lone cruisie lamp on a table cast a feeble light. The room had the familiar smell of such places, a bitter odor of sour milk and sweat and unwashed flesh, of lurking angers and festering hopes. The priest felt his stomach lurch. Though he had been in similar homes a thousand times, they always repulsed him. Several black-shawled women from the neighborhood murmured off in one corner, while the men congregated near the fire smoking clay pipes and talking animatedly in their strange tongue. Scrawny, raggedly dressed children of various ages huddled in the shadows playing some sort of game. With her back to him, a slight woman with reddish-blond hair squatted before a blackened pot suspended over the fire. He recognized Finola Daley, Dominic's wife.

When they saw him, a hush fell over those in the room. Some of the men removed their caps and nodded deferentially, while the women made the sign of the cross and bowed their heads. None came up to greet him.

Tom led him into an even smaller room at the back, no bigger than a cell. There was no window in the room, and it smelled strongly of sickness. Lying in a narrow bed, a rosary wrapped tightly around a plump hand, a gray-haired woman smiled when she saw him. It was Rose Daley, Tom's wife. On a night table burned a taper in a tin stand. Beside it was a bloody rag. With difficulty the woman sat up, her face brightening a little.

"Ah, God keep you for comin' out on such a night, Father," said the woman.

"Good evening, Rose," the priest replied, taking her hand. The skin was cool but rough as that on a dogfish. The foul odor of the sickroom was overpowering.

"Tom," she commanded, "don't just stand there like an egit. Take Father's cape and give it to Finola to hang by the fire," she directed. "And tell her to come in here. Please sit down, Father," Rose said, indicating the only chair in the room.

Rose Daley was a sturdy woman, with a large sagging bosom, fleshy, pink arms, and a belly that strained against her unclean shift. Though she was probably only fifty, she looked much older, wrinkled, her hands gnarled, weather-scarred. Her puffy cheeks shone with an unnatural brightness from the disease that was slowly ravaging her lungs. Her mouth was pinched and sunken, her nostrils flared, straining for breath. She wore a dark shawl loosely draped over her head and shoulders. Her gray eyes were red-rimmed, hollow looking. He saw nothing of her son Dominic in her except perhaps for the smile. Despite her illness, she gave one the formidable impression of some large immovable object: a tree trunk struck by lightning, a boulder. Whenever Cheverus spoke with the woman—in the street, the confessional—her sheer force of will always intimidated him a little.

Finola Daley poked her head in the doorway. "Yes, mam?" she said.

"Would you care for something to drink, Father?" Rose asked.

"No, thank you."

"Are ye quite sure? A bit o' the craythur p'haps. The best thing on a night like this," she said with a mischievous wink of a young girl.

The Irish, he knew, were fiercely hospitable. They took offense easily and held grudges for ages. Though his stomach hardly felt like whiskey, so as not to offend the woman, he said, "Well, perhaps just a little."

"Bring us some whiskey, *macushla*," the old woman said to her daughter-in-law. "And a nice hot pot a tay."

"Yes, mam," the young woman replied and left.

"Tom just made up a batch of the stuff. Take the nip out of your bones, it will."

"It is cold out," Cheverus offered, blowing on his hands.

They sat silently for a moment. "So Tom told you we heard about the trial?" she said at last.

"Yes."

"Three days is all they're givin' 'em. Three blasted days," she cursed. She shook her head, holding her mouth pinched tight, like a purse that contained coins she wanted to guard. Her dull gray eyes flashed with sudden anger. "Why they—" but she began to cough. Her shoulders lurched, her large bosom heaving. This soon led to a paroxysm of coughing that made the color blaze in her plump cheeks while the rest of her face was transformed to a deathly pallor. She picked up the bloody rag from the night table and hawked something into it.

"Is there anything I can do, Rose?" Cheverus asked.

She held up one finger to show she would be all right in a moment. He waited patiently for her to catch her breath. Whatever it was Rose wished to ask him, he wanted to have it over, so that he could be gone, back in his own warm bed. After a while the woman's coughing fit slowly died down, and at last she was able to take several shallow breathes. Her breathing was irregular, punctuated by ghastly wheezing sounds.

Finola returned carrying a tray, which she set on the night table. She smiled self-consciously at Cheverus, the way she sometimes did after Mass or if she happened to meet him when she'd come to light a candle and pray. But there was something else to the smile that he wasn't sure of. He nodded to the young woman. Finola went over to her mother-in-law and began rubbing her back.

"Are you all right, mam?" she asked tenderly. "Did you have another fit?"

"Aye. A wee small one. I'm fine now, love."

From a stone jug on the tray, she poured some saffron-colored liquid into one of the cups and handed it to her mother-in-law. The cup's handle had been broken off.

"Drink this, mam," she said.

"Oh, thank ye, *alannah*," the old woman replied, taking a sip. The draught seemed actually to regulate her breathing a little. And it brought some normal color back into her face.

"Good evenin' to you, Father," the young woman finally said.

"Hello, Finola," he replied.

"Much obliged you could come. Especially on such a foul night. I gave your cloak a good brushing. It's drying by the fire."

"Thank you."

In her twenties, Finola was a slight, somewhat retiring woman. She wore a dirty apron over a blue skirt of homespun material. Where her mother-in-law was heavy, thick-waisted, substantial despite the wasting effects of her illness, Finola was frail, almost fragile looking. She wasn't pretty, her face too angular, fleshless and drawn, the bones straining against the pale, almost transparent skin. Her dull, yellowish-green eyes were too large for her thin face and always appeared startled somehow. Despite this, there was something not altogether unpleasant about her looks. Her mouth was oddly generous, full and soft and pliant, and there was something about her that suggested an intimacy with suffering. Without her husband working, she'd had to find employment to support her and the baby. She'd taken a job in the ropewalks making ropes. Since her husband's arrest, she had come several times to the church to pray for her husband. Once or twice Cheverus had joined her. Her eyes glossy and tense, she looked as if she might cry at any moment, though usually she didn't. He felt pity for her, her husband in jail, her six-month-old child Michael perhaps to be left fatherless. But she would stare at him in such a way that also made him uncomfortable. He couldn't say why. Did he detect in it some sort of scorn, unstated though it may have been? The younger woman poured some more whiskey into a second cup and handed it to the priest.

"Here we go, Father," Finola said. "You'll want to go easy on that."

He'd partaken of their wretched-tasting homemade brew before, though not in some time. He took a quick gulp of the whiskey, hoping to get it over in one swallow. He should have known better, though. The strong-tasting liquor scorched the back of his throat and made his eyes water. When it hit bottom, for a moment he thought he would be sick. "Heavens!" he cried.

"It does take some gettin' used to," offered Rose, suppressing a smile. "G'on and have you a bit more, Father. Good for what ails you."

Finola refilled his cup. He took another sip, more cautiously this time. As the burning liquid slid down his throat, now a sweet warmth spread across his chest and fanned out luxuriantly throughout his entire body. He felt the chill of the night being slowly driven from his bones.

"Yes, indeed," he offered, smiling.

"We call it *usquebaugh*, Father," Rose said. "It means the water of life."

"The water of life," he repeated.

The young woman sat on the bed beside her mother-in-law and placed her arm around her. Finola stared silently at him with her too-large eyes, a challenge almost. Finally, the priest said to Rose, "So Dominic is to stand trial at last."

"Yes, Father," Rose said.

"Let us pray he is found innocent," he offered.

"*Ochone,*" Rose scoffed. "They're bound and determined to see him hang."

"You mustn't talk like that, mam," the younger woman pleaded.

" 'Sure and we know it's the truth, love. What chance do the poor lads have?"

"We got to keep up our hopes," Finola said, looking over at him.

"Finola is right," he said to Rose. "You must pray to God. Ask Him for strength."

"Been doing that night and day for five months," the old woman replied. "I think He's turned a deaf ear on us."

"He always hears us," the priest said. Yet he recalled the silence in his room earlier when he'd invoked God's name. The dark silence that seemed to surround his prayers lately.

"I still can't believe any of this is happenin'," Rose said. "Dom was always a good lad. Never done nothin' bad to nobody."

"That's true," agreed Finola. "Dom always had a good heart in him."

Cheverus noted the tense of their verbs. They didn't even seem to be aware of it.

"My son was a good Catholic, Father. You know I speak true."

He nodded. What else could he do?

"As bad as it was back home, I wish we'd never left," Rose lamented. "Least there when we died, we could rest in our own soil. I curse this land, Father."

"You mustn't despair," he said.

"It has stolen two of me boys."

He thought he would try to get her to see things from a different perspective. "We mustn't forget, another mother lost her son, too."

Rose shot him a hard, searing look.

"I feel bad for any mother losing a child. But my son had nothing to do with that. He's *not* a murderer," she hissed. "I raised him up a good Christian. You know Dominic, Father. You *know* him. He'd not a done something like this."

"Trust in God," was all Cheverus said in reply. Her son's guilt or innocence was not a matter for him to weigh in on. "Would you care to pray with me, Rose?"

"Forgive me, Father, but I'm not in a praying mood," she said, waving her fist in the air. "I'm mad at them what's done this to me boy."

"They've not been treated right," Finola Daley said. "The government's had all this time to prepare their case and my husband just three days. Does that seem fair to you, Father?"

"I suppose not," the priest said hesitantly, wanting to keep his distance. Not wanting to commit himself or the Church to a course that he would come to regret.

"You speak the God's truth, Father," Rose said.

"When was the last time you saw him?" the priest asked.

"Not since his arrest back in November," Rose said. "We took the stage out there a couple of months back, Finola and the little one and me. To visit with Dom. Only the jailer there wouldn't let us in. Six dollars we spent for the coach and lodging."

"Why wouldn't he let you see him?" Cheverus asked.

Finola shrugged. "Only that he had orders from the attorney general the prisoners were to have no visitors."

"So we went to see himself. That Mr. Sullivan," Rose said scornfully. "The fellow who wants to be governor."

"He wouldn't even talk to us," Finola scoffed. "We was told he was too *busy*. The filthy *mac diabhail*."

"What would it hurt to let us see me son, Father?" Rose asked. "He's been locked away in that stinkin' jail for months. Him and the other poor devil. What's his name, Finola? The one who writes such a fine hand."

"Halligan, mam," she replied.

"Aye, that's it. Halligan." Rose was breathing hard again and she paused to catch her breath. Her eyes strained with each intake and her nostrils turned white at the edges. She looked over at Cheverus. "Would you be willing to talk to him, Father?"

"To whom?" he asked.

"That Sullivan fellow."

So, he thought. They did want him to help with her son's case.

"Rose," Cheverus began, "I'm afraid the Church really can't get involved in legal disputes of this nature."

"In Ireland when we had a problem with the law, we'd go to Father Morin."

"This is not Ireland, Rose. The Church and State are separate here."

"But we got no one else to turn to," Finola said, her bony face held rigid, a fragile mask that might break into pieces at any moment.

"I can appreciate your situation," the priest said.

"Appreciate!" the young woman mocked. Rose touched her hand. "Sorry, Father. I meant no disrespect."

"You ought to have an attorney speak for you. Not a priest. What do I know about the law?"

"This ain't about law," Finola said. "It's about what's right and wrong."

"Please, Father. Help us," Rose pleaded.

"I would like to. Really," he said, the lie turning sour in his stomach. "It's just that the attorney general and the Church, well, we have not exactly seen eye to eye," he offered. The fact of the matter was Sullivan and the Church had been at loggerheads for some time. The attorney general had been involved in two legal actions against the Diocese of the Catholic Church in the past, and little love was lost between the two men. The last thing Cheverus wanted was to have to go and plead their case before a man he disliked as intensely as he did James Sullivan.

"But you and Father Matignon are important people in this city," Rose pleaded. "The man'll have to listen to you."

Shaking his head, he said, "I think you overestimate the Church's influence. Sullivan is hardly a supporter of Catholics."

"But you're my son's priest," Rose said. "And they're being treated like dogs."

"Worse than dogs, mam," said Finola. "My husband writes they've not been allowed out of their cell, not to bathe nor walk about nor anything, in all this time. Dom says the cell stinks like a hog's pen. Mother o' God," she sighed. She closed her eyes for a moment. Her lips were parted, her face angled upward, an expression of inconsolable sorrow on her thin, haggard countenance. When she did this, she reminded Cheverus of something he'd seen before. Mary Magdalene in a painting he'd seen at the Louvre? Some grieving Madonna in a pietà? "Oh, my poor Dom. My poor love," she wailed. Sudden tears streamed down her cheeks and fell onto her dirty apron. Her sobs convulsed her slender body.

"There, there, darlin'." Now it was Rose doing the consoling. "*Asthore*, love. It's all right." The old woman stroked Finola's hair, wiped the tears from her eyes.

"Here, Finola," the priest said, offering the young woman his handkerchief.

"Thank ye, Father," she said, wiping her eyes.

"I wish there was something I could do, Finola," he offered. "But . . ."

They were silent for a moment. Then Rose said, "Finola and I are planning on taking the stage out there for the trial."

"Do you think that's wise?" Cheverus asked of Rose. "I mean, in your condition?"

"My son needs me there, Father," she said determinedly. "I have to go."

"It might not be safe for the two of you," Cheverus advised. "There might be trouble."

"Father," Finola said, staring at him, her olive eyes narrowing. "Our place is there. We'll take our chances."

The two women looked at each other. Cheverus suddenly felt an overwhelming pity for them. What would it hurt to talk to Sullivan, he thought. Just talk. You're their priest, he told himself. They've come to you for help.

"Perhaps I could speak to the attorney general after all," he offered. "But I would first have to get permission from Father Matignon."

"Of course, Father," said Finola, smiling through her tears.

"If I am able to speak to him, what would you wish me to ask?"

"If we could be allowed to see him," said the old woman.

"And try to get them more time before the trial starts," Finola added. "So they'd have a fighting chance. Oh, and if they might have a bath and some clean clothes."

"I shall look into the matter."

"Oh, thank you, Father," Rose said, folding her hands in prayer.

"I cannot guarantee anything," he explained. "With the trial this close, the attorney general may already have left for Northampton. Or he may not have time to see me."

"We'd appreciate anything you could do, Father," Rose said. "Anything."

He nodded, wondering if he would come to regret his decision.

"Would you care to take communion?" he asked. He hadn't seen Rose at Mass for a while.

"Aye, Father. If it's not too much trouble," the old woman replied.

After he had given her communion, he said, "I should be on my way."

"Finola, love, get Father's cape. And have Tom see him home."

"That's not necessary," he said.

"Are you sure?" Rose asked. " 'Tis a devil of a night. And the neighborhood, well, it ain't so safe to be walkin' about by yourself."

"I'll be fine. Goodnight, Rose."

"Bless you for coming, Father."

Finola got his cape and walked with him to the door. The men were still seated around the fire, drinking and smoking pipes; the women were huddled together on their knees, rocking back and forth, saying the rosary.

"Thank you for agreeing to help us, Father," Finola said to him softly at the door, as if telling him a secret. "I can't tell you how much it means to us."

"I don't know how much help I can be. Sullivan may not even agree to see me."

"At least someone's on our side. With the whole countryside against us, it's good to know someone believes them innocent."

He nodded, unsure whether he did or not. Then again, that wasn't his job. That was the job of a court to decide. His was to prepare them for the next life.

"Dom hasn't said confession in a while, Father. Maybe you could come with us?"

He pursed his lips. "I am very busy, Finola."

"Of course. Och, I nearly forgot. Here," she said, taking from her pocket his handkerchief. "I could wash it for you and bring it by the rectory tomorrow."

"That won't be necessary."

He looked up into her face. She was taller than him by half a head. Her too-large eyes made him think of the nervous eyes of a deer, wary, about to bolt. They were glossy, filled with a liquid sadness, the flesh around them drawn and wan-looking. He stared at her mouth, the ample lips slightly parted. This close the severity of her face took on a certain comeliness—the sort inspired by pain, the transcendent glow of suffering. He had seen such a face somewhere before. Where, he wondered. Perhaps a fleeting glimpse of a woman's face, some aristocrat he'd seen in a cart approaching the guillotine in the Place de la Revolution? He stared at her until it became awkward for both of them and then, coughing, he averted his gaze.

"God bless you, Finola," he said. "I'll pray for your husband." He drew his hood up and was about to go out into the night when she laid her hand on the bare skin of his wrist. Her fingertips were cool, surprisingly so, and a shiver went coursing through him. His head swirled, both from her touch as well as from the liquor he'd drunk. She leaned into him, her full mouth slightly parted, her large eyes fixing him. She was close enough that he could smell her: a peculiar odor of smoke and sour breast milk. But of something else, too. Something sweet, a honeyed ripeness.

"I'll pray for you, too, Father," she said.

He pulled his hand back from her as from a flame. He stared at her for another moment. Then he turned and hurried out into the cold, dark night.

TWO

He awoke in the small hours of morning, in that slippery, blue-black territory between night and day, when a man's heart can fail him utterly. In the bunk next to his, Daley was snoring away. It always amazed him how soundly the fellow slept, as untroubled as the sleep of a child with a full belly. Occasionally Daley might call out something. *Finola*, he'd say, *where are me shoes?* But he hardly ever roused himself into consciousness, didn't so much as turn over. He woke in the same position he went to sleep in, on his back, hands locked behind his head. Halligan had trouble sleeping. His mind swirling with thoughts and images, half-recalled songs from home, scraps from a life which seemed as unreal, as distant as the moon. And when he did manage finally to fall asleep, it felt as if he were falling, plunging into black space. His dreams were tangled affairs from which he woke thrashing and fighting as if trying to free himself from a net made of sorrow.

It always took him the odd moment or two to get his bearings. Sometimes when he first woke, especially in the dark, he found himself back with the Franciscans, in that long, narrow, high-ceilinged room with the other orphans, old Brother Padraig passing among their beds, rousing them with his rough hands to morning devotions and chores. Other times he believed himself in the stables of some gentleman in whose employ he'd been, the reassuring snorting and snuffling of the horses in their nearby stalls gently stirring him. But other times, the worst by far, he thought himself in that quiet, secluded place among the willow and pine trees, lying on the soft cool moss that grew along the mountain stream. It was there he used to meet a young girl with raven-colored hair and eyes dark and luminous as opals. In the treachery of those first few moments between sleep and waking, he was teased into believing she was lying beside him, her presence so palpable, so unmistakable, he could almost feel the velvety down along her cheek and the smooth thrill of her thighs, could smell the apple fragrance of her hair. In the darkness, he would whisper, *Bridie*, and then again, *Bridie*. But when he reached out to touch her, the only thing his hand came into contact with was the cold stone wall of his cell.

He shivered in the frigid darkness, his feet swollen and aching with chilblain. The turnkey maintained a fire in the small room at the end of corridor where he slept, but not much of its heat reached them. So they were always cold, even with their boots and greatcoats on, their paper-thin, grubby blankets wrapped around them like shrouds. It was the one thing about America Halligan had never quite adjusted to. The cold. Back home, he was used to roughing it, tramping about from place to place, sleeping out in any sort of weather, in a hayloft or under a tree, walking barefoot to save on shoe leather, and it never really affected him. The cold back there was a teasing sort of thing, something just to make the warmth of a turf fire or a noggin of whiskey all the more inviting. But here it was grim and bone-wearying. Was it any wonder these Yankees had hearts of flint?

He got up and made his way in the darkness to the slop bucket in the corner. He unbuttoned his trousers and relieved himself. Daley stirred but continued to sleep. Once back in bed, Halligan pulled the blanket tighter and managed to doze for a while. He woke again, heard a cock crowing in the growing blue of morning. Outside the jailhouse, the town hadn't yet begun to stir, not even the hoof beats of the early post rider galloping for the ferry. Halligan lay there shivering, curled on his left side, his face inches from the damp stone wall. His belly growled from hunger. He pictured food, great heaping platters of beef and mutton, crúibín and ham, pratie oaten and cobbledy, with a strong pint of porter to wash it all down. He pictured standing in the sun on a warm day in

July, cutting turf, his shirt off and the sun baking his back. He pictured sitting around a blazing fire, sipping a warm spiced rum and staring drowsily into the flames. He dozed again, dreaming of the ocean off Slea Head, the deep blue stretching out dizzyingly to the horizon, like a carpet extending all the way to America.

Here's your grub, boys," said the turnkey, as he slid first one wooden trencher and then the other through the space in the bars on the floor. His name was Dowd. He was a short, balding man, with red whiskers streaked with gray. Chatty and high-spirited, Dowd would often show up whistling or talking about the weather. He was, despite his position, a decent sort, even kindly, providing Halligan with books to read and paper and ink with which to write, occasionally even sharing a pot of tea with them. He had to walk a half mile to the center of town, to a tavern called Pomeroy's, to get their twice-a-day meals. If he were busy, sometimes an old humpbacked crone would bring their meals down. It was usually cold gruel and a crust of stale bread, a piece of moldy cheese, on Sunday a hunk of some brown thing that passed for meat. And a pitcher of water that tasted of tallow.

"Thank you, sir," said Daley, picking up his plate and Halligan's as well.

"You'll need to eat up quick lads," the man explained in an undertone, as if conveying a secret. "The sheriff is to bring you to court today."

"Court, sir?" Daley asked in disbelief. "Today?"

"That is what I understand."

When the turnkey left, Daley glanced at him. "What do you make a that, Jamy?"

Shoveling the food in with his fingers—they weren't allowed utensils for fear of hurting themselves—Halligan replied, "About bloody time I say."

"Ain't we supposed to have counsel first?" Daley asked.

"Maybe it's just a hearing or something."

"Or another rumor."

For months they'd lived for this day. Yet their lives till now had been dominated by rumors, the odd bit of gossip that reached them—from the turnkey or from one of the other infrequent prisoners, or from the old woman who showed up now and then with their food. Rumors that their trial was imminent or that it had been put off yet again. That the attorney who was to defend them would be arriving on the noon stage. Even that it had all been just a terrible mistake, and that Daley and he were about to be released. One night they'd even heard distant shouts and cries coming from somewhere up the road, toward the center of town. The woman who'd arrived with their suppers informed them that a mob was gathering on the town square. According to her, they had torches and carried pitchforks and ropes. Their intention, she was only too eager to tell them, was to break the two out and administer their own brand of justice, and not to wait for the next session of the Supreme Court. The woman, a wizened, bent-backed old crone, took particular relish in telling them of this. "They'll soon be comin' for you, Irish," she taunted, sticking her blackened tongue out and making a hideous face as if she were being hanged. The truth, they would later learn from the turnkey, was that while a crowd had gathered, it hadn't amounted to much, just a few drunken farmers that the sheriff and his men had forced to disperse before they gathered any momentum.

But this? This sounded like the real thing.

They didn't have to wait long to find out. The guards came for them before they'd even had a chance to finish their breakfast. They entered noisily, their boots resounding on the flagstones of the corridor, their sabers and guns clanging and rattling. The high sheriff of Hampshire County appeared at their cell door, surrounded by a half-dozen armed militiamen, all crowded into the narrow space. Major General Ebenezer Mattoon, the man who'd led the posse that had captured them, was tall and athletic in appearance, with a gristle-like leanness to his still-handsome, windburned face. Mattoon looked impressive in his uniform. Around his waist he wore a red sash, which held a gleaming saber on one side and on the other the same navy pistol he'd pointed at Halligan when he'd arrested them five months earlier. The turnkey opened the cell door, and the sheriff strode in, his bearing officious.

"Gentlemen," he instructed them, "I am to conduct you to the courthouse."

"But we've not met with counsel yet," Halligan said.

"That's not my concern. Step lively. We don't want to keep the judges waiting."

Manacles were placed on both their hands and feet, and the two were led out into the street. They had to take short, mincing steps, so as not to trip. Besides that, their legs were weak from lack of exercise, and it took a moment or two for them to get used to walking again. Outside, the militiamen shouldered their muskets and took up positions in two lines around them. The sheriff mounted his horse, a large bay mare with four white stockings, and the group began moving north toward the center of town.

Halligan glanced around. The early spring day loomed cloudy, with a light rain falling out of a tattered gray sky. The air hung chilly, smelling of wood smoke and ash and of the earth slowly thawing. The street was muddy, deeply grooved by wagon tracks, and they had to be careful not to turn an ankle. On each side of the street, the still-naked trees and houses appeared dull and drab after the long winter. Despite the overcast, the sudden vastness of the outside world nearly overwhelmed him. He'd forgotten just how expansive the sky was.

Daley leaned toward Halligan and whispered, "Me guts are rumblin' something awful. I got to use the jakes."

"A fine time you picked to have to shite. You'd better hold it."

"I don't know if I can."

"Quiet there," cried a stocky beared guard to their right. He glared at them.

They were marched north along Pleasant Street toward the center of Northampton. It was the route they had taken when they were first brought here, though they'd been on horseback then instead of on foot, and in the confusion Halligan hadn't taken much notice. Now he thought the place reminded him a bit of Dingle town—the hilly streets, the houses packed close together, the mountains he could spy in the distance. He noted the shops and businesses along the way. A saddlery and a cooper's shop, a wig-makers establishment, a goldsmith and a bookseller, a blacksmith's dark-looking den with smoke curling from the forge.

Because of the rain, only a few were out and about. A large-bosomed, spindly-legged woman, one of the Osborn sisters who ran a milliner's shop on the corner of King and Main streets, happened to be tossing a pan of dirty water into the street. She paused to watch the procession, her hand covering her mouth in muted surprise. A young boy herding some hogs toward the slaughterhouse just west of town appeared to fall in beside the group. He stared at the two prisoners with dumb fascination as he swatted the animals with a hickory switch. And the blacksmith, a squat, dark-featured man named Wallace, came lumbering out from his forge to stand defiantly in the rain, his sleeves rolled back over massive forearms and a hammer clutched in one beefy hand. Somehow he caught Halligan's eye, and a smile seemed to pass over his dusky face.

The small procession turned onto Main and made their way up the street toward the squarish courthouse building. A little ways beyond it, standing on the very summit of the hill, was the much larger Protestant meetinghouse, its white steeple pointing like a bony finger toward the sky.

Inside the large courtroom, a few men up front were standing about, engaged in conversation. They turned to look at the prisoners as they entered. The place was oddly empty, hushed, unlike the sort of busy, crowded justice halls Halligan had seen back home. The guards took up their position along the back wall, while the sheriff escorted them forward. The jangling of their chains scraping the floor echoed throughout the high-ceilinged room. At the front was a plain, oaken table, slightly elevated on a platform, with two chairs behind it, now empty.

"I am going to remove these," the sheriff said as he took hold of Daley's manacles and held up a key. "You're not going to give me any trouble, are you?"

"No sir. You'll get no trouble from us," Daley replied.

"Good." Only then did he remove the manacles and have them sit at a table by themselves. He stood a few feet behind them.

Off to their left, two men, one seated, the other standing, were engaged in conversation. The one standing was a stout, ruddy-faced individual who wore small clothes, yellow satin breeches and white stockings held up by garters. The second sat at a table covered with papers. This man was balding, with the jerky movements of a squirrel. Halligan recognized him as Mr. Hooker, the assistant prosecutor, a man who had come to their jail cell several times to interogate them about the murder. He glanced over at them now and nodded perfunctorily. Then he returned to conversing with the heavyset man.

The two Irishmen sat there waiting, awkwardly, warily, like animals caught in a trap. They looked ragged and unkempt, their long hair tangled and greasy, their beards hanging almost to their chests. They hadn't bathed once since being jailed. Halligan started to scratch himself, hardly aware of it. He picked a louse off his shirt and crushed it against a nail, the blood—his own—staining the tip of his finger. He wiped his hand on his coat. The garment was filthy. So, too, were his hands, the long fingernails encrusted with grime, looking more like the claws of an animal. He angled his nose toward his armpit and caught a sour, musky odor, like that released from the belly of a gutted sheep. He hadn't been aware of his own smell in the jail. But here, in the courtroom, among regular people, he realized he stank. He felt ashamed suddenly, and he suspected that's just what they wanted him to feel. *The bastards*, he cursed.

Daley touched his arm. "Jamy," he whispered anxiously.

"You'll just have to hold it."

"No, not that. What do we say if they ask . . . you know?"

"What we agreed on."

"But—"

"Shut your bloody gob," Halligan hissed. "We stick to our story, Dom. It's our only chance."

Halligan had met Dominic Daley the previous fall, only a few months before they were arrested. They had run into one another on the Boston Road as they traveled on foot looking for employment. Times were hard in Boston, what with the war in Europe and the terrible situation in Ireland forcing growing numbers of immigrants to come here looking for work. Many of the Irish traveled west to pick apples or to help with the harvest or the laying of roads, anything to make a little money. A Connemaraman, Halligan guessed as soon as he heard his broad, thick hill accent. Daley was a large strapping fellow, nearly six feet five and weighing well over two hundred pounds, with a sallow complexion pitted from having had smallpox as a child. Unrefined in his speech and manners, he had gray-blue eyes that looked upon all things with a child's unblinking sense of wonder.

"I'm Dominic Daley," the big man said to him, offering his hand.

"Jamy Halligan," he replied. From an inside pocket of his great coat, Halligan removed a bottle of rum and offered him a drink.

"Where do your people come from, Jamy?"

"Here and there," was all he could say.

They decided to throw in together. Walking the road in the early mornings, working in orchards, sleeping under the stars at night, they became fast friends. Halligan found Daley a boon traveling companion. Though unlettered, he had a cheerful, gregarious disposition, a good sense of humor, and a surprisingly fine voice. In the evening, around a campfire, they would play cards from a deck Daley carried or share Halligan's bottle of rum, and later Daley would sing a song. Some ballad or jig from back home. "Snowy Breasted Pearl" or "Green Bushes."

"Where'd you learn to sing like that?" Halligan asked.

Daley shrugged, told him it came natural as breathing. They would swap stories of home, of what they'd left behind and what they hoped to find here in America. He learned that Daley had come over in '99, the year after the failed Uprising, and the large, close-knit Daley clan had settled in Boston. His friend was forever going on about his family, talking about his beloved mother, his siblings. But he especially liked to talk about his wife and newborn son. He was always bragging about Finola, about her cooking and how well she could sew, how much he missed her. "Finola's a right fine woman," he'd say. "I'm lucky to have her."

Halligan wasn't nearly as tall as Daley, but he was solid, broad through the chest with sloping shoulders and arms well developed from his labors. He had a wide, squarish face and deep-set, almost pretty blue eyes, eyes at once pensive and a touch jaunty. He was good looking in a gypsy sort of way, with a head of curly brown hair and a lusty mouth always ready with the hint of a smile, one that men found a challenge and women an invitation. Something of a ladies' man, he amused Daley with stories of his rakish past. Of this conquest and that. The time he'd nearly been shot by a jealous husband or run off by an irate father.

"Don't you have a girl?" Daley asked him once as they sat around a campfire preparing their supper.

"I wouldn't want to be tied to only one," he'd joked. "It wouldn't be fair to all the others."

"Listen to himself. You get one as knows how to cook it'll change your thinkin'."

"I can cook just fine," Halligan replied with a coy smile. "It's the other thing I can't do for myself."

In November, they had set out together from Boston, bound for the city of New York. Daley knew someone there who owed him some money, money he was planning on putting aside for a piece of land he wanted to buy up in New Hampshire. Halligan went along simply to keep him company, for the adventure of it. He had never seen New York. He'd heard it said it was bigger even than Dublin, though he found that hard to believe. He thought he might sign on with some merchant ship and sail around the Horn. He was free, unattached, all his worldly possessions slung over his shoulder. The autumn days had stretched out fine and clear, and the traveling had been pleasant. They'd taken their time walking west, stopping to have a pint of porter and play some cards in a tavern, sharing a room at various inns. At night, Daley would get down on his knees and say his prayers. In fact, Halligan had never seen a man so damned religious. But each to his own, he felt. Things went well until they reached Rye, New York, where they'd stopped at an inn to have supper. They were to take the ferry from there to New York City. But a large party of heavily armed riders came swooping down on them, guns drawn. Halligan could recall thinking that whoever they were after must have done something terrible. The posse's leader, the high sheriff of Hampshire County, pointed a large-bore navy pistol at Halligan's chest and said they were under arrest.

"On what charges?" Halligan asked, incredulous.

"We have a warrant for your arrest on the charge of murder."

Murder, they exclaimed, thinking at first it had to be some kind of joke. But it was no joke. They were clapped in irons and placed on the back of an old piebald mare who staggered under her dual burden and brought back to Springfield. There, at the inquest, a nervous, scrawny young boy pointed a finger at them and said they the ones he'd seen leading the murdered man's horse into a field near where the crime had happened. That was enough to convince the authorities they had the right men. They were conducted twenty miles north to the county jail in Northampton. They were told they would be held here until the next session of the Supreme Court, which tried capital cases. They had waited in jail for five months, not allowed to see or speak to a soul, except for the assistant prosecutor and a minister by the name of Williams.

After nearly a half hour's wait, a door to the left opened and two men entered, one walking briskly, the other slowly, gingerly, as if he had a bad back.

"All rise," cried the stout man, who took up a position to the left of the table. "The court of Hampshire County in the Commonwealth of Massachusetts is now in session," he droned in a mechanical voice. "The honorable Judges Theodore Sedgwick and Samuel Sewall presiding. Be seated."

The Supreme Court justices wore scarlet robes with black collars, and upon their heads white silk wigs, old looking and yellowed from smoke. One judge, a tall, slump-shouldered man in his sixties, wore a sour expression on his long, wrinkled face. He had dark eyes set deep beneath graying, shaggy brows, long side whiskers, and a large nose that seemed to be displeased at some odor. The other was a short, rotund man, with ears that protruded from beneath his wig and a small pink mouth held in an attitude of mild consternation. Neither one looked at the prisoners, almost as if their presence there was superfluous. Instead the judges spent some time shuffling through papers, occasionally writing something down or turning to the other to ask a question or make a comment. Finally, the tall judge with the dark eyes looked up and spoke to the assistant prosecutor. "Mr. Hooker," he began, "is the government ready to proceed?"

The assistant prosecutor stood. "We are, your honor," he replied.

"Where is Mr. Sullivan?"

"He's not here, your honor."

"I can see *that*," the judge scoffed. "Does he plan to grace us with his presence? Or will you be trying the case by yourself, Mr. Hooker?"

"No, I will be assisting Mr. Sullivan. He very much wished to be here for the arraignment but he had certain other pressing affairs of his office he had to tend to."

"Of his *current* office?" Judge Sedgwick said, raising one of his furry eyebrows.

"I would assume so, yes."

"If the attorney general would put half as much time into performing the duties for which he is currently being paid by the commonwealth, instead of campaigning for the governor's office, then perhaps such crimes as this would not even take place."

"Yes, your honor," Mr. Hooker replied meekly. "The attorney general wished me to express his sincerest apologies to the court for his unfortunate absence today. And he would like to assure you he will be here on Thursday. That is, if it is suitable with your honor."

"No, it is *not* suitable, Mr. Hooker," retorted the judge. "In fact, it is highly *un*suitable. You have had five months' time to prepare the government's case. I would think that would be quite sufficient given the circumstances."

"My apologies, your honor," Mr. Hooker said, his bald skull turning red. His hands trembled, his face twitched in spasms.

"Let the attorney general's Republican cronies handle his campaign," Judge Sedgwick berated the man. "He has duties which require his presence—"

The plump judge to his left touched Sedgwick on the shoulder then. The two spent a moment conferring in an undertone which grew heated. When they were finished, Judge Sedgwick turned back to the assistant prosecutor. His mouth pinched in annoyance, large nostrils flared, he stared down at Mr. Hooker for several seconds. "If it is not too much to ask, please inform the attorney general that his presence is required here on Thursday," he said, with a dismissive flick of his hand. Then he looked to the stout man wearing the yellow breeches. "Would the clerk kindly read the indictment against the defendants."

"Yes, your honor," said the man, rising to his feet. He held an official-looking document before him, from which he read in the same mechanical voice as before:

At a court holden at Northampton, within and for the county of Hampshire, on the fourth Monday of April, in the year of our Lord one thousand eight hundred and six, before the Honorable Judges Theodore Sedgwick and Samuel Sewall, Esquires, Dominic Daley and James Halligan come on to be tried for the willful murder of Marcus Lyon, a resident of the state of Connecticut. On motion by the Honorable James Sullivan, Esquire, Attorney General of the Commonwealth, they are to be arraigned on an indictment charging them with having, on the ninth of November in the year of our Lord one thousand eight hundred and five, at Wilbraham in the county of Hampshire, killed one Marcus Lyon, in the peace of God and of this Commonwealth, then and there being:

~ The first count states that Daley, with a pistol, gave Lyon the blow of which he instantly died and that Halligan was present, aiding, abetting, and encouraging;
~ The second, that Daley gave the blow as aforesaid and immersed the body in the Chicopee River so that Lyon died, as well by reason of the immersion as the blow, and that Halligan was present as before;
~ And the third, states that both Daley and Halligan, with each a pistol in his right hand, gave the mortal bruises and wounds of which Lyon instantly died.

When the clerk finished reading the indictment, he came over to the two and said in a whisper, "The judges will now ask you how you plead, and you are to say guilty or not guilty. Then they will ask how you are to be tried. You must answer, 'By God and my country.' Nothing more. And when you address them you are to call them 'your honor.' Do you understand?"

They nodded that they did.

"Beggin' your pardon, sir," said Daley, "do ye think I might use the jakes?"

"Not now. We are about to begin."

Judge Sedgwick looked down at the prisoners for the first time.

"I am Justice Sedgwick of the Massachusetts Supreme Judicial Court," he explained. "Justice Sewall and I will be hearing your case. Today you are being formally arraigned. Do you understand the charges that have been read to you?"

Daley looked at Halligan, deferring to him.

"We do, your honor," replied Halligan.

"And how plead you to the charges?"

"But your honor, we haven't been allowed to speak to counsel yet."

"In good time, sir. I am now asking how you plead to the charges," he repeated.

"But your honor—"

"Silence!" cried the judge, wagging a threatening finger at Halligan. Color rose again to his pale cheeks and his thin mouth wrinkled in anger. "In my court, sir, you will speak only when I ask you a question. Do you understand?"

He wanted to tell the stinking old bastard he didn't care a tinker's fart for his court, but he figured he'd better not. "Yes, your honor," he replied instead.

"Now. How plead you to the charges?"

"Not guilty," they both replied at once.

"Not guilty to all the charges?"

"Yes, your honor," said Halligan. "Not guilty to all the charges."

"Very well." Staring at Halligan, he asked, "Dominic Daley, how will you be tried?"

"Beggin' your pardon, your honor," Daley interrupted this time.

"I warned you already, did I not?" the judge cried, scowling at the two. "I'll indulge no further interruptions."

"But sir, *I'm* Halligan," Halligan explained. "He's Daley."

Glancing from one man to the other, the judge frowned, as if he could tell their names just by staring at them long enough. He then shuffled through the papers on his desk, before resorting to a quick appeal to the sheriff, who shrugged. Finally, the judge turned toward the clerk. "Mr. Lyman, I thought the tall one was Halligan."

"No, your honor," the clerk replied. "That's Daley. The other one's Halligan."

Judge Sedgwick paused for a moment, shaking his head in annoyance at this oversight. "Very well. Dominic Daley," he began again, this time looking at Daley, "how will you be tried?"

"By God and my country, your honor." He then asked the same of Halligan, who responded in kind. After that the judge said, "God send you a good deliverance." He next inquired of the prisoners if they wished to have counsel. They said they would and the judge assigned them a man named Francis Blake, of Worcester, Massachusetts, a town some fifty miles to the east. Finally Judge Sedgwick set a trial date for Thursday, three days hence, to begin at nine.

"I hope that is *convenient* for your esteemed colleague, Mr. Hooker," Judge Sedgwick offered sardonically.

"The commonwealth appreciates your gracious indulgence, your honor."

The judge stared at Mr. Hooker to see if he was trying to be sarcastic. When he couldn't decide, he remanded the prisoners to the custody of the high sheriff, then the two judges stood. They left the courtroom the same way they had entered it.

The sheriff placed the prisoners in irons, and led them out. Word having spread about the two being brought to the courthouse, more people had assembled in the street despite the rain. Small groups had gathered here and there, in front of shops and on porches to get a look at the prisoners. Young boys ran alongside the procession now. Just outside the jailhouse, a small crowd of some fifteen or twenty had congregated in the street. Somebody called out, "There they are!" and several heaved rotten eggs, one of which hit Daley on the back. The sulfuric stink rose up around them. "A curse on ye," he cried. "Come and fight me like a man, why don't ya." But the guards easily kept the men at bay and hustled the prisoners into the jail.

As soon as they got back to their cell, Daley rushed over to the slop bucket in the corner, unbuttoned his trousers, and squatted. As he emptied his bowels, he cried, "Jesus Mary and Joseph. I thought I'd shite me pants there for a minute."

Halligan sat on his bunk. He unlaced his wet boots and took them off. His feet were hurting, cold and blistered from the unaccustomed walk.

"So we're finally to have our day in court, eh, Jamy boy?"

"Looks that way."

"We'll just get up on the witness stand and tell 'em the truth."

"You reckon it'll be that simple?"

"It'll be our word against theirs."

Halligan didn't say anything.

"If they had anything on us, don't you think they'd of tried us long before this? Mark me words, Jamy. In a few days we'll be home."

Home, Halligan thought.

Daley wiped himself with a piece of old newspaper, pulled up his trousers, and went over and lay down on his bunk. He put his hands behind his head and stared at the ceiling.

"Yessir. Won't be long now."

They were the only prisoners in the small jailhouse of this western Massachusetts town. For some reason the turnkey allowed them to share the same cell. Perhaps to give them some company, as they were allowed no visitors. Since their arrest back in November there had been other prisoners. The most recent being an old man, a frail bag of bones clothed in a ragged watchcoat and an old-fashioned tricorn hat from the revolutionary days. As old as Atty Hayes's goat, Daley had called him. He'd been brought in a few weeks before for hitting somebody during a drunken argument. And there had been a man arrested for stealing a horse. He had a look in his eyes of one teched in the head. He would stare through the bars at Halligan and curse, "What the hell are you looking at, paddy?" But then he was taken off somewhere, to trial or to another prison, they couldn't say. Back in the winter, there had even been a young Irish lad from Clonakilty, an indentured servant who'd run away from a harsh master down in Springfield. For the two Irish prisoners, it was good to talk to someone from home. His master eventually came for him though, put him in irons, and dragged him back to serve out the remainder of his contract. For the last few weeks, the jail had held only the two of them.

The turnkey appeared before their cell.

"This come by the morning's post rider," he said. He slipped a letter through the bars and dropped it on Daley's bunk. It was from his wife. Even from across the cell, Halligan recognized her handwriting. She wrote to her husband nearly every week and he saved the letters in a packet, tied with a piece of string. He kept the packet inside his shirt and, though he couldn't read a word of them, would take the letters out from time to time and fondle them, put them to his nose as if he could smell her.

Daley sniffed the envelope. "Would you do the honors, Jamy boy?" he asked, as he always did, handing the letter finally over to Halligan to read.

Halligan felt in a playful mood for some reason. He took the letter and passed it under his nose, in imitation of Daley. Then, when he began to read it, he did so in a breathy, comical way. "Oh, Dominic. I miss your big—"

"Just read the bloody letter, before I crack yer head for you," Daley said, pretending to be angry.

In a regular voice Halligan started over.

My Dearest Dominic,

How are you, my love? We are all fine here and in good spirits. Even your mother, whose cough appears to have improved somewhat. Your folks send their love and miss you very much. Michael grows bigger with each passing day. You would hardly recognize him. And quick, too. Though but six months, he's going to be very intelligent, I can tell. I am trying to get him to say "Da" so he can surprise you when you come home.

We spent a lovely Easter together. The weather has been unseasonably cold and rainy. Back home it would already be like summer, the air *smelling of gorse and the hills green. What is it like out there? Are you getting enough to eat? Did you receive the pair of socks I sent you with my last letter? I know how your feet get cold.*

Your mother and I have been to see the Attorney General on several occasions to ask permission that we be allowed to visit with you. But alas, he has not even extended us the courtesy of hearing our petition. Have no fear though, we shall keep trying.

I have missed you terribly these past few months. I am so lonely without you. I am able to keep myself occupied during the day but the nights I have a devil of a time. I sometimes think of that song you used to sing when you were courting me. "The Banks of the Roses." Do you remember it, my love? I sing the words at night to help me sleep. Each morning before I go to work I stop in the church and say a prayer to the Virgin, asking Her to watch over you and to send you safety back to us. I do not know what I would do if anything were to befall you. Take care, macushla.

Always and forever your wife,
Finola

When he finished reading, he handed the letter back to his cellmate. Daley lay quietly, brooding, fondling the paper and staring at the ceiling. His eyes were moist, a look of terrible sadness on his long face.

"Dom, are you all right?" Halligan asked.

"I hate thinkin' she's all by herself."

"She's got your family there."

"Still. She gets lonesome. She's the sort of woman needs someone around."

"Aren't they all like that?" Halligan said, kidding.

"No!" he snapped, suddenly angry. "You don't understand. Finola's not like that."

"Easy, Dom. I'm only fooling with you."

"She's not been the same since we lost Eva."

Daley had told him about the child that had died of fever back in Ireland. How Finola had cried for months, how it had almost destroyed her.

And it was only with the birth of their second child, Michael, here in America that she was able finally to move on.

Like always, Daley had Halligan write a letter in reply. The turnkey provided them with paper and writing implements, and Daley told him what he wanted him to write. The big Irishman was clumsy with words, handling English as if it were a piece of thread he were trying to guide through the tiny eye of a needle. Often he'd say to Halligan, "Put it so it has a nice ring to it, Jamy boy. So a woman will like it." For his part Halligan did his best, though he wondered what it would be like to write to a woman he was in love with as much as Daley was in love with his wife.

When Halligan had finished, Daley put his X on the paper and folded it. He would have Dowd give it to the post rider tomorrow.

Halligan held up the well-worn deck of cards and Daley nodded that he wanted to play. They used Halligan's bunk as a table and had to keep track of what one owed the other by making scratches in the stone wall with a piece of chicken bone. So far, Daley, a wild, daring gambler, perhaps because nothing was at stake, was in debt over a hundred dollars. They played just to help pass the time.

"Who learned you to read and write like that?" Daley asked.

"The brothers that raised me."

He thought of them: Brother Padraig and Brother Sebastian and little Brother Simon who always smelled of the barn and had a loony smile of someone not right in the head. Kind-hearted, serious men of faith. They were among the last of the Franciscans in all of Ireland, after Cromwell and William of Orange and a hundred years of the penal laws. It was a small community west of Cahirciveen, in the remote mountains of Kerry. They lived in an old abbey, one that through the influence of a local landlord had been spared razing like all the other Catholic buildings throughout the country. The brothers took in orphans and taught them to read and write and do their figures. Old Brother Padraig used to read *Robinson Crusoe* or *Gulliver's Travels* to the boys at night and then listen to their prayers.

"'Tis a grand thing," Daley said, "to open a book and know what it says. Do you think you could learn me someday?"

"You want to learn? To read and write?"

"Aye. Do you think I could pick it up?"

"A big dumb ox like yourself!" Halligan scoffed, smiling. "Hell, it'd be easier to teach a pig to stand on its hind legs and play the pipes."

Daley didn't smile. "But would you? Would you learn me to read an' write?"

"You're bloody serious, ain't you?"

"I am."

Halligan shook his head. "Why all of a sudden this interest in reading?"

"I'd like to write a letter to me son."

"I could write one for you."

"No. I mean, something in me own hand. Something he'd have from his father."

Halligan furrowed his brow. "I suppose. Are you gonna play or not?"

Daley looked over at him. "Do you think they'll let me folks come? To the trial."

"I don't see how they can stop them. It's a free country."

"Free country," he snorted. "Would be nice to see 'em." He stroked his long beard in thought. "I haven't seen Michael in a while. Finola says the lad is gettin' big."

"He'll favor you. Just hope he's got your wife's brains. Now are you going to play cards or flap your bloody gob?" Halligan said.

Before bed that night, Daley got down on his knees, his rosary wrapped around his hand, and prayed. He had taken a piece of twine and tied knots in it, fashioning a crude rosary, which he called his *paidrín*. For a cross, he had tied at right angles two gray pieces of chicken bones left over from a meal. He would kneel on the cold stone floor, bow his head, and give thanks to the Lord. Thanks for His manifold gifts, both large and small—for the food he was about to eat, for his wife and little boy and for his dear mother who was ill. And he would pray for the arrival of the priest from Boston, a certain Father Cheverus.

"Join me, Jamy boy," he would say, inviting Halligan to pray with him. But he never would. Halligan couldn't remember the last time he had prayed, really and truly prayed. That wasn't counting of course the odd bit of wishing and hoping and bargaining a fellow did from time to time, like during the fighting he'd done in the Uprising. And the last time he'd made confession or received the host was when he'd lived with the Franciscans all those years ago. Though he'd been raised Catholic, and even now, if asked, he supposed he'd call himself one, it was more an indication of what he wasn't—a bloody Proddy-dog—than anything he was, than anything he believed in. But as far as the particulars of Catholic belief, that was something else entirely. The not eating meat on Fridays, when most of the Irish he knew couldn't afford to eat it the other six days either. Or turning the other cheek or the horseshite about the meek inheriting the earth. The only earth the meek would inherit, he knew, would be six feet of it piled right on top of them—if they were lucky. If not, a pauper's grave. Or the priests, lording their power over you. Saying you couldn't do this or that, especially if it made you feel good, made you feel alive. Like drinking or gambling, or sleeping with a woman, when they were just jealous that they couldn't. To Halligan, there was just oneself. That's all you could count on. All in all, it wasn't such a bad life if you knew that.

"Watch over me wife and child, Lord," Daley said.

Then he got into bed, put his hands behind his head, and within moments he was snoring. Halligan closed his eyes, hungry for sleep. But it didn't come. Outside, the rain made a mournful sound against the prison walls, rustling like silk over a woman's thigh. He had to admit he envied Daley a little, his having a woman to write to, to think about, people who cared whether he lived or died. He supposed that was something to be thankful for. Then again, it had to be a burden, too. In some ways, it had to be harder this way—having loved ones you had to worry about, to think of them managing without you, if and when the time came. You hadn't just yourself to think about, to take care of, you had them, too. You had to think about how they would suffer at your suffering, how they would be afraid at your fear, so your own pain was increased many fold. He himself had no one to worry about, no one whose suffering he had to consider in the least. Just himself. And that had to be better, hadn't it?

As far as he knew, he had no kin in the world. He was what they called a merry begotten, a child of a woman who hadn't been married. He'd never known a father, and he had only a single memory of his mother—or at least a woman he took to be his mother. In it, he was a small boy, three or four years old, sitting on a dirt floor in a cottier's hovel in some back-of-beyond place in the west of Ireland. She was stirring something in a large scorched pot, an intoxicating smell he could still recall. His mother had long dark hair that glistened in the firelight and thin, pale arms, the skin smooth and white as that which forms on boiled milk. He couldn't remember her face or her voice, though for some reason he imagined she must have been pretty. That was all he had of her, this lone image in his mind, a thing polished smooth from handling. He never knew how she died or where she was buried. He wondered if she had loved the man who was his father, even whether or not she had loved her son. Sometimes he thought he missed her, but he knew that that was impossible. What he missed was just the *idea* of a mother, the notion that there was a warm, protective place to come back to, a safe harbor. Yet if being an orphan had taught him anything, it was this: that we were all, in one way or another, at one time or another, orphans. If not now, then later. We were born alone and we died alone, and in between a man's heart navigated by itself as best it could.

After his mother's passing, the world became an even harder place. He could vaguely recall a series of grim, smelly homes where he was always hungry and treated miserably. Someone grabbing him by the scruff of his neck, a harsh word, the back of a hand stinging against his mouth. He wound up somehow with the Franciscan brothers. The brothers were austere men, disciplined and stern, but in their own way not unkind. They wore rough habits and lived simple, pious lives of prayer and hard work and self-denial. Of all of them, he'd liked Brother Padraig best. He was a tough old bird, with a grizzled face and scaly hands like the claws of a rooster. But he took a special interest in the young Halligan. He used to take him fishing in Dingle Bay, in a small canvas-sided coracle that seemed too frail to keep out the cold Atlantic waters. At night he would tell the lad the names of the constellations and the history behind each one. "You see those seven stars, James," he would explain, "they were the daughters of Atlas, you see." He taught him a bit of Latin and some of the old language, before the British came: *Ta ocras orm* (I'm hungry), *Ta tart orm* (I'm thirsty), *Deoch eile* (another drink). He taught him things he would need to get by in the world, like how to shoe a horse or mend a harness, how to ride, how to plow a straight furrow, how to read and write and figure sums. Perhaps the most important and ultimately the most dangerous lesson he'd taught him, especially for a poor boy living in a country run by wealthy masters: self-respect. "Remember, Jamy," he had told him, "you're as good as any of them. Don't let 'em tell you any different."

The brothers also taught him things he came to feel had no use at all: the Latin of the Mass, the names of the saints and the martyrs, how to make a good confession, above all, how a piece of bread could be changed into the body of Christ. They would tell the young boy about God's love. How He so loved us He let His only son die on the cross for our salvation. Yet Halligan wondered what sort of father would let his own flesh and blood die. And if God really loved us as much as the brothers and the priests and everyone made out, why would He let innocent children starve during the yellow famine? Or permit landlords to throw whole families into the cold? Or allow the English to live on the sweat and toil and backs of the poor? Or let a mother die so her only child became an orphan? What sort of loving God would do that?

The brothers used to tell them the tale of Piaras Feiritéar, the heroic Catholic rebel during Cromwell's brutal campaign in Ireland. In every pub and small shebeen, in every hedgerow school and open-air chapel, they spoke with pride and with awe of the man who had defied the Protestant invaders. How the English had hunted him down like a dog, finally cornering him in a cave on the remote Blasket Isles, though not before he had managed to kill no less than fifty of the depised English. The story went that they brought Feiritéar to a hill west of Killarney to hang him. But a priest, disguised as a commoner, had slipped by the guards to give the condemned man the last sacrament and God's blessing. The noose was placed about his neck, and Feiritéar seemingly dropped to his death. But the rope broke. They tried a second time, and again the rope broke. " 'Twas a miracle, James!" Brother Padraig had told him. According to the old man, and to most Irish, the breaking of the rope that was to hang Feiritéar signified that God was on the side of the Irish. "Did they let him go?" the young Halligan had naively asked. "No, lad," replied Brother Padraig, "they finally got a strong enough rope."

Such stories only convinced Halligan that there was only one conclusion a person of reasonable mind could make: that there wasn't a god. Or if there was, He must have been an Englishman, for He sure as hell didn't lend an ear to an Irishman. When he told this to Brother Padraig, as he had once, the old man placed his hand on the boy's shoulder. "James," he said. "Be a hard and lonely life if you don't have Him there."

The truth was, Halligan didn't mind being alone in the world, dependent only upon himself, answering only to himself. In fact, he actually preferred his own company, quiet nights looking up at the stars, days spent alone staring off at the sea. There was in his heart a strain of wanderlust. Even as a boy, he was curious about what lay just beyond the next hill. At night as he lay in bed in the long room with the other orphans, he wondered what the rest of Ireland looked like, what the rest of the *world* looked like. Sometimes, tending sheep from a hill overlooking the Atlantic, he would stare for hours out at the blue-green water. He'd heard talk of Amerikay, a magical place where a man could stand on his own two feet and be the equal of anyone. Someday he swore he'd go there. Yes, he would. Eventually this natural restlessness proved too strong. He was just thirteen when, in the middle of the night, he packed his few possessions in a blanket, lifted a couple shilling from the collection box, and took to the open road. He would miss Brother Padraig and a few of the others, but he needed to be moving on. He'd been moving on ever since.

He traveled all over Ireland and some of England, too, sleeping under the stars or in someone's stables, never staying long in one place. He worked when there was work to be had, he stole when he had no other choice. One time he hadn't eaten for two days, and he stole an apple from a vendor's stall; he ran like the clappers while two men chased after him. Caught, he managed to give one a good kick in the bollocks but the other got hold of him, and they ended up beating him within an inch of his life. He learned that his existence wasn't worth the price of an apple. Another time, he gave away his last farthing to a starving woman and child he came across in a fetid alley in Macroom. Later, when he himself was hungry, he considered it a foolish gesture and vowed never to do it again.

He remembered one time, he must have been fifteen. It was winter and bitter cold, with the gray rains flogging the countryside like an English cat-o'-nine tails. It was in the Burren somewhere, that rock-scarred, blasted, godforsaken place, so desolate and unforgiving even the Irish themselves pitied those whose fortunes cast them there. Half-starved, his privities almost froze clean off, he was seated around a meager peat fire, eating what was left of a rabbit he'd managed to catch, when this scrawny yellow tomcat wandered in. The thing was skin and bones, half of its fur having fallen out. It meowed pathetically looking for food, and came up to Halligan. He felt sorry for the thing and stroked its back. He'd never had a real pet of his own before. The creature wound itself between his legs, looking up at him imploringly. "You're worse off than me, ain't you boyo?" Halligan said. He gave the thing a few scraps of rabbit. They became friends. It stayed with him for several days, until Halligan's hunger grew overpowering. He would always feel a twinge of regret when he thought of the cat, but only a twinge.

Yes, he'd done things he wasn't proud of, things that shamed or humbled or reduced him in some measure, but most of what he did, if given the opportunity a second time, he'd have done again. That, he came to believe, was morality, the real difference between right and wrong: what you'd have done over if given the chance had to be right, and what you wouldn't, had to be wrong. It was that simple. All the rest of it, the heaven and hell, the going to this church or that or none at all, why, it was just so much rot.

Sometimes, seeing as he knew his way around horses, he'd find employment as a groom for some wealthy landlord. He preferred the company of horses to that of people anyway. They had a quiet dignity, an air about them that most humans lacked. He loved the smell of them, the feel of their coats as he brushed them, the deep snuffling sounds they made at night when he slept nearby in the stables. And they knew his smell and touch as well, and his soft voice beside their ear. When they were frightened during a storm, he would whisper to them, "Hush, darling, I'm right here now."

Other times, when nothing better presented itself, he worked as a spalpeen, a common laborer, cutting turf or digging potatoes, paid a shilling a day plus meals, a place to rest his head at night, as well as the occasional scullery maid or cottier's daughter he could talk into meeting him out in the barn. He was never lacking in that department. He was a good-looking lad with that cocksure smile of his, those broad shoulders and strong arms. He liked to drink and play cards and have his fun.

When he was seventeen, he was employed as a groom for a Mr. Fitzgibbons, a well-to-do gentleman in Enniscorthy. There was already talk of trouble brewing, especially up north in Ulster, of the poor rising up against their masters. Halligan had had his share of harsh masters, those who regarded Catholics as little more than beasts of burden. And like most Irish, he'd had the occasional run-in with some loudmouth Proddy or had heard the stories of people driven from their houses by the Peep o' Day boys, the Protestant secret group known for raiding Catholic houses at dawn. But he mostly kept to himself, didn't bother anyone who didn't bother him first. If things turned bad, he would move on. He looked after himself and didn't stick his nose in where it didn't belong. His employer, Master Fitzy, as the help called him, was a decent enough skin, benevolent, generous, fair to his tenants and those who worked for him. Occasionally he would even let Halligan borrow one of the books from his grand library. His son, on the other hand, was an arrogant and haughty youth, hot tempered, prone to sudden tantrums if he didn't get his way. Behind his back he was referred to as the "squireen" or "half-sir." He was about Halligan's own age, a pale, effete-looking young man with long blond hair which he powdered heavily. He always smelled sweet, like a bawdy house. As Halligan saddled his horse for him, he had to avoid looking the young man in the eye so as not to show him his contempt for the stinking little podgreen.

One day, the half-sir was in a terrible rage because an expensive bridle turned up missing from the tack room. His suspicions fell for some reason upon a small boy who polished the masters' boots. They were in the yard of the demesne, and the half-sir had taken to whipping the boy with his riding crop.

"I'll teach you, you thieving Irish bastard," the man cried, beating the boy savagely. The boy stood there crying, protesting his innocence. He looked at Halligan, as if he might help him.

"There's no call for that," said Halligan.

"What did you say?" the half-sir exclaimed, turning on him.

"I said there wasn't any call to do that to the lad, sir."

"You'll keep your nose out of this, if you don't want a few good ones yourself."

Halligan would have liked simply to keep his nose out of it. After all, it wasn't his business. But somehow he couldn't. Not with the boy staring imploringly at him. And he had never forgotten what Brother Padraig had told him, about his being as good as any man. He smiled contemptuously at the young master and said, "And I suppose you'd be the fellow to try it?" Halligan had spoken loud enough that some of the help could hear his words. Incensed, the half-sir turned on Halligan and whipped him across the shoulder with his riding crop, as if he were nothing more than a dog or a mule. Instinctively, Halligan grabbed the man by his beaver-trimmed lapels and pummeled him. He probably would have killed him, too, had they not pulled him off. Later, when he came before the sessions, the judge asked him if he was connected to any of the agitators then becoming prevalent in the country, one of those United Irishmen come down from the North to cause trouble. Halligan said no, he was just defending himself, as any man would. The judge was unimpressed. He sentenced him to two years at hard labor and told him he ought to consider himself lucky not to receive transportation to New South Wales.

He got out of prison in 1798, just before open rebellion broke out in the North and soon spread to Wexford. Now his hatred of the British burned within him, fanned by his time in jail. He joined with the United Irishmen, became one of the insurgent croppies, as they were called.

They were finally going to take back their country; they were finally going to expel their centuries-old oppressors, send them packing just as the Americans had done, and the French to their aristocrats. He had never felt part of anything larger than himself before. But now, for a short time anyway, he was part of a cause he was willing to fight and die for. Though the Uprising only lasted a few months that spring and summer, it was a glorious time to be Irish. Their morale was high. The French, it was said, were to land an army to support them. The Irish fought admirably at the battles of New Ross and Arklow, most wielding only a pitchfork or a pike, bravely throwing themselves against the might of the British guns. He saw priests fight and die side by side with their parishioners, and he gained a new respect for those who did.

Then came Vinegar Hill and the inevitable end. The superior English forces routed them, scattered them like chickens before their cavalry and their cannons. Along with many of his comrades, he managed to escape through Needham's Gap and went into hiding in the mountains. Yet when he'd heard their captured leaders were to be hanged on Wexford Bridge, he and a few others slipped back into town to be there out of respect. Their hats pulled low over their faces, they stood among the vast crowd to witness Father Roche, Bagenal Harvey, John Kelly, and the others hanged up on the bridge. The sight of them dying miserably sickened him.

After that, he wandered slowly westward, avoiding the militia and the British soldiers, sticking to the back roads. He crossed a countryside of devastation: razed churches, destroyed homes and slaughtered livestock, starving families wandering the roads, their possessions in a small donkey cart or borne upon their backs. Hanged croppies, their bodies rotting in the breeze. On every tree, wanted posters showing the sketches of rebels. He'd heard how the loyalist yeomen would torture people, even women and children, using the pitchcap to get information on other rebels. How Father John Murphy had been caught and hanged, his body mutilated. Those were hard times indeed. He thought of leaving Ireland altogether, that it was no longer a place where a man could live. Maybe slipping away to America as soon as he'd saved up the passage fare.

He drifted from place to place, surviving as best he could. Working a few months here, a few there. Never staying long in any one spot, always worried that someone would recognize him, turn him in as a croppy to get the reward. Making just enough to get by, and sometimes not even that. He reached Dingle in the hard winter of '02. There in the market he had gathered with a shabby-looking group of other men looking for work, waiting to be chosen by farmers or stewards who needed help. Besides a raw potato a widow woman had given him for some work around her place, he'd not eaten a thing in three days. As it turned out, the steward from a large estate approached him and asked, "Know anything about horses, do ye?" Halligan nodded. The steward was an old man with moist yellow eyes and large teeth stained brown from tobacco.

"You'll do odd jobs around the place, as Mr. Maguire or meself sees fit. Pays a half shilling a day plus meals and a glass of whiskey."

"I got a shilling the last place I worked."

"Times is tough. Take it or leave it."

His hunger made the decision for him. He followed the man and they climbed into a two-wheeled trap, the back of which was loaded with supplies, and rode west out of town. The old man must have read his thoughts, for he reached into a burlap bag in the back of the wagon and handed Halligan a dirt-covered onion to eat. "I'm Morrissey. I pretty much run things up at the Maguire place. What's your name, lad?"

Though it was almost four years since the Uprising, still you never knew. Informants were everywhere. They'd hand over their own mother to the British to save their necks. "O'Shea," he replied at last, remembering the name on a sign in town: *O'Shea, Harness Maker.*

"You're not one o' them troublemakers they had over in the east, are you?" the old man asked.

"No," he said.

"You're a Catholic though?"

Funny how they always knew. He didn't wear any outward signs, no cross or rosary, and he hadn't practiced the faith since running away from the Franciscans. But still somehow it showed through. As if it were an odor he carried with him, as if the smell of incense from his days with the brothers had become ingrained in his flesh.

"In a manner of speaking," Halligan replied.

The old man frowned. "Jaysus. 'Tis like being in a manner of speaking with child. You either are or you ain't, lad."

"Does it matter?"

"Not to me, it don't. Long's you're not one of those rabble-rousers," he said, giving him a look. "Do your work, O'Shea, and keep your mouth shut, you'll do just fine."

After that they rode in silence, though the old man hummed occasionally. The day was cold and damp, with a thin crust of ice along the roadside. The ground cracked as the wagon's wheels rolled over it. Soon they were climbing up what the old man told him was the Mam Clasach road, the steep mountain road that led to the Maguire farm. It wasn't as large an estate as some of those he'd worked on back east, but it was big enough. Mr. Maguire, he was told, was a well-to-do landlord, known throughout Dingle. His farm was made up of high meadows and broad fields and undulating pasture land, separated by hedges and neat stone walls. Fat, black cattle grazed in one field, sheep in another. In the valley below, a grove of pine and willow and white oak grew along the banks of a fast-moving stream which churned and boiled as it cut down through the hills toward the sea. To the west was a sheer wall of sea cliffs—Slea Head, he learned they were called. And above them, framed against a gray sky, rose two peaks, the larger of which was dusted from a recent snowfall.

"What do they call the mountain?" Halligan asked, making conversation.

"Mount Eagle," the old man replied.

They passed through an ornate iron gate, over which a sign said *Devonshire Park*, and into the demesne proper. They headed up a long stone drive lined with tall Lombardy poplars, toward the Big House. The grounds were well tended, with manicured lawns and shrubs, neat flower gardens, a pond before the great oak front door. They rode around behind the house and into a muddy courtyard where pigs and chickens moved freely about scratching for food. A pair of collies began to bark at them. To the right of the *cúl a' tí*, the back door used by the help, a hugely obese woman was washing clothes in a large kettle on a fire. She stirred the clothes with a peggy's leg stick, her face swollen and pink from the steam. She eyed the newcomer suspiciously.

"I already fed the help," she cried out to Morrissey.

"Shut yer mouth, woman," he said. "You can wash yourself there," the old man said to him, pointing at a pump near a water trough. "There's a room off the tack room where you can put your things. Are you hungry, lad?"

He nodded. "Who's she?"

The old man smiled for the first time. "That be Dora. She's in charge of the kitchen. Don't pay her no mind."

Halligan stepped down from the trap and took his bearings. He could see right off that Devonshire Park was a well-run operation. Everything neat and well-ordered, not fancy or ostentatious, but functional. Stables, outbuildings, a barn, smokehouse, cold cellar, a structure that looked like it housed a blacksmith's forge. Situated halfway up the slope of the mountain, the demesne had lovely views east toward the bay and Dingle town, the Slieve Mountains turning a pale, blurry purple. He gazed up at the Big House. It was a large Georgian-style structure, with a slate roof, ornate cornices and entablatures, half a dozen chimneys all spewing smoke. Over the first-story windows hung the heavy iron grating many of the landlords had put up since the Uprising.

Despite the cold, he took off his shirt and began to wash himself. He hadn't bathed in a long while. The water was brutal, stinging like nettles against the skin. But no water was ever so refreshing. His skin turned pink as he scrubbed the filth from his body. The fat woman Dora stared at him, frowning. As he happened to look up, there in one of the third-story windows, he caught sight of a figure. A young girl. She was staring down at him. She had olive-colored skin, and black hair that fell to her shoulders. She wore something white about her shoulders, making her skin appear all the darker. She continued to look down at him for another moment or two. So he gave her his best smile. With this she stepped back from the window, perhaps embarrassed that she was trading glances with a hired hand, maybe offended that he would have the audacity to smile at her in such a way. Still, when he cast a sideways glance up at the window a few moments later, there she was again, peering down at him. *Well, now*, he thought.

Morrissey came hobbling out from the kitchen and gave him a madder of buttermilk, a boiled pratie with a bit of salt, some brown bread.

"Who's the dark-haired lass?" Halligan asked.

"That'd be Mistress Bridie. Mr. Maguire's daughter," the man explained. "And you'd best keep your eyes to yourself, lad, if ye know what's good for you."

"Oh, I know what's good for me," he said, smiling at the old man.

That night, trying to sleep in the stables, he would play that image of her in the window, over and over in his mind. That was how it started.

THREE

The rain had let up a little, now falling in a soft gray drizzle like ashes from a fire. Except for the occasional coach or solitary rider, the streets were deserted and silent, the rain seeming to absorb any sound. Cheverus felt the need to walk, to be alone with his thoughts. He was still conscious of the weakness in his legs and the throbbing in his temples, but the strong drink the Daleys had given him had revived him a little. He experienced an odd but welcomed surge of energy.

He thought again of Finola Daley: the gaunt face, the large, restive eyes, that ample mouth so full of sadness. That piercing look she had given him as she said, *I'll pray for you, Father.* Was it that obvious, his need for prayers? Did the secrets of his heart show so plainly on his face? It came to him then, what it was she made him think of. On a trip to Rome once, he had visited the Cornaro Chapel of the church of Santa Maria della Vittoria. In the niche before the altar, he'd seen Bernini's great work, the statue of St. Theresa in her ecstasy. He remembered the saint's beautiful, tortured face, the gaunt features, the full lips parted in agony and rapture as the angel of divine love struck her in the side with its arrow. He could recall standing there gazing on the statue for the longest time, a sublime feeling swelling in his chest at how the saint had been transformed by her suffering. *Whom the Lord loveth he chasteneth.* That's what Finola Daley's face reminded him of, Bernini's lovely saint.

. He had wandered, as he often did, into the Beacon Hill section of the city, an area of impressive mansions and stately homes overlooking the

Common to the south. Here lived the rich and powerful of Boston, those stodgy conservative Federalists, wealthy merchants and sea captains, lawyers and doctors and statesmen. Men like Harrison Gray Otis and Thomas Amory, Gardiner Greene and Dr. Joy. The neighborhood's opulence and grandeur stood in stark contrast to the penury and filth and brutishness he had just left behind at the Daleys.

And yet, it was here where he felt closest to home, closest to the life he had known back in France. Passing by in the street, he might catch a few exquisite notes of a harpsichord playing Handel. Or through a window he might glimpse a book-lined study or a room that glowed with delicate and beautiful things—Louis Quatorze furnishings, Chinese vases, tapestries from Turkey. Though Cheverus's family had not been wealthy, they had been comfortable, and the young Jean had been raised amid culture and education and refinement. His parents had seen to it that their six children had been instilled with an appreciation for beauty, for things of the mind and heart and soul. There were outings to the opera and to the theater, to museums and galleries, even the occasional trip up to Paris, a hundred and fifty miles away.

He regretted not so much the hardships he had to endure in this new land. Not the poverty nor the privations of the most basic of needs. Not the discomforts brought on by the brutal New England winters. Not even the long and dangerous journeys he had to make into the wilderness of the north, where he went each summer to minister to the Indians of Maine, his *cher sauvages*. No, all of that he had expected, even welcomed with a missionary's zeal, when he had accepted Father Matignon's request to join him here. What he missed simply was the grace of his former life, the proximity to elegance and beauty that his native country had offered. The sublime feeling that stole over him while kneeling in the vast solemnity of some medieval cathedral, with its stained glass and centuries-old paintings and frescoes. The pleasant strolls he used to make along the public promenade of the Royal Palace. Seeing a play by Corneille or a painting in the Louvre. Here in America, everything was rough and coarse, unfinished, unpolished. He missed his beloved France, and no more so than now.

As he walked along the Common, his thoughts returned to the

Daleys. The sight of the two women had affected him deeply. But what, ultimately, could he do for them? He was their priest, not their lawyer. Besides, publicly supporting the accused murderers in such a notorious case could prove troublesome for the Church. And personally, Cheverus didn't relish having to go before Mr. Sullivan to supplicate on their behalf. He disliked the attorney general, an arrogant and difficult man. Yet what else could he have done? He couldn't very well have refused Rose Daley's request, could he? They were his parishioners, his flock. Who would speak for them if not he? *Please, Father. Help us.*

Just then a carriage approached, its calash raised to protect its two finely dressed occupants, a man and a woman of obvious means. As it went by, Cheverus heard the woman's laughter, a light, airy sound that clutched at his heart. Something about it made him think of his mother's laugh. Twice in the space of a few hours' time he'd thought of her. Why, he wondered. Why did her memory cause him such anguish now, so many years after her death? In the past few weeks, he recalled her often and with such vividness, such tenderness, that a great and shapeless melancholy descended upon his spirit. Sometimes when he thought of her, he found tears inexplicably rolling down his cheeks, the pain he felt at her absence as fierce and raw and unmitigated as it had been when he was a boy.

Of her six children, Jean had been her special one, her *petit chou.* Perhaps because he was her first born, or because he was so small and frail and prone to illness. Or because he had such an inquisitive mind, a heart receptive to beauty. More likely it was because, from an early age, he shared her own deep faith. It had been due in large measure to Mme. Cheverus that her son chose to enter the priesthood and devote his life to God. He could recall accompanying her to Mass, where they would kneel side by side in prayer, the silver cross dangling from her slender neck, her piety gathering as moisture in her pretty, sepia-colored eyes. Or sitting under a willow tree along the banks of the Mayenne River, his maman reading to him from a book on the lives of the French Jesuits in the new world, those heroic black robes. He would listen with rapt attention to the stories of men like the blessed martyrs Jean de Brefeuf and Issac Jogues, their remarkable lives of courage and faith, their glorious martyrdoms, their bravery and stoicism and abiding faith as they faced, what was to the young boy, unimaginable tortures. He pictured himself someday ascending to heaven, a martyr to his faith, a devoted servant of God. Once, his mother had turned to him with an expression of joy tinged with sadness, and said, "Someday, Jean, you too will perform a great deed in His service." What great deed, he would always wonder. He was so small and frail and timid, and the world so large and terrifying—what great deed could he possibly do in His service? And yet, he never forgot her prophecy.

He recalled the last time he'd seen his mother alive. With his papa, he was about to board the coach that would take him to the seminary in Paris. He was twelve, a small, pale, sickly child with faltering eyes. A boy still afraid of the dark. "You will be very brave for me now, won't you, Jean?" He nodded uncertainly. Madame Cheverus removed the cross from around her neck and placed it over his own. "I want you to have this," she had said to him. "But Maman," he had told her, fighting back his tears, "I do not want to leave you." "You will never leave me, my love. I will always be there. Always." She fell sick of a fever and died while he was away at school.

Except for the cross, he had nothing of hers. Not even her likeness, a small pendant with her portrait, something which would help him conjure her face. One of his last official acts before the Jacobins stripped him of his clerical authority was a Mass said for her soul, in the grand cathedral in Mayenne. The whole town had turned out to pay their respects to Madame Cheverus, even those who had sided with the Jacobin clergy. Before he'd been forced to flee France, he used to visit her grave. He would kneel beside her stone, talking to her, recalling the sweetness of her voice. How near she had seemed at those moments, as if he could reach out and touch her face. And how far away she seemed now. How far away they all seemed—his father, the rest of his family. He felt suddenly so alone, so isolated here in this distant land.

He knew the reason, of course. Why lately he thought of her, his former life—it had to do with the letters that sat unanswered in his desk drawer. One was from the vicar of his former diocese, Reverend Dumourier, entreating him to return home to assume his old duties. The vicar spoke of how much his former parishioners needed him. How much his country, his Church, his God needed him. *Of course, it is not the same Church you left,* his colleague had written. *That is gone forever, I fear. But things have improved under the Emperor. It is high time that you came back and helped us to rebuild what was destroyed.* Even more compelling was the letter from his father. Monsieur Cheverus's words tugged at his heartstrings like leaden weights. *My Dear Son,* Vincent Cheverus had written, *I am an old man and have not many more years left. My fondest wish is to see you again before I am called to join your mother. If a Father's love has any influence over you, please heed my request and come home at once.* The letters had rekindled his thoughts of home, and of the past.

Yet they had sat unanswered in his drawer for weeks. As much as he would like to board the next ship bound for France, it was hardly that simple. In the ten years he'd been in Boston, he had formed loyalties here as well. Friendships. Responsibilities. Undertakings half finished or just begun. How could he leave his people here, his surly, distant Irish? Or the school he planned on starting? Or what of his beloved Indians in the north? Surely they needed him. Above all, what of his dear friend and mentor, Father Matignon? How could he abandon him? After all the man had done for him. After he had nursed his spirit back to health following the terrible malaise he'd suffered because of the Revolution back home. After all the struggles they'd been through together trying to establish the Church in the face of such antagonism. He tried to tell himself that, if he did go, it would not be an act of betrayal, that he was merely following the dictates of conscience and the needs of the Church. Hadn't his superior himself given him his blessing? "Follow your heart, Jean," Father Matignon had said. He had even written to Bishop Carroll, in Baltimore, asking for advice. "Dear Sir, My mind is perplexed with doubts, my heart full of trouble and anxieties." Yet the bishop had left it up to him, saying he would pray to God to assist him in arriving at the right decision.

Of course, he wouldn't even be in this predicament if not for that misbegotten beast sired by the devil himself: the French Revolution. He cursed it, blindly, dumbly, the way one might curse an illness or a rock one had struck one's toe against. If not for it, he'd still be at his old parish

in Mayenne, presiding over a quiet ministry filled with prayer and con-
templation, morning matins and evening vespers, confession and Mass,
baptism and marriage, with time for reading and study, for pleasant din-
ners with his family on a Sunday, tranquil walks in the park, trips to the
theater and the museum. Playing chess with his father. Visiting his
mother's grave. Yes, that's what his life would have amounted to had
things worked out differently, a modest and quite unremarkable existence. Despite his mother's prediction, he was not someone to have lived
a bold life; he was not cut out for martyrdom or sainthood, for suffering
agonies or experiencing visions or miracles. He had wished merely to
serve his Lord, quietly, loyally, within his own modest abilities. God
knew of what he was capable and would not have demanded from him
more than he could give. But the Revolution had denied that peaceful
life to him, had cast him adrift in a boiling sea of uncertainty and chaos.
And like a castaway, he had landed on these distant shores, but always
maintained an eye toward the sea, as if waiting for the ship that might
carry him home again.

Lately, too, his thoughts had turned more and more to those final dark
days before he fled France, that period which later they would aptly call
the Terror. The letters asking for his return had conjured not only tender
and loving memories of his childhood and his family, but bleak and
painful ones as well. The mere thought of returning to such scenes of terror had unleashed memories he'd certainly not forgotten—could never
forget—but which he'd managed to lock away for years. Now they were
set free again to terrorize him. Now he'd begun to recall those days once
more. More than recall, relive them—for they had the feel not of static
images in the mind but of life being lived all over again. He relived the
chaos and fear that it was to be under the Jacobins' capricious and bloody
rule. Relived the daily rumors of them rounding up nobles and aristocrats, and finally even the king himself. Relived the terror of the mass
arrests of clergymen. Relived the growing violence which spread
throughout the city like a conflagration, consuming everything in its
path. Relived the dread of walking the streets with his head covered so as
not to draw the attention of the savage *sansculottes* roaming Paris in
bands, carrying pikes and axes. Relived the rabble crying out, "*Calotin*"

whenever they saw a priest. Relived the smell of pine-pitch torches and the terrible *whooshing* sound of the guillotine's blade as it fell on another neck in the Place de la Revolution, or the heavy clank of the wheels of carts filled with corpses bound for mass graves. Yes. Oh, God, yes, he had begun to relive all that again.

And worst of all, he relived his own private shame, the disgrace of his secret renunciation, a perfidy known to none save God. For in his heart, even after all the years since then, he had not fully been able to exorcise the demons that resided there, that accused him of treachery for betraying his Church, his fellow clergy, most of all, his Lord. It didn't matter that he was just one man, that he could do little against the inexorable march of events. That he had tried, in his own humble ways, to confront the Jacobins, first by refusing to sign the loyalty oath, then by carrying on with his pastoral duties right up until he was arrested and thrown into prison. It didn't matter that so many other priests had fled with him. Or that, of those who had remained and weren't butchered, most had so compromised themselves and their faith as to be worthless servants of the Church. No, that didn't matter at all. He had run. He had scurried away in the night like a rat into a Paris sewer. Worst of all, he had denied God to save his own pathetic existence. During the four years he'd spent in exile in England, Cheverus had prayed endlessly, fiercely, begging His forgiveness. With tears streaming down his face, he would pray until his knees bled. He would fast for days sometimes, until he became faint from hunger. He would scourge himself until his back was raw. He would make pilgrimages to holy shrines. He even considered returning to France, though his family warned it was tantamount to a death sentence. He asked God over and over to absolve him, to acquit him of his secret act of betrayal.

So when he'd received the letter from Father Matignon inviting him to come and help establish the Catholic mission in Boston, he had taken it as God's will. A sign he was being given another chance. He thought he could finally put those dark times behind him once and for all and make a new start in a new land. After all, other French émigrés had done it, begun new lives dedicated to God's glory elsewhere, far from home. *Come, Jean,* God seemed to be saying after his painful years of exile in

England, a period when He seemed to have turned a deaf ear to him. *You are forgiven.* Maybe coming to America was what He had intended for him all along. Maybe there, he would finally accomplish that great deed in His name. His superior's letter spoke bluntly of the many hardships and difficulties and sacrifices he could expect in the New World. Yet these only made him hunger to go all the more. On board ship, he pictured converting savages and saving souls from damnation. He even imagined being chosen for a martyr's death in the wilderness, like those saintly black robes of old he used to read about. He pictured the Indians burning him at the stake while he recited the 23rd Psalm, and thanked God for this second chance to show his faith. If He wished that, then His will be done—and this time he would not fail Him.

Of course, the new mission would not ask for his martyrdom. The Indians he ministered to turned out to be friendly converts already; the work he found difficult and ceaseless, but hardly cause for sainthood. Once, it was true, while traveling in Maine his canoe overturned, and he nearly drowned. And several times during the yellow fever epidemics that struck Boston every few years, he had gone into the homes of those afflicted to comfort them. But he had not been asked to sacrifice his life. Nothing nearly so dramatic. Still, as the years passed, God seemed pleased with him, with his work here, seemed to accept this as his penance. And if Cheverus never quite forgave himself, he had at least managed to bury the shame so deep in his heart he hardly felt it, or at least not often and not with the same urgency. Like a wound it had scarred over: the touch of it didn't hurt, though it recalled an earlier pain.

Now all the doubt and self-recrimination returned with a vengeance. At night, he would stare into the opaque darkness above his bed, that leaden weight upon his heart, the cool silence of God's condemnation blowing over him like a dry, parching wind. Or during the day sometimes, this odd feeling would steal over him and he would be seized as if by an apoplectic fit. He might be saying Mass, and his hands would begin to tremble; he'd lose his place, stumbling over the Latin he'd said ten thousand times before. Or while walking the streets of Boston, he might catch the raw stench from a butcher's shop, and he would suddenly be back there, smelling the rank odor of blood that had hung in the air like a pestilence as he'd passed those slaughtered in the street before the abbey at St. Germain des Prés, where the September Massacres had actually begun. His heart would beat faster, his throat constricting so that he could hardly breathe. And it was then that he might hear the voice, the guttural, disembodied voice he knew so well: *Vous etes l'un d'eux, n'est-ce-pas? You are one of them, are you not?*

His dreams were similarly affected, populated by scenes from those early days of the Terror. In some, he watched from a window as carts filled with the condemned, women and children, passed before him, bound for the guillotine. Those about to die cried out for help, but, of course, no one came to their aid. In others, he found himself being pursued by a faceless mob, running madly through the streets of Paris, his legs moving slower and slower until finally they were unable to move at all. One dream though was worse than the others: the dream of the white-walled garden. Oddly, in it nothing happened. No violence. No bloodshed. In this dream, he saw the beautiful courtyard garden, the one that had been attached to Convent of the Carmes, where so many of his fellow priests had been imprisoned and later lost their lives. The high, whitewashed walls enclosing a bucolic scene of flowers and shrubbery and fruit trees, a small orangery planted by the Carmelite nuns. The late summer's drowsy air, the light reflecting off the walls, the grounds shimmering and wavering in the languid afternoon. He could even hear the buzz of the bees going from flower to flower, the soft rustling of the wind among the treetops. Sometimes in the dream the garden was empty and still. Other times the imprisoned clergy were at their devotions, kneeling in prayer, rosaries or breviaries in their hands. It was a quiet and peaceful image, like a Watteau painting. Still it filled him with a formless dread, a terror that rose from his belly and pushed up into his throat like a muffled scream. Because, of course, of what he sensed would happen, of what, even in the dream, he knew would happen, the inevitability of it more frightening somehow than its actual appearance. He would wake from it, his nightclothes bathed in sweat, that terrible weight on his chest so that he could hardly breathe. Sometimes in the darkness, he would hear that voice near his ear, the guttural peasant voice, the shaggy head always haloed in light but which left the face obscure, indefinable as a foul mist.

You are one of them, are you not?

He heard it now, as he walked along in the rain. It always seemed to lunge upon him whenever his mind had wandered into this dark abyss of the past. He tried to ignore it. Sometimes he could put it from his thoughts by a sheer act of will. Hadn't he managed that all these years? *It is over*, he would tell himself. Just a thing of the past.

Nonetheless, it came again: *You are one of them?*

Without realizing it, he'd begun to walk faster. His heart began to rap within his breast. He turned and headed east, across the Common, his pace quickening. It was then that he thought he heard something behind him. At first it was barely audible. But then it came again, louder. Yes, he was sure of it now. A sound like footsteps behind him. He turned to look over his shoulder. He saw nothing, though. Only darkness.

You are one of them?

He broke into an awkward trot, his cloak catching about his legs. The ground was soft from the rain, and he slipped in the mud, nearly falling. His head pounded, his chest burned with a jagged blue fire. Several times he found himself glancing back over his shoulder. He continued to run, the voice coming to him again and again, each time more insistent: *You are one of them?* He hurried across Park Street, slipped down an alley behind the Park Street Church, and rushed on into the Old Granary burial grounds, a shortcut back to the rectory. It was then that he heard another voice, this one quite real. "Who goes there?" Turning, he saw the familiar lantern of the one-armed night watchman, an old man named Lemuel. Cheverus often passed him on his nightly walks about the city.

"Oh, it's only you, Father," the man said, as he drew near. Holding his lantern aloft, he inspected the priest's face closely. "Is something wrong?"

"No," Cheverus said. "Nothing is wrong."

"What are you doing here at this hour?"

"I was just returning from making a visit to someone who is ill."

The man stared suspiciously at him for another second or two before saying, "Well, good night to you," and continued on his rounds.

When he was out of sight, Cheverus glanced around the unfamiliar cemetery. The Old Granary was a Protestant cemetery. Catholics didn't have their own, having to be buried at Copp's Hill in the North End or in the city's Central Burying Ground, reserved for, as the city's selectmen said, "foreigners, Roman Catholics and Freemasons." He knelt on the soft wet ground and bowed his head in prayer: *O Lord. Thou has sent Your servant here to this land to do Your work. I beseech Thee, do not abandon me in the wilderness. Help me to see Thy light. To know Thy will.*

He was surrounded by silence, vast and featureless as a sea becalmed after a storm. Instead of the voice of God though, he heard once more that of the faceless *sansculotte*, guttural, jagged as a rusty blade: *You are one of them, are you not?*

It was nearly midnight when he finally reached the rectory. He was wet and cold, shivering, his shoes soaked through. From his capote, water dripped onto the floor in the entryway. Father Matignon came in from the parlor where a fire blazed.

"Where have you been, Jean?" cried the older priest, taking the cape from Cheverus's shoulders. "I was beginning to worry."

"Out walking."

"*Mon Dieu!* In such weather! You'll catch your death."

"I thought I'd walk a bit."

"*Tu n'as plus aucune chance,*" he scolded with the patronizing smile of a parent. They slid into French, hardly aware of it. They reverted to it whenever it was just the two of them. It was comforting and reminded them both of home. "Well, come and warm yourself by the fire then."

Cheverus followed the elder priest into the parlor. Abbé Matignon limped slightly from the gout in his toe. Cheverus sat in front of the fire in a high-backed chair.

"Your hands, Jean," the elder priest said in French. "They are filthy. What happened?"

Cheverus looked down at his hands. They were covered with mud from the burial grounds. He brought them to his nose and sniffed. He thought of that line from *Lear*, when the old man puts his hands to his nose and says they smell of mortality. "I fell," was all he gave for explanation.

"Are you all right?"

"Yes. It was nothing."

"Would you like some tea?"

"Thank you, Father, no."

Abbé Matignon drew up a chair and sat on the other side of the fire. The flames shimmered in the old priest's chalky blue eyes, clouded now by cataracts, and the light cast his deeply lined face in a series of jagged shadows. He did not speak for a time but gazed into the fire like a man into a pool of water studying his own reflection.

The rectory, which was attached to the church on Franklin, was small and spartan but certainly preferable to the cramped quarters they had rented from Mrs. Lobb when Cheverus first arrived in America ten years earlier. The parlor had a few pieces of second-hand furniture, two chairs, a drop-front writing desk, a bookcase, on the wall a painting of the Mayenne River by an unknown French artist, sent to them by Cheverus's brother Louis. The bookcase, the only hint of largesse, held a modest library, volumes in English and French, in Latin and Greek and Italian, and even a few in Hebrew. When they had a little extra money sent to them from relatives back home, they permitted themselves one of their few indulgences: the purchase of books from the second-hand book-sellers in the city. There were the *Summa* and Augustine's *Confessions* and Melchior Canus's *De locis theologicis,* as well as books by Aristotle and Cicero. *Utopia* sat next to the *Commedia, Paradise Lost* next to a ragged folio of Shakespeare in the original English.

"You should have hired a coach," Father Matignon said after a while.

"The night air was refreshing," Cheverus replied.

"I meant it might not be safe for you to be out at this hour."

"You worry too much, Father," the younger priest said, waving off the notion.

"One of us has to," he said, a gentle upbraiding. "Catholics are being harassed."

"I was perfectly fine. Besides, a coach costs money."

"We can afford it."

"Huh! We can hardly afford to pay Yvette," Cheverus scoffed, gazing into the fire as if trying to see what Matignon saw there. "Or to buy missives or candles."

"What I cannot afford is for anything to happen to you, my friend."

Father Matignon stared over at him, his ashen gaze full of some vague meaning. Cheverus looked back to the fire.

"Do you realize how much I have come to depend on you?"

The younger priest shrugged, not so much in feigned modesty as in simple weariness of all the statement implied.

"Sometimes I wonder what little good I do here, Father."

"Nonsense. You've accomplished so very much, Jean."

"What?"

"*This*, for one," he said, holding his hands palm up and looking around the room. "The church and rectory wouldn't exist save for your efforts, Jean. We'd still be living with Mrs. Lobb and saying Mass in the old Quaker chapel."

"We have no cemetery of our own."

"In time."

"No formal school."

"But you have some eager disciples. Young Máirtin, for instance."

Cheverus nodded, thinking fondly of his star pupil. "But we have no real classroom, Father. Few books or slates."

"God will provide, my friend," he said, what he always said. *God will provide.* "We must look at how far we have come, not how far we still must go," Father Matignon said philosophically. He was guided by a cautious optimism, avoiding extremes, something he tried to impart to his younger, sometimes more moody colleague.

"They still scorn us, Father. These . . . Yankees," Cheverus said.

Drawing his mouth together, Father Matignon looked over at his younger colleague. "Yes, we have our detractors," he conceded, and when Cheverus seemed about to jump in, he held up two fingers. "But we also have our friends now. Good friends. Mr. Bulfinch, for instance. Where would our church be without his generous support? Or Gardiner Greene. Even Mr. Adams. Think of it, Jean. You have broken bread with a former president of these United States. I would call that progress. And we have *you* to thank for that."

"*Pfft*," he said, frowning. "As always, you overestimate my contribution."

"And as always, you're being far too modest. It was your efforts during the fever outbreak that helped to change people's attitudes."

"I only did what I was called upon to do. No more."

"*Allons donc!*" Father Matignon said. "You did a great deal, Jean."

When the yellow fever outbreak ravaged Boston a few years before, those who were able abandoned the city for their summer residences, leaving the poor to fend for themselves. Fathers Cheverus and Matignon, along with a handful of Protestant clergymen, had gone into the poorer sections of the city—Fort Hill, the waterfront in the north, the old poor house near Park Street—where the fever was rampant, and offered what help they could. Cheverus had entered homes, not asking if the people who lived there were Protestant or Catholic, only if they were ill and needed assistance. He had brought food to the hungry, medicine to the sick, comfort to the dying. He had helped to wash and wrap the bodies of the dead before accompanying them to the burial grounds where he said a few words over them. He threw himself into his duties as he did everything else since coming here—with a fearsome passion that Father Matignon couldn't decide was divinely or demonically inspired. But when the fever subsided, attitudes toward papists did seem to warm a little—at least for a time. People were less openly hostile. Then came the troubles in Europe, Napoleon, and the crushed rebellion in Ireland, and when the Catholic immigrants started to appear on these shores in unprecedented numbers the attitudes toward papists cooled once more.

"I don't think you quite realize how many people depend upon you," Father Matignon said. "I for one could not manage without you."

"You did before I arrived."

"It was different then," his superior said. "We were a tiny mission. A handful of communicants. Now we number almost a thousand. One thousand Catholics! We have more than a foothold. And that is due in large measure to your diligent work. It is I who am expendable."

"You *are* the Church here, Father."

"No, no, my friend. The Church could get alone quite well without a purblind, half-crippled pastor," the elder priest said with a chuckle. He looked over at Cheverus and both knew what was on their minds. Father Matignon was aware of the younger priest's dilemma, which was also his own. He would have to replace Cheverus if he returned to France. And while he was hardly a disinterested party, he had told his colleague he would abide by whatever he decided. He wanted only what was best for his friend, and he believed that returning home, to family and ecclesiastical responsibilities, was what was best, though of course he wouldn't admit this. The thought of losing his young, talented assistant, now his closest friend, filled him with a deep sorrow.

"Did you eat, Jean?"

"I am not hungry."

"You need to eat to regain your strength."

"I am hungry only for sleep."

Abbé Matignon had known Jean Lefebvre de Cheverus since he was a child. He'd heard the boy's confession, and later the young man had been a student of his in Paris. Before the Revolution, Dr. Matignon had been a distinguished professor of theology. He had found in Cheverus a brilliant student, a young man with a first-rate mind and a deep faith and ardent passion for serving his God and his fellow man. The abbé knew the young seminarian would make a remarkable priest, perhaps even someday being raised to the red robes of a cardinal. When Cheverus had fled to England, Father Matignon had written to him from Boston, beseeching him to join him here. There was plenty of work to be done. And for ten years, they'd worked side by side struggling to establish a Catholic diocese, to sink down roots and to nurture the frail seedling Church in this barren Protestant soil. Cheverus threw himself into his labors in the new world like a man possessed. He worked with indefatigable energy. Father Matignon would often have to rein in his younger colleague's fervor for his own good.

The two priests sat silently staring into the fire. Entire nights sometimes slipped by like this, with no more than a few words passing between them—Father Matignon reviewing the church ledgers with his magnifying glass or writing correspondence, Cheverus with his nose in a book or working on a sermon. Sometimes Cheverus would read to his friend, Montesquieu or the Bible. He especially liked Exodus, for obvious reasons. Sometimes they might play cards or chess, though the old abbé's eyesight was bad and he took forever to move his pieces. But often they just sat silently together—such was the comfortable familiarity they found in each other's company. The elder priest was by nature a circumspect, deliberate man, one who viewed things from all sides, carefully weighing all considerations before arriving at a balanced decision. Like Cheverus, he had fled France during the Terror but had come to America four years prior to his friend, entrusted by Bishop Carroll of Baltimore with the task of carving out a Catholic mission. But where the French Revolution had darkened Cheverus's outlook, for Father Matignon it had only made him more cautious, more pragmatic in his dealings. *Les temps noirs*, as he called them—the black times—had caused him to be more vigilant, more politic. He said to Cheverus that even a man of God must always be on his guard.

The two men had become close friends over the decade of their work together. Their personalities complemented each other's. It was Father Matignon, the more analytical and practical, who handled the church finances and negotiated the complexities of local politics, while Cheverus, whose English was nearly flawless, gave passionate Sunday sermons, drawing large, curious crowds to hear him. In fact, many Protestants came to listen to the small priest hold forth on matters of Catholic dogma. Cheverus also had a sharp wit and an equally sharp tongue, which Father Matignon would sometimes have wished to moderate. Several times he had gotten into verbal jousting matches in the city's newspapers, defending his faith against virulent, usually unsigned, anti-Catholic diatribes.

"Yvette told me you were called to the Daley house," Father Matignon stated.

"Rose wanted to speak to me."

"How are they taking the news?"

"You have heard then? About the trial?"

"It's all over the city. Terrible business. Just terrible. How is Rose faring?"

"Angry that her son has been given so little time to prepare a defense. Frightened, too."

"The poor woman. What that son of hers has put her through. And she not well. What did she want of you?"

Cheverus paused for a moment, wondering how best to present what Rose Daley had asked of him. Finally he decided on the direct approach. "I would like your permission to meet with the attorney general regarding the prisoners, Father."

"For what purpose?" the elder priest asked.

"To ask for better treatment."

"Is that what they wanted to see you about?"

"Yes. They would like to be permitted to visit with Dominic, too."

"They have not been allowed to visit him?"

"Evidently not. They have gone to see Mr. Sullivan but he has refused to meet with them. So they asked if I would go on their behalf."

"I see," Father Matignon said, rubbing his chin. "And you agreed?"

Cheverus nodded. "Of course, with your permission, Father."

"Do you think that prudent? That we get involved in this . . ." He paused, searching for the right word. At last he settled on "situation."

"But we aren't involved. Not really. I just thought I could see if Sullivan would permit them to have visitors. And perhaps grant the defense more time to prepare a case. The government, after all, has had five months."

"I appreciate that, Jean. But the Church needs to handle this situation with great delicacy. We don't want to lose the gains we've made. Certainly you understand that."

"I agree, Father. But—"

"Then you would also agree that we cannot be perceived as using our influence to aid a couple of murderers."

"Accused murderers, Father. They have not been convicted of anything yet."

"From all I've heard the case against them seems rather strong."

"But even if they are guilty, they deserve a fair trial. And to be treated humanely."

"Of course. No one is debating that. I am merely saying that it may be in our best interests if the Church remained neutral."

"Neutral, Father?" Cheverus asked.

"Yes. If we simply permitted the law to take its course."

"The law has not exactly been protecting the prisoners' rights. They've been kept in jail for months without due process. There is a little matter of *habeas corpus*. They haven't been allowed the opportunity to consult with a lawyer or to question their accusers. Heavens, the two prisoners haven't even been permitted so much as to bathe in all that time. I am only saying they have certain legal rights."

"You know, I am hardly a supporter of Sullivan. But perhaps he has his reasons."

"Reasons!" Cheverus said a little too forcefully. "Excuse me, Father." The elder priest waved the supposed offence away. They were always free to speak their minds with each other. "You know what sort of man Sullivan is. His only reason is that they happen to be Irish and Catholic. That is his sole reason for treating them like this."

"Yes, I know Sullivan. But this crime has stirred up bad feelings against all Catholics. People are frightened. Some in our parish are afraid to come to church. They fear being harassed. Need I remind you of Declan O'Brien?"

The younger priest leaned toward the fire. He took up the poker and jabbed a birch log. He didn't want it to seem as if he were blaming Father Matignon for not taking action. What, after all, had he done till now? Nothing. He knew his superior was only pursuing the most reasonable course of action, one that placed the best interests of the Church and their parishioners before those of two men who had, in all likelihood, committed a vicious crime. In most ways Cheverus agreed with him, too. They had to protect the image of the church. Yet he kept seeing the searing look of emptiness in Rose Daley's eyes. *Please help us, Father?*

He turned to Father Matignon. "Who will speak out for them if not us?"

"By speaking out, it might look to some as if we are condoning such behavior."

"We are not condoning their actions, if they did what they are accused of. We are merely being compassionate, Father."

"Jean, your compassion for them is commendable, but we must be very careful not to confuse compassion with foolhardiness. People will think Catholics defend their own no matter what. The Church must protect itself if it is to survive."

"But at what cost?"

The abbé made his hands into fists, placed them knuckle to knuckle, and brought his fists to rest beneath his large nose, a habit of his when he pondered a question.

"The least little spark could set off a blaze. There could be real violence."

"I know, Father. I know."

"But you still believe we should get involved?"

"Our involvement is really quite minimal. Just asking Sullivan to improve the conditions the prisoners are being held under. But if you think not . . ."

Father Matignon held up his hand in a kind of surrender. "All right. You have convinced me, Jean. As usual, your rhetorical skills far surpass mine." Father Matignon conceded a smile, not so much in defeat as in pride—the pride of a teacher in a gifted student. "When would you plan to meet with him?"

"Tomorrow if possible," he offered. "He may have already left for the trial."

Father Matignon nodded his head. "Then go with my blessing. Just remember to exercise discretion, Jean. We do not want to make him more of an enemy than he already is. He may be an insufferable bore, but he is an influential one nonetheless."

The two priests laughed at that.

"You should get some rest, Jean."

Oddly enough, he was no longer tired. At least his mind wasn't. It was alert, restless with thoughts.

"One more thing, Father," Cheverus said, glancing over at the old abbé. "Do you think it advisable for me to accompany the Daleys to Northampton?"

"Did they ask you again?"

"Yes."

"I thought we already decided that, Jean?" he said, furrowing his brow.

"My presence might be of comfort to the prisoners. Finola said her husband desires to make confession."

"About the crime?"

"They believe him to be innocent."

"They would. But do you?"

"I couldn't say. If guilty, perhaps the crime weighs on their conscience."

"There is so much work to do here before you leave for Maine. Besides, passions will be running high. It might not be safe for a priest to be seen out there."

"Do you really think so?"

"Indeed. I think there is the very real potential for trouble. If anything were to happen to you, I could not forgive myself. I will not prohibit you from going, Jean. But please, for my sake, do not go out there."

Cheverus acquiesced, nodding.

They sat quietly for a moment. Out on Franklin a hackney coach could be heard clattering over the cobblestones.

"Have you made a decision yet?" the old priest asked. "About returning home."

"No," Cheverus replied with a sigh. "Not yet."

"Whatever you decide, I want you to know you have my full support. I will miss you if you go, but I understand your reasons completely."

"Thank you, Father."

"Would you like me to hear your confession, Jean?"

"I think not. It is very late."

"You haven't in many days." When Cheverus looked over at Matignon, the abbé said, with a knowing smile, "You might sleep better."

The elder priest was his closest and dearest friend. He knew him as few other human beings did. Besides that, he was his confessor, someone he poured his soul out to, someone who listened to his sins, acknowledged his frailties, gave him the soothing balm of absolution. He kept few secrets from his friend. But for a decade, he hadn't told him of those things that had most troubled his soul. The awful guilt that lay hidden in the core of his heart, gnawing away at it like a worm in a piece of rotten wood. But those were things he had never shared with anyone.

"Another time."

"As you will."

Cheverus rose from his chair. As he passed by the elder priest, he leaned over and patted him on his shoulder. "Good night, Father."

He left the room but stopped just outside the door and turned. He watched the back of Father Matignon's graying head. If only he could unburden to him what was in his heart. How much better he would feel.

"Yes, Jean?" the elder priest asked, as if reading his mind.

"I was just wondering, Father. Do you ever think of those times?" Cheverus asked. "You know . . . before we left France."

"Ah. The black times." The elder priest stared pensively at the flames dancing in the fireplace. "Ancient history. I try not to think of them."

"Are you able to . . . not think of them?"

"Mostly. Sometimes they come back despite my best efforts." Father Matignon turned in his chair to look at him directly. He squinted to make out the expression on the younger priest's face. "And you, Jean? Do you think of them?"

"Yes. Especially of late. I suppose because of the possibility of going home."

"And what about those times troubles you?"

He shook his head. "I guess I feel guilty."

"Guilty?" Father Matignon repeated, seeming to watch him like a blind hawk.

"Yes. That I lived, and so many good priests died."

"You mustn't blame yourself for that. That was not your fault."

"But I could have done more."

"Don't fool yourself, my friend. No earthly power could have stopped it."

"I think of the compromises I made."

"We all compromised ourselves, Jean. Look at the king. Even he tried to flee for his life."

"But some remained true to their ideals. To their vows."

"The dead! They are the only ones. For the rest of us we did what we had to. What we *could*. He understands."

"Does He?"

"Of course. When they demanded we sign the Civil Constitution, I did the noble thing and refused. And when I chose to leave for America when the Terror began, I told myself it was also out of noble principles. That I would not submit. The truth is, Jean, I was afraid. I didn't want to have my faith put to the test and find it lacking. Like the king, I had my own Varennes."

"But you did what you thought was right."

"*Tssh*," he said, scornfully brushing the thought aside with his hand. "Did I? Do you see this?" he said, touching a V-shaped scar in the middle of his right palm. Cheverus had seen it before, many times in fact. Whenever he took the host from the old priest's hand, he saw the scar. "It is the only mark I received from the Revolution. In Le Havre, I was hurrying up the gangplank. We'd heard rumors of the government closing the ports and arresting priests even with the right papers. And the clumsy fool that I am, I fell and cut myself," he said with a self-mocking laugh. "A great many of my former students and colleagues, some of my closest friends even, they stayed behind and died for what they believed in. Did you know a Jean Pierre Marchand?"

"Yes, I knew Father Marchand. He was imprisoned at the Carmes."

"A dear friend of mine. We attended seminary together. He believed it was his duty to stay in France and defend the Church. He perished in the massacres."

Cheverus allowed his gaze to fall to the floor. *Tell him*, he thought. *What better moment? Get it off your chest once and for all.* And yet, he secretly feared losing his friend's respect. He feared the old priest could never again think of him in the same way. It was the worst sort of vanity. Instead he said, "But Father, you couldn't have known what would happen to those that stayed."

"Perhaps. Yet he was butchered for his beliefs, and I have a tiny scar on my palm for mine. So you see, Jean, I think about those days, too. But it does no good to dwell on them. We did what we could. He knows we are weak."

Cheverus nodded. "Good night, Father."

"Good night, Jean."

PART II

Mr. Marcus Lyon, a young man of peculiar respectability, about twenty-three years of age . . . was attacked by two merciless ruffians and murdered in a most barbarous manner. . . . Having thus far gratified their infernal disposition, they robbed him of his pocket-book (how much money it contained we are not able to inform). The villains who perpetrated the awful crime are supposed to be two foreigners in sailors dress, who were seen that day by a number of people making their way towards Springfield. We are happy to learn that his excellency Governor Strong issued a proclamation offering a reward of five hundred dollars for the detection of the villains.

—MASSACHUSETTS SPY
WORCESTER, 20 NOVEMBER 1805

And hath it come to this? Have things gotten to such a pass, in this infant country, that it is dangerous for a man of decent appearance and equipage, to travel on the highway in mid day, through fear of being murdered and robbed for his money? This is alarming indeed. And what shall we come to next. Must we all arm ourselves and procure guards in order to travel in safety? In such a state of things, who of us all is safe; and who of us is to fall the next victim? We are doubtless justified in saying that a great portion of the crimes abovementioned . . . are committed by foreigners. . . . Since the rapid increase of our intercourse with other nations, and the great increase of foreigners . . . we have ripened, apace, in all the arts of vice and depravity.

—DISCOURSE DELIVERED IN WILBRAHAM,
MASSACHUSETTS, OCCASIONED BY THE
MURDER OF MARCUS LYON, BY PASTOR EZRA
WITTER, 17 NOVEMBER, 1805

That the minds of the good people should be shocked with the late murder of Marcus Lyon on the high road is perfectly natural and would be right to a certain extent. But the panic excited by this event goes to the extreme. It magnifies every assault to a manslaughter— every sudden or accidental death to a bloody assassination.

—HAMPSHIRE FEDERALIST, JANUARY 1806
NORTHAMPTON, MASSACHUSETTS

Catholics are only tolerated here and so long as their ministers behave well, we shall not disturb them. But let them expect no more than that.

—JUDGE THEOPHILUS BRADBURY
MASSACHUSETTS SUPREME JUDICIAL COURT

FOUR

Late in the afternoon, an older, heavyset man showed up at their cell. Rain dripped from his dark-gray riding coat and pooled on the floor around him. At first glance he gave the appearance of a gentleman of some means. He wore a high, beaver-trimmed hat of the latest European fashion and a silk cravat tied in a large bow around his thick neck. His yellow waistcoat was also silk, and his long, fitted pantaloons were tucked into knee-high riding boots. In one hand he held a cane with a scrimshaw handle, in the other a leather valise. Yet upon closer inspection his clothes appeared somewhat shabby. His neck cloth had stains on it, his topcoat was coming out at the elbows, and his boots hadn't been oiled for some time, the leather cracked and worn. Dowd opened the cell door, and said, "There they be, sir." Squinting, the heavyset man cast a doubtful glance into the murky cell, as if reluctant to enter it.

"My good fellow," he instructed the turnkey, in a supercilious tone accustomed to giving orders. "Would you be so kind as to procure a chair for me? And something to see by. It's rather dark in here."

The turnkey locked the door and left. He returned in a moment with a small milking stool and a taper. "This will have to do," he said of the chair. "Call when you're done."

Once in the cell, the man removed his hat, gloves, and rain-slicked overcoat. "May I?" he asked Daley, but didn't wait for a reply before tossing his things on Daley's bunk.

"Go right ahead, sir," Daley said. "You'd be Mister Blake?"

"I would. Francis Blake, Esquire," he said, extending his hand to Daley.

Daley rose from his bunk. "Dominic Daley, sir."

Turning to Halligan, Blake said, "And you must be Mr. Halligan then."

He nodded, shaking the man's proffered hand. A soft, womanish hand, one not much accustomed to work, Halligan thought.

With difficulty Blake lowered himself onto the small stool, expelling a loud exhalation of air. He placed the taper on the bunk and took a moment to situate himself. He rubbed his nose and snuffled, coughing several times. In the light of the candle, Halligan looked him over more closely, the way you might inspect a boat you'd be using to cross a fast stretch of water. He was younger than Halligan had first taken him to be. Perhaps forty, the difference due in large measure to the wasting effects of drink. His corpulent face was flushed, the nose pitted and red, the broad forehead damp and slightly febrile looking. He had drowsy, slightly bulbous eyes that looked on things with the unruffled equanimity of a country squire. They were, however, of a remarkable azure blue color, with long lashes. Pretty eyes, Halligan thought. Though his clothes were worn, they were of good quality, and he had the voice and refined mannerisms of a gentlemen. One that must have fallen on hard times. Otherwise why would he be taking on such a case as theirs, which offered little in the way of financial reward?

Blake picked up the candle and held it aloft, peering first at Daley, then at Halligan. Now it was his turn to inspect them. A dilatory smile began about his lips.

"What, sir?" Daley asked.

"You're not exactly what I expected," he replied.

"How's that now, sir?"

"In the press, you've been made out to be a couple of bloodthirsty highwaymen."

"Blood an' ouns," Daley said. "Is that what they're sayin' about us? Highwaymen?"

"Indeed. Why, the newspapers have made you out worse than Thomas Mount," the lawyer explained. The smile broadened to include the eyes and cheeks, carving his face into overlapping folds and creases. Even his forehead wrinkled into a fleshy M. Did the blasted egit think this all a joke, Halligan thought. Were they just a couple of Irish swine to him?

"Do ye hear that, Jamy?" Daley said. "They think we're bloody highwaymen."

Halligan nodded.

"They may even try to link you to a number of other robberies in the area," the lawyer added.

"We didn't rob him or anybody else," Halligan said sharply.

The attorney glanced over at him and pursed his lips noncommittally. He set the candle down on the bunk again and opened his valise. He removed several papers and spread them out on the bunk. From his waistcoat pocket he took out a small tin box, removed a pair of spectacles from it, and put them on his broad nose. He then began to inspect the papers. Now and again, he brought the candle close as he perused a certain document, muttering a "yes" or a "hmmm," and raising his eyebrows. From the valise he also removed a quill pen, and with a pocket knife he sharpened the tip to a fine point. He performed this with a punctilious exactitude. He then took out a small pewter inkstand and a leather-bound writing tablet, and began to make some notes. During the entire interview, Blake jotted things down on this tablet, in an unsteady hand, the letters stumbling drunkenly across the page.

"How have you been treated?" he asked perfunctorily.

"Could a been worse, I suppose," Daley replied. "We've no complaints."

Blake nodded but didn't look up. He was studying one document in particular. He frowned, tugging on his lower lip. He had a habit of taking the lip between his thumb and forefinger and pulling it down when he was lost in thought. The gesture looked almost painful but the man didn't seem to be aware of it. Every once in a while, he would withdraw a small silver box from his pocket and apply some snuff to each nostril. He would then sneeze violently several times, his face turning a bright red.

"Mr. Blake," Halligan asked. "Why is it we are only now getting to speak to you?"

"What?" he said, looking up. "Oh, I was notified only yesterday. I came as soon as I could. The road from Worcester is bad with the recent rains."

"What I mean is, the prosecution has had all these months to get ready."

"Yes, of course," Blake said absently, while jotting something down in his writing tablet. "You are quite right. I have asked the court for a postponement so that we can have sufficient time to prepare our defense. I am not sanguine about our chances, however. Therefore, I think we should proceed with all due speed. Are we in agreement, gentlemen?"

They looked at each other and nodded.

"Very well then," said Blake. He picked up one document from the pile before him and held it under his nose. "Since I have not had time to adequately study your case, I'd like to begin by a review of the facts."

"We didn't kill that feller," Daley said.

"Well, that's what I hope to prove, Mr. Daley," Blake replied with an ironic smile.

"We're innocent," Halligan cried. "That's the only fact you need to know."

"Indeed," Blake offered, giving him a critical glance. "Now, according to the coroner's inquest, the deceased, Mr. Lyon, was riding east along the Boston turnpike, when he met his end in Wilbraham, on the ninth of November last. The prosecution has several witnesses who can place him on the road just before his death. Now, both of you were traveling west at approximately the same time, were you not?"

"We didn't keep track of the time, sir," Daley explained.

"But you were in this general vicinity on the day Mr. Lyon was murdered?"

"Aye, we passed through there on Saturday," Daley said. "Where the turnpike road comes down close to the river."

"Mr. Lyon's saddled horse was discovered by a . . ." Here the man paused as he riffled through several papers until he found the one he was looking for. He read from it. "Discovered by a Mr. John Bliss, a farmer, in whose pasture the victim's horse had wandered. When the owner didn't appear to claim the horse, foul play was suspected and a search was conducted on Sunday morning but which turned up nothing. According to witnesses," and here Blake angled the paper for better reading light, "a pistol was later discovered near the river, and the search was resumed Sunday night by means of lanterns. Eventually a second pistol was found covered with blood and hair, and soon thereafter a body was discovered submerged near the banks of the river. Now, according to Dr. Merrick, the examining physician who opened the body, Mr. Lyon had been shot in the side but that the ball hit a rib and didn't prove lethal. The victim was subsequently dispatched by being bludgeoned to death by said pistols and by his submersion in the water." Blake stopped reading and looked up at them. "These are the facts I have to work with, gentlemen."

The lawyer removed a handkerchief and dabbed his forehead. Though the cell was chilly, sweat rolled down his face. His eyes appeared inflamed, glowing from some inner heat.

"Did either of you own a pistol?" he asked.

"No," they both replied, almost in unison.

"Neither of you purchased a pistol from a certain dry-goods establishment of a . . ." He paused to look over the papers again. "A Mr. Syms, of Boston?"

"No, sir," replied Halligan. "We did not."

"According to Josiah Bardwell, who was among the posse that arrested you, you have pockets in your coats that are made for the purpose of carrying a weapon."

"True enough, we got pockets there," Daley said. He opened up his coat to show Blake the pocket on the inside of his greatcoat. "They're but for carryin' our bottles."

"Your bottles?"

"Aye, sir. A feller gets awful thirsty trampin' about the countryside. There ain't no crime in that."

"Hmmm," the lawyer said, pinching his lip and writing something in his tablet. "Help clarify one point for me, Mr. Daley. The first count in the indictment says you were the one to have administered the lethal blow to the deceased."

"I done what, sir?" Daley asked.

"You struck and killed Marcus Lyon with the aforementioned pistol."

"No, sir. I done no such a thing. Like I told you, I don't own a pistol."

"Well, how did they conclude that it was you and not Mr. Halligan that struck the blow?" he asked.

"I dunno. When they brung us back to Springfield, they put us in a room and asked a lot of questions. They said somethin' about a gun. I don't recollect plainly. But I told 'em, like I'm telling you, I had no gun and I niver struck nobody."

Blake took off his glasses and squeezed the pink bridge of his nose. He looked up finally and asked of Halligan, "Where were you headed the day of the murder?"

"To New York, sir," he replied.

"What was your business there?"

Halligan shrugged. "I was keeping Dom company. Thought I'd look for work."

"And you?" he asked of Daley.

"I had to collect a debt from a friend."

"What was this friend's name?"

"Sweeney, sir. Matthew Sweeney. He owed me from back home. For a cow I sold him when we left to come here."

Blake wrote this down.

"And yet when the posse arrested you in Rye, New York, they found a sizable amount of money on you already."

Daley hesitated before replying. "Yes, sir. I had some money on me. It was . . . money I earned."

"Yet a number of the bank bills in your possession," Blake continued, "were drawn on the very same banks as those stolen from the victim. How do you explain that?"

"I . . . I couldn't rightly say," he replied.

"Don't you think it odd?"

"I suppose," Daley replied, glancing over at Halligan.

Halligan held his gaze. *Don't be stupid, Dom,* he thought. *Stick to our story.*

"Mr. Daley," said Blake, "if I am to represent you to the best of my ability, you shall have to be completely forthright with me. Your very life may well depend upon it."

"I cannot explain it, sir. I can only tell you it was me own money."

"You're certain of that?"

"Aye," he replied. Yet he didn't sound convincing, and Blake's prying stare lingered on him for several seconds.

"And you?" he asked, turning to look now at Halligan. "How did you come to be in possession of such a sum of money?"

"Same as Dom," Halligan said. "I earned it."

Blake pulled on his lower lip and sighed nasally. "Do either of you recollect passing Mr. Lyon along the turnpike road?"

"No," Daley replied. "I mean, we might a passed him, but I couldn't say for sure."

"He was . . ." Blake repositioned his glasses on his nose and fumbled through the papers. "Going east on 'a bright bay horse.' With new saddlebags."

"I don't remember any rider on a bay horse, Mr. Blake," Daley replied.

"But the prosecution has several witnesses that can place both of you just to the east of the murder site at approximately noon on the ninth. You had to have passed him, Mr. Daley."

"Not," Halligan interjected, leveling his gaze on Blake, "if he was already killed."

The lawyer looked at him and frowned, annoyed at being interrupted.

"The state has a witness, a young boy by the name of Laertes Fuller, who saw you, Mr. Daley, with this very same horse. He swears that you led a bay horse under an apple tree, which was up on a hill near the spot where Lyon was slain. And he spied another man," he said, turning to look at Halligan, "pushing said horse from behind, though he couldn't recognize the second man. What do you say to that, sir?"

"I dunno, Mr. Blake," Daley replied. "He's got to be lyin' then."

"What possible reason could the boy have to lie, Mr. Daley?"

"Maybe he mistook us for somebody else. With them as done this terrible thing."

"But after you were brought back to Springfield, he picked you out of a group. He identified you as the man leading the dead man's horse, did he not?"

Halligan snorted. "Huh!"

"What is it, Mr. Halligan?" the lawyer asked, turning to look at him.

"We were the only ones in irons."

"What do you mean?"

"When they brought us back to Springfield they didn't bother removing the irons. The lad who picked us out of the group saw us with them on. It wouldn't have been hard for him to think we were the guilty ones already."

"Hmmm," said Blake, scribbling in his tablet. "Yes, that would make sense."

"Anyways, it'll be our word against that boy's," Daley said. "We'll just get up on that witness stand and say he's lying."

"You won't be permitted to take the stand."

"Why not?" Daley asked, on his long face an expression of outraged incredulity.

"The accused isn't allowed to testify in a capital trial. It will fall to me to state your case and to challenge the prosecution witnesses during cross examination."

Blake spent another hour asking them questions. About Daley's friend Sweeney, whom they were to meet in New York; at which inns they stayed before reaching Wilbraham and where they stayed afterwards; to whom they spoke during their journey westward; if they ever got drunk or were in fights or if there was any sort of other damaging evidence that could be brought against their character. When he asked if they'd ever been in trouble with the law before this, Halligan told him of the time he'd spent in prison back in Ireland.

"You struck the man?" Blake asked.

"Aye. But he had it coming."

"And here? Have you ever been in trouble here?"

"No sir. Nothing before this."

"Well, I doubt they will have your records from Ireland."

At last, Blake said that would be all for today. He was feeling rather fatigued from his long ride and needed to rest for a while. He stood and put his coat and hat on.

"I shall return early tomorrow," he said, as he gathered up his notes and papers. "We have a good deal of work to do, gentlemen."

"Sir," Daley said, "have you had no word if me family will be at the trial?"

"I have had no communication from them whatsoever."

Daley sighed, his eyes downcast.

Blake then went to the cell door and called for the turnkey. Before he left, though, he turned and said, "I won't mislead you. Our chances are not promising. The evidence against you is quite damaging. They have some two dozen witnesses and we have none. But it is not entirely hopeless. There are some points in our favor. And I will do my best. You have my word on that."

After he was gone, Halligan said in an undertone, "We got to stick to our story about the money."

"I didn't tell him nothin', Jamy."

"For a minute there, I thought you might."

Daley sat silently for a moment, hunched over on the edge of his bunk, his elbows resting on his knees. "Maybe we ought to," he said finally. "Tell 'em the truth."

Halligan stared across at his cellmate. "Have you lost your wits man?"

"Mr. Blake said we have to tell him everything if he's to do his best for us."

"We don't even know if we can trust him."

"He seems like a decent sort."

"Dom, use your head. Do you really think they'll believe it happened like that?"

"But it's the truth."

"To hell with the bloody truth. If we tell 'em we were lying before, we got no chance a'tall. None. We might as well just skip the trial, and they can take us out and hang us and be done with it. Don't you see, we're just a couple of lyin', thievin' Irishmen to them."

Daley shook his head. "Hell, I wish I'd never laid eyes on that blasted money. The devil's own hand in it, I tell you."

"What's done is done," Halligan said. "We stick to our story. Agreed?"

Daley hesitated but finally nodded.

Strange how at first it had seemed like a wondrous gift. It was Daley who had spotted the purse, as he stopped to urinate down by the river.

There, in the high weeds a few feet off the turnpike road, lay a silk purse stuffed with money. Nearly one hundred dollars in bank bills, some loose coins. A fortune for a pair of poor Irishmen. A gift from God, Daley would later call it. An answer to his prayers. Halligan thought it simply a matter of luck. At first, Daley talked of finding its rightful owner, inquiring along the way, perhaps even turning it in at the next tavern they came across. Halligan argued why look a gift horse in the mouth. But even Daley knew they wouldn't be giving it up. And why should they? They'd found it. It was rightfully theirs now. Lady Luck, which had been so long absent from both of their lives, had decided to shine her sweet light on them. After all, this was America. The fair land of opportunity. So they kept the money and treated themselves to a bottle of rum and a splendid meal at the next inn. Daley talked of putting down his half on that farm he'd always dreamed of. Halligan didn't know what he'd do with his share. Perhaps he'd buy a good horse and head out west, wide open country where a poor man could still make his fortune. Later, sitting in that tavern in Rye, New York, watching ships ply the water of The Sound, he'd had a very odd thought: *Perhaps he could send for her. Aye, but would she come? Or, after all this time, was it too late for such a possibility? Still, he thought, he would buy a ticket once they reached New York, to prove he was serious, and send it to her. He'd write a letter, too, apologizing for his foolishness, telling her he'd finally come to his senses and asking her to join him. It was a crazy idea, he knew, but the thought thrilled him nonetheless.*

Then the posse came swooping down on them, and they were charged with the murder of a man they'd never laid eyes on, and the wonderful gift turned suddenly into a curse. If they told the truth now, the preposterous tale of happening upon a purse of money just lying there, who would believe them? They hardly believed it themselves. The authorities would conclude what any reasonable person would: that they had held Marcus Lyon up and then killed him when he'd put up a fight. No, that would be pure suicide. They couldn't tell anyone that. So when asked about the money, Halligan told them it was theirs, earned by the sweat of their brow. Later though, on the long ride north, the heavy manacles biting into his flesh, Halligan kept wondering at their bad luck. How had the purse of money come to be lying by the side of the road in the first place? Had it fallen from the dead man's pocket during the struggle with the real thieves? Had whoever robbed and killed him dropped it in their haste to get away? Had they hid it there thinking to retrieve it later? No answer seemed plausible. But more importantly, why them? Of all the travelers passing on the road that day, why had it been their lot to find it? Halligan was not a believer in omens or in signs or in the usual sort of superstitious nonsense that most of his fellow Irish adhered to, but it seemed almost too coincidental even for him. It was as if it had been planned by some unseen agency whose sole purpose was to see the two men standing on the gallows. As they rode back to stand trial, what puzzled him most of all was whether he'd actually have sent a ticket to Bridie or not. He supposed he'd never know now.

Τhat evening, Daley and Halligan talked well into the night. Though excited by the prospect of their trial looming ahead of them, they avoided the subject. Instead they spoke of home, their childhoods. Better times. The Maamturk Mountains in the spring. A rainbow Halligan had once seen off over Ballinskellig's Bay. Fishing on the Eriff. The sweet taste of bonny-clabber over a steaming lumper. Drinking hot whiskeys with sugar after a cold day working in the fields. Playing games of hurley on a Saturday afternoon.

"I was pretty fair at hurling," Daley said.

He told Halligan how it was after a hurling match that he met his wife at a small out-of-the-way shebeen where he'd gone to have a pint. A scrip-scrape man was playing fiddle, and he had gotten up to sing along.

"Finola come up to me later and said I had a wonderful voice. I fell in love with her then and there."

Halligan nodded, trying to picture the scene. Daley standing there, the big lout tongue-tied, and falling in love with some bog-girl because she liked his voice, of all things. Still, he had to smile inwardly at the thought.

"Have you never had a special girl, Jamy?" Daley asked him.

"I liked my freedom too much."

"Someday you'll be wanting a wife, mark my words."

Someday, Halligan thought ruefully. Like there would be a someday for them.

"What about a family?" Daley asked.

"What about it?"

"Wouldn't you like a son, Jamy?"

He shrugged.

"Someone to carry on the Halligan name."

"It's getting late," he replied, suddenly cross. "Go to sleep."

He pulled his blanket over his head and turned toward the wall. He was tired, but his mind wouldn't shut off. It kept swirling with thoughts, with memories. He thought about what Daley had asked him, if he'd ever had a special girl. He'd had plenty of girls. Pretty girls and plain ones. Young ones and those that had been around the track a time or two. Some had to be sweet-talked out of their virginity as if it were some precious gem, while others were only too happy to give it away. There was a shy blond girl named Siobhan, from Wexford, when he worked for Mr. Fitzgibbons. And a hot-tempered redheaded wench named Maraed who had a shapely calf. He'd always had a way with women. He'd smile and they would smile back, and he'd say he liked their hair or their eyes, and one thing would lead to another.

Now, though, he could hardly recall any of them. They receded into his mind like dreams after a night of too much drink. All, that is, except Bridie. He remembered her all right. The silky touch of her skin, the smell of her hair, like fresh-cut apples. The dark gleam of her eyes. Such earnest and taciturn eyes. At first glance, she gave every appearance of being the prim and proper daughter of a well-to-do Protestant landlord. The modest way in which she carried herself across the yard into the stables, the assured tilt of her head, the way she spoke to the hired help, with courtesy but also with the confidence that came of having money and status, with knowing how to command without commanding. Later, how that façade would fall away when she was in his arms and she would startle him with her passion. She was like a wild animal, biting his neck, digging her nails into his back. Afterwards whimpering and purring softly deep in her throat. Yes, how could he forget her?

Have you never had a special girl?
What about a family?
Wouldn't you like a son?
Someone to carry on the Halligan name.

Daley's questions were like a knife blade in his gut. He'd never told Daley about her. He couldn't even say why he hadn't told him, his best friend, his only friend, and here the two of them had been locked up tighter than a couple of doves in an osier cage. In fact, when Daley had once asked him about a name he had cried out in his sleep, Halligan only shrugged it off as some girl he'd known back home. Just some girl. Nothing more.

Wouldn't you like a son?

For some reason, when he let himself think about it, he pictured a son. A lad, though he never permitted himself to imagine what he might look like, his eyes, the sound of his voice, whether he had Bridie's raven-black hair. Just how old would the child be now, he wondered. Three? He'd been gone almost four years. The lad would be about his own age when his mother died and left him all alone. But this boy wouldn't be alone, of course. He'd have a family, a wealthy one at that, to see that he didn't go without.

He remembered the last time he'd seen Bridie. It was up on Mount Eagle behind her father's estate, overlooking the sea. Sometimes he used to work up there cutting turf, hauling it down the mountain in a cart pulled by a donkey. He liked working there, all alone, the salt breeze off the water, the vast expanse of the ocean stretching to the pale blue of the horizon. Why, you could almost see all the way to Amerikay. *Meet me tonight up on the mountain near the old bothan*, her note had said. *We must talk!* She had hurriedly pressed it into his hand in the stables as she mounted Tristan, her white charger, to go for a ride earlier that day. He wondered at its urgency. Was something wrong? Had her father found out about them? But if that was the case, he'd already be knowing it. Her da would have cut off his bullocks for him right quick.

He waited for her that night at the old shepherd's stone hut, just below the crest of the mountain. A warm summer moon bathed the Dingle hills in a pale, silvery glow. When she finally arrived on foot, a shawl tossed over her white gown so that she reminded him of a ghost, she threw her arms around him.

"Do you love me, James?" she demanded, her voice filled with an unsettling gravity, even for her. Her arms around his neck clung so hard they almost cut off his breath.

"What?" he said, pulling her away so he could look at her.

"Do you love me?"

"What's all this?"

"Do you?"

"Of course."

She was young, seventeen, a naïve girl inexperienced in the ways of the heart or the soft unctuous words of men. Sheltered by a widowed father who doted on her and shielded her from the roughness of the world. What did she know of love? And the truth was, he was fond of her. Very fond indeed. This serious, raven-haired, dark-eyed girl had cast a spell on him. In fact, he was more fond of her than he had been of any of the other women he'd been with. That's why, perhaps, he'd stayed as long as he had. Seven months. He hardly ever stayed that long anyplace. No matter what, there always came that moment when the pull to be moving on grew too strong. But with this girl things were different. He didn't want to leave. He found himself wanting to stay where he was, his will made torpid by Bridie's charms.

"Really and truly, James?" she asked a third time. "Tell me the truth."

"Yes. I love you," he replied, kissing her eyes, her cheeks, finally her lips. "Now what in blazes is this all about?"

She looked up at him, her expression an odd mixture of fear and excitement. He stared into her dark eyes, iridescent in the moonlight. And then, she told him the thing that would change everything, the thing that would make his heart stop: *she was carrying his child.* She told him with this naïve expectancy, almost as if she actually believed he would be excited by the news. Instead he felt sick to his stomach. *Sweet Jesus,* he thought. Now there would be hell to pay. When her father found out he would kill him. Bad enough that he, a dirt-poor Catholic, was fucking the man's daughter. But getting her with child was too much. His goose was cooked, no two ways about it.

"How long?" he managed to get out.

"I don't know. A couple of months."

"Jaysus," he said, holding his head in his hands. "Why didn't you tell me before?"

"I didn't know. For sure anyway. Don't be mad," she pleaded, beginning to sob. "Please don't be mad, James."

"I'm not mad. I'm just . . ."

"What are we going to do?"

We, he thought. "I don't know," he said.

"We could go away."

"Where?"

"To America."

"*America?*" he scoffed.

"You've talked about it before."

"Yes, but . . . by myself."

"We two could go. I have a little money saved."

"And what would we do there?" he said, sarcastically, bitterly, wanting to hurt her now for some reason. As if it were all her doing, this child of theirs. As if she had planned this, as he knew some women did to snag a man.

He turned and gazed out at the sea with its moon-dappled skin, glimmering like black ice. It looked almost firm enough to hold a man's footstep, as if he could walk across to America if he had to. The option had always seemed more a dream than anything real, more a hope that sat in every Irishman's heart like a trump card he would never use, in a game he could never win.

"We could get married," she said. "We could have a life there together."

"And what about your family, Bridie? Could you leave them?"

"Yes," she replied, hesitantly. Then more confidently, as if trying to convince herself too, she added, "Yes, I could. I *could*."

"Could you really leave all this behind? Everything you knew."

Tears slid down her cheeks. "I don't care, James. I'll go wherever you go. Just as long as we're together. That's all that matters."

"Oh, my dear sweet girl," he said, kissing her tears. He felt then a wave of genuine tenderness for her, this beautiful, frightened girl. "I'm sorry. I didn't mean for this to happen."

"I know. I love you, James. Just as long as the three of us are together."

The three of us, he thought. How could he fix this? How could he get out of the bind he'd made for himself? Finally, he saw the only way out. It was like a door, the only one that opened for him, and he grabbed it and opened it, ready to run through.

"All right," he said calmly. "We'll go away together."

"Do you mean it, Jamy?" she squealed with delight. "Do you really?"

"Aye," he said. "But I'll need to take care of some things first."

"We can't wait long. I'll be showing soon."

"Not long. I promise."

They worked out a plan. She would give him some money to book passage for two out of Cove, a port town just south of Cork, two days' journey from Dingle. She would meet him there in a fortnight. She would tell her father she was going to visit a cousin in Cork and then slip away and join him. Together they would board a ship bound for America. They worked it all out.

He kissed her one last time, tasting her salty tears on his lips. He had never seen a more beautiful, a more touching sight in all his days than that of Bridie at that moment. She was like the most perfect day a man could imagine, bright and cloudless, one where the air smelled of heather and your heart beat with hope, and there was not even the possibility of pain or loneliness or hunger or death anywhere in the world. In her dark lovely eyes he might have lived forever. He would miss this girl, he knew. More than all the others. More, perhaps, than he'd ever know.

"I love you, James," she said one last time.

He wanted to reply, but the words stuck in his throat.

He left the next day, telling Mr. Maguire he had some personal business to attend to in Cork. When he reached Cove, he booked passage on a ship sailing that very day for Boston. On deck, looking back over the stern as the green hills of the land he'd never see again faded into a fuzzy memory, he told himself he'd done the right thing. The only thing. What else could he have done? Their plan would never work. If they caught him running off with the seventeen-year-old pregnant daughter of a wealthy Protestant, he could only imagine the trouble he'd be in. But even if they somehow did make it to America, what then? What sort of life could they have had? They were too different, the worlds they came from too far apart. She was used to elegant things, servants and a great big house, a fine horse to ride. A life soft as velvet. Never getting her hands dirty or having to work to put food on the table. And he was a penniless spalpeen, a man who could claim only the clothes on his back and some big dreams. What sort of life could he have provided for her or the child? What chance of happiness could they have had with him? No, it was for the best. She'd be better off without him, he convinced himself. He pictured her standing on the dock, holding a valise with her things, waiting for him to come. Waiting and waiting. How long before she realized the truth? He knew when she found out he'd lied, it would break her heart. He felt awful about that and about the child he was leaving behind—as his own father had no doubt left him behind. In time she would come to understand the rightness of this decision. As the years passed and she fell in love again, as he knew she would, and got married and had more children, maybe she would think back on that brief time with him, and no longer hate him. Maybe she would look into the eyes of their child and realize it had been the only thing possible. Maybe.

Now, as he listened to the ragged snores of Daley, he had two thoughts, separate but connected to each other like a pair of manacles. He didn't believe in any sort of divine justice, whether it be rewarding the good or punishing the bad. There was luck, of course, good or bad. Some men were lucky and others weren't. But mostly he thought a man made his own way in life, had only himself to blame. Still, if he had been a believer in such things, he'd wonder if his current situation had anything to do with what he'd done. It was something to puzzle over. And there was the other thing: that odd notion he'd had right before he was arrested at the tavern. Of sending for her. Had he been serious? Would he have actually done it? Or was it something he told himself exactly because he knew it was too late?

· · ·

Blake didn't return until mid-morning the next day. This time the turnkey was able to scrounge up a regular chair for him to sit upon instead of the stool.

"Good morning, gentlemen," the lawyer grunted as he entered the cell. He wore the same clothes as he had the day before, which looked as if he'd slept in them. He appeared haggard, his blue eyes red-rimmed and glassy. His pantaloons were wrinkled and grease stained, his cravat askew, his overcoat fouled by mud, as if he had fallen in the gutter. And he brought with him a stale tavern smell of rum and smoke.

He sat down heavily in the chair. He held his head in his hands for a moment, silent except for his labored breathing. Daley and Halligan exchanged glances.

"Are you all right, sir?" Daley asked solicitously. "Could I get you some water?"

"No, I'm fine," he said. "It's just that I've come down with a cold in this dreadful weather. Up all hours of the night with it." And as if to prove it, he coughed several times, covering his mouth with a filthy handkerchief. His puffy cheeks flushed with color, the broken blood vessels a spidery web across his face.

"Oh, you'll want to take care of that, sir," Daley said. "Don't want that cough to get down in your lungs. That's what happened with me mam. A cough got down in her lungs, and she's not been the same since. Melted butter is what you want."

"Melted butter?" Blake asked, the very thought seeming to make him sick.

"Aye. That'd be just the thing for a cough. Some melted butter with just a spot o' whiskey in it, sir."

"I would just as soon skip the butter," he said, smiling wearily. He reached into the inside pocket of his coat and pulled out a small silver flask. He unscrewed the top with practiced movements of his pudgy fingers and took a long draught. "Ahhh," he said, reviving a little.

Once more he used Daley's bunk as a writing desk. From his valise, he removed his papers and spread them out and arranged his writing instruments. As he perused the papers, he gnawed on a fingernail until it bled. He fixed his spectacles on his red, splotchy nose and jotted something down on his writing tablet. "Hmmm," he said to himself, nodding. "Yes. Here we are."

"Mr. Blake," Daley interrupted. "We ain't talked yet of your fee."

"My fee?" the man asked, looking up from his papers. His eyes were distorted behind his glasses, the whites looking large and slimy as the belly of an eel.

"We ain't wealthy men, as you can well imagine. But we'd be willing to work off the debt, whatever it be."

"That won't be necessary," Blake said. "I am being remunerated by the state. Now according to statements you gave when arrested, it took you five full days to travel on foot from Boston to Wilbraham, the scene of the murder, a distance of some eighty miles. And yet, from Wilbraham to New York, which is over one hundred and thirty miles, it took you a mere two days. How do you explain that?"

"I don't know, sir," Daley replied. "We just walked till we got tired."

"But you can see how one might interpret such a fact. Your pace was less than twenty miles per day before the murder but nearly three times that after it. The prosecution will make it look as if you were fleeing from something."

"We weren't fleeing from anything," Halligan interjected.

"But how do you explain it then?"

"There were hills we had to cross east of there. The road south of Springfield was flat and easy walking. So naturally our pace was a bit faster."

"More than a bit," Blake challenged.

"And it had been raining the days before . . ." Daley said, pausing, "the murder. The road as far as Palmer was muddy. And later in the week the weather was clear."

The lawyer reached into his waistcoat pocket, removed his snuff box, and took a pinch for each nostril. His lids fluttered and his eyes rolled way back in the sockets, then he sneezed vigorously several times into his handkerchief.

"I think," Blake said, "I shall be able to handle that issue without too much difficulty. However, the bank bills found on you might pose a problem. Tell me where you got them again?"

Daley glanced furtively at Halligan and quickly averted his gaze. "I earned that money doing honest work."

"Where?"

"Some was from digging on the Mill Pond Dam. Some I got working on the South Boston Bridge. The rest here and there. I don't remember it all."

"And you?" he asked of Halligan.

"Same. Here and there."

"Do you have anyone who can vouch that you earned it as you say? An employer that would be willing to testify on your behalf?"

"Oh, I doubt that, sir," Daley said. "I'm just a common laborer. The only time they remember you is when you done something wrong."

"If you could prove the money was yours, it would greatly aid our cause."

"Why do we have to prove it was ours?" Halligan jumped in. "Shouldn't they have to prove it wasn't?"

"One hundred dollars is a good deal of money to be carrying about."

"What you're saying is," Halligan offered, "what's a lazy Irishman doing with that sort of money? He must have stolen it from somebody, right?"

"Gentlemen," Blake said, taking his glasses off his nose and looking at the two. "I'm only trying to be prepared for what they'll ask in court. And yes, the jury will wonder how a pair of unskilled laborers came to be in possession of such a considerable sum, and drawn on the very same banks as those bills carried by the victim. I would prefer to offend your sensibilities and save you from the gallows. Is that clear?"

" 'Tis, Mr. Blake," said Daley, glancing at his cellmate.

"In any case, I don't suppose the prosecution," Blake continued, "will spend a great deal of time on this issue of the bank bills. It is rather remote from the central circumstances of the case, and it could actually confuse the issue, particularly if they thought we might be able to call a witness of our own proving the money was legitimately earned through gainful employment. So we'll leave that for the time being." Blake shuffled through his notes. "All right," he said, "the rest of the prosecution's case seems rather circumstantial to me. They have a number of witnesses who saw people fitting either your description or that of Mr. Lyon at various points along the turnpike on Saturday the ninth of November. And then they have that merchant from Boston who claims that an 'Irishman' came into his store and purchased pistols similar to those found at the murder site. However, he cannot say with any degree of certainty that it was either of you, nor that the pistols he sold were those found at the murder site. Again, such presumptive testimony will be of dubious value at best. So what the state's case will largely rest upon will be the testimony of the Fuller boy."

The lawyer spent a long time going over the statement the boy had given during the inquest. That he said he'd seen the two passing along the Post Road heading west. That he spotted them returning some "short time" later leading a large bay horse with a "handsome saddle." That he followed them up a hill toward an apple orchard where he got a good look at Daley's face but not Halligan's. That one of them rode while the other pushed the horse, driving it into the pasture of John Bliss.

"The outcome, I believe, will largely hinge on the boy's testimony," Blake said. "To be perfectly frank, left uncontested it will be quite damning. An eyewitness always carries a great deal of weight with a jury."

"He's not tellin' the truth," Daley exclaimed.

"But he swears that he saw you, Mr. Daley, leading the dead man's horse. In the courtroom tomorrow, he will point his finger at you and say you are the one he saw." Blake looked at Daley with those sleepy blue eyes of his. Despite the lethargy in them, there was a certain hard subtlety about them now, a sly cunning, like those of a cat quietly sunning itself. It was almost as if he half expected the Irishman finally to give up this unconvincing pretense of innocence and admit his guilt at last.

"He's lyin'," Daley repeated. "I cannot say why, Mr. Blake. P'haps the boy knows who done it, and he's protectin' him."

"That's just speculation. Even if it were true, I will not have time to mount a credible alternative theory. It will come down to whether they believe him or not."

"But he's just a boy," Daley said.

"A *Yankee* boy," Blake countered. "And every single member of the jury will be Yankees, too. As was the dead man. They will listen to him and then they will look at the two of you. And do you know what they will see, gentlemen?"

"A pair of stinkin' Irishmen!" Halligan cried out, angry.

Blake looked sternly over at Halligan. "See that you keep your temper in check tomorrow, Mr. Halligan. What they will see will be their prejudices. Everything they hate and fear. A pair of foreigners who have come to this country to rob and murder. To take what they've worked so hard to establish. To corrupt morals with their strange Catholic ways. That's what they will see, gentlemen. Since the murder, there has been in these parts, in fact, in the whole of the commonwealth, a growing sentiment against immigrants. Especially the Irish."

"I thought we left all that behind," Daley said with the stubborn naïveté of a small child. "I thought over here we're supposed to be good as the next fellow before the law."

"In theory, yes," Blake said. "You should know as well that both sides will be looking to use the trial for their own political ends."

"Both sides?" Daley asked.

"I speak of the Federalists and Republicans," Blake explained.

"I don't understand," said Daley. "What does politics have to do with whether we done what they say we did or not?"

"A great deal, I'm afraid, Mr. Daley," Blake replied, glancing over at him. "The Federalists have controlled the governor's seat for the past sixteen elections. However, their hold on the state, as with the country as a whole, is waning. The man who will be prosecuting you, James Sullivan, ran a very close race as the Republican candidate against Governor Strong in the last election. And he will be running against him in the next as well. Caleb Strong, on the other hand, hails from Northampton. A favorite son, if you will. He's quite wealthy, well connected. The town remains a stronghold for Federalists, one of the few remaining ones in the state for his party. In the last election Strong took every single vote from this town, which undoubtedly spelled the difference in the Federalists' narrow victory. But he's worried now that his hold on the town and on the entire western part of the state is slipping. For his part, the attorney general would like to make inroads in his opponent's advantage out here in the west by winning a conviction. Beating Strong in his own backyard, so to speak. A good showing in the trial might win enough votes to swing the next election in his favor. That's also why Strong offered a five-hundred-dollar reward for your capture and conviction."

"Five hundred dollars!" Daley exclaimed. "Do you hear that, Jamy boy? Five hundred they're givin' for our necks."

"There's your reason why the boy said it was us," Halligan said. "For the reward."

"I've considered that possibility. Unfortunately, I have no proof."

"A lot of people would turn their own mothers in for that kind of money," said Daley.

"By putting up such a large reward, Strong hoped to take advantage of the growing animosity toward foreigners. He feels it would help his chances for reelection. At the same time, he's one of the biggest investors in the turnpike."

"How's that?" Halligan asked.

"Well, the murder happened on the turnpike. If people are afraid to travel it, tolls will be down. Profits will be hurt. So it's to his advantage to see to it that these sorts of crimes are not allowed to go unpunished. Strong can't very well afford to have highwaymen accosting paying customers. It's bad for business."

Blake smiled at this, as if he had made a joke.

"And then there are the judges in the case," he continued. "Sam Sewall is openly anti-Catholic. He was one of the judges in a case that brought suit against the Catholic diocese of New England, forcing it to pay tithes for the support of a Protestant minister. The other is Judge Sedgwick."

"Tall fellow with coal-black eyes?" Halligan said.

"That's him. I've argued cases previously before him. He can be very exacting. And as a staunch Federalist, he is a solid supporter of the governor and a man who doesn't like Sullivan."

"That explained the business in court yesterday," Halligan said, glancing at Daley.

The lawyer frowned.

"The judge lit into Sullivan for not being there," Halligan explained. "Said he was too busy with his campaign."

Blake nodded.

"Sullivan's a skilled attorney. He's quite experienced. I look forward to such a formidable adversary. And I will do my best by you."

"Is there nothin' to the good, Mr. Blake?" Daley asked.

"I have a few cards I plan to play. It is not completely hopeless," he said, and then realizing how pessimistic that must have sounded, added, "not by a long shot. The boy's statement, though damaging, is not without certain inconsistencies that I shall try to exploit on cross-examination. Besides, they have no actual eyewitnesses to the crime. It is all presumptive evidence. Nor can they connect you to the murder weapons. These particulars are very much in our favor. And there is the fact that you put up no resistance when you were arrested. That looks good. So all in all, you needn't give up hope. We have better than a fighting chance, gentlemen."

The attorney began to pack up his things.

"Mr. Blake, sir," Daley said. "That fellow. The one who was killed. Did his people get his things back?"

"What do you mean?"

"His horse and saddle and such. Did his folks get them back?"

"I would imagine so. What they didn't keep for evidence. Why?"

"Just wonderin' is all."

Halligan shot him a warning look, but Daley wouldn't meet his gaze.

"Then I shall meet you in court, gentlemen," he said. He stood and removed the flask from his coat, and took another sip. He was going to put it back when he looked over at the two. "As you can see, I, too, have an inside pocket for carrying refreshments." He smiled, giving his fleshy, liquor-haunted face an oddly boyish look, youthful and mischievous. He unscrewed the cap and held it out to Daley. "Would you care for some?" he asked.

Daley hesitated, then said, "If'n you please, sir." He accepted the flask from him and took a short sip. "Ohhh," he cried, shivering. " 'Tis grand stuff that."

Halligan then took the bottle and drank. It was West Indian rum, cinnamon-flavored, sweet and filled with fire. The liquid burned his mouth and throat but slowly warmed his insides, fanning out like a warm sea breeze.

"Thank you, Mr. Blake," Halligan said, wiping the top on his sleeve and handing it back to the man.

"To our mutual success, gentlemen," Blake toasted, formally holding up the flask before taking another sip. He returned the flask to its pocket. Then he gathered up his things and put his coat on.

"Get a good night's sleep, gentlemen," he said. "It is likely to be a long day tomorrow. May God be with you."

"And you, sir," Daley offered, making the sign of the cross. "Take care of that cold. Have you some melted butter."

The man smiled and left. After he was gone, Halligan whispered, "What in the hell was all that about?"

"All what about?"

"If that fellow's family was going to get his bleeding things or not? What concern is that of yours?"

"I just . . . I feel bad about the money."

"Jaysus. We didn't do nothing wrong."

"We lied about it, didn't we?"

"What else could we have done, Dom?"

"But by rights it should belong to his folks now."

"We don't have it anymore, remember? They took it from us. Let them do with it what they will. It's no business now of ours."

"I still don't feel right about it. I feel like we stole it. I don't want that on me head."

They both fell silent for a moment.

"All right, listen, Dom," Halligan said finally. "If we get out of this, they'll have to give us the money back. We'll put it in an envelope and send it to them. We won't say who it's from. And if they find us guilty, well, it won't matter anyway. What do you say?"

Daley looked over at him and nodded. Then he lay back on his bunk, put his hands behind his head, and closed his eyes. He was so still that

Halligan had thought he'd fallen asleep. But then he started to hum. It was an old tune from back home. "Cossey's Jig." Pretty soon Daley began to sing the words to it.

> *Ma'am dear, did you ever hear*
> *Of pretty Molly Brannigan?*
> *The times are going hard with me,*
> *I'll never be a man again.*
> *Not since Molly's gone and left me*
> *Here alone for to die.*

FIVE

Cheverus rose in the chill pre-dawn darkness of his room. He knelt at
the foot of his bed, his rosary wrapped tightly around his hand, and
prayed. He prayed for the soul of his beloved mother. He prayed for those
of Father Landry and Archbishop Dulau and for all the hundreds of martyred priests who had died during the September Massacres. He prayed
for the two Catholic prisoners, Dominic Daley and James Halligan. May
God grant them a fair trial. May He forgive them their trespasses, whatever they might be. May He lead them from the darkness of sin into the
light of His everlasting love.

When he was in the seminary in Paris, he had liked this time of day
best, by himself, praying on the smooth stone floor of his narrow little
room. The still, sanctified air of early morning infusing his prayers with
solemnity and holiness. His heart quiet, his soul becalmed. The day's
busy labors awaiting him, but right then alone with his God. At such
times he could almost feel His presence, not as a thing abstract and transcendent, not as fire or light or love, but actual and corporeal, a presence
almost human. He felt he could hear God's heart beating, could feel His
breath warm upon his face, like a baby feels his mother's. Lately though,
his prayers seemed to hang unheard in the air around him, like so much
flotsam. Sometimes he wondered if He even received his words anymore.
He preached that God forgave even the worst sinner, as long as he confessed his sins and received absolution. So why hadn't he confessed? Was
it vanity? Fear? Willfulness of spirit? What? *Help me, O Lord, to know Thy*

wishes. I am ignorant and need instruction. I am weak and need Thy strength.

Finished with his morning prayers, he set about his toilet, washing himself briskly in a basin of icy water on his night table. Next, with a small handheld mirror, he shaved, the first time since his illness. With difficulty he hacked at his beard with the unstropped straight razor. Despite its dullness, he managed to cut himself along the angle of his jaw. The blood flowed freely down his neck, appearing bright red against the pallid skin. As he stanched the bleeding with a rag, he stared appraisingly at himself in the mirror. He felt the usual vague dissatisfaction with what he saw: a frail-looking man with a head too large for his dwarfish body, the melancholy, slightly down-turned eyes, the weak jaw, the absurdly boyish features belying the fact that he was rapidly approaching the middle years of life. He was at that stage when most men had something to show for their time on earth—a wife, family, career, a certain measure of success—when a man knows the rhythms of his own existence, when the feel of it is as familiar to him as the roof of his mouth, when he can look both backward with satisfaction and forward still with hope and anticipation.

Cheverus had never really cared to weigh his own life against those common scales of worldly success or failure. He had only wanted to serve his Lord, to carry out His will—regardless of however slight or unimpressive it might look to others. It would have been his success, his accomplishment. Even in that, how had he fared? He had toiled ceaselessly to further His Church in this harsh, unforgiving land. He had thrown himself into his work with a passionate intenstiy. But why? Was it for the greater glory of his Lord or for his own aggrandizement? Did He look with satisfaction on his life? The world saw a dedicated, hard-working, deeply devout man of God. He knew that many in Boston—Protestant as well as Catholic—held him in some regard. In his innermost soul, though, he questioned himself. In some ways, he couldn't help feeling his life a sham, that he was a charlatan, a fraud hiding behind the cloth. He was weak. He could be petty and vain. He yearned for the love of his flock though he felt himself above them. He often lacked humility or patience or understanding. He felt desire for women, even now after all these years of celibacy. Despite what others may have thought, he knew himself to be a coward at heart, and that when acting out of what seemed to be principle or conviction—as in the case with the Daleys—it was more that he feared to do otherwise, feared what people would think of him. The face that looked back at him seemed to mock him.

When he had finished dressing, he sat at his escritoire. He penned a note to the attorney general asking that he might have a word with him this morning about the prisoners. He left it vague, so as not to give Sullivan the advantage, but added the word "urgent." As he sat there, he glanced at the letters from home. Perhaps, he thought, he would leave for France in early autumn, when he'd returned from his mission work with the Indians in Maine. That would give everyone enough time to adjust to his going. By then, Bishop Carroll could have arranged for a suitable assistant for Father Matignon. His friend would not be left empty-handed, and he himself would have time to tie up loose ends here. Finish the Catholic manual he was working on. Perhaps get the school up and running. Give his Irish time to adjust to the idea of his leaving—though he doubted that would take much. More importantly, he would have time to get acclimated to the notion. Once the decision was made, he could then begin to set his sights on returning home. Who knows? Maybe going home was just what he needed. Maybe it would clear his mind of these brooding meditations, these troubling memories of the past. Facing the thing he feared. Courage, after all, was merely an act of will.

Yvette was up already, tending to the fire in the kitchen by the time he came downstairs. She said in English, "I made for you breakfast, *mon Père.*"

He found to his surprise that his appetite had returned. He sat down to a meal of fried cod, baked beans, and gruel, with a cup of tea. He ate ravenously.

"Good?" she asked, placing before him a copy of the *Columbian Centinel,* one of Boston's weekly papers.

"*Oui, très bon,*" he replied, smiling at her. He handed her the note he had written. "Yvette, I would like you to take this message to Mr. Sullivan. He lives on Summer."

"Now?" she asked.

"Please. Wait for his reply. *Très important.*"

"*Oui, mon Père.*"

After she left, he opened the *Centinel* and began to read, the first time in nearly two weeks that he had perused a paper. There was news about Napoleon's latest conquests. About a French frigate spotted off the Maine coast. About a possible embargo of all trade with Europe. There was the usual bickering between Republicans and Federalists, especially with the upcoming gubernatorial election still very much contested. Then on the second page, he came across a small article: "Irishmen to be Tried for Murder."

> Dominic Daley and James Halligan, two men lately from Ireland and now of the Commonwealth of Massachusetts, are to be tried this week in Northampton for the murder of Mr. Marcus Lyon, who was brutally slain at Wilbraham this past November. It is highly probably the accused persons were concerned in several highway robberies in this vicinity.

Yvette returned in a half hour's time with a note saying the attorney general could spare a few minutes to meet with him at nine. He put on his cassock and left the rectory, making his way along the alley toward the front of the church. The early spring morning was cool, especially in the shadows of buildings, but overhead the sky was a deep blue and the day promised to be much more seasonable than the past several. To the east, above the harbor, a determined sun had already broken through the usual mists that hung above the water. Yellow light glistened in the still-wet limbs of the maples and white oaks out on Franklin. The rain from the previous night had left the roads smelling sharply of sewage.

Rounding the corner, he came upon a group of boys heading off to work in the ropewalks, clutching their lunch potato and bit of bread wrapped in oil cloth. He recognized several from his parish. They were jostling and pushing one another and didn't see the priest right away. One boy, Danny Cahill, the youngest of the Cahill clan, called out, "I'd kick the bloody bastard in the arse, is what I'd do."

"You would not," cried another.

"What are ye talking about, yer mother's nothin' but a whore," taunted the Cahill boy. When he finally spotted the priest though, his face turned crimson and he lowered his gaze. "Mornin', Father," they all said in contrite, singsong fashion. The priest smiled at them and bade them good morning. He wasn't out of earshot before they fell once more to cursing and fighting.

He passed the impressive Tontine Crescent, a curved row of stately homes designed by his friend, the architect Charles Bulfinch, to imitate the grand rowhouses of Bath, England. The Crescent had been one of the new marvels of the city when it was completed a decade ago. Even now, people came from as far away as New York and Philadelphia just to see it. In front of one residence, a Negro coachman waited in the driver's seat of an elegant phaeton drawn by a matched pair of chestnut-colored geldings. He was dressed in red velvet livery and a white peruke beneath a cocked hat. It was now quite the fashion, especially among well-to-do Federalists, to dress one's servants in the style of an English manor lord. The Negro glanced down at the priest and nodded.

As Cheverus turned down narrow Arch Street and passed beneath the rooms of the Boston Public Library, his heart sank when he saw who was approaching him: Nell O'Rourke. It was hard to keep a conversation short with the woman, and he had little time and less patience this morning for her insipid blather. She was busily making her way along the street with a basket on her elbow, no doubt heading for the market in Faneuil Hall.

"Father!" she cried, surprised to see him out that early. She had a slightly guilty look on her face, which was as dark and scabrous as an oyster shell. "'Tis good to see you're feeling better. You've been in me prayers."

Nell was in her thirties, a sturdy woman with a fleshy neck and arms, thick ankles below her long, already-sullied apron. Cheverus didn't particularly like her. She was an ignorant woman, full of superstitious nonsense, like so many of them. More than that, she was the worst sort of gossip. She keened the loudest at wakes, and in the confessional she spent more time talking about her neighbors' sins than her own. And though she was always fawning and obsequious in his presence, he'd heard from Mrs. Lobb, another parishioner, how the woman thought the two French priests considered themselves above the common sort.

"Good morning, Nell," he said unenthusiastically.

"Sorry for missin' Mass, Father. I been awful busy. Me mistress is with child—again," she said with a conspiratorial wink. She was employed in the household of Sarah Wigginson, a well-to-do woman whose husband owned several merchant ships. "Herself with three little ones already. The master can't keep his hands to home." Then, lowering her voice as if someone might hear, she added, "Though for the life of me, I can't see reason for it. A face like a pig's rear end. Pardon me tongue, Father." But she laughed in spite of herself, tossing her head back to show a mouthful of rotten teeth. "On'y means more work for me."

"I'll see you at Sunday Mass then?"

"Aye. If she lets me off."

He didn't want to be late for his appointment with the attorney general, so he wished her a good day and tried to slip by her.

"By the way, Father," Nell said, cutting off his escape. "Those lads. Daley and the other one. Word is they're to be put on trial finally."

"I don't know anything about it," he lied.

"A terrible thing. Just terrible. Poor Mrs. Daley. And herself losing her younger boy, too. A cryin' shame. Now to have this one branded a thief and a murderer. A curse is what 'tis." Then leaning close to him so he could smell the oniony odor of her breath, she said in an undertone, "But it don't surprise me none. No sir. Them Daleys always was a bit wild, if you know what I mean."

Cheverus stared at her, surprised by what was, even for her, vicious gossip. "Dominic was a good Catholic," he offered. *Was*, he thought.

"Not what I heard, Father. I heard he had a wild streak in him," she said, nodding. "Me mistress says they'll get the rope. Do ye think so?"

"I don't know. Good day now," he said, moving on.

"They're as far back as Couneenole," she said, walking with him back the way she'd come. Cheverus had heard the expression before. It meant something hopeless. She continued talking as she walked along beside him. "Me mistress says they ought to do it and be quick about it, too. Afore there's trouble."

"What trouble would that be?"

"You haven't heard, Father?" she said, raising her eyebrows.

"No," he said, stopping again. He wasn't sure he wanted to get into this, but then again he was curious. "What are you suggesting?" he snapped.

"I wouldn't want to be the one to spread rumors now." She glanced over her shoulder before continuing. "There's talk about some of our lads going out there and helpin' them."

"Helping them? How?"

"Why, to escape."

"Escape! That's nonsense."

"I heard it with me own ears, Father. The other one, that Halligan fellow, it's said he fought in the Uprising. A blasted croppy, he was, begging your pardon. And some of our boys as fought with him are going out there and breakin' the two out of jail."

"I don't believe that."

"'Tis true, Father. I won't breathe a word who told me but I have it on quite good authority, too." She winked again. "Me mistress says they're going to send a whole regiment of soldiers out there. In case there's trouble."

"Well, I wouldn't trust every rumor you hear, Nell."

"The God's truth," she said, crossing herself. "Do you believe 'em to be guilty, Father?"

"That's for the court to decide."

"I got a feeling they done it. And if so, by rights they should swing. The sooner the better, you ask me."

"I have to be going." He pushed by her and continued on his way.

"I'm prayin' they're found guilty, Father," she called after him. "Otherwise, I fear it'll go hard on the rest of us Irish."

When he reached Summer Street, the road was crowded with wagons and peddlers' carts and women carrying baskets of eggs and baked goods. People were shouting and calling out, and there were the cries of vendors selling milk and fish and charcoal, as well as the clatter of hooves and the rattling of iron wagon wheels over the cobblestones. The priest turned west, and headed toward the Sullivan residence. The street here was quieter, more residential. It narrowed to a tree-lined way just wide enough for a single carriage to pass along. Lindens and elms and a few tall cedars bordered the street. The houses were elegant three- and four-story brick mansions in the Federal style. While some of the houses stood right on the street, most had small gated areas, pretty gardens, that led up to their front doors.

He heard the bells of the Park Street Church sounding nine times. Now he would be late. As he hurried along, the woman's words kept echoing in his brain: *I'm prayin' they're found guilty, Father. Otherwise, I fear it'll go hard on the rest of us Irish.* Pay no attention to her, he told himself. She was just a foolish, malicious woman who liked to spread gossip. Still, there was an element of truth to her callous remarks. Things might, indeed, go hard for the Irish if the two were found innocent. And what if some *were* planning on doing something as reckless as trying to set the prisoners free? The authorities would seize any excuse to crack down hard on them. On all Catholics, for that matter. There was no telling how bad things could get if something like that were to happen. He made a mental note to mention in his next sermon the need to avoid acting rashly, for cool heads to prevail.

Cheverus did not look forward to this visit. The attorney general would, he knew, make it unpleasant in various subtle, and not-so-subtle, ways. Neither man liked the other, though they usually pretended a gloss of mutual respect, at least in public. For instance, Sullivan, president of the Massachusetts Historical Society, and Cheverus, one of the founders of the Boston Athenaeum, sometimes had to appear together at fundraising or social gatherings and act cordially to one another. But with Sullivan now riding the Republican wave of popularity that had spread across the country since President Jefferson's victory, he could afford to be less than cordial to a priest whose standing in the community had fallen because of rising anti-French sentiment. With his recently acknowledged political aspirations, the attorney general would doubtless try to turn to his advantage the always-present anti-papist, anti-foreign resentment which simmered in New England's Protestant hearts. With the war in Europe, with Catholic France seizing American vessels on the high seas, and with the mass of immigrants streaming into Boston Harbor, that suppressed resentment had come to a full-fledged boil once again. Though the attorney general and Strong were not much different when it came to their views on Catholic immigrants, Sullivan would wish to show the citizens of the commonwealth that if he was elected, Irish Catholics who broke the law could expect little leniency from him.

Ironically, the Sullivan clan had come from Limerick as Catholics two generations before. His grandfather had been one of the "Wild Geese" who had fled to France. The Sullivans had settled in Maine as farmers, worked hard and prospered. Somewhere along the line, they did what many before them had: realized the unacceptable burden of their faith and abandoned it in favor of one less onerous. His brother, General John Sullivan, a governor of New Hampshire and a Revolutionary War hero, had called Catholicism that "cursed religion," and like his brother James, thought it was bent on destroying "the pure race of Protestants." Having come from Catholic stock, James Sullivan made the most formidable sort of enemy—the kind of man to turn his back on his past with the narrow-minded zeal of a convert. And he was a self-made man, one of the few men of power in Boston that had risen from modest beginnings to become the most influential Republican in the state. He, like many a self-made man, held in contempt those not so able to rise above their station. Though a Republican like Jefferson and thus someone who should have been more sympathetic to the plight of the poor, the common man, he felt nothing but disdain for them, especially immigrants. Even before this case, Sullivan had been unapologetic in his prejudice against Catholics and other "foreigners." In particular, he viewed the Irish with downright animosity, a form of self-loathing which hated the roots from which he had sprung. Whenever a poor Irish laborer or scullery maid broke the law and came before him in his role as prosecutor, he always sought the harshest penalty: the stocks, a good whipping, cutting off of an ear, a hanging on the Common.

It wasn't only the poor laboring class or just-off-the-boat immigrant who brought forth his ire. It was all Catholics, including its ministers. As a Republican, he had supported—at least in theory—the French Revolution as an attempt to throw off the dual chains of monarchy and Catholicism. In two previous court cases involving the diocese, Attorney General Sullivan had made it abundantly clear that he held only contempt for any brand of papist. One case arose out of a controversy involving tithe taxes in the commonwealth. The Church brought suit to have Catholics legally exempt from having to pay taxes for the support of the Protestant clergy. It was a matter, Fathers Matignon and Cheverus had tried to argue in court, of the fundamental separation of church and state. Why should Catholics have to pay for a Protestant minister when they attended a Catholic church? Yet the court found against them, and they had to pay several hundred dollars not only for the taxes but for the court costs as well, money which they could ill afford to lose.

The other case involving Mr. Sullivan was even more troubling. It stemmed from an incident up in Maine, which was under the jurisdiction of Massachusetts. Besides ministering to the Indians, Cheverus spent a part of each year up north administering the sacraments to a handful of Catholics who had settled around Newcastle, Maine. While up there several years earlier, he had performed the marriage ceremony for two Irish Catholics, James Smithwick and Elizabeth Jackson. According to law, marriage was only legal if performed by an acknowledged minister or by a justice of the peace. Hoping to avoid a legal conflict, Cheverus had advised the couple to have their marriage offically sanctioned in a civil ceremony before a justice of the peace, just to be safe. Which they did. Nothing happened until the following year, when Cheverus returned for his mission work in Maine. The attorney general then served him with a warrant for his arrest, taking, to Cheverus's mind, a more than professional interest in the case. The priest was charged with marrying a couple without legal authority and placed in jail like a common criminal. It was the second time in his life he'd been in jail. In court, Cheverus had to prove himself a "settled" minister, that is, one legally sanctioned and recognized by the state. Mr. Sullivan had hoped to win a guilty verdict so that he could show everyone that New England was, is, and always would be a Protestant realm that wouldn't stand for, as he put it in court, "popish harlotry." Fortunately, Silas Lee, a member of Congress and a skilled attorney, defended Cheverus and won him an acquittal. Even so, when dismissing the case, one of the judges, Justice Bradbury, had stared down from his bench at Cheverus and declared spitefully, "Nothing would have delighted me more, sir, than to see you spend a pleasant hour in the pillory."

Though there had been some significant concessions made in the laws of the commonwealth over the past twenty years regarding Catholic rights, Cheverus had learned not to expect much. Under Father Matignon's tutelage, he had come to be ever wary, ever cautious. Even in 1806, he knew that Catholics were still considered second-class citizens, trespassers in this Protestant country, and that something like the Daley-Halligan case had the potential to make things only more difficult for all. Still, he'd given the Daleys his word. He had told them he would talk to the attorney general, and they had no one else to speak for them. He realized, too, that it was partly his own pride that made him waver now. He didn't like the thought of going to Sullivan and asking him for his help. Yet he must swallow his pride, he thought: *Pride goeth before destruction.*

While he was debating with himself, he had reached the Sullivan residence. The attorney general's mansion was one of those newer, Federalist-era houses that had changed the face of Boston during the past decade, turning the city from a simple Puritan village of plain wooden structures to an English-style municipality with grand brick houses preaching the new faith in materialistic success. Cheverus went through the wrought-iron gate and up to the impressive front doors. The building was enormous, a four-storied, double house with long windows recessed into the white-painted, brick bow fronts—a home befitting someone as substantial as James Sullivan. He was after all, the most important Republican in the city, in fact one of the most important men period, wealthy, highly connected to many of Boston's most influential families. One didn't want to make an enemy of such a man. Remember to be discreet, he told himself.

Cheverus struck the gleaming brass knocker and waited. A Negro servant answered the door.

"Yessuh," the man said. He was tall and lean, with graying hair and loose, jaundiced eyes. The priest stated that he had an appointment to see the attorney general.

He gave his name, and the man had him step into a foyer. He had him wait there while he went off to see Mr. Sullivan. He returned after a moment and said, "Mr. Sullivan is with his barber now. Please to wait here, sir."

Cheverus glanced around. He had never been in the attorney general's residence. It was an impressive home, high-ceilinged, elegant, with Italian marble floors. A chandelier hung from the ceiling while a curved staircase with ornate balusters wound its way to a second story. On the walls were various portraits of men and women, several appearing to be in the style of Gilbert Stuart, for whom many of the city's elite sat. One on the wall opposite happened to catch his eye. It was of a young woman wearing a mull cap and a dark shawl drawn slightly down off one pale, angular shoulder. She had sharp features but was pretty in a severe sort of way. She stared at Cheverus unabashedly with large, dark, candid eyes. There was about her stare a kind of challenge.

His forehead felt damp with sweat. The fever was upon him still. He reached into his pocket, took out his handkerchief, and dabbed his face. As he did so, he smelled something odd. A too-sweet odor. It took him a moment to realize what it was: the scent of Finola Daley. Her tears, that odd smell she gave off. He remembered the night before, that suffering, saint-like aspect of hers. *My poor Dom. My poor love.* And he remembered as they stood at the door, her leaning into him, her cool hand on his wrist, whispering that she would pray for him.

After making him wait the better part of an hour, the attorney general finally appeared.

"Good morning," the man said curtly, without offering his hand. His face glowed a bright pink from having just been shaved, and his gray hair was freshly powdered and held in place at the neck with a black ribbon. He was of the newer style of men who went without a wig, though he still had his hair powdered so that his scalp appeared a grayish white. "I hope I have not kept you long, Mr. Cheverus." The priest knew that the absence of a title of respect was intended as a slight, as was the time he had been made to wait.

"Not at all . . ." Cheverus replied, hesitating, then deciding finally to address him in kind. "Mr. Sullivan."

"We'll be more comfortable in here." The attorney general led the priest into a front parlor directly off the foyer. The room was bright and gracefully furnished with Queen Anne chairs, an expensive Persian rug, a gilt taboret before a Hepplewhite sofa. Over the mantel hung another portrait, this one of an elderly woman wearing a simple shawl over her head.

"Please, have a seat," he instructed Cheverus, though he remained standing. It was a calculated move on his part. He wasn't a tall man himself, perhaps only five-six, but standing he could lord his height over the seated priest. He also didn't offer Cheverus anything to drink, which was a customary hospitality.

The attorney general was a distinguished-looking man in his sixties. Though short, he gave one the impression of size, of substance, perhaps because of his erect bearing and the long, perfectly tailored coat he wore. Underneath his coat he had on a gray waistcoat, a white frilled shirt with a high collar and silk necktie, and long trousers that fitted his slender form. He had an angular face profoundly lacking in any softness, with a sharp nose and chin that made him resemble some bird of prey. Save for a pronounced widow's peak, his forehead was high and shiny, except for the powder at his hairline. A narrow, pursed mouth formed words with great frugality. Before uttering something of note, he had a habit of crossing his arms over his chest, the right elbow supported in the palm of his left hand, the index finger of his right hand pressed against his lips, as if he were asking his listener for silence. His most prominent feature, though, was his eyes. They were dark, all iris, made darker still by the contrast to the pale, bluish-white skin of his face and the powered hair, and they gazed at you without blinking or giving any indication of what was going on behind them. Cheverus thought it was like looking into a lump of coal.

"If you don't mind my saying, you don't look well, Mr. Cheverus," Sullivan noted, giving him a patronizing look.

"I have been ill."

"Nothing serious, I hope."

"No. A fever. I am nearly recovered."

"You must take better care of yourself. Your colleague Matignon has already far too much to do." His gaze lingered on Cheverus, as if his statement implied more. The man pulled a silver watch from the pocket of his waistcoat, glanced at it casually, then returned it to his pocket. "I'm afraid," he said, "I am rather pressed for time this morning, Mr. Cheverus. My carriage shall be leaving for Northampton shortly."

"Yes, of course," Cheverus replied. "I will only take a moment of your time."

"Your note mentioned that it was of an urgent nature. Something concerning the Irish prisoners, I believe?"

"Yes, I have come to speak on their behalf."

"In what regard, sir?"

"Their treatment."

"Treatment?" he said, the dark eyes fixed, expressionless, though the thin mouth drew itself into a slight grimace of vexation. "With all due respect, sir, I do not see what concern they are of yours."

"Daley is a member of my parish. And the other one is a Catholic as well."

"This is a legal matter," he lectured. "Not one of concern to a minister of God."

He said "minister of God" as if he were trying to expel an irritating grain of sand that had somehow found its way into his mouth. Though he told himself not to, that he didn't want to antagonize a man of Sullivan's importance, Cheverus went ahead and said it anyway. "That was not your position when I married those two Catholics. You made a union under God a matter of state law."

"As indeed it was," the man said evenly, with great restraint. "You broke the law of the commonwealth and as attorney general, I had no alternative but to prosecute you. I was merely carrying out my elected duties. No more, no less."

"You seemed to take particular interest in my case."

Cheverus saw a momentary glimmer of emotion break the placid surface of those eyes. He wasn't sure if it was anger or amusement or some other emotion. Whatever it was, his eyes quickly regained their cool composure and he even managed a thin smile. "Merely the interest of performing one's duties to the best of one's ability. Similar, I would imagine, to your giving a sermon."

Before Cheverus could reply, the man turned his back to him and proceeded to the front window. He moved with a noticeable limp, one leg obviously shorter than the other. Yet he was vain enough not to use a cane, and he tried to hide the flaw in his carriage by walking slowly, a kind of crab-like shuffle, pulling the bad leg stiffly after its fellow and canting a little to one side, like a ship taking on water. Sullivan stood at the window looking out onto Summer Street, arms crossed, a finger placed contemplatively to his lips. He watched the passage of people and vehicles as if with profound interest. He didn't speak for several seconds, allowing the awkward quiet of the room to make his guest feel nervous. An old courtroom trick of his. In a trial, he would do just that—turn away from the jury and stand as if lost in deep thought for a moment, the courtroom growing uneasy with the silence, wanting him to speak just to break it. Cheverus had heard it said of Sullivan that he wanted to run for office partly because he feared the prospect of a chaotic future, a time when masses of filthy, ignorant, immoral foreigners streamed onto these shores, bringing their backward religions and decadent ways, befouling the gem-like purity of this once-Protestant Eden. Doubtless he saw this trial as nothing less than a conflict between two incompatible ways of life. There were the Yankees, rightful heirs of the Puritans, and then there were the "others."

Sullivan finally broke the silence. "Now what about their treatment so concerns you, Mr. Cheverus?"

"Am I to understand their trial is to take place on Thursday?"

"That is correct."

"It is hardly giving them time to prepare a defense."

"They have been given adequate time."

"The prosecution has had five months to ready its case."

"If you must know, the trial was to commence tomorrow. But I was able to have it delayed, at considerable personal inconvenience, until Thursday so they would have more time."

"That still only gives them a few days."

Sullivan took a deep breath and exhaled loudly through his nose. "You are a man of God. Not one trained in the intricacies of the law. I would suggest, sir, you stick to saving souls." Then he added with a sardonic sneer, "It would seem you have your hands full doing that."

"It doesn't take one trained as a barrister to understand that the circumstances are not favorable to the defense. Have they even been assigned counsel yet?"

"They have. They will have a fair trial, I can assure you of that."

"*Fair*, Mr. Sullivan?"

"Indeed fair!" he snapped, annoyed at having his word questioned.

"Would justice not be as well served if the trial were postponed to give them sufficient time to ready a defense? A fortnight, perhaps."

"An innocent man need only a moment to prove his innocence."

"But the state has had five months to prove them otherwise."

"The trial proceeds as scheduled," he declared. "Now if that is all you came here for, Mr. Cheverus, as I said, I am rather busy."

"There is something else." He paused for a moment, careful to choose his words. "Daley's family would like to ask that they be permitted to visit him before his trial."

"Out of the question," Sullivan said, brushing the request away as if it were an annoying fly.

"But why?"

"I will not take the chance of a bunch of Irish ruffians trying to break them out of prison."

"Ruffians? I am only asking that he be allowed to see his immediate family."

"I have dealt with Irish prisoners before, Reverend Cheverus," he said. "If I permit one, fifty of his reprobate countrymen will come and there is no telling what will ensue. There is already talk abroad of a band of their compatriots planning to go west and help them escape."

Cheverus thought again of what Nell O'Rourke had told him. Could it be more than a rumor?

"That's absurd."

"Is it?" Sullivan picked a piece of lint off his coat, inspected it between his thumb and forefinger, then flicked it away. "Can you assure me that won't happen?"

"I'm only asking that he be permitted to see his immediate family— his mother, his wife and child. Certainly they pose no threat to the security of the commonwealth."

"They might try to smuggle in weapons."

"You can have their belongings searched."

"I am sorry. But it is quite out of the question."

"Why?"

"I don't have to explain my reasons to you, sir."

"The family deserves the right to see their loved one."

"Dare you speak of rights?" he said, his voice growing sharp as a knife blade. "What about Marcus Lyon's rights? Did he not have the right to see his loved ones once more before he was so brutally dispatched?"

"You are assuming that they are guilty. In America, I thought one is innocent until proven guilty."

"I don't need to be lectured on the Bill of Rights. My family fought in the War for Independence. I supported your own revolution until it grew into madness."

"It was not my revolution, Mr. Sullivan."

"No, I suppose a movement that freed people from the oppression of the Catholic Church would not be," he replied contemptuously.

"You don't know of what you speak," he flung back in anger. He quickly chastised himself for losing his temper. "Forgive me," he said, swallowing his pride. "What if I were to assure you nothing will happen?"

The attorney general placed his hands behind his back and let out a mocking little laugh. "How can you assure that? They are followers of the papist religion and you could not keep them from slaying their fellow man over a few dollars. They are like the rest of their kind."

Their kind, Cheverus thought. He reached into his pocket and took out his cross. "My mother gave me this when I was a boy," he explained. "A long time ago. It came across the ocean with me. Did you have one?"

"I do not believe in such idolatry."

"But your people did come from Limerick, Mr. Sullivan? They were Catholic, were they not?"

Cheverus saw that he had struck a nerve. The man glared at the priest, offended that he would dare bring up such a fact.

"Fortunately for my soul and for those of my children, my forebears saw the error in believing in such false images."

"It is a sacred image to me," Cheverus said. "What if I were to swear on the cross that nothing will happen?"

"I'm afraid I cannot take the chance. It is as much for their own safety. Given the public outcry against this dreadful crime, someone might try to do the prisoners harm. Or their relatives. I don't want to be responsible for another riot."

"He has not seen his wife and small child since November. And his mother is ill. What harm can come from allowing him to see them?"

Sullivan pursed his lips. He seemed to be entertaining the idea, weighing the political consequences to himself.

Cheverus seized the moment to continue. "Such a gesture will be looked on as an act of kindness in a political leader. Especially one campaigning for governor."

"Or as weakness."

"You'll recall after the Shays rebellion. Two rebels named Parmenter and McCullough."

"Indeed, I remember them."

"You defended them."

"That was a long time ago. I was in private practice then. My position now is to see that the laws of the commonwealth are enforced."

"And yet, when they received the death penalty, you personally recommended to the governor that he grant them clemency."

"That was different. They weren't cold-blooded murderers."

"Merely traitors and rebels." Cheverus paused for a moment, wondering if he should simply give it up. He could go back to the Daleys and say he had tried. But then he said, "In the last election you lost by a handful of votes. There are a thousand Irish in Boston now. Many will have the right to vote in the next election. They will remember how you treated their countrymen."

"That rabble. Most are illiterate and have no political awareness."

"Ah. Perhaps I could put in a good word."

Cheverus withheld a smile. As Sullivan stared at the priest, a hint of a smile came to his own sharp features.

"Well, well. I wonder if I underestimated you, Mr. Cheverus." He thought for a moment, then said, "Very well then. One short visit. Just his wife and child."

"And his mother, too. I beg of you."

"All right, his mother, too," he conceded. "But only after the trial. Not before. And I will hold you personally responsible if anything happens. Do I make myself clear, Reverend Cheverus?"

"Yes."

"Now is that all?" he said testily.

"There is one more thing."

"What?" he hissed, exasperation finally winning out.

"They would like to be allowed to bathe."

"To bathe?"

"Yes. For the trial. And they would need some clean clothes."

He shook his head, then said, "Yes, I will grant them permission to bathe. You may have the clothing delivered to the jail."

"Thank you."

He turned and started for the door, his limp more noticeable now. Before he reached it, he stopped abruptly and turned around. "I must warn you," he said, wagging a thin finger at him. "If there is any more trouble with you papists, there will be hell to pay, Mr. Cheverus. Do I make myself clear?"

"Quite clear," the priest said.

"Good day to you, sir. I think you know the way out."

After leaving the Sullivan residence, Cheverus headed north to tell the Daleys the news. The day was warming, the sun bright and high in the sky over the city. The harbor was crowded with schooners and sloops, merchant ships and whalers. The docks were a flurry of activity. People passed by with carts and wheelbarrows and wagons. He saw shipwrights and caulkers, sailmakers and mastmakers, all smelling heavily of tar and salt. A fishwoman pushing her cart called out, "Fresh cod for sale. Eels for sale."

When he reached the Daley home, he found himself half hoping that Finola would be there, but it turned out she was away at work. She had left the baby home with Rose and with Dominic's little sister, Pegeen. Cheverus found Rose seated in a rocking chair by the small fire. Despite her illness, she was smoking a clay pipe and knitting something.

"Hello, Father," she said. "Back so soon?"

"Good morning. How are you feeling?"

"Better, thank you."

"I have some news, Rose," he said. "I was able to see Mr. Sullivan today."

"Will he postpone the trial?"

"No, I'm afraid not. But he will let you see Dominic. He says it'll have to be after the trial though. He assured me you will be allowed in to visit."

"And Finola and the baby, too?"

"Yes."

"Arrrah!" she said, folding her hands in thanks.

Cheverus reached into his pocket and took out a few coins and put them in Rose's palm.

"What's this, Father?"

"You'll need some money for the stage. And for lodging and food."

"We couldn't take your money, Father."

She tried to refuse, but he made her accept it

"Buy your son some new clothes with it then. And the other one as well. Bring the clothes to the jail. They'll see that they get them for the trial."

"Oh, thank you, Father. You've done so much for us, I don't know what to say."

"I've done nothing. Give Dominic my love."

"I will, Father. Indeed, I will."

"And tell him he'll be in my prayers."

"You won't be comin' out then? For the trial."

"No," he replied. "I'm afraid I can't."

The old woman took his hand and kissed it in gratitude.

"Bless you, Father."

SIX

The next morning, the turnkey brought their breakfast earlier than usual, just before dawn. He carried a lantern in one hand, the basket of food in the other. The meal was more substantial than the standard slab of stale bread and watery gruel. This morning it consisted of fried cod, a piece of cheese, boiled turnips, corn nocake, and a pot of warmish tea.

"Rise and shine, lads," Dowd said, sliding the trenchers of food through the narrow space in the bars. "You got a long day ahead of you."

Daley got up from his bunk to get their breakfast.

"I hear they expect a fair crowd today," offered Dowd.

"You don't say?" the big Irishman replied.

"A second coach arrived last night from Boston. And there's not a room to be had in town."

"Here just for the trial, are they?"

"Why, you boys are famous," Dowd said with a good-natured chuckle. "You'd better get crackin'. They'll be coming for you shortly. Good luck."

"Here, Jamy," Daley said, handing him his plate. "Lookit all they give us today."

Halligan sat up, rubbing his eyes. He was still half asleep, his head dulled with dreams he could not remember. Though he woke hungry as always, the greasy smell of the food turned his stomach. Since he didn't have any idea how long the trial would last or if they'd take time out for lunch, he figured he'd better eat. Before Daley began on his, he got down on his knees.

"O Heavenly Father," he prayed, "thank you for the food we are about to eat. Be with us today. Watch over me family. Let nothin' happen to them. Amen."

Daley started eating ravenously, shoveling it into the hairy hole in his face. Food slopped down into his beard.

"So this is the day we been waitin' for, eh Jamy boy?"

" 'Tis," he replied.

"They'll see they got themselves the wrong fellers. They'll have to."

"Let's hope so anyway."

"That lad that says he saw us with the horse, I want him to look me in the eye and say that."

Halligan continued eating.

After a while Dowd returned, followed by a half dozen guards. All of them shouldered muskets, save for the leader, a captain in the militia. He was young and good looking, freshly shaven, with long side whiskers and his blond hair tied at the nape of his neck. A cavalry saber with an ornate baskethilt dangled from his belt. He had a certain swagger about him, but his eyes betrayed a vague uneasiness.

"James Halligan and Dominic Daley," he said in an overly punctilious tone. "You are to be tried this day in court. I am to escort you there presently."

Out in the corridor they offered their wrists, expecting the irons to be clapped on them, but the captain motioned them to move along without them. Instead of heading up the road to the courthouse, the guards led them out a back door of the jail and down a narrow alley between the jail and a barn next door. Daley shot a quizzical look at Halligan, and he could only shrug at the meaning of this unexpected detour.

A small muddy paddock was connected to the barn. Off to one side a dungheap steamed in the frigid morning air, while up near the barn, a pair of broad-chested Percherons stood curiously watching their approach. Chickens wandered about, pecking at the ground for food. They entered the paddock through a gate and crossed to the far side where a water trough lay against the fence. The dark water had a thin coating of ice on it. The rain had stopped, but the day was overcast and chilly. A light frost lay on everything like a sugar glaze. On the other side of the pen, the land sloped down to a river and a swampy area of cattails and reeds. Upriver was a bridge and a gristmill, its wheel slowly turning. Beyond the river lay fields and pasture land, then a forest of hardwoods and pine. Way off in the distance, hazy and gray in the morning, rose the mountains, scallops of lighter and lighter blue fading to gray at the horizon.

"Take off your clothes," the captain said to the prisoners.

"Our clothes, sir?" asked Daley.

"That's right. You are to have a bath," he said, pointing at the water trough. "Sergeant," he said, turning to one of the guards, "See to it that they are made presentable. And they are not to have any contact with anyone. Is that clear?"

"Yes, sir," replied the sergeant. He was an older man, a veteran with a weather-beaten face, and it was obvious that he bristled at taking orders from his young superior. The captain then turned and headed out to the street.

"Here," the sergeant said, handing them a bar of lye soap. When they didn't move right away, he snapped, "Don't just stand there like you're daft."

They undressed quickly in the crisp morning air, hanging their tattered clothing on the fence. They stood barefoot on the frozen ground, hopping from one foot to the other, hunched over. Embarrassed at their nakedness, they tried to cover their privates with their hands. Their bumpy skin was a ghostly white.

"Get a move on," the sergeant barked. "We ain't got all day."

They cracked the ice with their fists and dipped their hands into the water, which burned painfully when it first touched their skin. They moved quickly, shivering, their teeth chattering. But it felt good finally to be scrubbing off the months of dirt and filth, the putrid odor of the cell. They ducked their heads into the trough and washed their hair, too. They worked in silence, not uttering a word. Up toward the barn, Halligan noticed that a group of young boys had congregated, staring at them. They carried things in their hands: stones, clumps of dirt, rotten vegetables.

"Run along now," the sergeant called to them. None moved. "You hear me?" When they still didn't move, he took off after them. They broke and scattered like chickens as the sergeant chased them for a short distance.

While the sergeant was gone, one of the guards said, "Have you ever smelled anything as foul as a stinking Irishman?" He was a boyish-looking man with long red hair pulled back behind large ears and freckles across the bridge of his nose.

Several of the guards made sniffing noises and laughed.

"Smells worse than a goddamned pig sty," said another.

The others nodded in agreement.

"And look at the tiny yard on that one there," said the red-haired one, pointing at Daley's cock.

A guard with a mouthful of crooked and broken teeth said, "D'ye think an Irish whore would have a hankering for such a small cock?"

"You'd have to ask his mudder," the red-haired man said, leering at Daley.

There was more laughter, raucous, obscene.

Bent over the trough, Daley stopped washing, turned his head, and glared up at the red-haired man. Halligan put his hand lightly on Daley's arm, but the big Irishman didn't seem to notice.

"Do you fuck your dear ole mudder, paddy?" said the red-haired man, putting on an Irish brogue. They all laughed again.

Daley rose slowly to his full height so that he towered over the guards. His raw, pink fists, clenched by his naked thighs, were large as hamhocks.

"He's a big bastard, ain't he," exclaimed the snaggle-toothed guard.

"Dom," Halligan warned. "No."

"I won't let the podgreen talk that way," Daley said, staring at his friend. He had an expression in his normally sanguine eyes Halligan had not seen before. A wild unpredictable look.

"Think of your wife and son, Dom."

Gradually, Halligan could feel the muscles begin to relax in Daley's body.

"Go ahead and try it, ya stinkin' Irish dog," the red-haired man challenged, holding his musket at the ready. "It ain't the two of you against an unarmed man now."

"That'll be enough, private," said the sergeant, who had just returned then. "And you two, hurry up."

They fell to washing themselves again. A guard appeared and gave them some rags with which to dry themselves. He also carried a brown paper sack.

"You're to put these on," he told the prisoners.

Inside the package they found new clothes, shirts, trousers, two pair of stockings.

"Who brought us these?" Daley asked.

The sergeant said, "I don't know. Just mind what you're about."

When they were dressed, the sergeant put the manacles on their hands and feet, and they were marched back down the alley, this time toward the front of the jailhouse. They halted just short of the street. From the alley, they could see more soldiers waiting out there, a company or better. With them were Sheriff Mattoon and the captain, both seated upon horses. The two men were engaged in conversation. They were looking up the street at something Halligan could not see from where he stood in the alleyway.

The sheriff finally turned in his saddle to face his troops. His features were tense, almost grim. "Hold your formation," he commanded. "And remember, no one is to discharge a weapon without my orders. Is that clear?"

At this, the guards exchanged anxious looks.

Then the order was given, and they moved out into the street to join the others, where the guards formed lines on either side of the prisoners. Halligan could then see what had worried the sheriff. A huge crowd lined Pleasant Street its entire length, all the way to where it met Main. In some places people stood three and four deep, craning their necks and pushing and jostling to get a better view.

The captain pulled out his saber and cried, "Forward," and they started toward the center of town. People had taken up positions on porches and on the beds of wagons, and some leaned out of upper story windows. A number of boys had climbed into the lower branches of the elm trees edging the road. One had even shimmied up a flagpole near the intersection with Main Street. As they approached the center, the boy on the flagpole could be heard crying, "They're coming!" and a great murmur went forth from the crowd. Some spectators called out things, taunts and epithets and curses, and a few even held crudely painted signs. Halligan noticed one that said, IRISH GO HOME, while another proclaimed, PAPISTS BURN IN HELL. Others waved their fists or made obscene gestures. A pretty girl in a second-story window stuck out her tongue at them as they passed.

The noise increased in volume and the crowd began to stir uneasily. When they reached Main Street, a torrent of rotten fruit and clods of earth rained down upon guards and prisoners alike. Their only protection was to shield themselves with their manacled hands. Some in the crowd actually brandished rakes and hoes, and a number held freshly hewn cudgels. As the procession moved up Main, the crowd began to press in upon the group from either side. A cry, at first low and inchoate, rose up from those assembled, gathered strength and clarity, and soon turned into a chant that swelled up and down the street: *Hang them! Hang them!* Then a man wearing a buckskin jacket and a blue voyageur's cap rushed from the crowd, wielding a club before him. "Give us those Irish murderers," he cried. Several guards had to fend him off using the butts of their muskets, knocking him to the ground. Others came to the man's defense, closing in on the group of soldiers. Just when it looked as if things might get out of hand, a gunshot exploded nearby. Startled, people froze in their tracks, and silence fell like a sodden blanket over the town. The sheriff had fired his pistol into the air. The bitter smell of gunpowder hung in a bluish cloud above the street.

"Good people of Northampton," the sheriff called from his horse. "Stand aside and let justice be done."

"Hand over those Irish murderers," a man called from the crowd.

"Yea, yea," several others cried.

"I give you fair warning," the sheriff said. And when they didn't immediately move back, he commanded his troops to fix bayonets, which they did.

"Men," said the sheriff. "Shoot the next person who gets in the way."

Realizing his threat was real, the crowd began slowly to fall back, though not without a certain aggrieved truculence. Before the crowd could recover, the procession was in motion again, marching rapidly in the direction of the courthouse. This day they passed by the courthouse and continued up the hill toward the Protestant meetinghouse that sat perched on a rise overlooking the small town like a sentry. As it turned out, it had been decided to conduct the trial there because it was larger and would hold more people. The meetinghouse was once the church of the famous minister Jonathan Edwards, whose fiery sermons in the previous century had put the fear of God into the town's citizens. Now it seemed somehow fitting that the two Catholics were to be tried there. The bell in the belfry sounded their coming, several deep, harsh peals that echoed throughout the valley.

They were led up the steps and into the large meetinghouse. The inside was plain, fierce in its austerity, unlike a Catholic church. The walls were unadorned, whitewashed, with no stained glass in the windows, no crucifixes or confessionals either. Halligan realized it was the first time he'd ever set foot in such a place. The building was already filled to overflowing, each pew crowded with spectators who had gotten there early to get a seat. When the crowd spotted the two, a low rumble floated upward, toward those seated in the balcony. The crowd was daunting, especially to men who had spent the past five months in a tiny dark cell by themselves. Faces pressed in upon them from all sides as the sheriff and the captain pushed through, escorting them to where their lawyer, Mr. Blake, sat at a table near the front.

"Good morning, gentlemen," their attorney said, standing. He wore a dark barrister's robe and a white wig atop his broad skull, which made him look slightly comical. As soon as the manacles were removed, he vigorously shook their hands. He had them sit down, Halligan next to him and Daley on the other side. "How are we today?" he inquired.

"Niver seen so many people for a trial," Daley said.

"Indeed. Quite a crowd," Blake said, turning eagerly to scan the audience. "I must admit I have never seen anything like it myself." Halligan noted that he seemed actually excited by the crowd. Then the lawyer began to sneeze, and he withdrew a handkerchief and blew his nose hard.

"Did you take the butter, sir?" Daley asked.

"Butter? Oh, no. I shall be fine though. Never felt better, in fact. I've heard that the governor himself is expected," he said, looking around again. "Can you imagine that? That's how important this trial has become in the commonwealth."

The man looked different today. Despite his cold, he appeared well rested, his spirits much improved. As he arranged his notes and wrote things down in his tablet, his movements were filled with a lightness and energy belying his cumbersome bulk. Though Halligan caught a whiff of rum on the man's breath, his eyes were sharp and clear, animated by some internal heat. He looked confident and at ease, in his natural element. Halligan could hardly believe the transformation. And then he realized what it was: the man liked this. He actually liked it. He looked forward to performing the way an actor would, and was excited by the large audience that would be watching him.

"Are you ready?" he asked, hardly able to suppress his enthusiasm.

"Ready as we'll ever be," Daley replied in a faltering voice.

Seated at another table up front were two men wearing an outfit similar to that worn by Blake. They recognized one as Mr. Hooker, the man who'd questioned them in jail and who'd been at their arraignment, but the other was unfamiliar. They'd not seen him at the inquest nor at the arraignment. He was an older man, distinguished looking, with sharp features, a thin mouth, a hooked nose.

"That is our Mr. Sullivan," Blake whispered, his tone both disparaging and reverential at once. "He has quite the reputation in capital cases."

"Excuse me, Mr. Blake," Halligan asked, "but how many murder cases have you tried?"

He looked over at them, drawing his lower lip down into a point. "Prior to this? Well . . . none actually."

"None?" Halligan said.

"Most of my previous legal experience has been wills and estates. Land disputes. That sort of thing. But the law is the law," he explained. *Jaysus*, thought Halligan, feeling his heart sink. "Now, no matter what happens," Blake counseled, "you are not to lose your composure. You mustn't show any signs of emotion regardless of what is said. The jury will be watching you very closely. Do you understand?"

They both nodded.

"Good. I see you received the new clothes. Your family brought them for you," he said to Daley.

"Me family? They're here?" Daley asked excitedly.

"They should be. They arrived on yesterday's stage."

Daley turned and began to scan the crowded room, looking for his folks. But there were so many faces. Outside, more people crowded about the church's long narrow windows to peer in. After a while, Daley cried, "There they are! There's Finola!" and he waved ecstatically. "And me mam, too. Over there, Jamy boy," he said to Halligan, pointing. In the back of the meetinghouse, on the same side as the defense, sat an old woman with a black *kiddhoge* over her head and a young woman holding a baby wrapped in a blanket. Both women offered up a little wave of acknowledgment. The wife, a skinny woman with large moist eyes, held up the baby and turned him so that Daley could see his son's face.

"She brung Michael!" he said. "That's me boy, Mr. Blake. Would you look at the size on him."

"Yes, I had the pleasure of meeting with them briefly this morning."

"How are they, sir?"

"They are all fine. They send their love. Oh, your wife wanted you to have this." From his waistcoast pocket he took out a piece of paper that had been folded into a square and gave it to Daley. Daley opened it to find a well-worn rosary, with shiny black beads and a small silver crucifix. On the paper was written a note, which he showed to Halligan. "God be with you, my love," Halligan read.

"But for heaven's sakes, don't let anyone see that now," Blake warned.

Daley slipped the rosary into his pocket.

"Will I get to visit with 'em?"

"After the trial," Blake explained.

"I couldn't just say a quick hello to them now?"

"No. Afterwards. It's all been arranged."

Halligan watched his friend smile at his wife and mouth the words, *I love you.* He scanned the courtroom, he couldn't say for what. In the faces of those staring back at him, he saw expressions of revulsion, of contempt, and not a few of curiosity. Immediately behind the prosecution table he saw several well-dressed men, dignitaries from town, he guessed. Among them he recognized Reverend Williams, a tall gaunt man with a pink face like undercooked pork. The minister had come to see them in jail once or twice. He had tried to get them to mend their evil papist ways and see God's true light while there was still time. In his long bony hand he held a Bible. Seated next to him was an older couple. The woman was dressed all in black. She wore a black bonnet, a long black skirt made of coarse homespun, and a black cloak over her shoulders. She was a farmer's wife, Halligan could tell, a plain woman dressed in her Sunday clothes for the occasion. Her hands were cracked and raw from hard work, her face windburned and wrinkled. The man he took to be her husband was also dressed in black. Several times Halligan noticed the assistant prosecutor turn to the couple and whisper something to them. They would nod soberly. Once the woman happened to glance in his direction and made eye contact with him. She seemed almost to flinch from the exchange.

Halligan leaned toward their attorney. "Those two behind the prosecutor, Mr. Blake," he said, indicating the pair. "Do you know who they are?"

Blake turned in his seat to look. "I believe they are Mr. and Mrs. Lyon."

"Who?" Halligan asked.

"The parents of the victim."

Halligan watched them for another moment or two. He wanted to go over and tell them he had nothing to do with it. That they were innocent. That he hadn't harmed a hair on their son's head. But then he recalled what Daley had said about the money. That it had been their son's money and now rightfully belonged to them. Hell with it, he thought. He knew the truth. That was good enough for him.

Right then, the clerk called for everyone to rise, as the two judges entered through a side door. They took their seats at a table that had been placed up on a raised platform where the minister normally would have given his sermon.

Judge Sedgwick gazed at Mr. Sullivan with a look of cool disdain.

"Is the state ready to proceed, Mr. Attorney General?" he asked curtly.

Sullivan rose slowly, offered a slight nod of his wizened head, then replied, "The commonwealth is ready, your honor."

"The court is grateful that you can take time from your other affairs to join us."

"I take the duties of my office with great earnestness, your honor."

"Of course," Sedgwick replied. Then he turned to Blake. "Your motion for a postponement, sir, has been closely reviewed and herewith denied."

"But your honor," Blake pleaded, "the defense has not had adequate time to prepare our case. We've had no opportunity to interview witnesses."

"We have not traveled all this distance, nor have all the people here today, to see the trial be delayed," the judge said flatly. "No, we will proceed as scheduled."

The prosecution and the defense spent the next hour or so picking a jury. As both sides asked questions of each potential juror, Daley kept turning around to look for his family. When he caught his wife's eye, she would smile demurely, and the color would come to her pale cheeks. Halligan watched her, too. She was a plain-looking woman with reddish-blond hair, too skinny for his taste. Still, he couldn't help thinking of all those letters he had read of hers. *My dearest, how much I miss your loving arms.* He seemed to know her in some intimate way he couldn't describe.

At last the jury was seated. They were common men, broad-shouldered farmers and hard-working craftsmen, merchants and shop-owners, even a blacksmith. Sober men with Yankee names like Elijah Hubbard and Jabez Nichols and Asa Spalding. Dressed in their finest homespun clothes, they were used to coming here each week to listen to their minister, Solomon Williams, speak of the terrible justice of God. But today they were as gods themselves, delivering their own justice, deciding the fate of two men. Uncertain in this new role, they perched awkwardly on a single row of hard benches that had no backrests, so that they had to sit upright throughout the long proceedings. They sat with their battered hands in their laps and their heads bowed slightly, the way they would in church. From time to time they would steal furtive glances at the two Irishmen, as if trying to read something in their countenances. One particular juror was Wallace, the town blacksmith, the man Halligan had seen in the street the other day as they passed by to the courthouse. He was a thick-necked, dark-complected man who kept glowering at them. He would look from Daley to Halligan and back again, a scowl on his soot-blackened features. The whites of his eyes gleamed.

The prosecution and the defense spent some time haggling over various technical issues with the judges, subjects Halligan could only vaguely follow. Occasionally Sullivan would smile and concede something to Blake, and sometimes it would be the other way around. Judge Sedgwick did most of the talking. The other one, Sewall, didn't say much. He belched occasionally and snorted now and then, but mostly he seemed content to sit quietly there.

Once this business was concluded, Judge Sedgwick told the prisoners to stand and raise their right hand while the clerk read the indictment again. After that, the judge said to the jury, "Good men and true, you shall now stand together and hearken to the evidence."

Mr. Sullivan opened the government's case. He rose and walked slowly toward the jury, his hands behind his back. Halligan noticed he had a decided limp. He stopped in front of the jury and gave something of a bow.

"May it please your honors, gentlemen of the jury," he began, his words measured and passionless, as if he were lecturing about philosophy. "It is unnecessary for me to make many observations to you in opening this cause, either on the importance of it to the prisoners, or to the government. A young man in the prime of life has been 'untimely ripped' from this worldly womb of ours. He will never know the joy of witnessing another sunrise, marking another spring, smelling another flower. He will not know a marriage bed. He will not savor the happiness of the birth of a son. He will not know what it is to have grandchildren. He will never again look upon the loving faces of his mother and father, who sit before us today." At this, he held his hand out toward the parents of the victim, his face assuming an attitude of bereavement. The mother whimpered audibly, bringing a handkerchief to her mouth. "No, gentlemen, these gifts of God are forever denied him. He has been cast down into the darkness of the grave. And for what? For *what*, gentlemen? But for this," he said, removing from his pocket a few bank bills. He held them up and waved them for the benefit of the jury. Each member stared at the money. "A few trifling dollars. That's all this poor young man's life was worth to these . . . these *men*," he said disdainfully, pointing at the two Irishmen. Though his features remained poised, cool as stone, his voice slowly began to warm to his subject. "They murdered for gain. They murdered simply because they wished to have the fruits of another man's labor. These men, these lazy *Irishmen*, came to these shores because they wanted the freedom and opportunity to make of themselves what they would. What their own hard work and God-given talents would provide. Instead of accomplishing it by the sweat of their brow, by industry and diligence, they took the primrose path and sought to gain by robbing another.

"Your situation, gentlemen, is one of the most solemn to which men are ever called. The destinies of two of your fellowmen are dependent on your verdict, and though you are selected and sworn to pass between the accused and the commonwealth on a question of life or death, yet you have this consolation—that you are sworn to try the issue according to the evidence. If you follow the dictates of your own understanding as influenced by the evidence alone, you will discharge your duty to yourselves and to your country, however afflictive the event may be to others."

He looked at each one of the jurors in turn, as if speaking personally to each. Though his voice had increased slightly in volume, his features remained placid, emotionless, a pale mask.

"There are three counts in the indictment." He then went over once more what the clerk had just read. When he was finished restating the indictment to the jury, he said, "Hence, gentlemen, if you shall find to your full satisfaction that the deceased came to his death in either of the ways I have specified, you will be authorized to find a verdict of conviction."

Next, the attorney general spent the better part of an hour going over the facts of the case in painstaking detail. With cool equanimity, he explained how at about one o'clock in the afternoon, on November ninth of the previous year, Mr. Lyon had been riding from Cazenovia, New York, returning to Connecticut, when he was waylaid by highwaymen. How he had been shot in the side by a large-bore pistol, but that the bullet struck a rib and had not proved fatal. How his demise had actually resulted from several vicious and premeditated blows to the back of the head, as well as by his having been immersed in the cold waters of the Chicopee River. How several witnesses the prosecution would produce could verify having seen him traveling east on a large bay horse with new saddlebags. How the defendants, too, were recognized by several witnesses traveling in the opposite direction along the same road, and how one man would testify that he had seen the two walking a mere seventy rods from the place where the man was killed, on the *very* day and almost at the *precise* instant of the deed. How the murder weapons, a pair of navy pistols, had been found near the murder site and matched exactly holsters sewn on the inside of the prisoners' greatcoats, and how the prosecution would call a witness who had sold similar weapons to a man with an "Irish accent." How bank bills were found in the possession of the prisoners when they were apprehended, bills which were drawn on the same banks and for the same amounts as those that Marcus Lyon had had on his person when he left New York. How it had taken the prisoners nearly five full days to travel only eighty miles from Boston to Wilbraham—the site of the murder—but only two days to travel more than one hundred and thirty miles to New York after they had committed their crime.

"We shall prove all of this to your full satisfaction. But most importantly, gentlemen . . ." the attorney general said, pausing, as he limped slowly over to where the two Irishmen sat. He came to a stop before their table, his arms wrapped across his narrow chest, a forefinger placed squarely against his lips. He stood there for several seconds, his gaze sifting the courtroom, weighing it appraisingly, before settling finally on the two men. He permitted the silence to continue, so that it seemed to expand and fill the courtroom, until all ears were craning and you could hear the *tck . . . tck . . . tck* of water falling somewhere. He gazed down at each of the prisoners in turn with a cool, penetrating stare. Up close, Halligan saw that the attorney general had small dark-brown eyes, the fierce, imperturbable ones of some great sea bird. A cormorant perhaps, like those he used to see diving for fish off Slea Head in Dingle. The man continued staring at them, as if, in fact, he actually intended to dive into their very souls, seize hold of their guilt as if it were some fish, and return to the surface with that guilt for all to see, to wave it about as he had with the bank bills.

"We shall call to the stand an eyewitness," he said, finally breaking the silence, "someone who saw with his own eyes these very men leading Mr. Lyon's horse into the pasture not far from where the murder was committed. This brave young man, who stood no farther from the accused than I do now, saw them in full possession of the victim's horse. The same witness who was later able to pick them out from a line-up and swear with complete confidence that they were, indeed, the men he saw with Mr. Lyon's mount. These, gentlemen, are the facts we intend to present to you today. If they produce in your minds a full conviction of the prisoners' guilt, as I am certain they shall, you will pronounce them guilty; if not, you will be happy in returning a verdict of acquittal. Thank you, gentlemen. May God grant you wisdom to know the truth and the courage to perform your duties."

He then went over to where Mr. Hooker waited and took a seat.

"Do you wish to make a statement, Mr. Blake?" Judge Sedgwick asked.

"Not at this time, your honor," he replied.   .

"Very well," said the judge. "The prosecution may call its first witness."

Mr. Hooker, the assistant prosecutor, now took over for the state. It soon became obvious that the attorney general left for his assistant the menial tasks of the trial, while reserving for himself those which offered more in the way of dramatic flair. Still, the assistant nervously sprang from his seat, eager as a spaniel on the scent of a rabbit. The first witness he called was Samuel Merrick, the physician who performed the autopsy at the coroner's inquest. Dr. Merrick came forward and placed his hand on a large black Bible the clerk held for him. After being sworn in, he took his seat, a simple chair that was positioned to the left of where the judges sat, near the jury. He was a well-dressed older man with a high stiff collar, a full pudding cravat, and the small clothes of the previous century. His eyes were gray and sunken, and his mouth kept working on his badly fitted ivory dentures. When he spoke, the loose teeth made a distinct clicking sound.

"Dr. Merrick," Mr. Hooker began, "would you tell us how you came to examine the body of Marcus Lyon and what your findings were?"

"On Monday morning, the eleventh of November," he began, his mouth going *click click click*. "I was called upon by the jury of inquest and went to Mr. Calkins's where the body was. Over the right eye of the deceased was a hole to the skull. On the left part of the head was another wound of similar nature, but the bone was not injured. On the back part of the head rather to the right side, the skull was broken. I applied a common probe and it went in the whole length of it without any obstruction."

"Did it enter the brain, sir?"

"Without doubt," he replied.

"Were these wounds caused by a bullet, sir?"

"They were not." *Click click.* "On Mr. Lyon's right side, against the third rib from the bottom when we took off his clothes, I observed a bullet hole. The inquest wished to have the body opened to see if it entered."

At this, Halligan heard a high, thin gasp, as from someone who had accidentally cut herself while peeling potatoes. He turned and saw the woman in black. She had her hand to her mouth and was quietly sobbing. Her husband tried to comfort her.

"Continue, sir," instructed Mr. Hooker.

"We opened the body, but the bullet did not penetrate beyond the rib."

Judge Sewall, who had been sitting quietly, his chin supported by the palm of one hand, sat up suddenly. "Would the wounds to the back of the head have been mortal, doctor?" he asked.

"Immediately, your honor."

"In your learned estimation, did such wounds require a substantial force?"

"Yes, sir. It would be my judgment that great force would be needed."

Judge Sewall, having gotten the response he was looking for, went back to resting his head on his hand.

"No further questions, your honor," offered Mr. Hooker, who walked over and sat down next to the attorney general.

"Your witness," Judge Sedgwick said to Blake.

Without getting up, Blake said, "Dr. Merrick, I would first like to thank you for taking the time from your busy schedule to come here today. Now, you mentioned that the bullet wound to Mr. Lyon's side was not fatal."

"That's correct," he replied, his teeth clattering away.

"Did you find the ball, sir?"

"We did. When we took off Mr. Lyon's clothes the ball fell to the floor. One of the members of the inquest jury picked it up."

"Did the bullet suit either of the pistols that were found at the scene?"

"It did not—it was too small."

Blake paused for a moment, rubbing his chin thoughtfully. "How do you explain that, sir?"

The man glanced around the courtroom. "I cannot."

"But you are certain it did not fit the caliber of either pistol found at the murder site?"

"That is correct."

"Thank you, Dr. Merrick," said Blake.

The physician stepped down and the prosecution called its next witness, John Bliss. He testified that he had found a horse, saddled but riderless, grazing in his pasture on the hill overlooking the turnpike road.

"It was an unfamiliar horse," the man explained. "I supposed it was a physician's from the saddlebags that were on him."

"What did you do with the horse?"

"I tied him by the road that people might see him as they passed."

"Did anyone lay claim to the animal?" asked the assistant prosecutor.

"No, sir. So I put him out to pasture. By Sunday morning I grew more uneasy. My brother came in and said—"

But Blake stood up then and objected. "Your honor, this man must not tell what his brother said."

"I defer to my distinguished colleague," said Mr. Hooker. "Mr. Bliss, was the saddle on the horse partly turned when you found the animal? As if its rider had met with some violence?"

"It was, sir."

"Thank you. Your witness, Mr. Blake," said the assistant prosecutor.

Blake, who had been writing something, glanced up, looked about to rise, then seemed to think better of it and sat back down. "No questions."

Several other witnesses also testified to seeing the horse, and making inquiries about its possible owner. Another witness said he'd found the broken pistol guard and ramrod near where the road runs along the river, and how a search party was convened and an inspection of that part of the road was made but which proved fruitless. The next witness was a man named Pliny Bliss, the brother of the earlier witness. He was short and wore a smart-looking gray coat and pantaloons tucked into high riding boots—a simple farmer who was trying to look impressive for his day in court.

"Mr. Bliss, would you relate the events of the tenth of November last?" asked Mr. Hooker.

"I was at my brother's," the man said, pointing at his brother seated behind the prosecution table. "He told me about the horse."

"What did you do then?"

"We concluded to go down to the river and make an examination. We went along by the stream that runs into the river there but could discover nothing. It grew dark, and we soon gave up. As I was going to bed, someone came to our house and told me what had been found."

"You mean the pistol guard and ramrod?"

"Yes, sir. So we procured lanterns and torches and went again in search. Near the place where the pistol guard was found, Mr. Bartlett went down to the river before me, with a lantern, and I followed with a torch. Very near the river, I found a pistol with some hair sticking to it."

The man glanced around the room, obviously pleased with himself for his role in finding the murder weapon.

"Did you not think that strange, Mr. Bliss?"

"Indeed, sir. Very strange."

"Then what happened?"

"Mr. Bartlett and I walked along the river's edge. That's when we spied the body. I don't know which saw it first, but I think I might have noted it before Mr. Bartlett. I can see quite well in the dark," he added proudly. "I observed not far from shore a greatcoat which lay partly out of the water. Then I made out the form of a body beneath. The head was towards the shore with the large stone upon the chest."

"How large was the stone?"

"Very large. I would say it had to weigh sixty-five pounds or more."

"What did you then, sir?"

"We called some other neighbors and proceeded to carry the body to Mr. Calkins's house."

"What did you do with the pistol?"

"Why, we gave it to the sheriff."

Mr. Hooker walked back to the prosecution table and picked up a pistol. Returning to the witness stand, he asked, "Is this the selfsame pistol?"

"It is."

"Where was the hair?"

"In the head of the screw pin that holds on the lock," the man said, indicating with his finger where the hair was.

"Was the stock thusly broken when you found it?"

"It was."

"What was the appearance of the shore near where the body was found?"

"The shore, sir?"

"What did the area look like near where the body lay? Was it trampled?"

"It was, sir. It looked as if one had drawn a log through a thicket of bushes. The mud was impressed and the low alders were bent towards the river."

"So a person or persons had dragged the body there to conceal it?"

"It would seem so, yes."

"Thank you, Mr. Bliss," said the assistant prosecutor.

Blake got up and walked over to where the witness sat, his broad back hunched over slightly. He carried a piece of paper in his hand. He looked at the man and permitted himself a hint of a smile. The man shifted nervously in his seat.

"What was the weather on that particular day, Mr. Bliss?" Blake asked.

"It rained as I recall."

"Did it rain hard?"

"I suppose you could say that."

"As hard as it did a few nights ago, for instance?"

The man shrugged. "I would say so, yes."

"Saw you the tracks of men along the river where the body was drawn?"

The man considered this for a moment. "I do not recollect particularly."

"So you did *not* see tracks there?"

"I can't say one way or the other."

"And yet you recall seeing the area flattened," Blake said, and here he referred to the paper in his hand, "'as if,' and I quote you sir, 'one had drawn a log through a thicket of bushes.' Those were your exact words, were they not, sir?"

"I suppose. I still don't recall tracks."

"That is all, sir," said Blake, glancing at the jury as he returned to his seat.

The prosecution called a number of other witnesses to the stand. Some described the second gun that was found a few days later, or the horse, or how the saddlebags were eventually opened and it was then that the victim's name was learned to be a Marcus Lyon of Woodstock, Connecticut. Several others testified to having seen Marcus Lyon riding east at various points between Springfield and where he died. Another witness, John Powers, was asked if he'd met the prisoners on that Saturday along the turnpike.

"I did, sir. They were just east of the bridge. Not seventy rods from the place where Lyon was killed."

"What time was this?"

"Not far from one o'clock, I'd reckon," Powers replied.

"Are you sure these are the men you saw?" Mr. Hooker asked, turning to point at the two prisoners.

"I am," replied the man, staring at them. "We spoke. They asked how far to the next tavern." With this there were a few nervous titters in the courtroom. Judge Sedgwick cast a stern warning glance around the room and things quieted down. "I recall they spoke with an Irish accent."

"Knew you them by anything else?"

"Their countenance, too. I recall the smallpox marks upon that one's face," the man added, pointing at Daley.

Halligan looked over at the jury. They were listening intently to the witness. All except the blacksmith. He was looking directly at Halligan, his face a darkened scowl.

Blake leaned toward Daley and Halligan and whispered, "Is he telling the truth?"

"We might have spoken to him," Halligan replied. "I recall speaking to someone just before we reached the bridge."

Blake pursed his lips and wrote something down in his writing tablet.

When Mr. Hooker had finished asking questions of the man, Blake stood up and approached the witness.

"Are you familiar with the area where Lyon was killed?" he asked the man.

"I am," replied Powers. "I have cause to travel that stretch of road often."

"How long would it have taken the defendants to walk from the place where you spoke to them to the place where Mr. Lyon's body was later found?"

"Not long. A minute or two."

"No more than that?"

"No, sir."

"So they were still quite close to you when they were alleged to have accosted Marcus Lyon?"

"Yes. Most definitely."

"Tell me, sir, did you hear the discharge of a pistol?"

The man looked over at Mr. Hooker, then at the jury, before turning to face Blake. "I did not."

"Are you sure?"

"I don't recall one."

"Yet you heard testimony that Mr. Lyon had been shot. Don't you think it peculiar that you did not hear the report of a gun from such a close distance?"

"I suppose."

"You suppose, sir?"

"I did not give it much thought."

"That is all, thank you."

Blake turned to the judges and pleaded, "May it please your honors?"

"Proceed," said Judge Sedgwick.

Blake approached the bench. "We can prove that within three or four miles from this very place, a number of other robberies had recently been committed. That stage coach drivers always feel apprehensive of danger when they are near this stretch of road. With submission to the court, we beg leave to introduce this testimony at this time."

Judge Sedgwick frowned. "Such evidence is not relevant," he said. "It cannot be admitted, for unless this murder be proved upon the prisoners they will be acquitted."

"But, may it please your honors, we wish to introduce presumptive testimony to counteract presumptive testimony. Such is the government's evidence."

"The testimony you offer has no direct bearing on the present case, sir. Furthermore, if it be proper for you to go into this evidence, it will be proper for the government to go into similar evidence to prove that the prisoners have been guilty of other crimes heretofore."

"But, your honor—"

"Sit down, Mr. Blake. The prosecution may continue."

The prosecution called witness after witness. One described the hats and greatcoats the defendants wore, while another said he saw two men fitting the defendants' general appearance hurrying along the turnpike just west of where Lyon was murdered. That their movements seemed to be made with "great haste," as he put it. Now and then Blake would interject something or cross-examine them, but mostly he sat quietly, pinching his lower lip and taking notes. Halligan could not have said whether things were going in their favor or not, though he thought the business about having been seen close to where the murder took place not especially good. And he didn't like the way the one juror, the black-smith, kept looking at them. As if he'd already made up his mind.

Around noon, the court adjourned for lunch. The sheriff placed the manacles on them again and the guards escorted them toward the back of the meetinghouse. They had to pass before the woman in black. She stood at their approach, her eyes narrowed. Up close Halligan could see that she had fine blue eyes, delicate and soft as bone china.

"I curse you," she hissed at them, waving a small red fist in the air. Then suddenly, she spat at them, catching Halligan on the cheek. He'd never had a woman spit at him before. The guards interceded and her husband pulled her back. "May you burn in hell," she called after them. He wiped the spit off with the back of his hand.

They went outside and were escorted down to a grove of trees, where they were allowed to use the privy. Afterwards, they were brought back inside and led through a door and down some uneven stone steps into the cellar of the meetinghouse. The place was damp and dark, lit only by a pair of smoky lanterns. It smelled like a graveyard, of old moldering bones. They sat on the dirt floor, their backs against the foundation wall. They were given a piece of bread and some cheese and a tin cup filled with hard cider. The cider was strong and bitter, but it warmed the belly. The guards lounged about talking and joking, some of them taking the opportunity to doze.

"They oughtn't to let that crazy woman do that," Daley said to him, chewing his bread.

Halligan shrugged, rubbing the spot where the spit had landed. The skin there seemed hot, like an ash had scorched it.

"Still. It ain't right."

Halligan took a bite of the cheese and then sipped on his cider. He thought of that woman. He wanted to hate her for what she'd done but he couldn't. She was crazy with her grief. He wondered what it had been like for her, to have to sit there and listen to how their son had been killed. How his brains had been dashed out and his body tossed into the river, like he was nothing more than a litter of kittens. If it were his child that was killed, he'd probably have done the same thing as she did. He just wished he'd had the chance to explain he'd not had anything to do with it.

After a while Blake came down to see them. He had a hard time negotiating the steps, moving like an old man with rheumatism. And his eyes seemed to have difficulty adjusting to the dimness there.

"They thought you'd be safer here than going all the way back to the jail," he said, glancing around. His bulbous eyes squinted into the darkness. He sniffed the damp air, his nose crinkling. He removed his snuff box and took some in each nostril.

"How do you think it went, Mr. Blake?" Daley asked.

"They didn't present anything too damaging. They still cannot connect you to the murder. Or the guns. It is merely presumptive evidence." Nonetheless, he shook his head somewhat dejectedly.

"What is it, Mr. Blake?" Daley asked.

"The governor sent word he won't be in attendance after all." He frowned, his blue eyes shadowed with disappointment. "Well, I have some work to do. I will see you shortly."

When he was gone, Daley said, "What'd you think of her?"

"Who?" For a moment he thought Daley had meant Mrs. Lyon.

"Finola."

"Oh. She's a fine-looking woman, Dom," he lied.

"I can't wait to talk to her. And to hold me little fellow. Did you see the size on the lad? I tell you, I hardly recognized him."

Halligan nodded.

Daley stared pensively straight ahead. His big lower jaw hung down and he breathed heavily through his mouth. His eyes seemed to glaze over. He had the odd expression his face sometimes took on when Halligan would read his wife's letters to him, part smile, part wistful longing, part something else.

Halligan finished off the cider and leaned his head back against the damp wall. He closed his eyes. He was tired, so very tired. He thought he would doze for a bit. But the bone smell was strong, seeping up from the floor, surrounding him. It made him sick to his stomach. He tried not to think: not of the woman spitting on him, not of the look the blacksmith had given him, not of the trial, not of the past nor the future. But to let his mind go completely blank, a quiet place, a dark emptiness where nothing could touch him, where he would feel nothing.

For a while he managed to stay there, in that silent darkness by himself. After a time though, a memory came slipping into his mind. It was a hot, scorching summer's day. They were in the trap, he and Bridie, riding into town together. The air shimmered and wavered in the heat, the horse's hooves kicking up small yellow explosions of dust. In the distance the dun-colored hills undulated toward the bay. She had asked him to accompany her. Some errand or other, some excuse to be together. They had been lovers for some time by then—meeting clandestinely at night in the stables, or out in the fields, wherever they could. It was dangerous, he knew, but that was part of the excitement, too. The fear of her father finding out.

Halfway down the mountain road, she pulled up on the reins. She jumped down off the wagon and took him by the hand. She led him through a hedgerow of gorse and across an open meadow toward a stand of pine and willows at the far side.

"Where are we going?" he asked her.

"Trust me," she said, excited as a schoolgirl with a secret. "I want to show you something."

She let go of his hand and, pulling up her skirts, started to run, laughing, taunting him to follow. He didn't know what else to do so he chased after her. A pair of children playing, that's what it felt like. She led him into a dense grove of trees that provided a shelter from the blistering sun. The ground here was cool and damp, soft, covered with ferns and moss. In the center of the grove was an open area, a glade, through which trickled a cool, sparkling mountain stream. There was even a small waterfall at one end where the water made a light gurgling sound. In the middle was a pool no more than a few feet across.

"What is this place?" he asked.

"Where I come to be alone," she said.

Bridie sat on a fallen log and unlaced her soft leather shoes and removed her stockings.

"What're you doing?" Halligan asked. "It's broad daylight, don't you know. Someone might see us."

"No one will see us here." She lifted up her skirts and waded into the stream. She splashed her face with water, laughing sweetly.

"Oh, it's absolutely lovely, James," she said to him. "Come in."

She had changed so much in the short time he'd known her. She'd become a spirited thing, daring and wild, ready for anything. Finally, he took off his boots and walked in, not bothering to roll up his trousers.

"Ga!" he cried, shuddering from the cold water. The stream was frigid, the mud and rocks cool beneath his feet. Small silvery minnows flashed here and there beneath the water like pieces of light. She cupped her hands and splashed him with water.

"Ouch," he cried, pretending it hurt.

"Such a big baby," she kidded.

He looked at her, and she came to him and put her arms around his neck and kissed him several times, lightly, playfully. "Isn't that better?"

"Aye."

She took his hand and led him to the far side of the pool. They sat on the bank for a moment, holding hands, their feet in the water. She kissed him again, slowly this time, her dark eyes staring into his. They fell back onto the cool, soft moss that ran along the stream's edge. He made love to her, slowly, tenderly, as if they had all the time in the world. As if, in fact, the world—his, hers, everything outside this cool shaded grove— didn't even exist. Only *they* existed. Afterwards, spent and panting, they lay for a while in each other's arms, looking up at the dappled, sparkling light that fell through the overhanging branches like diamonds. Birds sang in the trees. Her hair smelled of apples. Her eyes shimmered from the water, light and gay, glowing from her now spent passion.

"Remember this," she said, looking at him, her expression turning serious once more. Her lovely eyes took on a distant and mournful aspect.

"This place, you mean?"

"Remember us, Jamy. This moment."

"Aye," he said. "I will."

SEVEN

In the vestry, Cheverus was preparing for Mass. Before putting on his vestments, he knelt and prayed to the Holy Mother. He asked not for the usual things: humility, patience, courage. No, this morning he asked Her merely for sleep. The lack of it had left him exhausted, tentative, irresolute. The previous night he had slept badly yet again, and now fatigue hung heavily on him, making his movements as slow and ponderous as those of someone moving about beneath water. As he prayed, in fact, an image of a man lying beneath cold, fast-moving water sprung into his head. He saw him there, eyes open, staring up through the clear, rippling water, bubbles slipping from his mouth as if he were trying to speak, to tell him something. Though he'd never laid eyes on the man, for some reason he knew who it was: Marcus Lyon.

Sometime before dawn, he had climbed out of bed. He shivered in the chill air of the room, the floorboards like ice beneath his bare feet. He stirred the few live embers in the fireplace, enough to light a taper. Except for the occasional lowing of a cow over on the Common or the rattling of the stage as it rumbled along toward Roxbury, the city was quiet at this hour. He sat at his escritoire. He took out some paper and started several drafts of letters—one to the vicar of Mayenne, Reverend Dumourier, another to his father, a third to Father Matignon. He had hoped that the very act of writing would provoke him into making a decision, that all of his confusion and bewilderment would vanish and the ironclad will of resolve and purpose enter his heart. He would know exactly what it was God had meant for him to do. *Dear Reverend Dumourier,* he had written. *It is with great reluctance that I must tell you I have decided to remain here in America.* Or: *Dearest Father, Forgive my delay in penning a response to your earnest entreaties. It is a decision that has weighed heavily on my mind and heart, knowing full well as I do the obligation a son is under to his father. So it is with deepest regrets . . .* Yet he ended by tossing each attempt into the fireplace, where the paper burst into brilliance, seeming to mock the obscurity of his own muddled brain. His choice had become no clearer to him. So he tried his hand at a letter to Father Matignon. *My Dear Friend, In these past ten years I have come to look upon you not merely as a colleague, but with the affection and tenderness of a brother. It therefore pains me all the more to have to tell you . . .*

That's when he had heard a knock on his door.

"I saw the light," Father Matignon said in French, poking his wizened head in. "Am I interrupting you, Jean?"

"No, Father. Please, come in," he replied.

Father Matignon sat on the unmade bed. He was dressed in his woolen nightshirt, a quilt Mrs. Lobb had made for him thrown haphazardly over his slumped shoulders. His skinny, naked legs were cadaver-white, except for a patchwork of dark knotted veins along the calves. The old abbé squinted, the look in his chalky gray eyes that of one long at sea, searching the horizon for the prospect of land. He seemed very old and frail suddenly, a man worn down by all the demands of his position. How would the priest ever manage without him, Cheverus wondered, feeling a stab of guilt in his side.

"You could not sleep, Jean?"

Cheverus shook his head.

"Nor I."

On the desk lay the letter he had started to Father Matignon. The elder priest's squinting gaze fell upon it. Though he knew his friend could hardly make out what was written there, Cheverus still turned it face down.

"Have you come to a decision?" Father Matignon asked.

"No. Not yet, Father."

"Be patient. God will reveal it to you in time, my son."

"I am sure He has more important concerns than whether I go or stay," Cheverus said with a cryptic sigh. The abbé waited for him to say more but nothing was forthcoming from his colleague.

Father Matignon smiled benevolently. "Maybe when you return from your trip to Maine. The time away will give you a chance to reflect upon what is right for you."

"Perhaps," he replied with a shrug of his shoulders. Cheverus gazed out the window. He could see a few lights burning along Boston's Neck, a narrow strip of land attaching the city's ponderous head to the mainland. Across the water in Dorcester, he saw the beacon of the lighthouse.

"Father . . ." he said, pausing. "There is so much still to do here. And I would not wish to leave you alone to see it through."

"*Tsk*," the old man scoffed. "I will manage somehow. You must answer only to your heart, my friend."

He thought of telling his superior of his other reasons for not wanting to go, the bad memories, the fear of returning to the scene of his betrayal. But he only nodded. He crumpled the letter he had begun and tossed it into the fire.

Now, as Cheverus put on his vestments, he thought of what Father Matignon had told him: *You must answer only to your heart.* But what lay hidden in his heart? What was he himself reluctant to recognize there? Part of him wanted desperately, longingly, to return home, to his family, to his old parish, to the way of life he had once known. Yet was that even a possibility any longer? Hadn't that life passed into memory as certainly, as irrevocably as had the monarchy itself, severed as surely as King Louis's head? Besides, there were plenty of other priests recently returned to France. He wasn't needed there. Not as he was here, where Father Matignon depended on him. But was his own heart truly here, so far from everything he had once known and loved? Would he *ever* feel at home in this strange land, ministering to these strange people—the Indians, the Irish? The debate in his mind, and all the things it had aroused in him, had made him feel weary and old, his spirit a thing as dry and brittle as parchment.

He tried to think of his sermon—it was from Isaiah. But his mind couldn't concentrate. His thoughts turned again to that image which had haunted him all these years, but especially of late. The garden of the Convent of the Carmes. The garden of the martyrs, as he had come to think of it. He closed his eyes and saw it once again. . . . *The white walls of the garden surrounding him, seeming to close in upon him. The air, sickly sweet with the heavy fragrance of flowers and of ripe fruit, hung dense and torpid, shimmering and wavering in the September heat. The sky was a pale blue, diffuse, hazy. The only sound was the distant buzzing of bees, a soft ripple of wind high up in the treetops. But then, far off, he heard the faint rumbling sound, the distant but growing clamor of the mob approaching, the tramping of many angry feet over the cobblestones, coming closer. Closer . . .*

"We're almost out of missals, Father," he heard a voice behind him. Startled, he turned to see Máirtin Kelly, an altar boy, standing in the doorway of the vestry. "Sorry for disturbin' you," the boy said.

"It's all right, Máirtin," Cheverus said. "I'll shall have to see about getting more printed."

"There's not many here today anyway, Father."

"No. I wouldn't expect so. I shall be along shortly."

Yet out of the corner of his eye, he saw the boy remaining in the doorway.

"What is it, Máirtin?" the priest asked.

"Och. You're busy, Father," the boy said.

"No, I have a moment. What is it?"

Máirtin was twelve, though big for his age, tall and gangly, with the large, callused hands of a man already. Over his black cassock he wore a white surplice, washed so many times it was nearly transparent. His face shone pink from being recently scrubbed, and it now held an expression of mild consternation. Máirtin had been an altar boy since coming to America three years earlier, and his surplice, which his mother had made for him out of an old sheet, now only reached to mid-shin. He worked long days in the ropewalks on Myrtle Street. A couple of evenings a week after work, Máirtin and a few other immigrant boys would come to Holy Cross, where Cheverus conducted informal lessons in the church basement. Back home there had been only the hedge schools for boys like him. Besides their catechism, Cheverus was teaching them to read and

write, a little Latin, some history. He had for a decade now been hoping
to start a school. To educate them. To bring them out of the darkness of
their ignorance.

He was fond of Máirtin, his star pupil. He reminded him a little of
himself when he was a boy. There was a gentleness of spirit about him
that was unusual in boys his age. He was quiet and serious, eager to learn.
He would make something of himself, the priest thought. That is, if the
grinding poverty or the drink or the hopelessness of living in a country
that hated them as much as had the one they'd left—if all that didn't
crush his spirit first. Who knows, in time he might even decide to go into
the priesthood. The Church had been here for a decade and a half, and
as of yet no child had entered the orders. But Máirtin may have had the
calling, he felt. The priest saw it in the way he gazed at the cross, the way
he touched the sacred vessels, the way he acted around the two priests.
With reverence and awe certainly, but with something Cheverus could
only think of as love. A love of God.

The boy hesitated for a moment. "I was just wondering what you think
will happen to those two?" he asked.

He didn't have to explain who he meant by "those two." For the past
few days, the city had been abuzz with talk about the trial of the two
Irishmen out in the west. There were new rumors, gossip, wild reports
concerning the fate of the prisoners. One rumor making the rounds
said the two had already been lynched without so much as a hearing.
Another insisted the trial had been postponed again, something to do
with one of the judges taking ill. Catholics were justifiably nervous,
unsure what would happen next. Someone had hung a straw figure from
the steeple of the Old North Church with a sign saying, IRISH GO
HOME.

"God only knows," the priest replied. "Are you acquainted with either
one?"

"Me da knew the elder Daley from back in the old country. Will they
hang 'em, do you s'pose?"

"Perhaps. If they're found guilty."

"Me da says they're bound to swing no matter what."

"Why does he think that?"

"He says an Irishman's always believed guilty."

Cheverus was going to say something reassuring, but he offered instead only, "I don't know what will happen. We can only pray."

The boy nodded soberly, his eyes not moving from the priest. "How come they hate us, Father?"

"They don't hate you, Máirtin," he said, not a lie so much as merely a frail hope, a belief that might prove true in time.

"I think they do. I thought it would change when we come here but it has not."

"It's that they don't understand you. People fear what they don't understand."

"But I never done 'em any wrong."

"Never *did* them any wrong," the priest corrected, smiling affectionately. The boy's sober expression didn't change. "It's a very complex question, Máirtin," he said as he picked up his stole, kissed it, and placed it over his neck. He didn't feel up to explaining to the boy the several hundred years of conflict between Catholics and Protestants, or the equally long antipathy for the Irish, things he himself didn't quite understand either. Prejudice as deep as the bone.

But he saw Máirtin waiting earnestly for an answer.

"In my own country, Máirtin, we had a revolution. You heard of the French Revolution, did you not?"

The boy nodded.

"France is almost entirely Catholic. Was anyway. But during the Revolution, Catholic fought Catholic. Some people wanted to banish the Church completely. They wished to send every priest into exile or to kill those that remained. Near the end they hated us all. We were all the same to them."

"Why?" the boy asked, knitting his brows.

"Many thought the Church was corrupt. For the wealthy, against the poor."

"Was it, Father?"

Cheverus sighed. "In some ways perhaps. There were bad priests. Selfish. Some put the Church ahead of the people they were supposed to be serving. Ahead of God, too."

Máirtin stared at him. He was a handsome boy, with pale, light blue eyes and a certain presence about him. He held his head erect, looked you in the eye. Cheverus could picture him in vestments someday, standing before the altar, his own people sitting there, proud of him.

"They say you're going back there, Father?" the boy said. "To France."

"Where did you hear that?" he asked, surprised that his secret was out. But then again, he should have known. Few secrets remained in a small parish.

The boy opened his mouth to speak but then only shrugged.

"Perhaps, Máirtin."

"Don't you like it here, Father?"

"It's not that. It's . . ." he said, wondering how to explain it. "That was my home. Don't you ever miss home, Máirtin?"

"I suppose. But this is my home now."

Cheverus patted him on his head and said he would be along shortly. If he returned to France, he would miss Máirtin. He felt bad he wouldn't be there to help establish the school, help guide the boy along the path to the priesthood. But if it was to be, then it would be. If not, nothing he could do or say would make the boy answer the calling.

The altar boy had been right—there were only a handful in attendance for a weekday Mass. Cheverus said the confiteor, striking his breast as he did so, then the kyrie, followed by the gloria. The Latin tasted dull and slightly tainted in his mouth, the words like meat gone bad. His sermon this morning was from Isaiah: *Woe unto them that decree unrighteous decrees, and that write grievousness which they have prescribed. To turn aside the needy from judgment and to take away the right from the poor of my people.* Though he knew he must walk a fine line between being a voice for his people and an agitator, he couldn't simply ignore the day, could he? Pretend that nothing was happening? One of his communicants and another Catholic were being put on trial for murder today. He had to say something. Yet the passage from Isaiah was obscure, its meaning lost on those in attendance.

He could feel sweat running down his neck and dripping onto his chasuble. His face grew flushed. Was the fever upon him again? He was so tired. He wanted only to sleep. Perhaps he should have stayed in bed longer, gotten his strength back. At one point in his sermon, he paused, feeling light-headed, his hands beginning to tremble ever so slightly. He closed his eyes and grasped the lectern for support. A dark stillness seemed to descend upon him like a leaden net; the air grew thick and stale. *Heavenly Father* he prayed. *Show me the way of Your light.* A cough from a front pew interrupted his thoughts. He opened his eyes and, momentarily confused, gazed at those seated before him. For a second, he imagined that he was back in Mayenne, preaching to his former parish, his family sitting before him. But they were not there, of course. Instead, he saw strange faces, in them a look of mild consternation. With a hand-kerchief he wiped his forehead, hoping to cover the awkwardness of the moment. The smell of it recalled Finola Daley to him again.

"Dear friends," he said, looking out over the church. "We find ourselves in most difficult times. As you all have heard, two of our fellow Catholics, one a communicant of this very parish, are to stand trial today for murder." All eyes looked up at him, expectant, curious. There was a low but very definite murmur that rose from those in attendance. Except to ask for donations for the Daley family back in December, it was the first time he had said anything publicly about the trial. Although there were only a handful of the congregation present this day, he knew that what he said this morning would spread by word of mouth throughout the parish. By nightfall every Catholic in the city would know what he had said, and many of the Protestants as well. So he would need to choose his words with care.

"I cannot speak as to their innocence or guilt," he continued. "That is a matter for a court of law to decide. We can only hope and pray that justice will be done: that if guilty, they are punished according to the law; if innocent, they are allowed to go free and resume their lives without fear of retribution." As he said this, he glanced over at Máirtin, whose expression seemed to acknowledge their earlier conversation. "But I beseech you not to take the law into your own hands. I counsel you and those you know against rash acts which will only make our lot and that of our brethren in Northampton worse. As a community of the faithful, we must not do or say anything which will provoke others to take action against us. We must ask the Lord for guidance. Let us pray," he said, bowing his head. When he finished, he added, "And let us pray for the soul of the victim, Mr. Lyon. As well, I ask that you pray for the two men whose fates are to be decided today, Dominic Daley and James Halligan. We humbly beseech Thee, O Lord, that You grant them Your blessing. That You help those entrusted with their fates to act with reason and fairness and in good conscience. That You forgive these men their trespasses, whatever they may be. Finally, we humbly ask you, O Lord, to comfort the loved ones of these men. Amen."

After Mass, he had a full schedule of appointments, various obligations that had earlier been canceled because of his illness. The day broke clear and cool with a light wind out of the northwest. Several new ships sat in the harbor, including a large barque from the West Indies and a whaler just returned from two years at sea. He first headed for Corn Court and the shop of Isaiah Thomas, a printer, to see about getting more missals as well as catechism books printed. Then he walked north, toward the almshouse out on Barton's Point where a number of his parishioners were in residence. Along the way he passed wagons loaded with wood or carrying milk to Faneuil Market. He was hailed by Liam Broderick, who owned the booksellers shop on Cornhill. "Good day, Father," said Broderick, a large, white-haired man with a soft red face. "I have some new French volumes just arrived." Cheverus said he would be sure to stop by, and continued on his way.

The long, Greek-style building that was the poorhouse was set off by itself on a boggy spit of land that jutted out into the Charles. The town fathers had transferred it from the fashionable area on Park Street, so as to "remove from the sight of gentlemen and ladies the disagreeable prospect of mendicants begging for their supper." He passed through the high iron gates surrounding it and proceeded through the front door. Inside, it smelled the way he imagined Purgatory smelling—the rank odor of despair and lost dreams. He spoke with several there, listened to their confessions, gave the sacrament to those who wished it. Before he left, he removed from the deep pockets of his cassock some onions and potatoes he'd taken from the rectory pantry, and gave them away to those who looked most in need. He didn't ask whether they were Catholic or not. And he always remembered the sugared plums for the children.

Next, he made two sick visits. One was to ancient Mr. O'Shaunnessey, who'd been trying to die forever without much success. He was nearly blind and stone deaf, and would place his fingertips on the priest's lips to make out what was being said to him. Cheverus had given him the last rites on three or four separate occasions but somehow he always managed to change his mind at the last moment. The other visit was to old Madame Jariel, like himself a French émigré. Once a well-to-do woman before the Revolution, she now lived modestly in a sunny set of rooms on Spring Street. Her window overlooked the Charles. Old and forgetful, she would sometimes refer to the river as the Seine and the West Boston Bridge as *pont tournant*. Though she liked to chatter nonstop, he enjoyed visiting with her as the two would speak French and reminisce of days gone by. She would pour him a glass of fine Bordeaux she had somehow managed to get despite the restrictions of the war, and she would talk of home.

"I was an intimate of Madame de Tourzel's, you understand," the woman would remind him nearly every visit. Madame de Tourzel was the governess of the royal children. "We used to drink cognac in a café on the Rue de la Madeline. A charming woman with the most beautiful hands. She adored those children like her own. Especially the little dauphin."

Cheverus was next going over to Cambridge, to pay a visit to a woman sick with childbirth fever. The day was slowly warming. Along Cambridge Street, he smelled the teasing odors of food cooking in ovens. Breads and pork pies and corncakes. He felt a sudden sharp pang in his stomach and realized he'd forgotten to eat that morning, so he stopped in a baker's shop. He bought a penny roll and left the shop, heading for the West Boston Bridge. He paid the tollman at the gate and started across. He saw the tangled masts of more ships at anchor along the wharves, and the long low sheds of the ropeworks and sail-duck factories. Across the Charles he spotted the Naval Shipyards, a flurry of activity. Halfway to

Cambridge he sat on the bench along the railing and began to eat. He tore into the delicious roll, forgetting everything else. His own problems. Those of the Daleys. He forgot even to say grace. How strong were the needs of the flesh, he thought.

As he sat there eating, he recalled a meal he'd had up in the Maine woods once, on his first visit north after coming to America. He had canoed with his Indian guides several hard days' journey upriver to the Penobscot mission there. His body ached from the exertion, and he was wet and frozen and half starved from eating only jerked meat and the disgusting gruel the Indians called *sagamité*. And yet he joyfully accepted each trial God placed before him in this new land. He wanted to show himself worthy. When they reached the settlement, the Indians were eager to have him say Mass, which he did on a crude altar in a stinking, smoke-filled long house. He wondered how he would survive his stay there. Would he get used to the brutish accommodations, to the awful food, to the strangeness of the savages themselves? Only after Mass did they eat, the entire village dining from a large communal pot. He blessed the foul-smelling food. They didn't use utensils but ate with their fingers, wolfing the food, snapping at it like dogs. For plates they used sections of birch bark. They had served him first. A squaw had set before him something half cooked, gray and steaming. It turned out to be the boiled nose of a moose, a delicacy which the Indians had offered him as a sign of great respect. There was still hair and blood on the thing. He thought he would vomit. Yet, his strong repugnance at last overcome by his even stronger hunger, he had devoured it, finding it as sumptuous a meal as he'd ever eaten.

Sitting there now on the bridge, the sun lying drowsy on the back of his neck, he recalled another meal: a single sweet potato. He had gone into hiding to avoid being arrested by the Jacobins. He was lodged in a tiny garret room in the Saint-Eustache section of Paris. It was dangerous then for him. For all priests. The new government had just decreed that any clergy who hadn't signed the loyalty oath must leave the country or face ten years' imprisonment. The landlord, a man with obvious Jacobin sympathies, used to eye him suspiciously as he came and went, but an old peasant woman who lived in the room below his befriended him. Somehow she'd known he was a priest, perhaps by his voice or something in his manner. And though it was dangerous to be helping him, she would bring him whatever little she could spare—a piece of bread, a cup of milk, a boiled potato. Before returning to her room, he would listen to her confession and then serve communion to her. She would kiss his hand and, tears in her rheumy old eyes, say, "*Merci, père spirituel.*" Such a brave and decent woman, risking her life for him. The streets were dangerous, crowded with *sansculottes* and wild mobs of peasants, and he'd had little to eat for several days. He remembered her bringing him a sweet potato with a little salt and some milk. He could still recall the taste of the sugary flesh of the thing melting in his mouth. *And he took bread, and gave thanks, and brake it, and gave unto them, saying. This is my body which is given for you: This do in remembrance of me.*

The sunlight off the water hurt his eyes, so he closed them. He would rest just for a moment, he thought. A moment, and then be off again. He could hear the water sliding under the bridge, slipping by the piers and out to sea. Or maybe it was his own blood he felt, coursing through his veins. He felt himself sliding, too, slipping slowly away. Downward. Downward as if into the depths of a deep ocean. After a while, out of the darkness, it came to him: the bright, fragrant courtyard garden. The garden of the martyrs.

Sixteen years earlier, in 1790, the twenty-two-year-old Cheverus had graduated from the major seminary of St. Magloire in Paris and went on to receive Holy Orders in what would prove to be the last public ordination in France for many years. It was the happiest day of his life. Eager to begin fulfilling his vows, Cheverus returned to his small hometown of Mayenne that December. There he assumed the duties of vicar of Notre Dame, the beautiful medieval cathedral which overlooked the river. It was the church at which his uncle Louis-René had been pastor, and in which he had once knelt in prayer beside his mother. He said his first Mass on Christmas of that year, to a congregation that included family, friends, neighbors. He looked forward to a long and auspicious tenure in his native city.

He had no inkling of what lay ahead, though perhaps he should have.

After all, the Revolution had begun the year before. The National Assembly had already taken the Tennis Court Oath. The Bastille had fallen. There were riots in the streets of Paris. The king's reluctant acceptance of the new constitution. Even before those obvious signs, the winds of change had already been blowing for years. There were the scattered peasant uprisings, the food riots, the growing discontent and suffering of the Third Estate. Though he was a priest, the young Cheverus actually favored a number of the changes being called for. He could not help being influenced by the same heady idealism sweeping across the land. He believed in the need to improve the lot of the poor, in making changes. In one of those small ironies of history, several of the most important revolutionary leaders—men like Robespierre and Desmoulins, Saint-Just and du Tertre—had gone to the same college as he, Louis le Grand, which was to become known as the "Seminary of the Revolution." While he had for the Bourbons the same unquestioning loyalty he had for the papacy, he thought it high time to redress the inequities, the injustices, the grinding poverty he saw all around him.

He hadn't even considered himself political. He had only wanted to serve, quietly and faithfully, his God, his king, his pope, the people of his parish. He was so naïve, he hadn't even seen a contradiction in doing that. He had worked with the poor, so he was well aware of the appalling, squalid conditions most lived in. Equally, he was shamed by the lavish extravagances of the aristocracy, and in all too many cases, by his own fellow clergy. He was convinced that change was long overdue, both in the government as well as in the Church. He believed, as did many of his fellow clery of the First Estate, that the "movement" would lead to needed but relatively minor changes. It would be a slight revision to the social contract, one that would have little real consequence for the Church or for himself. Soon, he would come to realize that what the radicals—men like Marat and Danton and Robespierre—had in mind were not minor changes, a mere tinkering with a system that had some flaws, but rather, the total annihilation of a way of thinking. The new government would soon demand that all priests sign the oath of the Civil Constitution of the Clergy, declaring their loyalty to the new order. Those that refused to sign, to become jurored priests loyal to the new government, would be stripped of their authority, their parishes forcibly taken from them, and eventually arrested and thrown in jail.

But that would come later. At first, many in the clergy tried to go along with the new regime. They made concessions, minor compromises, small bargains. A brave few refused to compromise even then. There was, for instance, the shining example of Urbain-René Hercé, Bishop of Dol, who refused to go along with the oath. Or Cheverus's old seminary friend, Father Legris-Duval. They had both been *boursier* students on scholarship at Louis le Grand. They used to walk along the Seine together, discussing esoteric points of theology and preparing each other for the weekly sermons they would have to give before their superiors. After the arrest of the king, his friend had risked coming out of seclusion to go to the aid of the imprisoned monarch. Father Legris-Duval had openly traveled to Paris without the proper papers and without signing the oath. There he had the audacity to confront the Republican authorities by proclaiming his offer to be the confessor to the imprisoned "Citizen Capet," the new name by which the king was scornfully referred to now. Such courage and conviction. Such sangfroid, Cheverus thought, with wonder and admiration for his friend, and not without an element of envy. For if the time came when he himself were called to act in a similar fashion, would he have the nerve?

Cheverus had tried at first to go quietly about his priestly duties in Mayenne, thinking the movement, after it had achieved some modest changes, would eventually die of its own weight. In any event, the movement wouldn't concern itself with him, an unimportant priest in a small parish two days' ride from Paris. Pope Pius soon issued a papal bull threatening those clergy who signed the Civil Constitution with excommunication. For a priest that was worse than death. The Church, like the country as a whole, was now split in two. Cheverus realized he would have to make a choice: to go along with the government as many priests did, or to take a stand and defend the autonomy of the Church. In the end, he felt compelled to refuse signing the loyalty oath. He certainly didn't consider himself a brave or daring man, but he thought it his duty to object on grounds of conscience. He was officially stripped of his authority, which meant he couldn't perform the sacraments. Nonetheless, Cheverus continued "unofficially" saying Mass in his church, as well as performing the rites for those loyal Catholics in his parish who called on his services. As had begun to happen throughout France, violence soon erupted in Mayenne, pitting those of the old order against those that supported the new government. A radical priest accompanied by several guards went about the town gathering up the children of the wealthy and baptizing them with names like "Liberté" and "Égalité."

As Cheverus walked the streets in his cassock, he was intimidated by radicals who taunted him and threw rotten eggs at him, who called him a supporter of the old regime, a *calotin*. Threats were made against his life. On two occasions an angry mob had surrounded him while he was celebrating Mass, and he was saved only by the last-minute intercession of those loyal to him. Finally, the authorities took his parish church by force. They smashed stained glass windows that dated from the Middle Ages and confiscated sacred gold vessels, to be sent to Paris where they would be melted down by the new government. Secretly, he arranged for the priceless statue of the Virgin and Child—*Notre Dame des Miracles*—to be hidden so the Jacobins wouldn't destroy it. Despite the growing danger, he went on performing the sacraments, now in private homes, in barns and in cellars throughout Mayenne.

He was eventually arrested by the Jacobins and thrown into prison in Laval, where he spent several harrowing months. His cellmate was an old friend of the family, Father Urbain-René Hercé, Bishop of Dol. Republican guards would stroll through the jail poking the priests with their sabers and joking about whether they were fat enough yet for slaughter. One guard, a hugely obese man with a purple birthmark on his cheek, used to bring prostitutes and fornicate with them just outside their cell. Grunting like a dog in heat, he would yell out, "Will I go to hell, Father?" and laugh. Finally, through the intercession of his Uncle Julien, a lawyer and major of Mayenne, he was set free due to his frail health. Frightened and confused, he disguised himself as a merchant and fled to Paris. In fact, hundreds of priests made the same exodus to the city, hoping to hide out with relatives or friends while they waited for a passport. His brother, Louis, was a law student at Louis le Grand College, but Cheverus was too well known in that quarter of the city, so he went into hiding for several months in St. Eustache. While his Uncle Julien used his connections to secure a passport, Cheverus remained in his tiny room, hardly daring to leave, and when he did, only disguised in lay clothes. It was dangerous now for a priest opposed to the Jacobins to wear clerical garb openly. It was here that the old peasant woman would bring him food each day. Whenever his passport finally did come through, he wondered if he would actually go. Leaving his family, his colleagues, everything he'd known would be difficult. And yet, he did not know what would happen if he stayed.

While he waited in hiding, he found he couldn't turn his back on the hundreds of his fellow priests who had not been so lucky, who had been rounded up by the authorities and thrown in jail for refusing to sign the loyalty oath. Disguised as a student or common laborer, he would slip out of his room and visit his colleagues being held in the hastily converted prisons throughout Paris: the abbey at Saint-Germain des Pres, the seminary of Saint Firmin, the Convent of the Carmes. Since the murder of the Swiss guards in early August and the subsequent arrest of the king, travel about the city was perilous. As he made his way he stuck to the back streets, avoiding the main thoroughfares and the places where he knew revolutionary guards to be. Yet no part of Paris was safe any longer.

He kept his head low, his hood up despite the late summer heat, studiously avoiding the suspicious stares from the *sansculottes* who patrolled the city armed with sabers and pikes. He feared being stopped and searched, and having them find what he carried in his haversack: the breviaries and rosaries, holy water and hosts. The mere possession of those objects would certainly have landed him in jail—or worse. He brought the imprisoned clergy what food he could scrounge up, letters from relatives, forbidden newspapers, a book to take their minds off things. In the prisons, he chatted with friends and raised the spirits of those who had nearly given up hope. He read to them. He listened to their confessions. His fellow priests told him he shouldn't come, that it was growing too dangerous. Still, how could he not? So Cheverus returned again and again to his imprisoned colleagues, doing what he could to comfort them. This was where he belonged, he felt. Where God wanted him to be.

He especially liked to visit those clergy being held on the Left Bank, at the former Convent of the Carmes. Many of the prisoners there were his personal friends, several his former instructors from his school days. The Archbishop of Arles, Jean-Marie Dulau, was jailed in the convent, as were the two Rochefoucauld-Bayers brothers, the bishops of Beauvais and of Saintes. The king's personal confessor was there, along with the former head of Louis le Grand College, Father Berardier, and a few of Cheverus's old professors, too. There were priests and monks and brothers from all over France—those who had refused to sign the new government's loyalty oath. At the Carmes prison, Cheverus became close friends with a priest named Pierre Landry, a vicar from Niort. Only after bribing the guards with a few francs would he be allowed to enter. The grounds included a cloister and a small chapel, attached to a high-walled garden courtyard filled with flowers and finely trimmed shrubbery, chestnut and poplar trees, as well as a small orangery. Here and there were stone benches, and in a corner a grotto to the Virgin Mary. Daily, the clerics were forced out of their various prison cells and into the garden, at which time the guards would take a head count.

Cheverus happened to be there on the September day that would later become known as Black Sunday, the first of the September Massacres. The late summer day was warm, the air placid and still. A drowsy sunlight filtered through the leaves overhead and lay in broad swathes across the convent grounds. The fragrance of the late-summer flowers and the fruit from the trees hung heavy in the air, a lush, almost tropical scent. The high whitewashed walls of the courtyard seemed almost to be trying to keep at bay the growing anarchy that took place in the streets outside. Yet that day had been unusually still, he recalled. The silence almost overwhelming.

He was sitting on the ground in the garden beside his new friend Father Landry and another prisoner, August Berruyer, a Benedictine monk from Le Mans. They sat in the shade of an elm with their backs to the wall. Father Landry was a few years older than Cheverus, a tall, strikingly handsome fellow with thick dark hair and an engaging smile. He was well read, cultured, with the dignified bearing of a cardinal. He and Cheverus would talk about music and poetry and philosophy. Berruyer, on the other hand, was squat and heavily muscled, with the coarse features and plain speech of a peasant. His face was always greasy, and it possessed a surly expression. When talking of the revolutionary authorities, he would curl his lips and cry, *"Ces bêtes!"* and spit on the ground. He called Cheverus *"mon pauvre petit"*—my poor little chap.

As they sat there talking, the city's tocsin bell suddenly sounded in the distance. They wondered what it could mean this time. They had heard it often since that day three years earlier when the Bastille had been overrun. Just before this sound, they had been debating what was meant by the most recent decree of the revolutionary government, that disloyal priests would have a fortnight to get out of the country. Berruyer thought they were quite serious and said he would go in a heartbeat if they issued him a passport. Father Landry, on the other hand, held the belief that it wouldn't come to such an extreme, that it was just a means of scaring the priests into falling in line with those who had signed the new constitution. He said conditions would slowly begin to improve. An optimist, he was confident the worst of it was behind them. He mentioned talk of the Prussians' advance on the city, how the threat of an external army would force the Jacobins to come to their senses—to set the king free and sue for peace.

"The Prussians took Verdun," Father Landry had said. "They are not a hundred miles from Paris."

"Danton is calling everyone to arms," Berruyer countered. He was chewing on an overripe pear he had picked up on the ground, and the juice was running down his bearded chin. A bee flew about his mouth, after the sweetness. He didn't seem to notice. "The country is rallying around that madman."

"They can't declare war on all of Europe," Father Landry said. "What choice do they have but to free the king and call off this insanity?"

"They could put him on trial," Berruyer offered.

"The *king*? On trial!" Landry scoffed. "Are you insane, man?"

"I have heard rumors they intend to try him."

"*Mon Dieu!* They might as well put the pope on trial. No, that would be pure madness."

"Don't you understand? They *are* all mad," Berruyer interjected.

"No. They've made their point," Landry insisted. "Now they will listen to reason."

"Reason!" laughed Berruyer, throwing his great head back. "He talks of reason with mad dogs." Turning to Cheverus, he said, "And you, *mon pauvre petit*. What are your thoughts?"

Cheverus wasn't sure. He, too, thought the Jacobins were madmen. But maybe they would come to their senses before it was too late. Even a mad dog cowers before a boot to its ribs. Instead he said only, "Let us hope that Pierre is right."

"Of course, I'm right."

And that's when the alarm sounded throughout Paris. They exchanged anxious looks but decided it meant nothing. They continued conversing for a while, and then Cheverus and Landry read the breviary that Cheverus brought each time. Finally it was time to leave. He had a long walk, and he certainly didn't want to be on the streets after dark. Slowly, they became aware of another sound, at first low and muffled, but growing, coming nearer and nearer. It grew to a thunderous din, of countless feet pounding on the cobblestones and the frenzied cries of "A *mort!* A *mort!*" A priest watching from a window of the cloister hollered down that a mob waving guns and sabers and clubs was rushing down the Rues Vaugirard and Cassette. The prisoners wondered what this could possibly mean. What was happening? Only much later would they learn—those that survived anyway—that the Terror that was to rock the city, the country, the world even, had finally begun. The prisoners at the Carmes did not know that some twenty priests being conveyed to the nearby prison of the abbey of St. Germain des Prés had been pulled from their carriages, attacked by the mob, and summarily executed in the street, hacked to death, while government troops stood by and watched.

The *sansculotte* mob smashed down the convent doors and came storming in, yelling and waving their weapons in the air. Some in the crowd were already covered with blood. One man even wore a butcher's bloody apron. There were shouts and commands. Cheverus recognized two of the leaders. One was the lawyer, Stanislas Maillard, who had helped to organize the attack on the Tuileries. The other he knew by his red Phrygian cap—it was the wild, Catholic-hating Anacharsis Clootz, the self-styled "Orator of the Human Race." Holding his saber aloft, he shouted orders that the priests were to move quickly into the chapel.

"What do you think this means?" Father Landry whispered as they moved toward the chapel.

"What do you think it means?" Berruyer replied.

"Surely they will merely count heads."

"Or make them roll," Berruyer scoffed, a cynical smile on his rough features.

Father Landry stared at Berruyer in disbelief, but he saw that his friend wasn't joking. "They would not dare." But Cheverus could see that his friend was shaken.

The priests murmured nervously as they were herded into the chapel, the guards prodding them from behind with sabers and pikes. When one elderly priest who had been kneeling giving his confession to another was slow getting to his feet, a guard struck him in the head with a rifle butt, and the old priest fell just outside the chapel. The priest who had been hearing his confession, Alexander Lenfant, tried to help the old priest up, but he was shoved back, told to get in line. When he went to help a second time, the guard turned his musket and, casually, as if he were spearing a piece of fruit, thrust his bayonet into Lenfant's chest. The priest fell dead on the spot, the first of the martyrs that day. Cheverus and the others watched in stunned horror.

Inside the chapel, Clootz announced in a booming voice that he'd come here to put all traitors to France on trial. The Archbishop of Arles, the frail, seventy-nine-year-old Jean-Marie Dulau, calmly approached Clootz, and tried to reason with him. He said the priests there were loyal citizens, that they had done nothing wrong.

"I will decide who is guilty, old man," Clootz screamed at him, his face reddening with anger. Clootz took a piece of paper from his coat pocket and waved it in front of the old priest. "Will you sign the oath or not?"

The Archbishop shook his head.

"Sign it or die."

Father Dulau said he would not sign.

Clootz raised his already bloody saber. "I ask you one last time, old man. Are you one of them—or one of us?"

The priest crossed himself and got down on his knees. Looking up at his soon-to-be executioner, he said with perfect equanimity, "I forgive you, my son."

This seemed to enrage Clootz even more. "I don't need your damn forgiveness. May Lucifer accept your soul," Clootz cried, dropping the saber on the Archbishop's neck. The old priest fell over, his head nearly severed, his blood spurting in torrents onto the floor of the chapel. He was the second to be martyred.

Clootz next turned to one of the Rochefoucauld brothers, the bishop of Beauvais. He repeated the question: "Are you one of them? Or one of us?" When the Bishop said he would not sign the oath, he, too, was struck down with a savage blow that disemboweled him. His guts spilled out of him onto the chapel floor. Now, even the façade of a trial was at an end. A pent-up orgy of violence seemed to be suddenly unleashed. Gunshots rang out, splintering the torpid air, and sabers and pikes and axes gleamed and flashed in the small chapel. Some of the priests tried to make their way to the altar at the front of the chapel, as if the cross there would save them. A few were quickly dispatched by bullets, while others were slowly hacked to death, their limbs littering the floor of the chapel or the ground just outside. Some were bludgeoned to death by clubs, their brains strewn about. Some had their throats cut, others were beheaded, their heads impaled on pikes. Some were slaughtered where they stood or knelt in prayer. A few tried to fight back or at least to protect themselves, to ward off the blows. Cheverus saw the burly August Berruyer grab one of the *sansculottes* and throw him to the ground before a club crushed his skull. Others, having gained the courtyard, rushed headlong for the walls or the doors leading to the outside, hoping to save themselves. Most were shot trying to climb over the walls to freedom, or grabbed by their heels and pulled down, there to be bludgeoned or hacked to death. The whitewashed masonry of the wall was befouled by their blood. It looked like the insides of a slaughterhouse.

At the first outbreak of violence, Cheverus was overwhelmed. The unspeakable savagery had left him numbed, his limbs paralyzed. Somehow he managed to stagger outside the chapel. Standing behind a bush, he watched the hellish scene swirling around him, mesmerized by it, transfixed by such horror. He saw some of the priests aiding others, kneeling beside their fallen colleagues, praying, comforting those in their last agonies. Not far away, his friend Pierre Landry tended to one who'd been disembowled, his intestines lying strewn about the ground like those of a slaughtered pig. Father Landry gave him extreme unction and recited the prayer for a dead priest: *"Deus qui inter apostolicos sacerdos familium tuum."* Several of the assassins then fell upon him. He looked up at them, his eyes wide in terror but also with resignation. He started to say something but before the words were out of his mouth a saber descended upon his skull. Right before his eyes, his friend was hacked to pieces.

With Landry's death, something snapped in Cheverus. He seemed to wake from a terrible nightmare and into a reality even worse. He turned and fled across the garden, running right through the carnage, past the blood and gore, the severed limbs and heads, the steaming entrails, the cries and whimpers and death rattles of his colleagues. All the while bullets whizzed about him. Fellow priests dropped around him, bleeding, crying out in agony: *Help me. Dear Lord, help me.* He reached the wall and climbed a small pear tree. He scaled the blood-spattered wall, and flung himself over. He found himself in the Rue de Rennes, running, fleeing from the crazed mobs. He was not the only one. Of the one hundred and fifty priests in the Carmes that day, some forty managed to escape. Behind him he could hear the terrible screams and tormented cries of his dying brothers, as well as the shouts of the mob. "Get him," they yelled. "There he goes." He ran like a frightened animal, wildly, without plan or thought. His body took over, his heart pounding, his lungs burning, his brain hammering furiously. If he had one thought guiding him it was this: *to live.* Simply that. Everything else became unimportant. When Cheverus had managed to put some distance between himself and the Carmes, he stopped and vomited in the gutter. Then he ran on.

The *sansculottes* were everywhere now, roaming the streets, looking to kill any priest they saw. When, exhausted and out of breath, he could run no further, he tried to hide. He slunk furtively about the dingy alleys of Paris like a common criminal, knocking on the doors of houses only to be turned away by the terrified occupants: *"Allez-vous-en!"* they would cry. *"Go away, priest!"* He feared that any moment might be his last. *"There's one of them,"* he heard someone scream. *"Get him!"*

He took off again, fleeing in the direction of his old school, hoping to make the safety of his brother Louis's lodgings in the Rue St. Jacques. Sticking to the back streets and narrow, fetid lanes, he soon found himself lost in an unfamiliar part of the city. He turned and ran into an alley that he realized only too late had no exit. It was hardly five feet across and darkened except for a thin band of light that fell from straight overhead, a sordid place where prostitutes plied their trade at night and thieves lurked. Several doors led onto the alley. These he pounded on, calling for help, pleading, but no one answered his cries. He turned back the way he had come, hoping to avoid being trapped, when he heard the shouts of the *sansculotte* mob getting closer and closer. Finally, with nowhere to turn, he realized he was doomed. He knelt, closed his eyes, and began to pray, to pray as hard as he had ever prayed.

Is it my life You wish, O Lord, he asked. He thought of saying it was His, to do with as He wished, but his fear had so constricted his throat that no words came out of his mouth. He didn't hear God's voice, only the frantic pounding in his head. An icy hand seemed to grab hold of his heart, squeezing it. His soul trembled, quaking with a fear he'd never known before. He would die alone, he thought, in this sordid place. He should have stayed and died with his fellow clergy. If he had, it would all be over by now. At this very moment he would be sitting at God's right hand, a martyr like the others. Yet he had run, fled like a coward.

Before this moment, death—and especially a martyr's death—had been a mere abstraction to him, a lovely Botticelli painting framed by youthful notions of glory and splendid beatitude. If martyrdom were to come, he had always thought, it would be accompanied by bands of angels bearing him sweetly aloft to the glory of God. But *this?* This was pure horror. This was ugly and profane beyond words. He couldn't imagine heaven, and God seemed so far from this stinking alley. He took out his breviary and began to read from it, hoping that this would calm his soul. From memory, he recited the Twenty-third Psalm: *Yea, though I walk through the valley of the shadow of death, I will fear no evil.* Yet he did fear evil. The world had *become* evil. At that moment, the only image that came to his mind was the hellish scene he had just escaped from. He saw the courtyard garden strewn with the bodies of his fellow priests. He saw severed heads and limbs still twitching. He saw mutilated corpses. He saw blood spattered on the white walls. He saw all this and he trembled. His heart rebelled against such an end. He wasn't ready to die. No. He had just become a priest. God had so much for him yet to accomplish. With tears streaming from his eyes, he prayed once more, asking not for absolution for his immortal soul nor for the courage to face his end with dignity, but merely for his life. Life at any cost, in any form. *Dear God,* he had prayed. *I am afraid. Spare your humble servant, and I will serve you in any way you wish.* He closed his breviary and heaved it into a corner of the filthy alley, so that it would not be found on him. Then the mob came rushing upon him.

"*Vous etes l'un d'eux, n'est-ce-pas?*" demanded their leader, his voice that harsh, guttural accusation he would never forget, the voice that would follow him, haunt him, pursue him, for years, in dreams, in memories. "You are one of them, are you not?"

Cheverus remained silent, his head bowed, waiting for the blow that would send him to eternity. He didn't look up at them, because he knew he couldn't face what they were about to do to him. Or perhaps he didn't look up because he was afraid they would see their answer in his eyes— that he was one of them, that he was a priest. So he kept his head down. Yet he could smell them, the raw stench of fresh blood on their clothes, like iron heated in a forge.

"Are you one of them?" the voice asked again, insistent. The *sansculotte* put the side of his saber beneath his chin and forced his head up. In the light from above, Cheverus couldn't make out the face of the man holding the saber. Just a ragged beard, a perverse halo of luminescence surrounding his head. And his voice. The voice of Death, he would always later think.

"Are you one of them?" the man repeated.

Please, dear Lord. Help me.

"He is," said another. "He is one of them."

"Are you?" the first demanded.

"Just kill him," cried another.

"We are wasting time," said a third. "He dies."

"Wait," said the leader, holding up a hand. "Are you one of them? Speak or die."

The movement of his head from side to side along the blade that held his chin aloft was so faint at first he wasn't sure he had done it at all. His hands, still folded in prayer, trembled, and the breath in his mouth tasted foul.

"Don't listen to him," said one of them.

"The dog lies," another cried. "I saw him in the garden with the others."

"Kill him. Kill the filthy *calotin*," several chanted at once.

"Death to all priests."

"Please," he implored them.

"Kill him! Kill him! Kill him," they all cried.

"Are you one of them?" the leader asked a final time, his voice now oddly softened. It was almost seductive, silky, like a voice oiled by liquor or passion. A lover's voice. "Do you want to live or not? Speak: Are you a priest?"

The silence stretched out and out, pounding in his ears, exploding in his skull like one of those gunshots in the courtyard. *Where was God*, he wondered. *Where was He?* Cheverus saw the image of the archbishop, his throat slashed. And of Father Landry, his bloody, mutilated body. Is this what God wanted for him, to die here like a dog? His carcass hacked to pieces, his blood mingling with the sewage in the street. Was that really God's wish?

Finally, his voice barely audible, he uttered, "No." As soon as he said it out loud, he felt his soul contract inside his body, turn hard as a frozen stone that would never thaw out, not even in the flames of hell.

"What," the leader's voice cried, the faintest trace of pleasure in it, the joy of torture.

"No, I am not a priest," he said, a little louder this time.

"He is lying," the others said. "Kill him."

"Yes. Put him to the blade. Death to all *calotins*."

The leader, though, stayed their hands. "No. Leave him to his God," he said, and he laughed, a cynical sound Cheverus heard with a final sense of defeat. Then it was over. They turned, and, amazingly, left him kneeling there.

In a daze, he made it to his brother Louis's rooms, where he remained in hiding. There they would hear the reports of just how widespread the bloodshed of the September Massacres had become. Paris was now in complete chaos, fear reigned, its streets bathed in blood. The beast they would later call The Terror had begun in earnest. Having had a taste of blood, the creature went from prison to prison, slaying hundreds. At the abbey at Saint Germain des Prés alone there were more than three hundred martyred priests. At the Concièrgerie, a hundred. Nearly as many at La Force, at Chatelet, at La Salpetrière. The slaughtered priests were stripped, their bloody clothes given to their executioners, their crosses and medallions confiscated to be melted down by the government, their naked, mutilated bodies tossed onto carts and conveyed to a mass grave. The severed heads of a few clergy along with those of aristocrats and suspected loyalists, including that of the queen's friend, Princess de Lambelle, were impaled on pikes and paraded about. Those unfortunate enough not to be slaughtered on the spot were later brought before sham courts, tried on vague charges of treason, and sentenced to the guillotine. Peering from the window of his brother's rooms, Cheverus would watch those being led to their deaths. Envious of them, their deaths seeming to mock him. He had, like Peter, denied his Lord, not once, but three times. Oh, how he wished he had been one of the lucky dead. To have perished before his fear had got the best of him. At night he would get down on his knees and pray to God to take his life. *Please, O Lord, I am not worthy to be called Thy servant. Take me. Please take me.*

Then one day he put on his cassock and draped his cross about his neck. He said to his brother, "I must go to those still in prison."

"What! You will be killed, Jean," Louis cried.

"If God wills. Whatever happens, my place is there."

"Perhaps God meant for you to live," his brother pleaded.

Cheverus wanted to tell Louis the truth, that it wasn't God's will but his own cowardice that permitted him to continue alive. But he didn't. He was too ashamed.

In the end though, he was, above all else, a man guided by reason and logic, and those elements in his nature proved stronger than his wish to die. His brother was right, he argued with himself. What good could he do either his fellow priests or his God in dying now? The time for martyrdom had come and gone. He'd missed his chance. He convinced himself it would be mere vanity to die in such a way now, a pointless suicide rather than a true martyr's death. So he stayed in hiding for several weeks until his false passport finally came through. He was to pretend to be a grain merchant. Disguised once again, he journeyed in a farmer's wagon to Calais. Within a few days he'd managed to board a vessel and slip across the Channel to England, as did hundreds of other émigré priests. He remained there for four long years, working tirelessly, praying daily, trying to atone for his betrayal. And then came the letter from Father Matignon inviting him to come to the new world. In his heart, he looked upon the letter as a sign from God. This would be his penance, his second chance. This would be his absolution. So he sailed again, this time for Boston.

He never told anyone his terrible secret, his denial of his Lord, his faith, his martyred brethren. As much as he would like to have told someone, anyone, he hadn't even the courage to admit his sin. Not to his brother Louis, nor his father, nor any of his fellow émigré priests in England. Not even to his dear friend and confessor Father Matignon. Not to anyone. Only God knew of it. And He was silent.

EIGHT

After the recess for lunch, the trial reconvened. The sun had finally broken through the overcast and the day had warmed considerably. Garish beams of sunlight streamed in the long windows of the meetinghouse, the glare from the whitewashed walls as harsh as a winter morning after a snowstorm. The courtroom had grown uncomfortably warm, the air close and stuffy. Several well-dressed women fanned themselves, and a number of the men had removed their topcoats and hats. Outside in the street, vendors could be heard hawking baked goods and drinks to those gathered there.

The sheriff brought the prisoners over to where Blake was seated at the defense table and removed their manacles.

"Gentlemen," their lawyer said, without looking up. Blake had his spectacles on and was busy writing something. He was sweating profusely now, and his ears and cheeks had a high, flushed color to them. When he finally glanced over at them, Halligan saw he'd been drinking. His blue eyes were loose and distorted beneath the spectacles, his mouth agape, his breathing labored. Why the bloody fool is half-buckled, thought Halligan.

Blake removed his spectacles and put them on the table. He looked over Halligan's shoulder at Daley. "As I mentioned," he whispered, "we are holding our own. But they will be calling the Fuller boy this afternoon. His testimony worries me a great deal. I must ask you once again,

Mr. Daley: Have you no idea why he would lie about seeing you with the man's horse?"

"No, sir," Daley said nervously.

"None whatsoever?"

"I swear to God, I don't, Mr. Blake," Daley said, crossing himself.

"He never saw either of you up on the hill?" Blake continued, looking from one to the other, his glassy eyes nonetheless edged with concern.

The two shook their heads.

"And what of the money?"

"What about it?" Halligan asked.

"Are you going to persist in that absurd story that it was yours? I want to believe you didn't kill that boy. I want to believe you're not murderers. But even I have a hard time believing the money wasn't his."

He felt Daley nudge him in the back. "It was ours, Mr. Blake," Halligan said. "That's the truth."

Blake sighed heavily, his breath smelling sour. "Very well then."

In the afternoon, Mr. Hooker continued to direct the prosecution's case, while the attorney general sat stiffly in his chair, his hands folded in his lap, his expression one of haughty indifference. He seemed almost to have lost interest in the whole affair. From time to time he would glance out the window at the sky, or remove from his waistcoat pocket a silver fob watch and check the time.

The first witness that Mr. Hooker called in the afternoon was an Edward Syms, of Boston. He owned a dry goods store there. A slender, nervous man with long mustaches that nearly covered his mouth, he spoke so softly that on several occasions Mr. Hooker had to ask him to repeat his answers.

"Mr. Syms," began the assistant prosecutor, approaching the witness holding two pistols by the barrels, "are these pistols ones you sold?"

The man took one of the pistols and inspected it closely. "I believe they are," he replied. "The figure on the barrel is the same as those we sell."

"When and to whom did you sell them, sir?"

Syms fidgeted in his seat, glancing quickly about the courtroom. He mumbled something, and the prosecutor asked him to repeat his answer louder. "Sometime in the month of October last," he nearly shouted now, which seemed to startle him as much as anyone. "A man came into our store and asked the price of our pistols."

"Did you know the man to whom you sold them?"

"I did not. But he had on a dirty greatcoat. And he spake like an Irishman."

"What was his height?" asked the assistant prosecutor.

"He was of an uncommon stature. About like the prisoner," he said, pointing at Daley.

"Why are you able to recollect this sale so many months later?"

"Because it is unusual for a laboring man to purchase such pistols. So I took note of him."

"Your witness, Mr. Blake."

Without rising from his seat, Blake asked, "Sir, can you say with certainty what his countenance was like?"

"Not with certainty. He was big, as I have noted. And he spake like an Irishman."

"There are many big Irishmen," Blake said. "Can you say with any degree of certainty if either of the prisoners seated before you is the man who purchased these pistols from you?"

Mr. Syms mumbled something and Blake asked him to repeat his reply.

"I cannot say."

"Thank you. That is all."

Next, the prosecution called several witnesses that testified to having seen two men fitting the prisoners' description traveling west on the turnpike on November ninth of the previous year. One man recalled seeing them just east of where Lyon's body was found, and several had passed them to the west of the murder site. One witness, who was having his horse shod in the blacksmith shop just west of the scene of the crime, stated that he happened to see two men passing by and that "they walked very fast and were sweating." When asked if he could recognize either of the prisoners, he pointed at Daley and said, "That one, I can."

"Have you any doubt but Daley was one of them?" Mr. Hooker asked.

"I have not."

The prosecution then called Marvel Underwood, the man Marcus Lyon had worked for in Cazenovia, New York, since the previous spring. He testified to having seen the bank bills Lyon had in his possession when he left his house heading east. He said they had been issued from banks in Nantucket, Saco, Newburyport, and Bristol. The witness said Lyon kept his money in a small purse tied with a string about his neck.

Next to be called to the witness stand was Josiah Bardwell, the member of the sheriff's posse who had been the first actually to come upon the two Irishmen. He had the large, blank eyes of a fish and a prominent powder burn on his right cheek.

"Mr. Bardwell," began Hooker, "let me first extend the gratitude of the entire commonwealth for the brave role you played in the apprehension of these villains."

"I only did my duty," the man replied, smiling sheepishly.

"Would you kindly relate how you were able to capture the two suspects?"

"On Monday morning after the murder, we rode in hard pursuit of the prisoners. We heard of them at the lower ferry and again in Suffield on the west side of the Connecticut River. We continued on to New Haven and thence to Bridgeport, arriving at Norwalk by sun. We found the prisoners at Cross Landing Tavern, a public house in Rye, New York. They were about to board a ferry for New York. That one," he said, pointing at Halligan, "was seated on the stoop, and the other, the big fellow, was inside shaving. We disclosed what our business was and told them we had warrants for their arrest."

"Did you search their persons, sir?"

"We did. I found some silver coins and between them some eighty dollars in bank bills." He then cited the banks the bills had been issued from: a Nantucket bank, a Saco bank, a Newburyport bank, and a Bristol bank.

Mr. Blake objected then, stating that if the bills were of such importance to the prosecution's case, they should be introduced as evidence. But Judge Sedgwick overruled him.

"You earlier heard the testimony of Marvel Underwood," Mr. Hooker went on. "Were not these bills you confiscated from the prisoners drawn on the exact same banks as those Mr. Lyon had in his possession when he left Cazenovia?"

"They seem to be, yes."

Halligan glanced over at the jury. The blacksmith, his headed canted at a slight angle, was staring at him again. His massive dark hands lay curled in thick fists on his lap, as if ready for a fight.

"What else did you find when you searched them?" Mr. Hooker asked.

"We discovered in the inside of their greatcoats deep pockets made in the lining. I asked them the use of these pockets and they replied they were to carry their bottle in." Then he added with an ironic smile, "Though they had not a bottle with them at the time."

"Could these pockets have carried pistols?" Mr. Hooker asked.

"I suppose. They were shaped in the manner of holsters."

"Mr. Bardwell, how far is it from Wilbraham to Rye, New York?"

"One hundred and twenty miles thereabouts, sir."

"And from Boston to Wilbraham?"

"Eighty. Maybe ninety."

"Did you inquire of the prisoners, why it took them from Tuesday to Saturday coming from Boston, a mere eighty miles, but only two days in traveling all the way to Rye, New York, a distance of some one hundred and twenty miles?"

"I did. They did not assign any reason."

"What did you deduce from such a fact?"

"I must object, your honor," said Blake. "It calls on the witness to venture an opinion."

Judge Sedgwick pursed his lips. "I shall allow him to answer."

"I would think they were trying to run from something," he replied.

"Yes, indeed. To run from something. Thank you, Mr. Bardwell."

Now and then Blake would interject a comment, make an objection or cross-examine a witness with a few questions of his own. But mostly he sat quietly, dipping his pen into his inkwell and scribbling things down in his writing tablet. Once, both Blake and Hooker went up to the judges' bench to discuss some point of law. While they were occupied,

Halligan turned and surveyed the courtroom. He saw Reverend Williams sitting behind the prosecution table. He had his Bible in his hand and his eyes were shut, as if he was praying. Halligan looked for Mrs. Lyon but didn't see her. He saw her husband but not her. Had she found the morning session too upsetting? He noticed a man standing against the back wall, appearing to be writing in a tablet book. He was heavyset, with silvery hair, and he wore a long gray frock coat even in the heat of the room. When Halligan looked more closely he saw that he was actually sketching something. His hand moved freely over the page. He would look up from his work, stare at them closely, and then return his attention to his tablet. Probably drawing the courtroom scene and the portraits of the accused that would appear in various newspaper accounts and broadsides to be sold after it was over.

Then Halligan spotted the Daleys. The mother had her beads wrapped tightly around her fleshy hand and she seemed to be mouthing the words: *Our Father who art in heaven* . . . She looked ill, her face a mottled pink, the flesh around her eyes dark and sunken. Finola Daley sat next to the old woman, her son covered in a blanket in her arms. She had an expression of someone trying desperately not to be terrified. Her face was a tense, pale mask, her mouth held in a kind of grimace. Occasionally she'd bend her head, as if to whisper something to the child in her arms. Finola Daley happened to glance in Halligan's direction and their eyes met briefly. There was an awkward moment, when she didn't know how to acknowledge him, whether to smile or wave. At last she gave what he thought was a little nod of her head and the merest hint of a smile, the sort of look that passed between two people who shared an unpleasant secret. It seemed to imply some vague charge or other, an unspoken trust.

Around five there was another short break. Daley told the guards he needed to relieve himself, so they clapped him in irons and took him out back to the privy. Blake was hunkered over his journal writing something. The drink had worn off him now and he was simply tired looking, frayed, the flesh of his face sagging. *Don't*, Halligan warned himself.

Don't be a bloody fool. But he kept thinking of the look Finola had given him earlier, the one that seemed to imply something. And then he thought of the look in Bridie's eyes, that last time he'd seen her. *Do you love me, James?* Her look frightened and imploring.

He leaned over toward the lawyer and whispered, "Mr. Blake?"

The attorney stopped writing, glanced with bleary eyes at him. "Yes?"

"What if I say I did it?"

"Pardon?"

"What if I say 'twas me killed Lyon?"

"What are you talking about?" Blake asked, the skin of his forehead furrowing into that fleshy M. "Are you saying you want to change your plea, Mr. Halligan?"

"I'm asking what would happen if I said I did it. That Dom had nothing to do with it. That he was just going along with the story to protect me."

"Blazes man!" the attorney hissed in an undertone. "This is a fine time to be telling me this. Is it true?"

Don't, Halligan warned himself a final time. He wasn't used to putting anyone before himself. He'd never seen the sense in that. He'd come to the aid of that young boy who was being beaten by the half-sir and what did it get him? Two years' hard labor. But there was nothing to lose now. Better that only one of them went to the gallows. What, after all, was holding him here? What did he have to live for, except more years of the same? But it was different with Dom. He had something. Something to live for. That woman and child back there. Was that the look in her eye?

"Could you save Dominic?" he asked Blake. "If I said he had nothing to do with it."

"But is it true?" Blake asked again, leaning in close, his breath hot and foul.

"What if I said it was? Could you save him?"

"But *is* it true?"

"Is what true?" inquired Daley, who had just returned to his seat.

"Your friend here wants to say he killed Lyon," Blake explained, wagging his large head in exasperation.

Daley looked at Halligan in surprise. "What in God's name are ye talkin' about, Jamy?"

"Dom, you have a wife and child to think about."

"Get out with you now. I'll have none o' that."

"Think about it, Dom."

"No. There's nothing to think about. I'll not let you do it, James."

"Could it work, Mr. Blake?" Halligan asked of the lawyer again. "If I confessed to the murder, would it keep Dom from the rope?"

Blake shrugged. "I honestly don't know. They testified to seeing him with Lyon's horse, not you."

"But what if I say I acted alone? That Dom was just going along to protect me? Is there a chance you could save him?"

"I suppose there's a chance," Blake conceded. "We could ask to change your plea to guilty. They might accept it. And they might offer something less than death for Mr. Daley. Might, I'm saying. It might also just be the last nail in both your coffins."

"I'm willing to take the chance," Halligan said.

"Well, *I'm* not," Daley cried.

"Could we have a moment alone, Mr. Blake?" asked Halligan.

The lawyer sighed. "Well be quick about it. I'll get some fresh air."

Halligan turned to Daley. "It was my idea not to turn that money in," he explained. "And then to lie about it. If not for that, we might not even be here."

"We both of us wanted to keep it, and that's the truth. I won't let you do it, Jamy."

"But think on it, Dom."

"No!"

"If not for yourself, think of your wife and child then."

"Stop it!"

"Listen to me. You need to think of them. You need to live for them!"

Daley turned to stare at his wife seated in the back of the room. She was rocking the child in her arms. Daley gazed at them for several long seconds. His big Adam's apple bobbed twice as he swallowed hard. Halligan saw he was considering it. The offer was like a hand held out to a drowning man.

"Do you want to make your wife a widow?" Halligan asked. "Do you want your son to be fatherless? Is that what you want, Dom?"

"No, of course not. Christ Almighty."

"Then it's the only way. What do I have to lose? Nothing."

"You got your life to live same as me."

"I don't have anybody would care whether I lived or died. You do."

Daley was silent for a while, staring off into space. He was weighing things, thinking of that piece of land he was going to buy, seeing his son grow up. He glanced at his family again. Finally, he grabbed Halligan's wrist, squeezing it hard. "I wish to God I could let you do it. But I cannot."

"Dom—"

"No! I'll hear no more of this. We're in this together. We both live or we both hang." Daley touched Halligan's shoulder. "But thank ye anyway, Jamy boy."

After the break, the prosecution called their star witness, the young boy Laertes Fuller. He was obviously nervous before the large crowd. A thin boy of thirteen, Fuller had large ears, a sallow complexion, and the timorous eyes of a dog who knew well its master's boot. Blake objected to the prosecution calling a boy of such tender years, citing precedence that held fourteen as the usual age at which the law recognized mental competence in a witness. Judge Sedgwick overruled him yet again, saying the court would allow the boy's testimony and leave it to the jurors to decide the weight they would give to it.

As soon as the boy was sworn in, the attorney general took over for the prosecution. He rose slowly and approached the witness. His limp seemed more pronounced now, and he walked stiffly, with a slight stoop. He paused dramatically beside the boy and turned to view the courthouse. It was so quiet you could hear a horsefly buzzing, banging relentlessly against the glass of one of the windows.

"Do you understand the seriousness of these proceedings, Master Fuller?" he asked the boy.

"I do, sir," he replied, glancing sheepishly at the attorney general.

"Where do you live, Laertes?" Sullivan asked.

"In Wilbraham. On the mountain there."

"How far is your home from the place where the murder was committed?"

"Not far. Less than a quarter mile, I reckon."

"Please tell the court what you saw on the ninth of November last."

The boy glanced at the two Irishmen, then quickly averted his gaze like a hand drawn away from a hot iron.

"About one o'clock I spied two men on the turnpike going west. They passed on and left my sight. In a few minutes I went upon the same road and saw them coming back."

"What were they doing?" the attorney general asked.

"One was leading, and the other driving a horse. They turned up the old road that goes up the mountain and I followed them. When they were at the top of the hill, one of them stopped, and the other jumped on the horse and rode him off. I got over a stone wall nearby and took to gathering apples under a tree."

"Why apples?"

The boy shrugged his thin shoulders. "I had not eaten lunch, and I was hungry, sir."

Sullivan smiled benevolently. "Then what did you see?"

"That man," he said haltingly, pointing at Daley, "come up to the wall and looked directly at me."

"What did you do then?"

"I ran home."

"You ran? Were you afraid?"

"Not then, sir. I had not a reason to be afraid then. I only learned of what happened the next day. I was just cold is all."

"I see. How far were they from you when you first saw them walking along the turnpike road?"

"Some hundred feet or so."

"How far were they from the place where Lyon was killed?"

"Not far. I would say it was but fifty feet. Perhaps sixty."

The attorney general removed a handkerchief from his cuff and delicately dabbed the sweat that had gathered on his thin upper lip.

"At the top of the hill, did you observe the horse?" he asked the boy.

"I did not pay much attention to him, sir."

"But you took note of what color he was, did you not?"

"Yes. A reddish color."

"Did you see him afterwards?"

"Yes, sir. I saw him wandering loose in the pasture of John Bliss."

The attorney general limped back to his table and lifted up a sheet of paper. He looked at it for a moment, then returned to the witness.

"Which of the prisoners was driving him?"

"That one, sir," the boy said, pointing again at Daley.

"Did you see the other's face?"

"I did not."

"After their arrest they were brought back to Springfield," Mr. Sullivan continued. "From amongst a large group of men, did you not freely and of your own accord select Daley as the man you saw driving the horse?"

"I did, sir."

"You have sworn on the Bible to tell the truth, Laertes. Have you the least doubt but that Dominic Daley, the man who sits before you today, was the selfsame man whom you saw driving Marcus Lyon's horse?"

"No, sir. None," he said, gaining courage enough to stare at the defendants. "It was him, all right."

"Thank you, Laertes. You are a very brave young man," said the Attorney General.

Daley whispered to Halligan, "*Och*. Gimme five minutes with the little shite, and I'd make 'im spit out the truth."

Blake walked to the front, carrying a piece of paper on which he'd jotted down his scribblings. His head tilted downward, the boy watched the approach of the defense attorney's squat figure warily, eyeing him from beneath his brows.

"You must be tired, Laertes," the lawyer said. "After your long journey here."

The boy lifted his shoulders unevenly before letting them settle. "A little, sir."

"Given the lateness of the hour, I shall endeavor to make my questions as brief as possible. To begin, why did you follow the defendants up the hill?"

"I was curious."

"Curious? Yet you had no reason to suspect anything then, correct?"

The boy shrugged, glanced at the attorney general. "I don't know."

"But as you told Mr. Sullivan, you didn't learn of the murder until the following day."

The boy pondered that for a moment, then replied, "Like I said, I was curious."

"Yes, you seem like a very curious boy to me," Blake said, glancing down at his notes. "Now you said, and I quote, 'I spied two men on the turnpike going west. They passed on and left my sight. In a few minutes, I went upon the same road and saw them coming back.' 'A few minutes' are your precise words, are they not, Laertes?"

"Yes, sir."

"Exactly how long is a few minutes?"

The boy shrugged again. "I don't know."

"Well, from the time you first saw them walking west along the turnpike to the time you saw them leading the horse, was it five minutes? Ten? Fifteen?"

The boy thought for a moment. "I would say it was not more than fifteen minutes."

"You are quite certain of that, Laertes? That is was no more than fifteen minutes."

"I am, sir."

"When you saw the two men the second time, did you happen to notice if their trousers were wet?"

"Wet, sir?"

"Yes, were their pantlegs wet or dry?"

"I can't say one way or the other."

"Did you notice anything about their clothing, Laertes? Were their clothes muddy? Did they have blood on them?"

The boy glanced around the courtroom, confused.

"I don't know, sir."

"I see. Now between the first and second times you saw them, did you hear the discharge of a pistol, Laertes?"

He shook his head. "I can't say that I did."

"And yet they had only gone, to quote you again, 'a few minutes' before you saw them a second time. Surely they were close enough for you to have heard a pistol shot."

The boy frowned, looking as if he were trying to figure out the right answer to a math question. "Maybe I heard one and forgot it. It's been some months since."

"Yes, it has been a long time, hasn't it?" Blake said, smiling condescendingly. "Now, Laertes, you testified that after their arrest, you were able to identify Daley from amongst a large group of men assembled in the jail in Springfield. 'Freely and of your own accord,' my learned colleague, Mr. Sullivan, stated."

"That is correct, sir. I picked them out."

"But were not Daley and Halligan wearing manacles at the time?"

"They might of been."

"Were they not, in fact, the only two in the room who were handcuffed?"

"Maybe. Yes, I think they did have irons on."

"So in point of fact, it would have been easier to tell the accused from the others, would it not?"

"I remember him, sir," the boy said, fingering Daley. His tone now was peevish, almost truculent, but he also appeared on the verge of crying. "I saw him. I did."

"Did you indeed?" Blake said, smiling almost cruelly. "Now, Laertes. I wonder if you can help me with something."

The boy stared sullenly at Blake, from beneath his brows. He was wary of the man's questions.

"I am trying to understand exactly how this could have happened as you say it did. Between the time it took from when you first saw these men pass by on the turnpike and when you next saw them leading the horse up the mountain, you are absolutely certain that only fifteen minutes had elapsed?"

"Yes." But there was in his answer now a certain hesitancy, a tentativeness that hadn't been there before.

200 MICHAEL C. WHITE

Blake walked over to the jury, his broad back to the witness so the boy could not see the expression on his face.

"Are we to believe, Laertes, that it took a mere fifteen minutes for these two men to do all they are accused of doing?" He didn't wait for nor did he expect an answer. As he spoke, he passed in front of the jurors, pausing to eye each in turn. He counted off his points on his fat fingers. "To accost Mr. Lyon on a well-traveled road in the broad light of day. To shoot him and pull him from his horse. To engage him in what must surely have been a fierce struggle, Mr. Lyon having been a young laboring man of robust build who was fighting for his very life. To beat him so savagely that his skull was caved in and that one pistol was broken in the bargain. To rifle through his person as well as his saddlebags and portmanteau to find where he kept his money. Afterwards, to drag him down into the river, there to locate and place on him a stone weighing some sixty pounds. Having accomplished all of this, I might add, without getting their trousers wet or being splattered with what must have been an abundance of blood. Finally, to drive the horse up the mountain several hundred yards. And to do all of this in a mere fifteen minutes."

He had stopped in front of the blacksmith and was looking down at the man. The blacksmith in turn was staring at the boy, watching him intently. "Frankly, young man, your entire tale strains belief," Blake said. "What I also find puzzling is the fact that you are able to recall some things so vividly but others not in the least. You remember Mr. Daley's face with such unassailable assurance, but cannot recall hearing a gunshot. You were later able to pick out the horse as being the one you saw up on the mountain, but when you first spotted him, you did not remember much about the animal. You recall the men returning but not whether their trousers were wet or had any blood on them after such a sanguinary attack." The lawyer turned and walked back over to where Laertes Fuller sat. "Come, come, young man. Do you really expect us to believe that it happened as you say it happened?"

"Yes," the boy said, his voice near to cracking. His eyes were moist, and it was obvious to all he was fighting back tears.

"It has been a long day, Laertes," Blake said with a paternal air of kindness. The boy looked warily up at him. "We are all very tired. Why don't you just tell us what really happened that day so we can all go home?"

"But . . . I told you. I did."

"You told us a story that does not make much sense. What did you really see?"

The boy's face had reddened. He looked first toward the prosecution table and then over at the jury, before turning to look on Blake again.

"I told you what happened."

"Did you?"

"Yes," he said, "I've told you the truth. I have." But his voice was hollow, unconvincing. Halligan glanced over his shoulder at the people in the courtroom. They were staring at the boy with an element of doubt in their eyes now that hadn't been there before. *Well, I'll be damned,* Halligan thought.

"Are you sure you're not covering for someone else?" Blake continued. "The real perpetrators of this horrid crime."

"No," he said, and now he actually started to cry. Tears slid down his sallow cheeks. "I'm not, I tell you. I told you what I saw. I'm not lying."

"You've told us a nice story," Blake said condescendingly. "Thank you, Laertes."

It was late in the evening when the last witness had finished his testimony. Outside, darkness had already fallen, and it had turned chilly with a cool wind coming in from the mountains to the northwest. Yet most of the large crowd remained, eager to hear the verdict. Through the windows, the spectators in the courtroom could see torches and lanterns gleaming in the night. A large bonfire had been built on the center green, around which many had assembled for warmth. Some had taken to passing around jugs of hard cider. With it the crowd, which had been fairly sedate for most of the trial, had grown more boisterous and rowdy. There were shouts and cries, and the sound of drunken laughter drifted into the courthouse.

When Blake finally got up to give his summation, it was approaching nine o'clock. As he addressed the jury, he paced about the courtroom. Though he held his notes in his hand, he hardly referred to them, preferring to speak unaided. He went over the evidence again. He argued that the prosecution had produced not a single eyewitness to the murder, and that all the other evidence was merely presumptive in nature. He took issue with the guns found at the murder scene, saying that the only proof the prosecution put forward that they were owned by the defendants was that the buyer of the pistols "talked like an Irishman." More to the point, that Dr. Merrick had testified that the bullet that struck Lyon did not match either of the two supposed murder weapons, and that the prosecution had proposed no explanation for this. Likewise, Blake said, the prosecution did not even offer into evidence the money that was taken from the defendants. He forcefully argued against the point the prosecution had made about the speed with which the two traveled after the crime, saying the road was level and the weather much improved south of Springfield, and, he added, murderers would assuredly not have traveled so openly or carelessly as these two men had. He said the "supposed" holsters were merely pockets intended to hold refreshments for thirsty travelers. He spent a long while pointing out the flimsy nature of the rest of the so-called "evidence" the prosecution offered, which was mostly hearsay or conjecture. Finally, he spoke for nearly a half hour alone on the various inconsistencies and flaws and downright contradictions of the prosecution's main witness, Laertes Fuller.

Halligan had to admit that he was favorably surprised by Blake's abilities as an orator. The man spoke with clarity and reason in mostly measured tones. At the same time, despite his cold, he managed to infuse his voice with passion and fervor, and above all, with conviction. He made those listening believe that he believed the two were innocent. In fact, by the time Blake was winding up his summation, Halligan had felt a subtle but clear change come over the courtroom. As he glanced around, he saw some here and there nodding in agreement with the things Blake was saying, others whispering amongst themselves. The expressions on the faces of the jurors had also undergone a decided transformation. Before they had, to a person, a hardened, cynical look; now some had an expression that might best be described as uncertain. For the first time, a few of them had had their unassailable notions of the guilt of the prisoners challenged. Even the blacksmith was no longer staring at him, but seemed to be weighing each of Blake's words as if it were a piece of iron to which he would have to give shape. Halligan allowed himself a small measure of optimism. Perhaps they did have a chance after all.

Finally, the defense attorney walked over to where the jury sat. Some of them were yawning and fidgeting in their seats. After all, they had been there since nine that morning, and it was getting on toward eleven in the evening.

"In the investigation of every case," Blake continued, his hands folded over his belly, "the jury are pledged by their oaths, to guard every avenue of the mind against the approach of prejudice. That the prisoners here before the bar have been tried, convicted, and condemned in almost every barroom and barber's shop, and in every other place of public resort in the county, nay, in the entire commonwealth, is a fact which will not be contested. That the defendants have already received the penalty of death in many minds is also beyond dispute. But gentlemen, you have taken the oath to avoid such prejudices and to weigh the evidence carefully and impartially, and to discriminate between idle rumors and gossip, and the facts which have been this day presented to you.

"There is another and more dangerous species of prejudice it is my duty to warn you against. I allude to the inveterate hostility against the people of that wretched country from which the prisoners have emigrated, for which the people of New England are peculiarly distinguished. How far this hostility is the result of narrow and illiberal opinion, or how far it is justified by the character and conduct of those who have come among us, it is not for us here to decide. Whether they are wandering fugitives from justice or the exiled victims of oppression, do not, I beg of you, believe them guilty simply because they go by the name of Irishmen. Take, for example, the testimony of Mr. Syms. He assumed the man who came into his store was guilty of some wrong simply because he spoke in the suspicious dialect of their country. His mind is infected with the national prejudice which would lead him to prejudge the prisoners simply because they are Irishmen. Pronounce then a verdict against them! Condemn them to the gibbet! Send them 'to their great account with all their imperfections on their heads,' to paraphrase Hamlet. Hold out an awful warning to the wretched fugitives from that

oppressed and persecuted nation, saying despite our boasted philan-
thropy, we have no mercy for a wandering and expatriated fugitive from
that blasted nation! Tell them that the name of an Irishman is, among
us, but another name for robber and assassin, that when a crime of unexpected atrocity is perpetrated among us, we look around for an Irishman
to lay the blame upon.

"The lives of these men," Blake said, coming to stand before the prisoners, "are now consigned to your hands. You have been asked to pass
judgment not based on prejudice or age-old hatred of their countrymen,
but on 'plain, direct, and manifest proof—the sort of legal proof which is
deemed necessary by the law but which my esteemed colleagues have
clearly failed to present for you today. It is neither my right nor my incli-
nation to attempt to arouse your sympathy or passions for these poor
wretches. I may not therefore speak of the afflicted mother and wife and
child of one of the prisoners—who appear humbly in this courtroom
today." As he said this, he pointed toward the back of the room where
the Daleys sat huddled together. Everyone turned to gaze at them. "Their
lives are interwoven with that of Mr. Daley. They are tied to him by the
strongest threads of familial love and devotion, but threads which must
ultimately be severed by the same stroke that dooms him to the gibbet.
Still, I may, without incurring your displeasure, remind you of the various
lives your decision will affect. Before you proceed to your solemn duty, let
me remind you that there is another than human tribunal where the best
of us will have occasion to look back on the little good we may have
done in this life. In that solemn trial may your verdict on this day give
assurance to your hopes and afford you strength and consolation in the
awful presence of an adjudging God. I thank you, gentlemen."

When he sat down, Halligan could see the sweat pouring down his
reddened face. His collar was soaked and he was breathing hard.

" 'Twas a right smart piece of speakin', Mr. Blake," said Daley.

The attorney nodded. Though he looked like he could use a drink of
rum, his eyes were filled with that same earlier nervous energy. His fat
fingers anxiously tapped on the table.

The attorney general then rose and walked slowly over to the jury.

"Gentlemen," he said, "the solemnity of this trial tends to establish a proper estimate of human life. The counsel for the defense has urged, with irresistible eloquence, the importance of this trial for the prisoners. It now remains but for me to arrange the evidence. If in the performance of my office, there should appear to be a warmth of expression or a zeal of conduct, which would bear unreasonably hard on the prisoners, you will impute it to error, and not from any opinion I have of the prisoners' guilt. The judges are, by constitution and the laws, to be of counsel for the prisoners, and I am relieved from the apprehension I should otherwise feel, by the consideration that any undue impressions I may make on your minds will be fairly balanced by these men in their direction to you, and thus lead you into the path of your duty."

At this he glanced at Judge Sedgwick, who seemed to visibly stiffen.

"Your verdict will determine the fate of the prisoners as to life or death. You have sworn that you will well and truly try, and true deliverance make between the commonwealth and the prisoners whom you have in charge, according to the evidence. As my esteemed colleague," he said, casting a glance at Blake, "has stated, you are not to suffer any prejudice to have weight in your minds, and it is of no consequence to you what the opinion of the multitude attending the trial may be." Here the attorney general paused, glancing around the packed courtroom. The jury, too, followed his lead, surveying the crowd uneasily. "The very idea that you may be prejudiced against these men, as my esteemed colleague has implied, because they are foreigners, Irishmen and Catholics, can have no foundation but in a warm imagination. The supposition that such an idea could operate in a charge against *you* would be an ill treatment of your characters. The prisoners are men and as such are entitled to as fair a trial as men of the first rank. The law, gentlemen, must remain sacred."

Sullivan spoke for some twenty or thirty minutes more. Finally, he thanked the jury and hobbled over to his seat. Before sitting down, he threw a glance in Halligan's direction.

Blake leaned toward them and whispered, "They've not proved their case against you. I think we're all right."

Before the jury was sent off for their deliberations, Judge Sedgwick said a few words in his charge to them, about the presumption of innocence and of reasonable doubt and the categories of evidence. Near the end, he explained, "Your verdict must finally depend upon the testimony of Laertes Fuller. You have been told by the defense that this boy is not to be believed, that he is too young, that his story is inaccurate or incredible," he said, looking at Blake. "Of this, gentlemen, you are the judges. But we deem it our duty to observe to you that he hath ever been consistent. That the story he told to the coroner at the inquest and to the justices who examined the prisoners after they were apprehended and which he has related to you today has ever been uniform and consistent."

Blake stood and exclaimed, "With all due respect, your honor——" But the judge cut him short, telling him to be seated.

"Gentlemen of the jury," Sedgwick resumed, "this brings you to a point which leaves but little room for doubt. If you believe this witness, you must therefore return a verdict of conviction."

"Your honor, I really must object," Blake said, standing again. "The boy's testimony must stand on its own merit."

"Overruled, counselor."

"This is highly irregular, your honor. Sir Edward Coke, in *favorem vitae*, has written——"

"*Sit down*, sir!" Judge Sedgwick commanded, pointing his gavel at him. "I shall not warn you again." Blake finally complied, dropping wearily into his seat. He shook his head, a disgruntled look on his soft, fleshy face.

The cause was then submitted to the jury, and at the command of the sheriff two guards escorted the twelve men up the street to Pomeroy's Tavern, there to conduct their deliberations. When the crowd saw the jury emerge from the meetinghouse, a great roar rang out. A few called out to the jurors by name, reminding them of their duty to the dead young man or exhorting them to make those "paddies" pay for their crime. The prisoners were again placed in manacles and brought down into the cellar to await the jury's deliberations. Daley and Halligan sat on the dirt floor. Soon Blake joined them.

"What happens now?" Halligan asked the attorney.

"We wait," replied Blake, who remained standing. "Try to relax. It may be a while."

Halligan was going to ask him what he thought their chances were, but he decided not to.

"Your family may see you now," Blake said to Daley. "I'll go arrange it."

In a little while, Daley's family appeared in the cellar, escorted by several guards. Finola Daley was in front, with the mother behind her, holding the child. On seeing them, Daley's face suddenly brightened.

" 'Faith, 'tis good to see you, Finola," he cried, standing and going to his wife. With the manacles on he couldn't hug her, so he had to make do with holding her hands. She lifted his hands to her mouth and kissed them, her tears spilling onto his knuckles. His mother stood back, allowing them a moment together. Halligan thought of all the private things Daley had had him write to her, and all those she'd written back. Despite this, there was about them, he noticed, an awkwardness, a polite and distant strangeness as between two people just beginning to court. Perhaps it was due to the time they'd been apart or to his changed appearance, or perhaps because they were surrounded by strangers. She touched his long, straggly beard.

"They don't let us shave," he explained, embarrassed.

She smiled self-consciously, like a young girl. "It makes you look . . . I don't know. Handsome."

"Musha, dear," said Daley. "I missed you so."

"I missed you, too." By degrees, they lost their strangeness with each other. She put her arms around him and, standing on tiptoe as he was so much taller, kissed him lightly on the cheek. Then she turned toward the old woman and the baby. "Say hello to your mother," Finola said.

"Hello, Mam," he said, taking her hand, kissing her on the forehead. "Thanks for coming."

"How are you, son?" she asked, her gray eyes filling with tears.

"I'm all right. And you?"

"Fine," she said, wiping her eyes. "Look who we brung."

His mother unwrapped the blanket so that he could see his son's sleeping face.

"The poor thing is dead tired. It's been a long day for him," Finola Daley said.

"Sure and he's gettin' big," her husband exclaimed.

"Can he hold him?" his mother asked, turning to one of the guards. The man nodded, and Daley's mother handed him his son.

With the handcuffs on he held his son awkwardly, cautiously, as if he were a piece of fine crystal he feared dropping. He stared down at his son's sleeping face. "Would ye lookit the lad. Who's he favor?" Daley asked of no one in particular.

"I think he favors you, Dom," his mother replied.

"Why, he's the spittin' image of you, dear," his wife said.

Daley smiled proudly. He bent over and kissed the baby on the forehead. The child stirred, then woke up, staring wide-eyed at the strange figure above him.

"Hey, little fellow," Daley said. "It's me. Your da."

Warily, the baby continued to watch the face hovering above him.

"Where's your manners, son?" his mother chided him. "Ain't you gonna introduce us to your friend?"

"Sorry. This is Jamy Halligan. It's him as writes those fine letters."

Halligan stood and went over to them, the chains rattling on the floor.

"Glad to meet you, Mrs. Daley," he offered. "Much obliged for the clothes."

"Was the church bought 'em for you," the mother said. "Father Cheverus give us the money."

"I hope they fit," the wife said. Then, blushing, she added, "We didn't know what cut of man you were."

"They fit fine," he replied. "Thank you."

"When this is all over, Mr. Halligan," said the old lady, "will you not come and stay with us for a bit?"

"If you'd like."

"We would be honored, Mr. Halligan," said Finola Daley.

"Jamy can read a book this fat," Daley bragged, holding his fingers three inches apart. "He said he'd learn me to read and write."

"Wouldn't that be grand?" his wife said, smiling at Halligan.

They sat on the dirt floor and talked for a while, though not a word about the trial. They spoke about the baby. About Dominic's father, who regretted that he couldn't come but sent his love. About his brothers and sisters back in Boston. About his mother's health, which she said was improving day by day. About Father Cheverus and how it was thanks to him that they were permitted this visit.

"'Twas him got Mr. Sullivan to let us in," the mother said.

"Father's a good man," Daley said.

"A bit particular, he is," the mother added, "but a good man."

"How's the weather back home?" Daley asked.

"Rainy and cold," Finola replied. "How has it been out here?"

"The same. Though I don't get out much," he added, smiling sheepishly.

The old lady laughed awkwardly. "Would you listen to him. Have they been giving you enough to eat? You look like you lost some weight, son."

"I'm fine, Ma," Daley replied.

"You're hardly but skin and bones. I'll fatten you up when you get home."

Home, Halligan thought. *Bloody little chance of seeing that again.*

They chatted for another half hour. As they did, Halligan stole an occasional glance at Finola and her child. Up close, she wasn't much to look at. Plain like the baby, pale, gaunt featured. And so thin. Finola did have a pretty smile though. A sad smile, one that withheld something. While she didn't look a thing like Bridie, Finola made him think of her. He thought how, if by some stroke of luck he did get out of this mess, he might write to her. Yes, he just might. But what would he say? That he was sorry. That he'd made a terrible mistake. Maybe to show his sincerity, he would even offer to have her come now, that is, if she still wanted to join him. He realized that was probably asking too much. Leaving her the way he had, all alone, with child, shamed before her father, before her people. Not a word from him in nearly four years. No doubt she hated him, and had every right to. She'd probably already put him behind her, gotten on with her life, married someone else, someone more of her station. If not out of love at least out of necessity, to give the child a name, and her the gloss of respectability. It was crazy to think she would forgive him, much less come. Still, the idea glistened in the darkness of his mind like the first star at night, silvery and sparkling.

My Dearest Bridie, he thought. Then he decided not to use *my*. What right did he have to suggest any sort of ownership of her feelings now? *Dear Bridie,* he started over. *I haven't the words to explain to you my heart's feelings.* That, too, was wrong. Why would she care what resided in his heart now, or believe what he said of it? So he began a third time, saying simply, *Dear Bridie, Can you ever find it in your heart to forgive one so foolish?* Yes, that was better.

But Blake appeared then, huffing and puffing from the climb down the stairs. His broad face was blank and palid as a cheese wheel. "The jury has returned," he said flatly. "We must go up."

They stood. Finola Daley leaned toward her husband and whispered something into his ear which made him smile. Then she kissed him again, on the lips, pressing her thin body into his. She was smiling and sobbing both, her thin shoulders quivering.

"Let us say a prayer," Mrs. Daley said. They got down on their knees in a circle on the dirt floor. They held hands. "Join us, Mr. Halligan," the old lady offered.

He knelt, but he didn't pray. Instead, he thought of the letter to Bridie.

The clerk called the court to order. When everything was quiet, Judge Sedgwick told the prisoners to stand and face the jury. Then he asked the foreman, "Have you reached a verdict, gentlemen?"

"We have, your honor," replied the man, clearing his voice. He was a tall, bearded man with the gnarled, battered hands of a stonemason. Halligan kept his eyes not on him but on the blacksmith for some reason. The dark-skinned man returned his look, his gaze severe and unwavering. Halligan knew the verdict even before the foreman said, "We find the prisoners guilty."

"So say you all?" the judge asked.

"We do."

The courtroom buzzed. One man rushed outside to tell the spectators in the street of the guilty verdict. Immediately the church bells tolled and somewhere in the distance several gunshots resounded across the valley. Halligan glanced over at Daley, who was looking in shock at his family. His jaw hung open, his blue-gray eyes empty husks. "What will she do?" he said. "What will she do?" Halligan touched his forearm. "It's all right, Dom," he said, though he knew it wouldn't be.

The two judges conferred with each other for several minutes. As they did so, Blake leaned over to them and whispered, "I am sorry. I did my best." His face was sunken with gloom, his pretty blue eyes downcast.

Though he was numbed by the verdict, Halligan patted the attorney's arm and said, "You did a fine job, Mr. Blake. Nobody can say any different." He actually felt a certain fondness now for the fat man.

"Don't give up hope. I will appeal the verdict," Blake said.

The judge pounded his gavel to quiet the room.

"Before I pass sentence on you," he said, staring at the two, "I deem it my duty to observe that it is almost impossible to doubt of your guilt. Therefore you ought to entertain no hope of mercy from the government. The crime of which you are found guilty is the highest against the law of nature, of which a man in a state of civilized society can commit. For a crime so horrid, you have demonstrated that you are unworthy of the society of men. Therefore you must look beyond this life, to direct all your hopes to another and eternal existence. You will very soon appear before a tribunal infinitely more awful than that which has now investigated your guilt. I entreat you to seek for reconcilement and forgiveness from the Almighty. To this end, a learned and pious clergy will be most happy to give you instruction in the weeks ahead." As he said this, he looked toward the minister, Solomon Williams, seated there in the courtroom. "That you may repent your crime and be forgiven, I most sincerely and fervently pray.

"It now only remains that we do as our duty enjoins, pronounce against you the sentence of the law. Therefore, I order that you, Dominic Daley, and you, James Halligan, be remanded to the prison from which you came, to remain there until such a time as the court desires and from thence be taken to the place of execution and that you there be hung by the neck until you are dead. Furthermore, that your bodies be dissected and anatomized. May God Almighty have mercy on your souls." He slammed the gavel down on the table and the trial was over.

Chaos broke out. People were rushing about, talking, calling out, shouting. Some ran outside to inform the crowd of the sentence. When they heard it, another great cheer went up from those assembled. The guards quickly moved to surround the prisoners. Daley fell down on his knees. "Mother o' God," he cried over and over. He folded his hands and began to pray.

"Don't lose hope," Blake shouted above the din. "I'll file an appeal. It's not over."

Halligan nodded, but he knew otherwise. They were as good as dead already, that's all there was to it. It was as if a heavy steel door had closed shut on him.

PART III

The present week has been a very interesting one, as the Supreme Court [heard the case of] those unhappy murderers Halligan and Daley, two Irish Men, that have been guilty of murder. . . . the trial was very solemn, and affecting, and what added to the painful feelings was the presence of the wife and mother of Daley, one of the prisoners. But their sentence before an earthly tribunal is pass'd.

—JOURNAL OF MRS. MARY SHEPHERD

NORTHAMPTON, MASSACHUSETTS

FOR SALE AT THIS OFFICE

Price 9 penny single, 1 dollar per dozen
A Brief Account of the murder of Marcus Lyon;
The detection of the murderers, their trial, &c.
Written by a gentleman who resides near
Where the murder was committed

Man lifts his hand against his brother,
And brethren murder one another:
The bloody shafts of death are hurl'd,
From man to man, throughout the world.

—THE REPUBLICAN SPY

APRIL 29, 1806

Daley seemed to be in some degree agitated and immediately after sentence was pronounced fell upon his knees, apparently in prayer, but Halligan, who previous to the trial was by many supposed much the least criminal, exhibited stronger marks of total insensibility or obstinate and hardened wickedness than is often witnessed.

—HAMPSHIRE FEDERALIST

APRIL 26, 1806

Two men riding along, fired at an eagle and killed him; an Irishman coming by at the same time, says he, "You might have saved your powder and shot, for the very fall would have killed him."

—THE REPUBLICAN SPY

1806

NINE

Cheverus was in the parlor of the rectory making final preparations for his trip north to the Indian mission. He was packing things into a large battered trunk that had come across the ocean with him. He carefully laid all that he would need in the faraway forests of Maine—hosts, candles, holy water and oil, communion wine, breviaries, rosaries, missals, vestments, and various liturgical paraphernalia for Mass. He packed some books for his own perusal: a slender volume by Villon—his favorite poet—a book on the spiritual exercises of St. Ignatius, and of course the book he always brought with him when he ventured into the wilderness, the large, tattered volume called *The Jesuit Relations*, the collected letters the early Jesuits had sent back to France about their travails working with the Indians. No matter how often he read it, he never ceased to find it inspiring.

With this, his tenth visit north, he had learned to pack wisely, frugally, taking everything he would need but no more. The hosts and paper items he wrapped carefully in oil cloth. Fragile things, like the small, gilt-edged tabernacle he brought for the altar, he covered in linens and packed away at the bottom of the trunk so they wouldn't be damaged during the long journey. A few years earlier, he had purchased a beautiful two-foot-high marble and wood crucifix for the chapel in the Penobscot village. Yet when he arrived and opened the trunk, hoping to impress the Indians with the gift he'd brought them, there was the body of Christ in several pieces. The natives were saddened that *le sauveur cassé*—the broken saviour—could not be resurrected like in the magical story he told them of the tomb.

He would be leaving in three days and still had much to do. He would go by wagon to Newburyport, then take the ferry over to Pleasant Point, Maine, where he would spend several weeks with the Passamaquoddy tribe. From there, he would continue north along the Penobscot River by canoe with his native guides, to the village of the Penobscots on the island of Old Town. It would be, as always, an arduous trek, not without an element of danger. During his second journey north, one of the canoes had overturned and he'd nearly drowned in the frigid water. Even now, he could recall floundering in the frigid, fast-moving river, thrashing wildly about, all the while thinking any moment he would go under. But then, like a miracle, one of his Indian guides plucked him by the collar and lifted him to safety. As it was he'd lost all of his vestments, and the prayer books they did manage to recover floating in the river had been damaged beyond repair.

Despite the difficulties, Cheverus looked forward to going on the two-month mission into the north woods. While Father Matignon complained he couldn't spare him being gone that long, or worried the harsh living conditions might undermine his already frail health, Cheverus always enjoyed his time there. If anything, it seemed to have a salutary effect on his physical well-being. He worked hard, splitting wood and doing odd jobs about the small, bark-covered structure the Indians had made for a chapel. He went for long hikes in the forest. He found his muscles growing hard and knotted, his hands callused. He returned so darkened by the sun and weather-scarred by the wind that Father Matignon hardly recognized him. The fresh air of the forest provided a welcome change from the often fetid streets of Boston. At night, he slept soundly to the cries of loons, the howls of wolves, and the bugling of moose.

Besides, he delighted in working with the Indians. Ministering to them, helping lead them to God. Their ancestors may have slaughtered the first blackrobes who tried to convert them, but now they yearned for His light. Their faith was a simple and pure thing, brilliant as gold waiting to be harvested and hammered into something finely wrought.

Unlike the white man, they lived in a perpetual spiritual realm, negotiating the seen and unseen worlds as effortlessly as deer running through the forest. He especially loved working with the children, teaching them their catechism, playing with them, learning their songs. His time with the Indians seemed to benefit him as much as them. In fact, he sometimes felt closer to God there than in some great cathedral. In the profound stillness of the deep woods, he felt more clearly, more keenly the quiet presence of the Lord. There he felt a closeness to Him that he didn't in the noise and bustle of the city. Especially now, he thought, this visit might be just what he needed. Perhaps there, sleeping under the stars, amongst His children of the forest, that heaviness about his heart would leave him.

He glanced down at the thick, worn book he held in his hand, *The Relations*. He could still recall his mother reading to him those rousing narratives of Jesuit missionaries who had come to New France to save the souls of the savages. He opened it, his eyes chancing to fall on a passage he had read often before, the story of a young Huron Indian who had nearly been killed by his Iroquois enemies: *My God . . .* he wrote, *dispose of my life as you please. If I knew your will, I would present myself and tell them to burn me: and then I would offer you my torments . . . could I die a better death? Would I not go straight to Heaven?*

Cheverus still hadn't made up his mind about whether he would stay in America or return to France. He had been so busy lately with baptisms and confirmations, with communions and weddings, and, because of a number of cases of yellow fever, with ministering to the sick, that he hadn't actually given it much thought. He had taken Father Matignon's advice—to be patient, to wait for God to reveal His plan for him. He had considered it best to put off any decision until he got back from the north. He had hoped the time away from his hectic duties in Boston would help him make up his mind.

Things in the city had settled down since the trial, more than a month ago now. Other news had taken precedence. There was the war in Europe, Napoleon's latest battles. Also, the killing on the high seas of an American citizen named John Pierce by a British man-of-war had sparked an international incident. Many in Congress, particularly Republicans, were outraged, calling for reprisals against Great Britain. Closer to home, a dozen cases of yellow fever had been reported in the city, with several deaths already attributed to it. People were apprehensive about another major epidemic like the bad one of '98. Cheverus had paid visits to several of the affected families to do what he could, to give comfort and administer the last rites to the dying. Perhaps the most important news for Boston as well as the state was the election for governor. After a hard-fought campaign, the results of the close voting had dragged out for weeks, finally having to be decided in the Massachusetts legislature. By the narrowest margin in history, incumbent governor Strong had defeated the attorney general again. Heartened by his near victory though, Sullivan was already preparing for another run against him. His supporters were already attacking Strong for the arrest and trial of the publisher of the Northampton newspaper, the *Republican Spy*, on charges of slander.

Cheverus had not heard much about the two Irishmen. Of course, he'd been informed of the sentence—that they would hang on the 5th of June, now less than a week off. And there had been the usual smattering of editorials and broadsides and sermons, proclaiming God's terrible vengeance on those who took another's life, or blaming the loose immigration policies of the Republicans for the vicious crimes of foreigners. And just a few days before, Father Matignon had learned that the Daley family's petition for clemency had been turned down by Governor Strong. Cheverus was against the death penalty in principle, believing only God should decide when and under what circumstance a man should die. Yet if any crime ever deserved it, he supposed, this one did. Nonetheless, it was a tragedy for all concerned. Not only for the Daleys, but a stain on the entire Irish-Catholic community of Boston. And it would take a long time before people were able to put this behind them.

He had not seen the Daleys at Mass or in the confessional for several weeks. He wondered why. He felt a terrible pity for them. He had been meaning to pay them a visit, but he had been so busy tying up loose ends before he left for Maine he had not had the chance. At least that's what he'd told himself. Recently he'd received a note from Finola, asking if he would consider traveling out to the jail to hear the condemned men's confession and help them prepare to face death. He'd discussed the matter with Father Matignon, who felt it best to wash their hands of the whole sordid affair. He thought it would only stir up trouble for all concerned, not least the Catholic Church. So Cheverus replied to Finola by letter that, while he would certainly like to go, regrettably, he couldn't possibly make the trip as he had too many other obligations to meet. Secretly, he was relieved he would not have to attend the execution. He knew what it would remind him of: those poor devils driven through the streets of Paris in carts, crowds screaming for their blood, to face the guillotine in the *Place de la Revolution*. Cheverus didn't think he could go through that ever again.

He had seen Finola once. One evening not long after the trial, he was coming out of the vestry when he'd seen her praying before the statue of the Holy Mother. She was kneeling, her head bowed. He watched her for a moment. The flame of a candle lit her face, made it appear to glow palely in the otherwise darkened church, her bony face thrown into sharp chiaroscuro, like a painting by El Greco. He thought of going over and trying to comfort her. Saying a prayer with her as he had done before. He knew that's what he should have done, as a priest, a man of compassion. But something held him back. Wasn't it better, as Father Matignon advised, to keep a safe distance? To be mindful of the consequences? And there was, too, that awkwardness he felt around the woman, a certain unease he could not quite define nor dispel. Perhaps it was because of the way she stared at him, with that odd mixture of pity and . . . was it scorn? Did she revile him for not offering his help? In any event it would soon be over, and in many ways he would be glad of it. Not of the outcome, of course. But merely that it would be done, the entire disagreeable affair put behind them.

"Jean," he heard Father Matignon's voice. The old man entered the parlor, walking gingerly because of his gout. He patted Cheverus on the back, his touch frail as a feather. In French, he asked, "Are you all packed?"

"Almost. I have a few more things, Father," Cheverus said.

"You will be sure to say hello to my friends up there for me. What is that little one's name? The one they call Otter."

"Ki-wan-ik. He is hardly little anymore, Father."

"Yes, it has been some time since I was up there. Not since your arrival," he said, glancing at him meaningfully. "Give this to him," he added, handing Cheverus a small vellum Bible.

"He will like it."

The old abbé stood peering into the trunk.

"I suppose this will do me good," he said. Cheverus looked at him, perplexed. Father Matignon wore a rueful smile on his sharp, rawboned face. "Getting used to your being gone, I mean."

"I haven't decided anything, Father."

"True. But we both know it is for the best."

"Do we?"

"The Church there needs you. Your family, too. And you need them."

"Am I not needed here?"

"Of course you are, Jean. You don't know how sorely you will be missed, my friend. You have become my right hand. Both my hands," he added with a chuckle.

"Perhaps you, too, will return home someday, Father."

"No," he said, shaking his head resignedly. "This is my home now. When I left France I thought I would be gone for a year. Perhaps two. Just until the difficulties there were over. Now I know I will never return. This is where He wants me to serve Him. And whenever it is He chooses, this will be where I shall be buried."

"Your desire is to be buried here?" Cheverus asked.

"It is. Here among those I have served."

Cheverus felt a deep sadness at these words of his friend. "Lord willing, you shall have many more years to serve, Father."

"Perhaps," the old abbé offered with the insouciance of one whose fate was already determined. He appeared as if he would say something else, but Yvette came scurrying into the room then, her hands aflutter.

"Excuse me, Father," she said excitedly in French to Father Matignon. "You have a visitor. That Irishwoman."

"Who?" Father Matignon asked.

"The one whose husband is the murderer."

The elder priest glanced at Cheverus. "Tell her we are busy."

"I did. But she won't listen."

"Tell her—"

But before he could get the words out, Finola Daley was standing in the doorway of the parlor. She wore a long blue chemise gown, an apron, a neckerchief over her thin shoulders.

"Come in, come in, Finola," Father Matignon said with forced affability.

"Hello, Finola," Cheverus added, surprised to see her. He thought she'd be out in Northampton with the execution not a week away.

"Good day to you," she said to them politely.

"I am so sorry to hear about your husband, Finola," Father Matignon said, taking her hands in both of his. "Just terrible."

"Thank you, Father."

"Come and sit, my child," the elder priest offered. "May we offer you some tea?"

"No, thank you. I can't stay long," she said.

She had lost weight, he saw. The bones in her face and neck were even more pronounced, and there were dark circles under her too-large eyes. In the crook of one scrawny arm, she carried a basket with a cloth over it.

"How is Rose?" Cheverus asked.

"Not so good, Father," she explained. "She caught a chill going out to visit Dom and has been in bed ever since."

"I shall have to get out to see her," Cheverus said. She stared at him. Feeling himself caught in a lie, he lowered his gaze to the trunk before him.

She handed him the basket. "I made some nice pig's trotters for you both. To thank you for all you done."

"How very kind of you, Finola," Father Matignon said. Then, leaning toward her solicitously, he asked, "And how are things . . . ?"

She pursed her lips. "You heard the governor turned us down for clemency?"

"Yes, we heard," the elder priest replied. "I'm so sorry, my dear."

"We've not given up hope yet. There's still the appeal. Mr. Blake wrote us and said he believes we'll be granted a new trial."

"Yes, of course. Let us pray for that," Father Matignon said, shooting a quick sideways glance at Cheverus. "And how is Dominic holding up?"

"I've never seen him so down. I keep telling him he's not to lose hope. That we still got the appeal."

"So you have been able to visit with him?"

"Aye. Thanks to Father Cheverus," she said, nodding toward him. "I was out there just a while ago. I'll be heading back tomorrow. We don't have much time left, I fear. It's the fifth of June, you know. When they are to be . . ." she paused though, leaving the thought unsaid.

"Yes," Father Matignon said. "Is there anything you need? Do you have enough money, my child?"

"I'm doing all right."

"If there's anything we can do," Father Matignon said. "Anything at all, please don't hesitate to ask."

"Well, there is something, Father," she began tentatively. "Dom heard that on the day they're to be executed, they will have to listen to a sermon. A Protestant minister will preach to them. Is that true, Father?"

"Yes," Father Matignon replied for them. "A condemned man must submit to a funeral discourse on his crimes."

"But it's not right, Father," the woman said, her eyes flashing with anger.

"That is the custom here in America, I'm afraid," Father Matignon explained.

"My husband's a Catholic. He should have a priest there to see him off. That's only right, Father." She looked down at the paper in her hands. Then she held it out to Cheverus. "This is for you, Father," she said to him. "Dom asked that I see you got it personally."

He looked at what she held in her hand. Finally, hesitantly, he took the letter and opened it. He read it silently to himself.

22 May, 1806

Dear Father Cheverus:

While the judgment of men is liable to be deceived, we adore in the decrees of Providence. If we are not guilty of the crime imputed to us, we have committed other sins, and to expiate them, we accept death *with resignation. We are solicitous only about our salvation. To that end, we ask that you help prepare us to meet our Maker. It will be a painful task for you after the fatigue of a long journey, and especially after the sad impressions made on your heart by the sight of two young men about to die in the bloom of youth. Please do not refuse us this favor, and reduce us to the necessity of listening, just before we die, to the voice of one who is not a Catholic. It is in your hands. Come to our assistance.*

> *With humblest thanks and reverence,*
> *Dominic Daley & James Halligan*

When he had finished reading the letter, he knew it had to be the other one who'd composed it. Dominic could hardly write his own name in the church registry when his son had been baptized. The person who had written this had had some education. Cheverus finally looked up at Finola Daley. She watched him, waiting for his response.

"I know it's askin' an awful lot of you," the woman said to Cheverus.

"What does he write, Jean?" the elder priest inquired.

"He asks that I come out there, Father. They want me to be . . . to prepare them," he said, pausing to look at Finola Daley, "for their end."

She returned his look straight on, not even flinching when he said "their end."

"Will you do it, Father?" she asked, her olive-green eyes pleading with him. "Will you go to 'em?"

"I would like to . . ." Cheverus began, but then deferred to his superior.

"Of course, we appreciate the seriousness of such a request, Finola," the elder priest replied. "We do not take such an appeal for spiritual guidance lightly. Unfortunately, we must say no."

"But he *needs* you, Father," she pleaded, not taking her eyes off Cheverus.

"Much as we might wish to, we couldn't possibly go out to Northampton right now," Father Matignon explained.

"Why?" she pressed.

"There are just the two of us, and we have much to do," Father Matignon explained. "It's a busy time of year for us. Father Cheverus must leave for Maine in a few days. He shall be gone for several months, and I will be here alone to serve the entire diocese."

"My husband's always been a good Catholic, Father," she said, anger making her voice thin and brittle. "He believed everything the Church taught him. And now he needs you."

"Yes, of course. But we couldn't possibly, my dear," Father Matignon said. "Please try to understand."

"The only thing I understand is my husband oughtn't have to listen to a Protestant right before they kill him. He ought to have his own kind there."

"We appreciate how difficult this must be for you," Father Matignon sympathized.

"No, Father, you can't know what it's like," she said.

"No, perhaps not, my child," Father Matignon conceded, glancing at Cheverus. The younger priest remained silent. "Besides, they might not permit a Catholic to give the execution sermon. It's always done by a Protestant minister."

"What will I say to Dom?" she asked. "What will I tell him?"

Father Matignon turned to Cheverus and said in French, "Tell her you cannot do it. Tell her you are too busy."

"We sympathize with your situation, Finola," said Cheverus, reaching out and placing his hand on her shoulder. She looked at his touch as if it somehow hurt her. He pulled his hand back. "But as Father Matignon said—"

"What kind of men are you?" she cried.

"Finola, please."

"Have you not a heart?"

"You must try to understand," offered Father Matignon.

"Those two are beggin' you. I'm beggin' you, Father." Her face broke and she started to cry then. Tears slipped down her gaunt cheeks and fell onto her neckerchief. "Who will hear his confession? Who will give him the last rites?"

"We can say a Mass afterwards," the elder priest said.

"What good will that do 'em?" she wailed. "The bloody bastards are not even gonna let us have his body for a decent Christian burial.

They're gonna butcher me husband is what they're gonna do. And then they're gonna throw his bones to the dogs. Sweet Jesus!" she moaned. She wiped the tears away from her cheeks with the back of her hand. She looked up at Cheverus. "Don't let him die alone, Father. Please. I beg of you. Don't let him die alone."

"He won't be alone," Cheverus offered. "God will be with him." Yet the words were chaff in his mouth. He almost choked on them.

"He needs someone *there* with him," she said savagely. "At his side when he walks up those steps to the gallows. How can I make you understand?"

"Try to stay calm, my dear," Father Matignon advised.

"You call yourselves priests," she flung at them, but kept her eye on Cheverus. "Those boys need you. And you're not going to go to them?"

She got down on her knees before Cheverus and took his hand and kissed it. "Please, Father," she said. "In the name of God." She buried her face in his cassock and sobbed. Her body quaked against his knees, her shoulders lurching. He looked over at Father Matignon. Cheverus took a breath, exhaling slowly. He felt that terrible weight pressing down on his chest so he could hardly breathe.

"Perhaps we could discuss the matter," he said after a while, trading looks with the old abbé. The elder priest furrowed his brow and mouthed the words *"Mais non!"*

"I'd appreciate it, Father," Finola said.

"Please. Get up," Cheverus said, helping her to stand.

"We shall have to discuss it, Finola," Father Matignon said. "We will inform you of our decision tomorrow."

"Thank you, Father. I know Dom would thank you too."

"We are making no promises, you understand," Father Matignon added, glancing sternly at Cheverus.

"I know. Help my husband, Father. Please, don't let him die alone."

After she left, Father Matignon sighed and placed his knuckles together under his nose. Cheverus could see he was annoyed with him and trying to form his words with care. "Why lead the poor thing on like that? It will only make it more difficult when we tell her we can't."

"Forgive me, Father. I just thought . . ."

"I, too, sympathize with their plight, Jean. But it's simply impossible. We have far too many other duties to tend to. We couldn't spare the time it would take."

"Of course, you're right," Cheverus said, nodding.

"You leave on Friday," the elder priest explained, as if he had been challenged. "You still have much to do in preparation."

"I know." He paused, glancing down at the letter he still held in his hands. His eye fell upon the lines, *We accept death with resignation. We are solicitous only about our salvation.* What did that mean? He opened the Bible that lay in the trunk with his other things. He slid the letter in but didn't close the book.

"What if I were to postpone my journey north?" Cheverus asked.

"They are expecting you."

"A delay of a week, two at most. It won't make much difference."

Father Matignon gathered his lips into a pinched oval.

"Jean, even if we were not so busy, there is still the question of how this would appear to the public. Things are just getting back to normal for us. Would we really want to go and call attention to ourselves, to our Church? For a couple of convicted murderers?"

Cheverus glanced down at the Bible again. It happened to be open to John, chapter 3. He read to himself, *Hereby perceive we the love of God, because he laid down his life for us; and we ought to lay down our lives for the brethren.*

To Father Matignon he said, "They still maintain their innocence."

"What condemned man doesn't?"

"The trial was hardly a model of justice, Father."

"That is not for us to say. They had their trial and they were found guilty. We must abide by that." When Cheverus remained silent, the abbé said, "Do you not agree?"

He nodded, but without conviction.

"Jean, they've taken a man's life. They've broken the law. It is a terrible tragedy for all, but they brought it upon themselves."

Cheverus could only shake his head again.

"And think of how it would look for the Church, Jean."

"We would only be offering spiritual solace."

"It may not appear as such to others."

"Should we be guided by appearance?"

Father Matignon shook his head wearily. "Besides, it could be dangerous for you, Jean. The authorities are preparing for trouble."

"Mere rumors, Father."

"Perhaps not. I have heard from one of the church wardens, Mr. Neelans—and he knows his people as well as any—that there is talk of some going out there to free them."

"It would be suicide. They know the consequences would be brutal."

"The Irish are seldom swayed by consequences. Whether it's true or not, I've heard the governor is going to send more troops out there just in case there's trouble."

Cheverus closed the Bible with the letter in it.

"Jean, I don't mean to sound hard-hearted. I feel badly for them, too. It's just that we've worked too hard to establish our mission here."

"I know, Father. I know."

"And they will not be alone. They will be provided spiritual sustenance."

"By a Protestant minister who would look to convert them so they don't burn in hell."

"They have only themselves to blame."

Cheverus nodded again. "I will tell her no then."

"It is for the best."

That afternoon Cheverus walked to Long Wharf to buy some candles and incense for his trip. It was a mild spring day. A few clouds floated out over the harbor like the unfurled masts of grand ships plying an expansive blue ocean. Boston was coming to life after a long winter. Women carrying parasols and wearing taffeta strolled arm in arm with men in elegant beaver tophats and long-tailed coats. Young boys whistled as they went about their errands, and servants girls haggled with fish merchants. Near the T Wharf a small crowd had gathered around a man selling ices. He thought of those fine spring days in Paris, the smell of hyacinth and tulips floating in the air. He found it hard to be disconsolate on such a fine day. He saw a large barque being outfitted for a voyage, men hauling supplies up the gangplank. Perhaps he would be boarding such a vessel in a few months, heading for home.

He was on State Street, heading back to the rectory, when he ran into Nell O'Rourke. She had her shopping basket over her arm. In it was a freshly killed goose she'd bought at Faneuil Market. Its white head hung limply, blood dripping from his yellow beak.

"I hear you're off to convert the savages again," she said with a mocking smile. "'Tis a Christian thing you're doing, Father. But I fear it's lost on them heathens."

"Is that so?" he said.

"Indeed. You might as well teach the leopard to change its spots. They're all going to hell."

"Thank you for the warning, Nell."

"You'd have as good a chance gettin' them two murderers through the pearly gates as one of those red-skinned savages. Are you goin' to the hanging, Father?"

"No," he said, surprised she would ask. "Of course not."

"A good many are making the trip out. My master's going. He says he wouldn't miss it for the world."

When he got back to the rectory, he found a note requesting that he come quickly to Mrs. Quinn's boardinghouse on Canal Street. Someone was sick with yellow fever and in need of a priest. When he got there, he found it was a newly arrived immigrant girl. One look and it was obvious she hadn't long to live. She was young, perhaps eighteen, and pretty, though the fever had turned her face into a frightful, jaundiced mask of fear and pain. Mrs. Quinn told him she was an indentured servant who'd come by herself from Kerry. She had no people here. "Not a soul," lamented Mrs. Quinn. "No one to keen for the poor thing." The dying girl stared up at him with lead-colored eyes, the whites turned a shocking yellow, like rancid butter. He held her hand.

"I have sinned, Father," she said. "I stole from my mistress. I am not a virgin."

He listened to her confession, and then he gave her sacramental absolution: "*Ego to absolvo ab omnibus censuris et peccatis in nomine Patris, et Filii, et Spiritus sancti. Amen.*" Then he anointed her forehead with oil.

"Father," she pleaded with him, squeezing his hand with a desperate strength. "I'm afraid."

"It's all right, my child," he said to her. He heard the line repeated in his head: *I am afraid.*

"Don't leave me," she said to him. "I don't want to be alone."

"I won't, my dear. I'll be right here."

He stayed with her until the end. After a while, her fear passed and her eyes became almost calm. Her body seemed to relax and accept the inevitability of her death. She died finally, her eyes wide and deep as oceans. He thought of those brave priests who had stayed behind at the Convent of the Carmes and gave extreme unction to their dying brethren. While he had run for his life.

In the evening, he packed some more, wrote a couple of letters. Then, as he always did before he left for Maine, he composed a short last will and testament—just in case he didn't come home. He left most of his modest library to the Athenaeum. His small savings to the church. His breviary to Máirtin. His mother's cross would go home to his brother Louis. And all of his other worldly possessions, few though they were, he left to Father Matignon. As always when he wrote his will, he felt both humbled by the prospect of his mortality and mocked by his flair for the dramatic. He would not die, he knew. Not for a long time. He would live to be an old man and pass quietly away in his sleep. That's what God had in store for him. A long uneventful life, as if punishing him for his betrayal.

When he was finished, he said his prayers, blew out the candle, and climbed into bed. He lay with his hands folded over his chest, staring into the darkness over his face. Outside in the streets of Boston, he heard the occasional clomp of horses or the rattle of wagon wheels, the wind blowing in from the harbor, bringing with it the melancholy smell of distant shores. He lay there unable to sleep, his mind astir with thoughts. He recalled the young girl to whom he'd given the last rites, the desperate fear in her eyes. Then he thought of Finola Daley, what she had asked of him regarding her husband: *Don't let him die alone. Please, Father.* Finally, he got out of bed and lit a candle on his night table. He sat at his escritoire, took out the prisoners' letter, and read it again: *we have committed other sins . . . we are solicitous only about our salvation . . . to expiate them, we accept death with resignation . . . It is in your hands. Come to our assistance.* Despite their stubborn denial of the crime, he thought they had to be guilty. The evidence had been substantial, even if the trial was biased. What if now, as they realized the certainty of their deaths, they wanted to unburden their souls in the privacy of the confessional? Without admitting to the world that they were guilty, without bringing shame down upon their families. What if they wanted only to confess to him and him alone? Lacking the intercession of a priest, without confessing their sins, would they not be doomed to hell? Here he could have gone to them and heard their confession and he had not. He would have lost two souls for God's glory. He was a priest. It was his duty, after all, to perform this sacrament. Though he was confused by many things—by his own long-standing guilt, by the distance he lately felt from God—he was certain of this: His love and the grace which followed from that. Only His grace could save them. He believed in that above all else. Maybe this is what God had brought him three thousand miles to do—to save the souls of these two men. Maybe this is what He wanted for penance. Yes, he would do this service for God.

His heart raced with these thoughts, and he could not sleep. His way was finally clear. It was a little after two in the morning when he finally walked across the hall to Father Matignon's room. He knocked on the door.

"Jean?" Father Matignon said, rubbing his sleepy eyes. "Come in." He lit a candle and had Cheverus sit in the only chair in the room. "Is something the matter?"

"No. Well, yes. I wish to talk to you, Father."

"Of course."

Cheverus didn't speak for several seconds. Father Matignon waited patiently.

"I think I should go, Father."

"To France?" his superior asked.

"No, I mean to the prisoners."

"The prisoners!"

"Yes. I've given it much thought, and I think I should be with them."

"I see," the old man said, rubbing his unshaven chin. "And what if they are guilty?"

"Then we can save their souls, Father. Think of it. 'Joy shall be in heaven over one sinner that repenteth, more than over ninety and nine just persons, which need no repentance.'"

"Of course," Father Matignon said, smiling weakly. He lifted his hands in the air, in an attitude both of defeat and of understanding. "You will need some money for traveling expenses."

"Thank you, Father."

"But promise me you'll be careful. And dress in lay clothes. There's no sense parading around as a priest, asking for trouble."

"Yes, Father."

The abbé looked at Cheverus and offered a tired nod of approval.

"Go with my blessings, Jean."

Back in his room, Cheverus knelt in prayer. Was he afraid? Perhaps a little. But if it was fear it was of a different sort. His heart beat with a strange surge of excitement. He prayed until the sun came up. He had decided to fast, thereby purifying his body and his spirit for the long, difficult journey that lay ahead. Often before going off on some arduous mission—to the Indian camp in Maine, for instance—Cheverus would pray to the Virgin and make a vow to fast. Denial of the body oftentimes brought a clarity of mind, a strength of purpose. He promised the Holy Mother that food would not pass his lips until he had blessed the two men. *Give me strength.*

TEN

Three days.

The thought was a nail driven into the base of his skull. Halligan had finished his supper, what he was going to eat of it, and now lay back against the clammy stone wall. He closed his eyes because he couldn't stand watching Daley eat. He tried not to think, tried to let his mind become an empty expanse: a field left fallow, a high, snow-covered mountain valley, those long stretches of endless gray ocean he had come across. A blank nothingness upon which his thoughts could find no purchase. He wasn't interested in playing cards or chatting with Daley. Nor could he read the books Mr. Blake had kindly brought him. He no longer took an interest in the pale lives of those imaginary people. His mind wandered, roamed freely about, yet somehow always, *always*, gravitated back to the solitary fact that governed his existence.

Three days. Three days was all that was left to him on this earth.

He tried certain tricks he'd picked up from his time in prison back in Ireland, to fool himself, to lead his mind astray. He added sums in his head, or he tried to remember the names of the constellations that Brother Padraig had taught him: Gemini, Orion, the Seven Sisters, Leo, that group of stars low in the sky over Ballinskelligs Bay, in the shape of a mule's head. Or he'd try to recall a song he'd heard in some pub or back-of-beyond shebeen.

Well it's all for me grog, me jolly jolly grog,
It's all for me beer and tobacco.
For I spent all me tin on the lassies drinking gin,
For across the western ocean I must wander.

Sometimes he would pretend that he was digging turf, settling into the pure, mindless rhythm of it—kicking the slean with the heel of his shoe, driving it down, bending, lifting, tossing a clod onto the cart. Over and over, the image so vivid he could almost feel the sweat beginning between his shoulder blades, could smell the strong, sweet odor of the earth's dark flesh giving up its secrets. For a little while anyway, he was transported thousands of miles away, to some hilltop overlooking the sea, a man whose life unfurled expansively, thoughtlessly before him like a cooling summer breeze. But then Daley would ask him something or Dowd would come by with his keys jangling at his hip, and he'd find himself right back in the cell.

Three days, the thought would come again, slicing into him, making him flinch. *Three days.*

He could hear Daley chewing now, his jaws working, his lips smacking. The mechanical sound annoyed him, as did most things lately. Since the trial they were being treated a little better, given candles and reading and writing materials, as well as a bit more food, enough so their bellies didn't growl throughout the night. Enough, Halligan knew, so it would look to all, as they stood upon the gallows, that they'd been well treated, better in fact than they deserved. Daley accepted this at face value, unquestioningly, no more than would a dog tossed a bone. He ate mindlessly, ravenously shoveling the food in with his fingers and then wiping his plate clean with a piece of bread. He ate with the unmindful eagerness of a laboring man after a long day's work, or as someone recently sick, determinedly hoping to regain his health by forcing food upon a reluctant body. Halligan wanted to say to him, *You're going to die, you bloody egit. Eat all the bloody food in all the bloody world and you're still going to be dead in three days' time.* He himself had lost his appetite. He ate only out of habit, out of some dumb animal need for routine, to quiet his belly's incessant demands. He thought it remarkable that his flesh continued stubbornly toward a future his mind already knew had ceased to exist: like a headless chicken still running furiously about, almost as if it might still avoid its fate if it ran fast enough. Yet ponder it as he would, even he couldn't quite get his thoughts around the notion of death. It was too large, too murky and cumbersome a thing.

"Are ye gonna eat the rest o' that?" Daley asked, indicating the trencher of food that lay hardly touched on Halligan's bunk.

Halligan opened his eyes, looked across at him. "You're welcome to it," he said.

Daley eagerly picked up the wooden plate and started to shovel the food into his mouth.

The early June evening was mild, leaving a sticky warmth on the skin. Through the small window of their cell drifted soft night sounds, the whir of crickets and the lowing of a cow in a pasture somewhere, the plaintive *who-who-who* of an owl. In the distance, the squeal and laughter of children at play. Also came the teasing odor of late spring wafting into the cell, bringing with it the fact of a world coming slowly, vibrantly to life: the richness of newly plowed fields, the fragrant sweetness of trees leafing out, of flowers, forsythia and honeysuckle and something that made him think of bog cotton, the rank odor of the barn next door carrying the pungent tang of manure and hay and horseflesh. Despite his best efforts to make his mind go blank, the world seemed to conspire against him. It was as if it wanted to remind him of all he would leave behind, to tease him with his loss in having so soon to bid it farewell.

During the past few days, he'd felt a growing anger in his belly, a hot, sour rancor welling up in him like a fever. The generalized frustration and bitterness he had felt since their imprisonment had altered, transformed itself into something black and terrible, something hard and localized as a tumor knotting his gut. He was an innocent man. He was going to die, and he'd not deserved it. He'd done nothing. Nothing at all. *Do ye hear me*, he wanted to scream. *Ya bloody bastards! Do ye hear me. I'm innocent!* If he had to die, he'd at least like it to have been for something. A reason. Some logic or justification to it. If he'd been caught by the British back in '98, and hanged with the other rebels on Wexford Bridge, that would have been understandable. Neither just nor fair certainly, but understandable. Or if Mr. Maguire had found him one night in the stables with his daughter and had shot him dead on the spot, there would have been cause. Or even, say, if they *had* murdered Marcus Lyon, while he wouldn't have liked his fate, at least he would have understood its necessity. But this? This was a bloody joke. Even now, this close to the end, his mind rebelled at the injustice of it. He wanted to strike out, to beat, to bludgeon, to choke the life from someone as his own would soon be choked out of him. But he could not think of anyone or anything to vent his anger upon. Though he tried to direct his hatred at one of the judges, even toward that Mr. Sullivan with his haughty demeanor and his grim hawk eyes staring at them as if they were no better than curs, he knew he didn't really hate them. So that black feeling sat festering inside him, and it ended up turning upon himself, feasting on his own innards.

"Bastards," he'd curse from time to time, slamming his fist into the stone wall until his knuckles were raw and bleeding. "Ya filthy bastards."

"Easy, Jamy boy," Daley would say. "No sense gettin' yerself all worked up. Mr. Blake said not to lose hope, remember."

His mind went back and forth: convinced one moment of the utter certainty of his impending doom, the next just as certain that the appeal, that something would save him yet. Their lawyer had paid them a visit a few weeks before to let them know how the appeal was coming. He brought them food and books and tobacco, even letters from a few loyal Irishmen who sent their thoughts and blessings.

"I still remain hopeful the verdict will be overturned on appeal," he told them, though the look on his face was hardly hopeful. He sat on Daley's bunk, his fat hands nervously rubbing the legs of his brown pantaloons. "It is not over yet, gentlemen."

"If this appeal business comes through, then what, Mr. Blake?" Daley asked.

"They would have to grant us a new trial."

"And we'd have to go through all that again?"

"Yes. But I would have more of an opportunity to prepare a viable defense. And this time we'd win. I am quite certain of it."

"You'd be willing to take on our case again, Mr. Blake?" Halligan asked.

"Why, of course," he said, smiling, his blue eyes animated with genuine fondness. Blake looked over his shoulder to make sure the turnkey was out of earshot. "Do you recall," he said, "I tried to introduce evidence during the trial that there had been other robberies in the area?"

They both nodded.

"Recently, I came into possession of information regarding the Fuller boy," he said. "It is said that he told certain people before your arrest that he had seen his uncle leading a horse up the mountain."

"His uncle?" said Halligan. "Leading a horse?"

"Indeed," Blake said, nodding. "It was only later that he changed his story and said it was the two of you he'd seen with the horse."

"Jaysus!" exclaimed Daley. "Do ye think it was the lad's uncle done it?"

"It's certainly something worth investigating."

"And that would explain why the little urchin testified against us," said Halligan.

Blake squeezed his lower lip between his thumb and forefinger. "Precisely," he said at last.

"Jesus, Mary, and Joseph!" Daley cried.

"Now you mustn't get your hopes too high," Blake added. "It's only a rumor, mind you. Besides, we will need to be granted a new trial to bring forth any such new evidence. While I am reasonably hopeful still, I would caution you to be prepared for the worst."

He told them he would be back as soon as he had some news and left. After he was gone, Daley said, "See, Jamy. What'd I tell you. It ain't over yet. He says we still got a chance."

Halligan shrugged. Though he wanted to believe it, he warned himself not to. If the worst did come to the worst, he wanted to be prepared, just as Blake had said. Don't get your hopes up, boyo, he cautioned himself. That was just setting yourself up for disappointment. No sir. You need to get accustomed to the notion you'll be finding yourself standing up on those gallows with a hemp collar around your neck.

But if he had to die, he thought, why should he go meekly like a lamb to slaughter, as if only confirming that they were right all along about them? Why not go kicking and screaming? Why not make the blaggards pay a price? Show 'em all you had some bullocks, that you weren't just another gutless Irishman led peacefully along to the gibbet, offering to thank them kindly for the pleasure of getting your neck stretched. Over the past few days he had even formed this plan in his mind. It wasn't so much a plan, really, as it was just a picture, a dazzling image that glittered brightly in his head. When the guards came for them, he saw himself rushing one, trying to get hold of a weapon. And then somehow or other, if he could just make it to a horse outside in the street, he'd take off for those hills west of town. He was a pretty fair rider. If he could make the hills, he'd have a fighting chance. He could hide out for a while, and then, traveling by darkness, head up to Canada. Once there, who knows? Maybe he'd head out west. Or sign on with a ship bound for Australia. And if he didn't make it, if he were shot down trying, what would be lost? At least he'd have died like a man, fighting to the last. Not like a bloody chicken getting its neck rung. The notion excited him, distracted him, too. He didn't share any of this with Daley though. Halligan thought the idea wouldn't hold much appeal to him. He was far too gentle a soul for that sort of business, and no doubt he'd try to talk him out of it. And Halligan purposely left it vague in his own mind, perhaps because he sensed that details would only make the idea seem as foolhardy, as reckless and implausible as he sensed it to be in his heart.

Now and then during the past few weeks, he had an odd thought. He wondered about the man they were supposed to have killed. Marcus Lyon. In all the previous months in jail, Halligan had never given him more than a passing consideration. And why should he? It was on account of him, after all, that they were here. In some ways, he was to blame for what had happened. Yet he didn't hate the man. How could he? Halligan now thought it extraordinary that he hadn't contemplated the man before. It seemed that his and their fates were linked in some bizarre way Halligan could only guess at. He traveling one way on the highway, they the other, a strange chance bringing them together near the river on that fateful afternoon. Stranger still, their finding that purse with the money, almost as if he had placed it beside the road for them to come upon. *Here*, he had seemed to say. *Take it. It's yours.* Was it just a coincidence? Or was there some dark meaning behind it all? And then he thought about how the dead man was innocent too, just as undeserving of his end. He was about Halligan's own age. A young man with a young man's hopes and dreams. To have it all cut short in an instant. Here he was riding home on a fine horse, his pockets filled with coin. Going to see his family. A girl perhaps. What had it been like for him, Halligan would sometimes find himself pondering. Was it just fear and panic, your heart pounding, the plain, simple instinct to live another moment, just as it had been for Halligan while fighting the British? At night, with the darkness sitting heavily upon his face, Halligan pictured him lying below the cold river water as the last bit of life slipped out of him, bubbles floating to the surface. What had been his final thoughts? Had he recalled his childhood? Some sweet memory. What in this life did he most regret taking leave of? Did he think of that poor woman in the courtroom, his mother? Or had his last thoughts been on some girl he was leaving behind? The touch of her skin. The color of her eyes. Something she had whispered into his ear the last time she'd seen him.

Three days.

On the fifth of June, they would be taken to the gallows west of town, a place called, appropriately, Gallows Hill, and hanged. Afterward their bodies would be cut down and carted off to the slaughterhouse where they would be boiled, their bones tossed away for scavengers. Before all that, they would need to sit in the meetinghouse for several hours and listen to Reverend Williams, who would preach their funeral sermon to them. He himself had told them all this during his visits to them. He would appear in the corridor just outside their cell, dressed in black, Bible in hand. He was tall and gaunt of feature, with a long scrofulous neck, a raw pinkish face, and eyes the oily-black color of stones scorched at the bottom of a campfire. Standing there he would lecture them about the awful danger their souls were in. "Soon you will come before the Almighty," he warned them. "Throw yourself upon His mercy. Renounce your false beliefs while there is still time." Sometimes he would quote something from the Bible. "He that smiteth a man, so that he die, shall be surely put to death." It was obvious that he'd hoped to scare them into an acknowledgment of their crime, into understanding the torments that awaited them in hell if they persisted in their obstinancy—an obstinacy not only as regards to their crime but as to their religion as well. "The hour of your fate approaches," he cautioned them. Daley told the man to get out and not come back, that he wanted none of his Protestant gobshite. But each week he would return and try to get them to see the error of their ways.

"Jamy," Daley said to him after the minister left one time. "I want you to do something for me. I want you to write and say we're innocent."

"What are ye talking about?"

"I want you to write and tell them all we didn't kill that feller."

At first he thought he was kidding, but he could see he was dead serious. Halligan snorted with disdain. "They won't believe us."

"I don't care. We niver had the chance in court to tell our side."

"And who's going to read this?"

"You are," Daley said, staring across at him, his normally dull blue-gray eyes sharp as the tines of a pitchfork.

"Me?"

"Aye. You're gonna read it from the gallows."

"From the gallows, am I?"

"If it comes to that. So everybody can hear."

Halligan shook his head. Finally, though he didn't see the point in it, he thought if that's what the bloody fool wanted, then that's what he'd do. He'd write a last statement proclaiming their innocence. It wasn't any skin off his arse.

I pray he'll come," Daley said, mopping up the last of the food with a piece of bread.

"Who? Mr. Blake?" Halligan replied.

"Not him. Father Cheverus." The week before, when Finola Daley had been there to visit, she said she would pay a visit to this Father Cheverus and beg him to come back with her.

"I dunno. It's a long way to travel just for two men."

"He'll come, you watch," Daley said. "It'll be good to talk to someone who doesn't think we're a couple murderin' thieves."

"I suppose," Halligan offered, though he didn't see as it made much difference.

"Finola said she would talk to him."

"That doesn't mean he's going to come, Dom. He didn't answer your last letter either."

"She said she'd place this one in his hands. You wrote a fine letter, Jamy boy. If that doesn't convince him, nothin' will."

" 'Twas your letter. I just said what you asked me to," Halligan replied.

"You don't want to see a priest?"

Halligan gave a little shrug.

"What about confession?" Daley asked.

"I'm not much on confession."

"You wouldn't want to go with your sins on your head, would you now?"

"I'll worry about me own sins."

"But what about . . ."

"What about what? Hell? Just where do you think we are now? With all your blasted praying, you're here same as me. And I never prayed a fart's worth."

Lately, Daley had started to get on his nerves. He found most things Daley did irritating in some way or other. His praying. His insistence that *he* pray, too. The way he slept so soundly and ate as if it mattered somehow. And he would ask all these stupid questions. If Halligan thought they would let them shave. If they would have them walk to the gallows or ride on a cart as he had seen men do back home. If they would place a hood over their heads. If they would hang together or one at a time. On and on. Last night they were playing cards when Daley had asked, "What do ye reckon it'll feel like?"

"What would what feel like?" Halligan replied, though he knew exactly what Daley meant.

"You know . . . to hang."

"How the bloody hell would I know?"

"Do you think it'll hurt?"

"Jaysus. What kind of foolish question is that?"

"Well, do you now?"

"I reckon it will. Some anyhow. It would have to. Now are you gonna bid or jabber?"

"I hear your neck breaks and you don't feel much of anything."

"Maybe. Maybe not. Nobody's been hanged and come back to tell me."

"I got a fish bone caught in me throat once," Daley said. "Do you think it'll be like that?"

"Ga!" Halligan snapped. "A fishbone! You're talking like a bloody egit now. They're not gonna powder our wigs. They're fixing to hang us."

"I'm just asking is all."

"Well, keep your foolish questions to yourself. You stupid bostoon."

"Who're ye calling a bostoon?" Daley said, scattering his cards as he scrambled to his feet. His large fists were clenched, and he stared down at Halligan, ready for a fight.

"Oh, sit down would you," Halligan told him.

"I'll not take any man's guff, d'ye understand. Not even from you, Jamy."

"Sit down, I tell you."

"You oughtn't to call me that."

"All right, all right. I'm sorry. Now sit down and pick up your cards."

Daley hesitated, still angry and not quite wanting to give it up. After a while though he shook his head and sat back down.

"I'm not an egit," he said.

"So you're not."

"Whose bid is it?"

"Yours."

Sometimes he'd get so mad at Daley he wanted to punch the stupid bastard. He wanted to tell him to just shut his bloody gob. But there were other times when he felt sorry for him. The big lout would lie there staring at the ceiling, his hands locked behind his head, looking so bewildered, so forlorn, like a child lost in a large crowd unable to find its mother. Sometimes he'd say out loud, "What'll she do by herself? Faith, what'll she do?" Or, "The lad'll never remember me." And Halligan would think of his own mother, how he could barely recall what she looked like. Just that image of her in his mind, kneeling beside the pot over the fire.

Daley finished eating. He licked his fingers clean and wiped them on his trousers. He took up the new rosary his family had given him, with its shiny beads and its small silver crucifix, and he knelt on the floor. He closed his eyes and began to pray. An Our Father, ten Hail Marys, and a Glory Be. Then he went on to say the mysteries: the Five Joyful, the Five Sorrowful, and the Five Glorious Mysteries. Vaguely Halligan recalled the Franciscans making the orphans say the rosary, touching the beads, the large one, the three small ones, the five decades. It was in the small room off the vestry, where they learned their letters. They would kneel and say the rosary, mumbling the strange words. The only mystery that he remembered at all, exactly because it seemed so strange, was the one in which Jesus was in the garden, and he broke out in a bloody sweat that ran to the ground. Strange as it was, he could accept the crucifixion and the moving of the rock and even the resurrection, but he'd had trouble swallowing that. As a boy he had tried to imagine it, blood that flowed from the pores like sweat, dripping to the ground. He had asked Brother Padraig about it once. If it was real. Could someone really sweat blood? "Yes, indeed, James," the old man had said, "I've seen it happen with me own eyes once. The man had blood come running right out of him like it was water. Just like Jesus." He always wondered if it was true, or just another one of the stories the brothers told them.

"Come, James," Daley offered, holding out his hand to him. "We'll pray together."

"No, not me."

"It'll be a comfort to you."

"It'll be no comfort to me," he snapped.

"You don't want to die like this, James."

"Like what?"

"Without God. Full of sin."

"He's been of little help to me so far. Or to you, for that matter. Every man dies alone anyways."

"Och! You don't believe that."

"But I do."

Daley shook his head. "Then I'll pray for you."

"Suit yourself."

How could he explain to Daley he didn't believe there was some fine, grand place waiting for him after they hit the bottom of that rope? A glorious province of clouds and light, where he'd see his mother again. Where there would be no pain or loss, sickness or hunger or regret. Where everything would be perfect and no one would ever die again. That was just a fairy tale, Halligan knew. There was just six feet of cool, dark earth waiting for him. Huh! Not even that. Not for them. There would be nothing left of them. It would be as if he'd never even been born. He was reminded of a young boy aboard the vessel on which he'd come over. He had died of ship's fever during the crossing. There'd been a small ceremony on deck during a cold gray morn in the middle of the North Atlantic. The dead boy's folks had placed some Irish soil in his pale hand, closed his small fingers around it, wrapped him in a fancy table cloth for a shroud, and dumped him over the side. The mother had been screaming and carrying on, keening wildly like someone possessed. They had to hold her back from jumping over the side and following her boy into the depths. Halligan could still remember watching from the railing as the small white object hit the water, hovered momentarily, and then sunk like an anchor below the surface. After a while, you couldn't tell the spot where he'd gone under, couldn't distinguish it from the vast surrounding gray of the ocean. Gone, he had thought then. Not just dead but vanished. As if the boy had never existed. That would be their fate, too. Not even to have a grave with a marker above it. Then again, maybe that wasn't so bad. To leave without a trace. Your existence wiped clean. Silence and darkness covering you instead of dirt.

He recalled being there in the crowd of spectators for Father Roche's execution, up on Wexford Bridge, along with Bagenal Harvey and John Kelly and the other "traitors" of the failed '98 Rebellion. The British had wanted to make a statement to the other Irish, to keep them from trying such foolishness ever again. For the priest it hadn't been a quick end either. The bloody bastards had seen to that, all right. The poor, brave priest who had fought so gallantly at Ross and Goff's Bridge had strangled slowly, kicking and grimacing and fighting with a mindless ferocity. All dignity, all humanity lost in the struggle to fend off the frightening approach of death. Then, after a last shudder, he stopped fighting finally, and hung limp and wretched as a slaughtered hog dangling in a butcher's window, the shit running down his legs. An old woman cried out, "God bless ye, Father Roche," but he hardly seemed blessed. And Roche had been a man of God, too, as decent and true and honorable a fellow as there was, a priest, but one who wanted only what was just for his fellow Irishmen and had been willing to die for it. Yet for all that, he still seemed to have feared his end, to have fought it tooth and nail. So what would that mean for someone like yourself, James Halligan, a man with more sins on your crown than you'd dare count? A selfish, good-for-nothing fellow who'd never given a thought to anybody but himself. But to hell with all that, he told himself. Truth was, he put little stock in notions of hell or of heaven, or any place after he was finished and done. There was just the silent darkness, and he had never been one afraid of the dark, not even as a boy. He used to like sleeping alone under the stars.

Dowd came by then to pick up the plates.

"Any word from Boston?" Daley asked him. "About our appeal."

"They've told me nothing, lads," Dowd replied.

"No mail today?"

"Sorry. No."

"Did the afternoon stage arrive yet?"

"Yes."

"Me wife was supposed to come today or tomorrow."

Dowd shrugged as Daley slid his plates through the slot in the bars.

Since the trial, Dowd had let Daley's wife in to visit him several times. Accompanied by armed guards which now remained on duty day and night, the turnkey would open the cell door, put the manacles on Daley, and bring him down the corridor to an empty cell. There Daley would spend a few minutes visiting with his wife. He'd return with a couple of pairs of socks she'd knitted for them or a letter from his mother. His eyes would be red and glossy, and he had the look of one who'd been staring too long into a fire. He had asked Halligan to read one of his mother's letters for him. *Dear Son*, she had said in what turned out to be Finola's hand, *I have not been feeling well. Otherwise I would be there to see you. I send my love along with Finola. You mustn't lose hope. I pray day and night to the Holy Mother, asking that she watch over you. God is with you. Remember*

that his own son, Jesus Christ, died on the cross for our sins, was buried, and
rose again. I miss you very much. With deepest affection, Your mother.

"You wouldn't happen to know if there was a priest on the stage?"
Daley asked.

"I couldn't say," said Dowd. "There's a lot of new faces in town."

During the past few days they had heard all manner of traffic passing
by on the road in front of the jail. Horses and wagons and coaches. Halligan could tell the plodding draft animals, their heavy hooves pounding
on the road, from the more dainty prancing of the roans and bays ridden
by lone riders or drawing some fancy cabriolet or elegant phaeton.
Another thing he would miss would be horses. He had always loved the feel
and smell of them, the sturdy muscles of their flanks. Their soft snuffling
and snorting. The quiet aloofness of their eyes. He pictured riding one now,
riding fast and hard toward those distant hills to the west. "Go on, boy," he
could imagine himself saying. "Just a bit more and we're there."

"Mr. Dowd, sir," Daley said, "do you think we might have some more
paper and ink? And a candle, too."

Dowd went off and returned shortly. "Here you go."

"Thank you, sir," he said. Then, turning to Halligan, he asked, "Could
we practice some more, James?"

Though he hardly felt like it now, Halligan took a seat on Daley's
bunk and tried to show his friend how to make words on the page.
They'd been practicing for some time. Daley was incredibly clumsy with
the pen, clutching it tightly but fearfully, as if it were a spike about to be
struck by a sledgehammer. Halligan would hold his hand, trying to guide
his gnarled fingers, but his letters came out looking more like the scratch-
ings of chickens in the dirt. Daley didn't care so much about learning to
write. He wanted only to compose a single letter—to his son. He'd told
Halligan what he wanted to say and Halligan had written it all out, in
large, plain letters, and now Daley was simply trying to copy it word for
word. So it would be from him, in his own hand. He wanted his son to
have a letter he'd written. He wanted him to think he knew how to
write, that he wasn't some unlettered bog-trotter from the hills of Con-
nemara. Even so, he was having a great deal of difficulty pulling it off.

"Faith," Daley lamented, throwing down his pen in frustration. "I'll niver get the hang of the bloody thing."

"You're making your b's like d's," Halligan said patiently. Instead of writing *Someday you'll be old enough to read this,* Daley had written *Somebay you'll de olb enough to reab this.* "You got them arse-backwards. One faces east and the other west. Looky here now." Halligan had written the following letter that Daley had been trying to copy in his own unsteady hand.

My Dearest Michael,

    Someday you'll be old enough to read this and to understand what happened to me. I want you to know that your father was neither a murderer nor a thief. I am sorry for having left you and your mother. I know you'll be a good boy and that you'll help her all you can. She'll need you and I have every confidence I can count on you. One other thing. Remember that I loved you. Farewell, son.

                             Always and forever,
                                Your Father

They worked on it until it grew late.

"We'll stop for now," said Halligan. "We're getting there." He felt bad that he'd been cross with Daley earlier. The big lout was annoying, but it had to be hard for him, leaving his family behind.

"Do ye really think so, Jamy?"

"Aye."

They both lay down on their bunks. It was warm so they lay on top of the blankets. Outside in the night, they could hear far-off noises coming from the center of town, the sort of inarticulate din of a large crowd of people heard from a distance.

"Sounds like they're gettin' ready for a county fair," Daley said.

"It does," replied Halligan.

"Do you suppose it's got to do with us?"

"I don't know. Maybe."

Daley seemed to chew on that for a bit.

"Did you ever go to the Galway Races, Jamy boy?"

"No."

"I went there with Finola once."

"I heard it's quite an affair."

" 'Tis. A grand time. I never seen so many people in one place. She liked looking in the vendors' stalls. The lace and pretty ribbons and such. Women like that sort of thing."

"That they do," Halligan said. He recalled once buying a ribbon in Dingletown. He had given it to Bridie. A red ribbon, and it made her dark hair glisten with reddish hues, as if on fire. Though she was wealthy enough to buy a whole store of ribbons, she loved it nonetheless. You'd have thought he'd bought her an Arabian stallion.

"I niver gave Finola much," Daley said. "We hadn't the money."

"She knows that."

"Still, I wisht I had. Now it's too late." Finally, he said, "G'night, James."

"Good night, Dom."

After a few minutes, he could hear Daley snoring, the air reverberating loudly as it passed through his nose. He'd be dead in three days, he thought, and he slept like a child, slept like someone for whom time didn't matter. Halligan had heard it said that a man who slept soundly had a clear conscience. He could feel his own heart beating—*dugf-dugf, dugf-dugf*—each beat bringing him that much closer to his last.

He tried not to think about what Daley had asked. About what it would feel like, being hanged. But he couldn't help wondering. Would it be quick and painless, a momentary shudder, like a man coming between a woman's legs and then the whole business over and done? Or would it be drawn out and terrible, as it had with Father Roche? Having the life choked out of you, your lungs exploding, your brains on fire. *Stop it*, he told himself. *For Christ's sake.* Still, he couldn't rein in his dark musings. He took several deep breaths and exhaled slowly. Trying to calm himself. *Like this perhaps*, he thought. Your life slipping from you like breath and then . . . *gone!* Vanished who knows where? He wasn't a believer in souls, at least not in the way the priests had made out. But he did believe there was something inside him, something which made him him, James Halligan, different from anyone else. Whatever that thing was within, the spark which separated the living from the dead, lying here on his bunk, he wondered if it would slip out of him that easily, smooth as a piece of silk, like a magician's trick at a county fair. Leaving him an empty husk. And all this, the familiar body, the hot blood coursing through the veins, that teasing itch down in the loins, these half-formed, swirling thoughts—all this would come to a sudden halt. Would *have* to, wouldn't it? If death were the end. If life were nothing more than eating and breathing, sleeping and fucking, a jangle of sensations and heat, urges and hungers. Then what? Afterwards? Just silence and darkness?

Once more he was getting way ahead of himself, the way he did when he couldn't sleep, when morbid thoughts seemed to prey on his unguarded mind. He needed to get hold of himself. He needed to be strong. It hadn't come to that yet. Maybe, if they were lucky, it never would. He had to keep up spirits. As long as there was life there was hope, right?

And yet . . . *three days.*

He had just three days in which to set things straight in his own mind. Three days to prepare himself to walk up those steps and take the plunge that would lead to everlasting darkness. That's what Daley was doing with his letter to his boy, wasn't it? Preparing. Tying up loose ends. What of his own loose ends? Halligan couldn't help thinking of his own child, his and Bridie's, the child he'd never seen. Would never see. He wondered what Bridie had named it, and what she would tell the child? Would she pretend that Halligan had never existed? That her child was that of some other man she would no doubt come to marry? Then, though he realized he had no right whatsoever to feel this way, he felt a great sadness come upon him. That the child he had sired would never know him, would never even know *of* him. It was like a second death. And yet he certainly deserved it. He'd gotten Bridie with child and then he lied to her and left her waiting on the dock. It was a bloody terrible thing he'd done, he knew, and he could only hope there wasn't a hell.

ELEVEN

The unpleasant couple boarded the stage at a change house just west of Worcester, where the driver had stopped to take on passengers and change horses. The small coach had already been crowded. Three passengers sat on one side: a young sailor in duck pants, a sleepy-eyed farmer who smelled strongly of the barnyard, and an old man wearing small clothes. Across from them were Finola holding her baby and Cheverus with a book open on his lap. Before the couple got on, the five adults had been content to doze or read or look out the window, only occasionally making an attempt at conversation. The old man was hard of hearing, and if anyone said anything, he would cup his hand behind his ear and exclaim, "What say ye?" When the new passengers climbed in, they all had to move over to make room. The sailor got up and, apologizing, squeezed in beside Finola, to permit the couple to sit together. Finola had to shift her handbag to her lap. They were packed shoulder to shoulder, so that when the coach took on a sharp curve in the road, Finola was thrown into the young sailor. She would glance at him and smile apologetically.

The new passengers were a middle-aged couple, smartly dressed, in fact overdressed for such a warm day. Though the air inside the coach was close and stifling, they were attired as if going to the theater. The husband, thin, weasel-faced, wore a topcoat trimmed in velvet and sat with a smug look of one contented with his lot. His wife was a fat, garrulous woman, who wore a satin gown with several lustring petticoats underneath that billowed outward, spilling over the seat. Whenever she spoke, which was often, the loose flesh beneath her jaw jiggled. She fanned herself with a silk Chinese fan and complained about how ungodly hot it was. She started jabbering as soon as she got on and didn't stop—about the outrageous price of European cloth due to the war or how hard it was to get good help these days, or how the driver seemed intent on hitting every pothole along the way. She spoke to no one in particular, least of all her husband, who appeared immune to her ceaseless prattle. It was obvious, too, from the way she kept crinkling her nose and covering her mouth with her cologne-scented handkerchief that she was offended by the odor that emanated from the farmer, who sat dozing unconcernedly next to her. Occasionally, the man's head would loll onto her shoulder, causing the woman to frown.

After a while, her gaze fell quizzically on Cheverus and Finola. "How old is the child?" she inquired.

Cheverus looked up from the book he'd been halfheartedly trying to read, Augustine's *Confessions*. Though he usually found Augustine deeply inspiring, he had brought the book as much to fend off exactly this sort of unwanted intercourse that travelers encountered during a long coach ride.

"Pardon?" he said.

"Your child," she asked, smiling condescendingly. "How old is he?"

It was the third time during the journey someone had assumed that they were husband and wife, and that the child was theirs. It was a natural enough conclusion. After all, they got on the stage together, and now and then they spoke in quiet, almost intimate, undertones. And, too, Cheverus was dressed in lay clothes. He had acceded to Father Matignon's wishes and arrayed himself like an ordinary traveler— trousers, a waistcoat over a white linen shirt, a laborer's floppy felt hat. In his trunk, stored with the other passengers' things on the back of the coach, he had packed the things he would need for communion, the cassock and surplice and stole, the pyx containing the hosts he had consecrated back in Boston. For the journey out, he had seen the wisdom in not proclaiming that he was a priest. No sense in asking for trouble. Still, it had reminded him uneasily of his flight to Calais during the Terror, pretending that he was a grain merchant. And he had not realized the implication of traveling with a woman and child dressed as he was, not until the sailor, who had gotten on just west of Boston, had asked the name of their child. Cheverus had replied simply that the child's name was Michael. Then last night, the innkeeper where they'd stayed had tried to put them up in the same room. Cheverus ended up sleeping in the stables, wrapped in an old horse blanket. Yet he had spent most of the night praying, trying to make himself pure and strong for what lay ahead.

He had told Finola that her accent might pose a problem, especially once they reached Northampton. When she said she'd not had any trouble before, he reminded her that "things" might be different now. He avoided the words execution or hanging. People would be coming from all over, and some would tend to be a little suspicious of any Irish showing up there, especially given the rumors abroad of a disturbance planned by the prisoners' countrymen. She had agreed and had spoken little, answering with a nod or a simple "yes" or "no," allowing Cheverus to talk for her as if he were merely an overly protective husband.

He answered for her now. "He is eight months, madam," he said politely, but with a cool tone in his voice that suggested he desired no more in the way of intercourse.

"He favors you, sir," the fat woman said, not taking the hint. "The eyes." He glanced at Finola, who seemed to fight back a smile, her mouth folding in upon itself like a wilted flower. Their private joke. Cheverus looked down at Michael, who had a full head of dark hair like his father's and the same long face, too. But he had his mother's large, startled eyes. The child began to fuss, and Finola jiggled him, humming softly.

"Did you get on in Boston?" the woman asked.

"Yes," he replied.

"Where are you bound?"

He hesitated, considered saying Stockbridge or Pittsfield or Albany, anyplace but where they were headed. Yet they would know soon enough their true destination, so it didn't make sense to lie. Instead he replied only, "Northampton."

"Ah!" she exclaimed. "So you are going to the execution?"

He felt Finola stiffen beside him, her reaction so subtle no one else noticed. However, the child must have felt it, too, for immediately he took to howling, loud belly wails that reverberated throughout the coach. All eyes fell on Finola and her child. The fat woman, momentarily forgetting her question, asked, "Does he have the colic?"

Cheverus said he did.

"Mine all had the colic, too." The woman smiled at the thought. "So you are headed for the execution?"

"No," he said. "We have business there."

"Why, it seems the whole of the commonwealth is going to it," she said excitedly, looking for confirmation to her husband, who was gazing out the window. "Doesn't it, Elias? Elias?"

"What?" he said. "Oh, yes. It should be quite edifying."

Edifying, thought Cheverus. Death was always edifying, especially for those who didn't have to die. In his pocket he carried the letter from Governor Strong authorizing him to visit the prisoners—"to attend to their spiritual needs." Cheverus had paid the visit to Beacon Hill just the day before. The governor had been actually gracious about it. "Please, Reverend Cheverus," he had said, "extend my sympathies to the family." With the closeness of the last election, he was no doubt merely trying to curry favor with Catholics. Every vote counted. Still, unlike Sullivan, he treated Cheverus with at least a gloss of civility. "I hope your ministrations will be of comfort to the condemned," Strong had said to him.

Cheverus's stomach growled from hunger. He'd permitted himself nothing save water since leaving Boston. He felt faint from not having eaten, as well as from the heat and the ceaseless jouncing of the stage. The overpowering stench of manure in the tight space of the coach nauseated him. He could hardly breathe the stale, sour air. Through his shirt, he fingered the outline of his mother's cross, the silver lying coolly against his breastbone. He recalled, with sudden vividness, another coach ride: the trip he had made when he'd left home as a boy to go to the seminary in Paris. He remembered holding her cross, thinking of her words, the prophecy of some extraordinary deed he would perform in God's service. He recalled he had hardly crossed the bridge in Mayenne when his loneliness overtook him, when he already missed her profoundly. Overwhelmed, frightened at the large world that loomed before him, he had started to cry. His father, a kind and gentle man, had tried to comfort the boy, but it was no use. And he had felt then somehow— though perhaps he was merely transposing what he would only later feel with the news of her death with what he felt then in the coach—that he would never see her again.

Cheverus hoped to turn the conversation away from the subject of the execution, so he made some passing comment about the weather. Across from him, the farmer, who appeared to have been sound asleep, suddenly opened his eyes, hacked some phlegm up, leaned across the old man, and spat it out the coach window. The fat woman next to him recoiled in disgust.

"I'm looking forward to seeing those boys swing," the farmer said flatly.

"As are we all, I'm sure," added the fat woman, from behind her handkerchief.

"The rope is the only thing most of them foreigners understand," the farmer explained. "We got laws here."

"What say ye," the old man said, cupping his hand behind his ear.

"You're quite right, sir," the weasel-faced husband said. "They arrive here expecting to have everything handed to them. And take to thieving if it isn't."

"They don't know the meaning of hard work," his wife concurred.

"Some's worse than others," the farmer explained.

"Spaniards ain't so bad," offered the sailor. He had been sitting quietly, looking out the window. "They work hard and don't cause trouble."

"I wouldn't give you two cents for a Spaniard," countered the farmer.

"I've worked with them," the sailor interjected. "They're good seafaring men."

"Papists," the farmer scoffed.

"How's that now?" asked the old man.

"We're talking about papists," said the farmer in a loud voice. "Catholics."

"*Ahhh*," said the old man, nodding pensively, as if he would say something profound. Instead he just fell silent.

"It has been my experience," the husband said in a hectoring tone, "that those from nations which fall under the sway of Rome do not make satisfactory citizens in a democracy such as ours."

"I wouldn't trust an Irishman," the farmer said.

"You don't mean, sir, those from Ulster," the husband said, taking issue with him. "My own grandparents came from the North."

"I don't mean them. I mean your papist Irish."

"They're quite filthy creatures," the fat woman added, holding the handkerchief close to her nose as if she could smell them even now. "And altogether ignorant."

Finola looked up. She appeared about to say something but Cheverus nudged her gently with his knee.

"I had a servant once from over there," said the woman, waving a gloved hand vaguely in the air. "We paid for her passage and everything. Took her into our house like she was family. And how does she repay our generosity? Silverware started to turn up missing. Why, I would rather hire a Negro. At least they know their place."

"We should never have let them in to begin with," the husband said. "It's only asking for trouble."

"Since November, I have feared for my very life traveling the roadways," the wife exclaimed. "I've told Elias I wouldn't venture out by night."

"My dear," her husband countered, "Mr. Lyon was killed during broad daylight."

"I don't care," she snorted. "Why even now I don't feel entirely safe. We women are particularly prone to the lustful intentions of ill-mannered immigrants." She looked toward Finola for support as a fellow woman but Finola kept silent.

"Don't you worry, ma'am," said the sailor, lifting his jacket to show a large-bore pistol shoved into the waist of his duck pants. "You're safe now."

"I hear a bunch of them paddies is headed out there to break them out of jail," said the farmer.

"They wouldn't dare," countered the sailor.

"They might. They're headstrong, them Irish."

"Governor Strong," interjected the weasel-faced man, "has the situation under control, I'm quite sure."

The conversation then turned to Governor Strong and politics, the recent gubernatorial race. All this time the woman was staring at Finola and Cheverus.

"What's the child's name?" the woman finally got around to asking.

Cheverus was going to answer but Finola spoke up first. " 'Tis Michael, mum," she said, not trying in the least to disguise her accent. Instead, she glared at the woman, her large eyes full of rage. Cheverus touched her hand to try to quiet her, but she wouldn't be quieted now. "He's Irish, too. And I'll have you know, he's neither filthy nor dumb, and as wee as he is, he has more manners than you'll ever have."

The plump face of the woman grew pale and she replied only by raising her eyebrows.

For a long while after that they rode in awkward silence. Some of them slept or stared out the window, avoiding looking at Finola or Cheverus. The weasel-faced man took out some sort of small account book and seemed to review figures. The sailor opened an oil cloth containing some fried cod and a potato. He offered some to Finola, but she politely refused. The greasy smell of food, however, made Cheverus dizzy with hunger. The purification he had hoped for, the clarity of mind and spirit, had not come. He felt only weak, his belly queasy, his spirit weary and disheartened. He closed his eyes, resting for a moment. He told himself once more that it is through suffering that we know His love, through an acceptance of pain that we enter into His grace. He felt himself on a mission for God. If he could get them to confess to their sin, he could then absolve them. He could save their immortal souls from perdition. Touching the cross beneath his shirt, he prayed silently: *O Lord, grant me the strength and the wisdom to lead them from the darkness of their sin, to the light of Your abiding love. Amen.*

Late in the afternoon, one of the lead horses threw a shoe, so they had to stop at a livery station along the highway to have it replaced. Grumbling at the inconvenience, the passengers climbed down from the stage and filed into the tavern to wait. The fat woman, appearing as if she would faint, had to be helped along by her thin husband. While Cheverus filled up a bucket with water from the well, Finola and her baby went over and sat in the shade of a large elm that stood along the side of the tavern. He carried the water over to where mother and child waited and joined them. It was a little cooler in the shade, though not much. Somewhere high in the trees a cicada's high-pitched, metallic clamor erupted, piercing the drowsy afternoon stillness. Finola had spread a rough wool blanket on the ground and laid the child on it, and was now in the process of changing his soiled swaddling rags. The acrid smell of urine and excrement fouled the air. The baby had a raw-looking rash between its legs and was howling so hard it almost couldn't catch its breath.

"Musha, love," Finola cooed to the baby, who nonetheless continued to cry.

"Here," Cheverus said, offering her the bucket of water.

"Thank you, Father."

"Is he hungry?"

"No. He's a bad rash though."

She dipped a rag into the water and wiped between her son's legs. The cool water seemed to sooth the baby, for the intensity of his crying abated somewhat. Finola reached into her bag and took out a small vial containing linseed oil and beeswax and spread the ointment over the rash. Then she removed a clean rag and swaddled the baby with it. She picked him up and rocked him. After a while he fell slowly into a fitful sleep.

"The poor thing is tired," she said. "He didn't sleep so good last night."

From the pockets that hung from her skirt she took out an oil cloth and unwrapped it. It contained a small piece of cheese, what remained of a crust of bread, an onion.

"Here, Father," she said, offering him some. He declined. It had only been in the last few hours that he'd begun actually to feel the beneficial effects of his fast—his thoughts had slowed and a certain clarity had begun to form at the edge of his consciousness. He had reached that point where the pain in his stomach receded, the dizziness was fading, and he was left with this calmness of spirit. He didn't want to lose that by giving in to his hunger. Not yet.

"Was it hot like this in France?" she asked, wiping her forehead with the back of her hand.

"It could be. But no, not usually," he replied.

"I been here five years and I still ain't used to it, Father. Nor the winters neither." For some reason, she smiled at him, and he smiled back at her. "Perhaps I'll go back after . . ." she said, her voice trailing off. "I got nothing holding me here now."

"What of your family?"

"They're Dom's relations. Not mine. Oh, they been good to me and all. But you see, Father, I come only because he wanted to. I'd a followed him anywhere."

"How long have you been married, Finola?" he asked.

"Be ten years come July. Would be." She chewed on the bread and took a drink of water. He thought she didn't appear old enough to be married that long. She still looked like a girl. And yet, in the harsh light of the late afternoon her pale, thin face showed tiny creases around her mouth, and sprinkled through her light reddish-blond hair were a few gray hairs.

Glancing at her son, she said, "We had another babe back home, Father."

"Another child?" Cheverus asked.

"Aye. A girl. Eva. The prettiest little thing you ever saw."

"What . . . happened?"

"She caught a fever and died. She was just three."

He had been her priest all these years and had not known that. In fact, he knew so little about her or her husband. About any of his flock. In the ways that really mattered. Back in France, he'd known everything about his communicants. The small, plain details of their lives. That old Madame Leroux, for instance, had that limp of hers because of a fall from a horse seventy years before. Or that the miller, Etienne Desauliers, had broken through the ice of the Mayenne River one winter morning when he was a boy and had nearly drowned.

"I didn't know, Finola," he offered. "I'm so sorry."

"I mourned her passing for a long time. Every day I went to the church and lit a candle and said a prayer for her soul. I thought I'd never get over me loss, Father."

"It must have been difficult," he tried to comfort.

She nodded, staring out across the dusty road in front of the tavern. The heat made the light wavy, rippling like water in a wind. In her eyes, he saw the wavering reflection, the still, dull leaves of the elm, the golden light of the afternoon.

"I can't imagine life without Dominic," she said. She said it simply, without emotion. A fact that was too awful to contemplate fully.

"Of course," he replied softly. "Tell me about him."

"What do you mean, Father?

"What sort of man he was." Then he caught his error and tried to undo it. "What sort of man he is, I mean."

She looked at him, then glanced down at the child in her arms. "Oh," she said, "Dom's a good man. Gentle. Kind. A good father, too." She thought for a moment. Then she smiled, inwardly at first, but quickly her whole face brightened like a young girl's. "And he always liked to sing."

"He liked to sing?"

"Aye. Ever since I knew him. He had a sweet voice. Like a songbird. I fell in love with him because of his voice."

Cheverus smiled, gazing down at her son.

The sun was just setting over the mountains to the west when they reached the ferry which would take them across the Connecticut River. From his seat in the coach, Cheverus found himself staring out at the dark-skinned, oily-looking water. A man was spearing eels from a flat-bottom punt, while an osprey did its own hunting, skimming low over the water, one talon poised to strike. A foul, pervasive smell, of dead fish and muddy water, polluted the evening air. He thought, almost inevitably it seemed, of Dante, of the river Acheron and the souls of the damned being ferried across. Was he, like Virgil, only visiting, he wondered. Or was he one of the lost souls?

They arrived finally in Northampton well past nine. Just outside of town they were stopped by a uniformed sentry who held a lantern aloft and looked into the coach. Only after asking a few questions did he allow them to pass on. The coach stopped in the center of town. The priest had been this far west in the state only twice before. A French Catholic couple from Quebec used to live just north of here. He had come out to marry them and later to baptize their baby. But they had felt isolated, with no other Catholics for miles and no priest to say Mass, so they had eventually moved back up to Quebec. Cheverus stepped off the stage, his legs unsteady and weak from the long ride. He helped Finola and the baby down.

Cheverus went around to the back of the coach, where the driver was handing down the passengers' trunks and bags. As he glanced along the town's Main Street, he was surprised to see all the people out at this hour. Yet he should have known. Hangings were quite popular, attracting people like maggots to a dead dog. When they had one on Boston Common, spectators would line the way from the prison to get a glimpse of the condemned riding along on the cart, sitting on his own coffin, the noose already draped around his neck like a thin cravat. Thousands more would gather on the Common to watch.

Now, two days before the execution, they had flocked to this small western Massachusetts town. They had come on horseback and on foot, by wagon and stage. They wandered the darkened streets in riotous bands. One man was selling things from a cart he had set up where two streets came together. He peddled trinkets and ribbons and scarves. Nearby someone had set up a Punch-and-Judy show and was entertaining a group who had gathered around it. Two puppets had ropes around their necks while a third puppet wearing a uniform beat them with a stick. The spectators laughed heartily. Groups of boys ran wildly about, some carrying lanterns, others holding pine-pitch torches. They were calling out, chasing each other, playing games. One group was throwing stones at something that hung from the limb of a great elm tree on Main Street. When Cheverus looked more closely, he saw it was a straw man with a crudely painted sign dangling from its neck: IRISH MURDERERS, the sign read. The boys were pelting the effigy with rocks, laughing uproariously when someone hit the figure and knocked some straw stuffing from its bulging chest.

A hundred yards to the west, in the center of the street, a large bonfire raged, and a crowd of several hundred people had congregated around it. They appeared to be listening to a man speak. The man, dressed all in black, stood on the bed of a wagon. The fire behind him outlined his form in silhouette, black against the shooting orange flames. From this distance, Cheverus couldn't make out what he was saying, but every once in a while there would be this thunderous applause and those in attendance would call out their support for whatever it was the man was saying. Nearby, a company of uniformed militiamen stood looking on, their muskets at ease beside them.

Finola was standing in the street, looking west toward the crowd gathered around the fire. "Are they all here for it?"

He nodded. "We should try to find lodging," he said. "It's past nine o'clock."

Cheverus and Finola went into the first inn that presented itself. The landlord, a heavy, swollen-faced man, told them he had no rooms. He suggested they try Pomeroy's Tavern a little farther west on Main. So they walked there. They found Pomeroy's to be a two-story inn with an enclosed courtyard in the English style. The innkeeper, an old man named Asahel Pomeroy, greeted them in the entryway. Behind him was a public room from which flowed the din of voices and raucous laughter. Pomeroy had the somnolent yellow eyes of a cat sunning itself.

"You here to see the Irishmen swing?" he asked indifferently.

"We would like two rooms," Cheverus replied.

"Got but one and that's in the attic."

"You have nothing else?"

"No. With everyone here for the hanging, you won't find another room in town," he said confidently. "The one in the attic's big enough to sleep the three of you. And the bed doesn't have lice."

Finola glanced at Cheverus. She looked exhausted, as did the baby, asleep in her arms.

"All right," Cheverus said. "I'll take it."

"How long will you be staying?" he asked, staring curiously at Finola now with those sleepy yellow eyes of his.

"A few nights."

"Dollar a night," he said.

Cheverus knew what he was charging was outrageous. But they had no choice.

"Fine."

"In advance," the man said, his eyes fixed on Finola. "Meals and drink is separate. Have I seen you somewhere abouts?" he asked Finola.

She shook her head.

"You look awful familiar. You from around these parts?"

She looked to Cheverus. "We're from Boston," he explained.

"I could swear I seen you before." He rubbed his unshaven chin pensively. "Were you at the trial?"

She shook her head again and turned partially away, drawing her shawl close about her face.

Cheverus took out his purse, hoping to pay the man before he realized where he'd seen her. He wanted at least to see to it that Finola and her child had a room for the night. He would figure out something for himself.

"Just a minute," the man said, his eyes lighting up with recognition. "I did see you at the trial."

"No," she said. "You're mistaken."

"Now I remember. You're that fellow's wife!" he said, pointing at her. "The Irishman's. I remember you had the child with you. You sat in the back of the court."

"May I pay you for the room?" Cheverus tried to interrupt.

"And who are you?" he asked, turning to stare at him.

"I'm . . . a priest."

"A priest!" he exclaimed. "Good Lord! What are you doing out here?"

"I have come to minister to the condemned."

The man stared suspiciously at them. "You wait here. I'll be right back."

He headed back into the taproom.

"Maybe we ought to go," Finola whispered. "I don't want to cause you any trouble."

"You and the baby need a place to stay."

"We could sleep under a tree. It's warm out. We'll be fine."

"No."

Pomeroy returned shortly, this time bringing a woman with him. She was small and shriveled, with a humped back and greasy, disheveled white hair. Cheverus couldn't tell whether it was the man's wife or mother.

"We don't let rooms to papists," she snapped.

"But, madame," Cheverus pleaded, "we've had a long journey. Think of the poor child."

"That's none of my concern. I couldn't hardly sleep thinking there was a papist under the same roof. Besides, we have no rooms."

"What about the one in the attic?" asked Cheverus, glancing at her husband.

"I said, 'we've no rooms,'" the women declared adamantly.

So they left. Though she said she could manage, Cheverus took her haversack and placed it over his shoulder, leaving his hands free to lug his heavy trunk. They headed along Main Street. The night had cooled considerably from the stifling heat of the day. Finola put her shawl over her head, wrapping it about the baby. People were milling about, shouting, laughing. They had to pass by the crowd in the center of the street. Standing on the wagon, the man dressed in black continued to address the crowd. They were now close enough to make out some of what he was saying: "We see the evil attending a continual influx of vicious and polluted foreigners into this country," he cried. Those listening yelled out with "yea" and "huzzah." "Many of the outrages we suffer proceed from this source. Foreigners break into our houses, in the unsuspecting hours of sleep. They set fire to our large cities and towns for the sake of plunder. They rob and commit murder on our highways." The crowd yelled their encouragement.

Cheverus and Finola moved on. They passed a narrow lane where a group of youths were gathered.

"Could you tell us where we might find lodging?" Cheverus asked of them.

They eyed the two suspiciously, perhaps because of Cheverus's accent. "There's the Red Tavern yonder," a tall, dark-haired boy of fourteen replied, pointing up the street. "And there's Mosher's farther on."

"Thank you," Cheverus replied.

They tried the Red Tavern and then Mosher's Inn. At each one they were told there were no rooms. They came at last to the edge of the built-up portion of town. Beyond in the moonlight they saw darkened fields and pastureland, the lights from scattered farmhouses flickering in the valley. In the distance was the darker outline of mountains. The baby started to fuss, and soon, despite Finola's attentions, the child was howling.

"We need to stop, Father. He's hungry."

They paused by the side of the road, near a stream. Finola sat down on the grass and unbuttoned the top of her shift and took out a small breast. She began to suckle the child. Cheverus permitted himself to look on for a moment, Finola's breast white as snow in the moonlight. Then, embarrassed by an odd stirring in his loins, he averted his gaze. He felt sick to his stomach again. *What sort of priest am I*, he thought.

"Are you hungry, Finola?" he asked.

"I could do with a bit of food, Father."

"I shall see if I can find something to eat. Will you be all right here alone?"

"I'll be fine," she said. "Father."

"Yes."

"I'm sorry for putting you through all this."

"I am only glad I can be of help," he said.

"A saint is what ye are, Father."

"I'm hardly a saint," he said. In fact, he felt guilty that he hadn't wanted to come in the first place, that he had carnal thoughts of her, that he wasn't a better man, a holier priest. His entire life seemed a sham to him now. People thought he was such a holy man, so pure of heart. So dedicated to his Lord. If they but knew the truth.

He left his trunk there and headed back toward town. He stopped at the Red Tavern where he had earlier inquired about a room. There he purchased what they had left over from supper—some boiled turnips, a hunk of moldy cheese, a gristly piece of mutton, some milk. The innkeeper, a whey-faced man with long side-whiskers, wrapped the food in oil cloth and gave him a wooden bucket for the milk.

"You were looking for a room?" the man said.

Cheverus said he was.

"There's a farm just west of town. The widow Clark lets rooms."

"Does she take in Catholics?"

"Long's your money is good. Bear right when you come to the fork in the road. Just past the slaughterhouse a ways."

When he returned to Finola, he said, "I think I may have found a place for us."

Finola started to eat the food he'd brought.

"Aren't you going to have some, Father?"

"I am not hungry," he said. Actually he was weak from not eating, yet he wanted to keep his vow to the Holy Mother. He thought if he kept his vow, remained true, She would help him to do what he had to. Besides, he wanted to reach that state of perfect calm that martyrs and saints attained, when the flesh is conquered at last and the spirit soars above earthly desires. He walked down to the stream, cupped his hand, and drank copiously from the cold, sweet water. Then he returned and sat down beside Finola.

"Why would He do this to us, Father?"

Cheverus knew who she meant. "It is not for us to understand His will."

"Dom never hurt a soul in his life. He's a good man. A good Catholic. For the life of me, Father, I just don't understand it. What sort of heartless God would do something like this. Take a father from his child," she said, looking down at her son. "And for nothing, too." By the moonlight, he could see tears sliding silently down her gaunt cheeks. Angry, bitter tears.

"He . . ." Cheverus began to explain, and yet he felt suddenly inadequate to the task. Every answer he could possibly give appeared trite to him, empty of meaning. All of his training, all his years in the seminary and all those he'd served as a priest, all the baptisms and communions, sermons and homilies, absolutions and last rites he'd given in the Lord's name—none of it armed him with an answer to Finola Daley's question. "I wish I could tell you. But I don't know. The only thing I do know is that He loves us."

She glanced at him somewhat skeptically. "Please help my husband, Father," she begged. "He's going to need you. It'll be a hard thing he has to do."

"I shall do my best."

She ate silently for a while.

"Afterwards, Father . . ." she began.

"What?" he replied.

"They won't let me have his remains?"

"No."

"Not even to allow him a proper Christian burial?"

"It is part of the sentence."

"A terrible thing it is not to be able to bury your loved one."

He nodded. "Try to put it from your thoughts, Finola. His soul will be with God."

When she'd finished eating, they started walking west. He could tell they were close to the slaughterhouse when the air became infused with the raw stench of blood, a close, secretive odor that chilled him to the bone. Shortly after that, they came to a farmhouse. The woman who answered the door was a tall, large-boned farm woman wearing a bed jacket over her shift. She didn't wear a bonnet, and her long black hair hung wildly about her shoulders. She held a lantern up and stared suspiciously out at them.

"We were told you have rooms to let," Cheverus asked.

"I might. You here for the hanging?"

They said they were. Cheverus asked if she had two rooms for the night and the woman looked quizzically from him to Finola and the baby.

"I have only one room left," she said. "Do you want it or not?"

Finola touched his sleeve. He leaned toward her and she whispered, "We could share it, Father. I could sleep on the floor. Really."

He smelled her fragrance again, that too-sweet, overly ripe odor. He thought of them together in a room. He looked at her mouth and recalled the Bernini statue of St. Teresa in her ecstasy. That odd mixture of purity and seductiveness the saint seemed to inspire. He thought of the snow-whiteness of Finola's breast, and he felt the terrible stirring down in his trousers once again. He felt polluted, vile, a contemptible wretch. *No!* he thought. *You mustn't have such thoughts.*

"You stay here, Finola," he said.

"What will you do, Father?"

"I shall find something. Don't worry. You wait here for me. It's not safe for you to be walking about alone. In the morning I shall go to pray with Dominic and then come for you."

She nodded. Cheverus paid the woman and headed back toward town.

But he wasn't able to find any lodging for the night. He tried the two remaining inns in town, as well as a somewhat disreputable boarding-house one of the innkeepers had referred him to down near the river. All were filled, or at least that's what he was told. Maybe it was already about that a priest was in town seeking lodging. In any event he found no place to sleep. While he was walking past a farmhouse, a large black dog came rushing out at him, growling savagely. He managed to keep the trunk between himself and the dog until the animal finally gave up and slunk away. And then a band of young boys carrying torches seemed to follow him. Some of them carried stones and all had a look of trouble in their eyes. One, the leader, a stocky blond boy with a callous mouth, called out "What are you doing here, priest?" and the others chimed in with, "Yea, yea." How had they found out he was a priest? When he turned down a darkened lane they turned, too, and when he sped up they increased their pace as well. They were laughing and taunting him. He felt his heart beating faster, his face heating up. He looked over his shoulder, and they continued after him, menacingly. One tossed a rock which struck him in the back. It hurt, but he stifled a cry and kept walking.

Luckily a pair of soldiers happened by and the boys took to their heels. By now, not having eaten anything in two days combined with the fatigue of a long journey, he was near to exhaustion. His arms quivered carrying the heavy trunk, his legs felt leaden. A swirling dizziness clouded his head, and he saw odd lights streaking before his eyes like shooting stars. He found himself walking along a narrow river that cut through the town. He thought of sitting down and resting for a moment, but he was wary of the youths' return. He was now beset by doubts and uncertainties. Was it all a mistake? Should he have listened to Father Matignon and not come? What was he trying to do after all?

He decided he would find some quiet place where he would wrap him-self in his cassock and fall asleep under the night sky, as he did sometimes when he stayed with the Indians in the forest. In the morning he would make his way to the prison. He would hear the confessions of the two men and he would give them communion. He would save them from hell. He would offer their souls as a gift to his Lord. When his task was done he would return home.

Near a gristmill along the river he crossed a bridge, and in the moonlight he made out a field just beyond. He would sleep there, he decided. On the other side of the bridge, he happened upon some soldiers sitting around a fire. They were eating something, talking, laughing raucously. They passed around a jug they took turns drinking from. They eyed him curiously as he approached. He touched the brim of his cap in greeting and was about to continue on when one of them called, "Halt."

He stopped, turned around.

"Where are you going at this hour?" asked one soldier, a youthful looking man with long red hair. He was eating, tearing strands of meat from a bone. In the firelight, his fingers and his mouth glistened with grease.

"I was just out for a walk," he replied.

"What is your name?"

"John Cheverus."

The soldier leveled a wary eye upon him. "Where are you from?" he asked.

"Boston."

"No, what country? You have an accent," the red-haired man said.

"I am from France," he replied. "But I am an American citizen now."

"What business do you have here?"

He considered telling them he was just a merchant. Or like so many, that he had come to see the execution. But then he thought, What if they search my trunk and find the religious objects. So instead, he said only, "I have come to visit the condemned."

"Under whose authority?" challenged another soldier, a man with crooked yellow teeth that glistened in the firelight like the fangs of a wolf.

"The governor's."

"The governor's!" exclaimed the red-haired man, whistling sarcastically. "And I'm Tom Jefferson."

They all laughed.

"Who the hell are you?" he demanded. "And you'd better not give us any shit."

Cheverus felt light-headed. He was so tired. He only wanted to sleep, to close his eyes and sleep for days.

"I am . . . a priest," he said.

"A priest!" one exclaimed. "Says he's a priest."

"You ain't dressed like a priest," said another.

"I am."

"What's a priest doing here?" the one with the crooked teeth asked.

"I told you: I have come to visit the condemned. I have a letter from the governor permitting me to visit them."

"Let's see it," commanded the red-haired soldier.

Cheverus walked over to where they sat. They were all young. Some appeared only a few years older than Máirtin. He took the letter out and handed it to the red-haired soldier, who seemed to be their leader. He held it up to the firelight. Cheverus could see he had difficulty reading and was embarrassed by it. When he was finished, he tossed the letter contemptuously at Cheverus's feet. Cheverus stooped and picked it up.

"How do I know this is real?" the soldier said. "This might be some trick by the friends of them Irishmen."

"It's signed by Governor Strong."

"You could a wrote this letter yourself. We have orders to be on the watch for troublemakers."

"I plan no trouble, I assure you."

"What do you got in the trunk?" the red-haired soldier asked.

"Nothing. Only some personal effects."

"I bet he has saints' bones in there," said another. They all laughed again, drunkenly.

"Open it," the red-haired man said.

"Yea," another soldier cried, "show us what you got in the trunk."

He considered obeying. What harm would it be to show this man his things? That would prove who he was. That would show them he meant no harm. Yet he thought, why should he debase the sacred articles he'd brought for their mere amusement? What if they were to take them out, handle them, with their filthy hands profane the hosts he had conse-crated. What would he do then? Would he simply stand by and let them? Instead he said, "Good evening, gentlemen," and turned and started to walk away.

"Just hold on," the red-haired man called after him.

He stopped walking but didn't turn around. Behind him, he heard one or two of the men snicker.

"I said, open the damn trunk, priest."

He waited for a moment, then continued walking away. He headed for the field in the distance. Perhaps they would give up, he thought. Per-haps they just wanted a little fun at his expense.

But the command came again: "Hold it!"

He kept walking. His head was starting to swirl. In his mind he heard the voice: *Vous etes l'un d'eux, n'est-ce-pas? You are one of them, are you not?*

"I'm warning you—*stop!*"

He thought he heard the metallic sound of a musket's hammer being pulled back, locking into place. His throat went dry with fear, his heart thrashing wildly in his chest. Still he kept on walking.

"*Stop!*"

Instead of stopping, though, he walked faster, toward the moonlit fields in the distance. If he could just make them, he thought. Somehow he would be safe there. He thought of dropping the heavy trunk, which slowed him considerably, but he could not bring himself to leave it behind. He would need his things to serve communion. So he struggled clumsily on, half running, arm-weary, leg-weary, his head spinning in faster and faster circles, his heart slamming against the walls of his chest. A picture of his own death floated before his eyes. The musket ball slam-ming into his back, tearing through flesh and blood and bone, finally shattering the heaviness that had surrounded his heart for far too long. As he continued moving away from the soldiers, he began to pray: *Hail Mary, full of grace, the Lord* . . . But a thunderous roar interrupted him, splintering the night. He started to look over his shoulder, expecting any moment the sweet, pure kiss of the lead ball, waiting for it like a lover for the lips of his beloved. And then he stumbled over something in the darkness, felt himself pitching forward. He could see the dark sky slowly pirouetting, the moon above him swirling across the heavens like the wild eye of a demon. He felt the ground suddenly open beneath him, and then he felt himself falling, falling, dropping toward what he knew had to be hell.

TWELVE

As the red-haired soldier and another carried the priest's small, limp body into the jail, the others stood ready with their weapons. Young and inexperienced, they gazed nervously into the night, looking up and down Pleasant Street, unsure whether or not this was some sort of trick to rescue the prisoners. Major-General Mattoon had warned them to be on the alert. Sentries had been placed at all roads entering Northampton. Even the townspeople were apprehensive. Each day brought new rumors. It was said that a band of the prisoners' countrymen had left Boston and was headed west, with plans of storming the jail and freeing the two. Supposedly someone had already spotted a ragtag group of men armed with pitchforks and cudgels camping out in woods on Mount Holyoke, just across the river. They were coming to set free the paddies, many in town believed. So Governor Strong had called up a full company of artillery as well as a detachment of militia to keep order and insure that the hanging proceeded without incident.

The turnkey now stood outside the prisoners' cell, holding a lantern and calling to them. Halligan, shading his eyes from the light, roused himself from sleep. *Was it time already*, he wondered.

"What is it?" he asked Dowd nervously, his voice catching in his throat.

"They just brought in a man who said he's come to see you."

"To see us? Now?"

"Yes. Calls himself a priest."

"Dom," Halligan called. "Wake up. The priest's here."

Daley climbed stiffly off his bunk and went to the bars. "Mr. Dowd, would his name be Father Cheverus?"

"I don't know. He's out."

"Out? What d'ye mean, out?"

"The soldiers told him to stop but he wouldn't. So they fired."

"Sweet Jesus!" Daley cried. "They didn't hurt him, did they now?"

"No. They fired a warning shot. They said he fell. He might've hit his head. He's got some blood on him."

"But he's not shot, you say?"

"No. I don't think so."

"And he said he was a priest?"

"Yes. Though he's not dressed like a priest. I was going to send someone for the sheriff, but I thought you should take a look first. I know you were expecting him."

"Must be Father Cheverus. Where is he?"

Dowd turned and called down the corridor. "Bring him down here, boys."

The guards carried the man along, one holding his arms, the other his legs. Halligan recognized one of the guards. It was the red-haired soldier who'd had words with Daley on the morning of their trial. The man stared at the tall Irishman.

"I told him to stop," the young soldier explained, trying not to sound defensive. "But he ran off. We had orders to stop anyone who looked suspicious."

"That be him?" Dowd asked the prisoners.

Daley looked at the tiny, disheveled figure the soldiers carried. The priest hung limply, as if dead.

"Aye," said Daley. " 'Tis Father Cheverus. He's all right, you say?"

"We told him to stop," the red-haired soldier repeated. "He just fell and hit his head."

"He seems to be breathing just fine," added Dowd.

"What're you going to do with him?" Daley asked.

"I don't know. I suppose I could put him in an empty cell."

"He can have me bed," Daley offered. "I'll sleep on the floor."

So the guards brought the priest into the cell and laid him down on Daley's bunk. He made a low moaning sound but didn't wake up. Under his right eye there was a jagged cut surrounded by an area of abraded flesh. Blood and dirt were caked on the wound, and a small flap of skin hung loose. Halligan looked him over. The wee fellow wasn't even dressed like a priest. And so tiny, frail looking. He had a high forehead, soft doughy features, a small mouth that reminded him of a girl's. And yet his face seemed very old somehow, haggard, careworn. So this is the fellow Daley's been waiting for?

Daley knelt on the floor beside him. "Mr. Dowd, could you get me something to clean him up a bit?"

Dowd went off and returned with a stone pitcher of water and a rag. He left them a taper to see by.

"Call me if you need anything," Dowd said, locking the cell door. He and the guards left, and they were alone with the priest.

"I told you he'd come," Daley said. "Didn't I tell you?"

Daley wet the rag and gently started to clean the wound. The priest moaned again. His lids fluttered, then opened wide. His eyes appeared startled, confused, wild-looking as someone with a fever. He glanced around, the way a man would who was waking in a different world from the one he'd gone to sleep in. And when he started to speak it was only gibberish, though Halligan thought he caught some French here and there.

"Father Cheverus," Daley said, hovering over his face.

The priest stared up at him, his eyes glassy but straining with a kind of fear.

"Are ye all right, Father?"

"I'm a priest," he said, grabbing at the fabric of his shirt over his chest, balling it in his fist, almost as if he had some great pain there. "I'm a priest."

"I know, Father. It's me. Dominic Daley."

"Dominic?" he said, staring fixedly at him.

"Aye, Father. You may not recognize me on account of the beard and all. You baptized Michael. Remember, Father? You baptized me son."

Slowly, the confusion seemed to leach out from his eyes, leaving them a clearer shade of brown, burnished as leather. "I baptized your son," he said, neither question nor statement.

"That you did, Father," Daley said.

Looking around the room, the priest asked, "Where's Finola?"

"Finola? I . . . don't know, Father. I thought she'd be with you."

The priest frowned, searching his memory. Then he said, "Yes. And the child, Michael."

"Aye. That's his name. Michael. Where are they, Father?" Daley asked, worry clouding his features. "Did they come on the stage with you?"

The priest's gaze fell on Halligan for some reason. Halligan had never seen a priest like this one, so small, and his face like that of a child waking from a nightmare.

"I . . ."

"Would you care for a drink of water, Father?" Daley got his own tin cup and filled it with water. He lifted the priest's head and put the cup to his lips. The priest drank, gulping the water too fast. He started to cough.

"Easy does it, Father."

The priest looked around again, staring curiously at the walls, the bars of the cell.

"Where am I?" he asked finally.

"You're in the jail in Northampton," Daley explained.

"What happened to me?"

"They said you ran. The soldiers. They carried you here. You got yourself a nasty cut under your eye."

The priest touched the spot, winced.

"My things?" he asked urgently. "Where is my trunk?" He grabbed at his chest again, only this time he reached down into his shirt and pulled out a heavy silver cross. He brought it to his lips and kissed it.

"I couldn't rightly say, Father."

"I'll need my things," he said, almost petulantly.

"Don't you worry now. We'll ask where they put 'em in the morning," Daley said, patting the priest's hand.

"But I must have my things."

The man struggled to get up, his muscles straining, quivering, in his eyes a look of great worry. Yet his eyes fluttered then and rolled back in the sockets, and he collapsed onto the bunk.

Daley placed a hand on his chest and said, "Rest ye now, Father."

The priest stared up at him, still dazed and confused but slowly coming back to himself. He seemed to slump a little, letting the muscles of his shoulders and arms go limp. His eyelids grew heavy, and yet he fought to keep them open.

"Finola, Father. Do ye know where she is?"

But instead of answering, the man said yet again, "I am a priest."

"Yes. Everything's going to be all right now, Father," Daley replied in a soothing voice. "Get you some sleep. We can talk in the morning."

Cheverus looked about to say something, but he'd lost the struggle to keep his eyes open. They closed and he fell fast asleep. Daley lay on the hard stone floor between the bunks, on his back, his hands behind his head. Halligan blew out the candle. The darkness rushed in like water past a broken dam, inundating their senses for a moment. After a while, Halligan could make out the light breathing of the priest while he slept.

"I wonder where she is. And Michael," Daley said.

"I'm sure they'll be here."

"She was supposed to come with him, though."

"Maybe she stayed in town."

"I don't like to think of them all alone. Not with all that sort out and about."

Halligan wanted to reassure his friend that his wife was all right, but he didn't know what to say. So he said only, "She'll be here in the morning."

Daley snorted. "Why do you suppose he's dressed like that?" he asked.

"Who knows?" Halligan replied. "He seems like an odd duck, you ask me."

"He's French," Daley said, as if that explained it. "But he's a good man. He always done right by us. When me little brother got the yellow fever, he come every day. And now he's come all this way so we can make confession."

"So *you* can," Halligan said.

"It wouldn't hurt you none, Jamy."

"Now why would I be doing that if I don't believe in it?"

"Supposin' you're wrong?"

"Wrong?"

"Aye. Supposin' there is a hell? Then what?"

"Then I guess I'll be going there."

"*Och*," Daley said, annoyed at the illogic of such a response. "Stubborn as a mule, you are. Make confession why don't you? He come all this way. What do you got to lose? If I'm wrong, there's no harm done."

"You missed your calling. You're worse than that pastor fellow, Williams."

It was all so damned queer, Halligan thought. The whole bloody, stinking mess. First their arrest and then the months in prison, followed by that mockery of a trial, and now this priest showing up the way he did, carried in like a dead man himself. It was like a joke or a bad dream, he couldn't say which. Except for the fact that he'd be dead in less than forty-eight hours, Halligan might even have thought it funny. No sense crying in your pint though, he told himself. This was the way things stood, so you might as well get used to it, boyo. Nobody lived forever. And there was something to be said for knowing the where and when and how of it. In some ways, wasn't that actually better? There'd be no surprises. It wouldn't sneak up on you when you weren't expecting it.

Remember us, Jamy, he thought, recalling her voice when she said it, the way her eyes shimmered in the dappled light of the shaded grove. The cool shock of the water, the feel of her skin against his. How could he have left her? How could he have done what he did?

Can you ever find it in your heart to forgive someone who loved you more than life itself, he thought as he lay there. That's what he would say if he were to write her a letter. Perhaps: *I was a foolish man to lose you, love.*

He fell forever, it seemed, fell as if he would never stop falling, as if falling wasn't an action but a state of being, something he had become. In his wildest imaginings, he had never thought hell to be so deep, so bottomless a pit. And yet when he came to rest, or at least when he'd stopped his dizzying plunge, he realized it wasn't hell at all that he found himself in. No. Here there were no flames, no fires, no shrieks of the damned. Everything here was hushed, still, like the dreadful silence that follows in the wake of some deafening noise. In the air hung the overripe smell of fruit and flowers, and of some other sickening odor he could not quite define. A hazy light covered everything like a fine powder. Then he saw them. They looked like birds at first, great black crows, fallen from the sky and scattered on the ground, their wings outspread, broken, covered with blood. Soon, though, he saw they were not crows at all but men. The fallen martyrs. They lay still, unmoving, in awkward, grotesque attitudes. And as he looked on, his heart shrank in terror. He wanted to run and hide. He wanted only to leave this hellish place that smelled of death. And yet he found that he couldn't move, that his limbs were frozen. So he did the only thing he could. He folded his hands and he began to pray.

Then he felt hands on him, lifting him, moving him. So he too was among the dead, he thought, and they were carrying his body with the others to the mass grave. Above him he had a glimpse of the sky, oddly darkened now, with a smattering of stars, the tangled limbs of trees against the night. He looked up and saw what must have been the face of the *sansculotte*, the one who had killed him. His bearded face shadowed, unrecognizable.

I'm a priest, he told his executioner. *I am one of them.*

After that everything became dark and silent again, and he was alone. All alone. At first he felt he was in his bed, in the rectory back in Boston. But then he knew he was home again, really and truly home, in his room in Mayenne. He was a small child, once more lying in the dark, afraid. He called out to his mother, "Maman, I am frightened." He waited there in the darkness for a long time, hoping she would come to him. Finally, though he could not see her face, he heard her voice whisper close to his ear, "*Je suis là, mon petite chou.*" And then another voice, one not his mother's, said in the darkness, "I am here. Be not afraid."

When he woke finally and saw himself surrounded by the stone walls and iron bars, he thought for a moment he was back in the jail in Laval. He recalled the fat guard with the birthmark, the one who asked if he were going to hell. What had happened, he wondered. Where was he?

"Good morning, Father," a voice said to him. He looked over and saw a large man with a long scruffy beard seated on the other bunk.

"Where am I?" he asked.

"The jail, Father. The soldiers brought you here."

Soldiers, he wondered. Ah, yes. The soldiers. It began to come back to him, parts of it anyway. The previous night had the disjointed, unreal quality of a nightmare. He recalled meeting them, their questions, their wanting him to open his trunk. Then running, being told to stop, the sound of a gunshot. And then what? The sensation of falling. How long had he been out, he wondered. What day was it? Had he been shot? He stared across at the bearded man whom he vaguely recalled. Was *he* the faceless *sansculotte,* the one who had lifted him in his dream and carried him? No, it was not him. Yet he thought he *did* know this man. He was wild-looking, gaunt and haggard, his features altered almost beyond measure. But he recognized him. Yes. Slowly, he realized it was Dominic Daley. Finola's husband. The man whose soul he'd come to save.

"Dominic?" he whispered, his throat parched.

"Aye, Father," he said with a reassuring smile. "How are we feeling today?"

"I . . ." Yet he couldn't say how he felt, except that his head throbbed and his body ached when he took a breath.

"Hungry are ye? They brought some breakfast."

With Daley's help, Cheverus managed to sit up. A wild pounding commenced inside his skull. He leaned over and rested his head in the palms of his hands until the noise quieted down a little. He'd never been drunk in his life, but this is what it must feel like, he thought. A sensation similar to the weakness following a fever, the disorientation, that hammering in his brain as if his skull would explode. He took a breath, exhaled slowly. The cell's stench was overpowering, and brought a sudden wave of nausea sweeping through him.

"Why don't you eat a bit, Father," Daley said, holding out a piece of bread to him. "Something in your belly is just the thing."

He accepted the bread from Daley and placed a small piece on his tongue. He forced himself to chew it. He thought for a moment he would retch, but he somehow managed to swallow it. Then he drank water from a tin cup Daley handed him. He was so thirsty. He drank that and asked for another.

"How's the eye?" Daley said.

"Eye?" he asked.

He fingered the tender spot beneath his eye. The flesh was puffy and his touch sent a bright wave of pain washing up into his skull.

"You got yourself a good one there. How come you're dressed like that, Father?"

"What? Oh," Cheverus said, looking down at his workman's attire. There was blood on his waistcoast. "Where are my things?"

"The jailor has your trunk. Beggin' your pardon, Father, but you said Finola and the lad were with you?"

He frowned, then said, "Yes." Now he remembered. He saw her sitting in the grass near the stream, suckling her child. He remembered the whiteness of her breast in the moonlight. He remembered her smell and the impure feelings he had had. And he remembered her begging him to help her husband. She had called him a saint. A blessed saint. Finally he said, "I was able to secure them a room for the night. She's fine."

"Faith," Daley exclaimed. "Thank ye, Father. I was worried something awful. I should a known you'd not let anything happen to 'em."

Cheverus then felt a cool flood of panic sweep over him. He wondered what day it was, how much time they had left. "How long have I . . ." he asked. "I mean, when is . . ."

"Tomorrow we hang, Father," Daley said flatly, as if he were talking about market day or a new moon. "I was gettin' a wee bit worried you'd not make it. But I should a known better."

"Forgive me for not coming sooner."

"You're here now, Father. That's all that matters. I can't tell you how much it means to us that you come."

Cheverus glanced over at the other prisoner seated beside Daley. He was shorter, but broad-shouldered, thick through the chest. Despite the hair and the scruffy beard, he was a handsome man with a squarish face, intelligent, deep-set eyes.

"That's Jamy, Father," Daley explained. "James Halligan. He's the one writ them fine letters to you."

"Hello," he replied, his throat dry.

"Good morning, Father," Halligan said.

They talked as Cheverus nibbled on the bread. He did feel a little better with food in his belly. Daley asked how his mother was, and Cheverus lied and said she was improving.

"That's good to hear," Daley replied. "She's had a rough go of it, these past few months."

"She sends her love," Cheverus said.

"Would you give her mine, too, Father?"

"Of course. She regrets not being able to make the trip out."

"*Och,*" the big Irishman lamented, batting the idea away. "I do miss seein' the old gal. But I'm glad she won't be comin'. I wouldn't want her to see something like that."

They talked for a while about Finola and Michael, about the rest of Dominic's family, about the weather in Boston. Holy Cross Church. People they knew in common.

Cheverus said, "We soon hope to have a school in the church basement."

"A school," exclaimed Daley. "That's grand. A school so they can read and write. D'ye hear that, Jamy boy?" he said to Halligan. "Jamy here is a big one for the books. He's been learnin' me to write, Father."

Cheverus looked to the man, who merely nodded. During the conversation Halligan didn't say much, would only shrug or nod occasionally.

"I remember me Da and meself pitching in to dig the foundation," Daley said.

"The church owes much to your hard work, Dominic."

"I've missed going to Mass, Father. Do you think I might be able to receive communion?"

"Certainly. After you've made confession."

Cheverus looked over at Halligan again. He didn't think he'd ever seen him before. Not in church. Nor around Boston. He was good with faces. A man of few words, this one. And yet, he was a writer of some articulation and skill. Someone who understood he was at the very end of things and wanted to unburden himself, make his soul right before God. He recalled one line in particular: *We are solicitous only about our salvation.* Cheverus thought he saw in the man's eyes the look of some terrible longing. He'd seen that look before plenty of times, in the eyes of the sick, the aged, the infirm. People breathing their last, when their lives seemed to them so paltry a thing, filled with missed opportunities. Things that hadn't panned out. Hopes that never came to fruition.

"How long have you been in the States, James?" Cheverus asked.

"Not long. A few years."

"Where did you settle over here? Not in Boston? I don't think I've ever seen you in church."

"No, Father. You wouldn't have," he said, an ironic smile playing about his mouth. "Here and there. I moved around a lot."

The three talked for a while. Small talk, awkward and strained. When they laughed, it was too hard, self-conscious, meant to hide their nervousness. Cheverus had sat by the bedside of the dying countless times before, giving comfort, listening to their confessions, easing their fears. He knew what that was like. He was experienced in the ways of illness and accident and old age, of sudden misfortune, unexpected calamity. But this? He had never given counsel to men that were about to be put to death, at least not to men who knew with absolute certainly that they would be, very shortly, dead. Those poor souls he'd visited at the Convent of the Carmes, while in danger surely, had never known with complete assurance that they would die. This was different. This was grotesque, an aberration of the natural order. Two healthy men who lived and breathed, hoped and feared still—these two would be dead in a day's time.

Mostly it was Daley who spoke, chattering nervously, occasionally turning to Halligan and saying, "Am I right, Jamy boy?" and the other would perhaps nod. Daley talked of this and that, of springtime back home, of what crops would be planted and when. They avoided the subject of why they were there—their sentence, the fate which loomed just beyond these prison walls yet was slowly, inexorably closing in upon them. Once or twice, the conversation lagged and Cheverus saw the condemned exchange furtive glances filled with some meaning he could only guess at. He thought now it would happen: that one or the other would bring up their crime, blurt out that they were sorry, and beg God's forgiveness. But strangely they didn't speak a word of their sin. He knew if he were to save their souls, he would have to get them to talk. He would have to get them to confess to their crime, ask for forgiveness, and receive absolution.

After a while Cheverus said, "Forgive me, but I feel I must speak frankly. The hour of your sentence approaches. Tomorrow you will stand before the Almighty. You must consider your immortal soul. I ask that you reflect upon your sins."

"Aye, Father," Daley replied. "I have been. That's all I been doin'."

"Very well," Cheverus said. "Is there some place we might be able to talk in private?"

"We could ask Mr. Dowd," Daley said. "When Finola visited he would let us meet in one of the empty cells."

Daley called down the corridor to the turnkey, who showed up with several guards.

"I would wish to speak to each prisoner alone, if that is possible," Cheverus said to Dowd. "Is there some place where we might have privacy?"

Dowd scratched his bald pate. "I could put you in another cell."

"That would be fine, thank you," Cheverus said. He turned to the prisoners. "Who would like to go first?"

Daley glanced at Halligan. "I suppose I'll go first. Since I'm the older one. And the better lookin'," he added with a loutish grin.

Though they were headed just a few paces down the corridor, the guards still placed the manacles on Daley, both his hands and his feet, and escorted the two into an empty cell.

"I believe this is yours, sir," the turnkey said to Cheverus, handing him his trunk.

"Thank you," he replied. "Could you remove the chains from the prisoner, Mr. Dowd?"

"Sorry. I got my orders."

He sat next to Daley on the only bunk in the cell. He was close enough to catch the sour odor of the man, like the ocean at low tide. He looked at Daley. While he was the spitting image of his father, coarse-featured, with that large underslung jaw, Cheverus noticed, for the first time really, that he had his mother's soft blue-gray eyes.

Daley folded his big battered hands, closed his eyes, and bowed his head. "Forgive me, Father, for I have—" he began, but Cheverus interrupted him.

"A moment please, Dominic."

"Father?" he asked, opening his eyes to look at him.

"I thought we might talk for a while. Before you make your confession."

"Oh," Daley said. "Whatever you say."

"How have you been, Dominic?"

"All right, Father," he said, then, pondering it a moment, added, "Well, not so good to tell you the truth."

"I imagine it's been hard. These last few months."

Daley nodded. "The worst is not being about to see Finola and me son. I've missed them awful bad."

"And I know she misses you, too. She loves you very much."

"I worry what'll become of her and the lad after I'm gone."

"They'll get on somehow."

"I just wish there was someone to kinda look in on them now and again."

"I would be happy to," he said.

"Would you now, Father?"

"Yes, of course. Have you been praying, Dominic?"

"Every day."

"Good. Remember, my son: 'Yea, though I walk through the valley of the shadow of death, I will fear no evil.'"

As Cheverus uttered the words, he thought of his own fears. He thought how easy it was to tell another that he should not fear death.

"Aye, Father," the prisoner said, tugging on his long beard. "But I am, a bit anyway."

"You believe in God's love, my child?"

"Indeed, I do."

"Then that is all you need."

Daley nodded thoughtfully. "Still and all I can't help wondering what it'll feel like. Do you think it'll hurt, Father?"

He wanted to be able to say it wouldn't. That dying would be an easy feat for a man of true faith. Nothing more than a taking off of one's mortal clothes and putting on the glorious raiment of Paradise. But he couldn't bring himself to say that. What did *he* know of dying? Who was *he* to tell anyone about what death would be like?

"I don't know, Dominic. Each man dies in his own fashion."

"Do you reckon it'll be quick?"

"Yes. But try not to dwell upon that. You must set your sights on the next life."

"Aye, Father. But I'm afraid still."

"That is to be expected. Ask God for strength."

Daley nodded.

Cheverus felt like a hypocrite. Had his thoughts been on the next life when his moment to die had been at hand? Or had he been thinking only about his own fleshly existence, the pain and torments of the here and now?

Daley looked over at him. "I've heard about men who had to be dragged screamin' and kickin' up to the gallows."

"You will be brave, I have no doubt."

"I would want me son to know I died like a man. Not like some bloody coward—beggin' your pardon, Father."

"I'll be right there with you," he said.

"Will you now?"

"Yes, I promise. Every step of the way."

"And afterwards, too, Father? When it's over and done?"

"Yes."

"But they're gonna . . ." Daley swallowed hard, "take and boil our bodies. That's the thing I have a hard time getting used to."

He looked imploringly at Cheverus, almost as if the priest had the power to change that fact. He put his hands to his face and began to cry, softly at first, then in big quaking sobs that made his shoulders lurch.

"Dominic," Cheverus said, reaching out and putting his hand on his shoulder. "Listen to me, Dominic. That is just your mortal shell. Not you. Not your soul."

"I know, Father," he said, continuing to sob. The tears ran down into his hand. "But . . ."

"Put yourself in God's hands, my son."

He nodded. "I'm sorry for crying like this."

"It's all right." Cheverus rubbed his back.

After a while Daley's sobs slowed and soon they stopped altogether. He took a deep breath and exhaled. "Mother o' God," he moaned. "Would you look at me now. Blubberin' away like some schoolboy." He wiped his eyes on the sleeve of his shirt. "I don't want 'em all to see me cryin' tomorrow. Them that's come to see us hang. I don't want to give them the satisfaction."

"I understand," said Cheverus. "God will give you courage."

"Do you really think so, Father?"

"Yes. And I'll be right there with you."

Because of the manacles, he reached with difficulty into his shirt and took out a packet of letters tied with a string. The letters were worn thin and dirty from handling. He gave the packet to Cheverus.

"Those are from Finola. I'd like her to have 'em back. They won't do me no good where I'm going. And they might be of some comfort to her in the future."

"I'll see that she gets them."

"And there's one in there for me boy. I wrote it."

"*You* wrote it, Dominic?"

"Aye," he said, smiling with pride. "Jamy learned me how to make me letters. And I copied what he put down, as best I could anyway. Would you pass it along to him?"

"I will be sure to."

"When will I get to see them, Father?"

"I shall go and bring them here later. Anything else you need?"

"Could you ask 'em if we mightn't be allowed a razor? I'd like to shave in the morning. I would like to look presentable."

"I will ask."

"Oh. One more thing, Father? Whatever happens, would you tell me mam I died quick like. That I didn't suffer none. I wouldn't want her to get upset."

"I understand. I'll tell her that . . . it went smooth like."

"I know I've been a terrible burden on her. Tell her I'm sorry, too."

Cheverus looked at Daley expectantly, waiting. "I will." Then, "Dominic?"

"Yes, Father."

"Do you feel true remorse?"

"Remorse, Father?"

"For what you've done."

"I feel I've let me folks down, if that's what you mean. And I feel bad for that man's mother."

"Whose mother?"

"That fellow's. Lyon's mother?"

"You feel bad for her?"

"Yes."

"Because of her loss, you mean?"

"That, too, I suppose. But mostly on account of the money."

"The money?" Cheverus asked. So he would tell him finally. The truth. The truth that would save his soul.

"Aye, Father." He paused for a moment, looking down at the stone floor. He swallowed hard again, his big Adam's apple bobbing in his neck. "It was rightly hers and we shoulda come clean."

"So it was his money?"

Daley nodded, his gray eyes appearing contrite. "We lied about it because . . . well, on account of how it would look and all. We were afraid."

"I understand. And yet, you feel remorse for that now?"

"Sure and I do, Father."

Cheverus felt his heart lift up, like a white bird taking flight. He felt the joy of bringing God's gift of mercy to this man.

"That's good, Dominic," he told him. "It is through remorse and sincere repentance that we are able to receive the Lord's blessing. Would you care to make confession now?"

"Please, Father."

Cheverus opened his trunk. He took out his surplice and his violet stole, the one he used for hearing confession, and put them on. Of all the many confessions he had heard in his time as a priest, this one, he sensed, was by far the most important he would ever hear. A soul teetered on the brink, the abyss of hell waiting below him, and he, Cheverus, was going to snatch it back. He was going to save it. He thought of his mother, her prediction when he was a child that he would do something great in God's service. That he would make her proud. Till now he had only brought shame upon himself and upon his mother's memory. Secret shame. Shame which only he and God knew. But shame nonetheless. Perhaps this was what he had waited so long for. What he had crossed an ocean hoping to find. When he was ready, he blessed Daley with the sign of the cross and said, "*Dominus sit in corde tuo . . .*"

Daley began. "Bless me, Father, for I have sinned."

He wandered over the sins of his life, offering up every curse and oath and blasphemy he'd ever uttered, every lie and falsehood he'd told since he was a boy. He confessed to stealing some eggs from a neighbor back home when he was eight. To not paying a debt of a half-crown for some seed he'd purchased on credit. To selling a heifer for twice what he knew it to be worth. Yet when Daley had finished his confession, he hadn't said a word—not one word—about the murder. He told him about the money, how it wasn't theirs, how they'd lied to the authorities about it, but to Cheverus's utter amazement, the prisoner didn't say anything about the rest: how they had held up Marcus Lyon, pulled him from his horse and bashed in his skull, then pushed his lifeless body under the water. Nothing at all about that. Instead, what he told him was a preposterous story about their having found the purse lying in the weeds by the side of the road. Found it! And that his deepest regret was for not having turned it in. He knew that it was not his money and that it was wrong— a form of stealing—and he didn't want that on his conscience when he died.

"You found the money?" Cheverus asked him, his eyes widened in astonishment.

"Yes, Father. It was just a-laying there off the road. Down by the river."

"How had it got there?"

"I dunno. That's the odd thing. There was no explainin' it."

Cheverus paused, wondering how to continue. Was he going to persist in this hardened obstinacy, one that would condemn his soul to hell? He needed to get him to understand the spiritual peril he was in.

"Is there anything else you would wish to confess before God, Dominic?"

"I don't think so, Father."

"Are you quite sure?"

Daley scratched his beard.

"I think that about does it, yes."

"You know that you must make a complete and full confession in order for me to absolve you and for you to be forgiven in the eyes of God."

"Why, yes, Father, I do."

"Dominic, I must warn you one last time. You would be placing your immortal soul in grave jeopardy if you were to knowingly leave out a sin, especially a mortal sin. You would not have benefit of absolution because you hadn't, in your heart, repented of the sin. Do you understand what I'm telling you, Dominic?"

He stared at Daley, waiting. The big Irishman looked down at his hands, his fingers slowly contracting into fists and then relaxing, doing it again and again, seeming to knead something invisible. Cheverus wanted to take him by the shoulders, as you would a child, and say, *If you want absolution, Dominic, you will have to confess to your crime. If God is to forgive you, you will have to admit to killing that man and show remorse for your action, before it is too late.* Daley finally looked up at him. His gaze was the simple, uncomplicated gaze of a dog.

"I know, Father," he replied.

"Very well," Cheverus said, discouraged. He decided he would leave it there for now. There was still some time. Not much, but a little. Time to save his soul.

"What's my penance, Father?" Daley asked.

"Say five Our Fathers and ten Hail Marys."

And then Cheverus went ahead and said the words of absolution.

THIRTEEN

One day, he thought. *One stinking day is all you got, boyo.*

While Daley was with the priest, Halligan lay on his bunk staring up at a tattered cobweb dangling from the ceiling. In it lay trapped the dry husk of a single fly, dead for ages yet he had not noticed it before. He thought that odd. Soon you'll be as dead as that blasted fly, he told himself. He didn't hold out hope about the appeal saving them at the last moment. No, that was pure fantasy, as of course were his thoughts about escape. There'd be no escape. That was just grasping at straws. He needed to abandon hope, as it was a tantalizing and treacherous wench that would only make it harder to do what he would have to do on the morrow. He needed to set his sights on death, to look it right in the eye, to get used to the bitter tang of it in his mouth. And yet he knew it was only with the arrival of the little priest that the last shred of hope had vanished completely. It was as if the man had carried the certainty of their end with him like a buzzard floating over a sick calf in a field.

He looked back on his life with sadness and regret, with yearning and confusion, and with an odd detachment, too, as if it weren't really his life but that of someone else, or as if it were merely a story someone had told him once around a campfire: *There was once this lad named Halligan . . .* What had seemed an infinite array of days stretching out, glittering and luminous, all those he'd squandered or frittered aimlessly away, tossed aside like so much chaff, spent in drunken abandon, in card-playing or gaming or whoring, thinking they would remain as plentiful as the grains of sand on the shore below Slea Head, that there would always be more, always a tomorrow. But the joke turned out to be on him—they could be used up. They had been used up—or almost. It wasn't as if he would have done anything particularly differently with his life, though maybe here and there he might have. Yet he would have done what he did knowing full well this day would come. *The last one. The very last.* He could almost feel the approach of death as a tingling sensation along the back of his scalp, so that the hairs stood on end.

He had not been afraid of much, perhaps because he'd never considered he had much worth losing. But he supposed he was afraid of this. At least a little. Not of the pain of the thing so much, not like with Daley, though he didn't look forward to that either. He just hoped it would be quick. Sometimes the memory of poor Father Roche dying miserably up there on Wexford Bridge slipped into his mind. *Jaysus,* he'd cry out. He didn't want to go like that. No sir. He'd rather be shot down like a dog running away. Perhaps it was more simply the unknown of it, the strange, dark mystery of the thing he'd be facing tomorrow. He felt there was nothing waiting beyond, neither joyful nor filled with terrors, only silence and darkness. Still a fellow couldn't help but wonder, could he now? And that was the thing that rubbed him the wrong way. The wondering and thinking on it.

Yet mostly what he felt today hadn't so much to do with fear, nor even with the rage that had burned so hotly in him just a short time before. Of course, he was angry still, but the anger had dissipated, become a thing muted and distant, a notion more grasped by the mind than felt by the heart. So what did he feel? A peculiar kind of resignation had stolen over him in the last day or so, a grudging acquiescence regarding his fate. He accepted both the injustice and the inevitability of his end, not willingly, not gladly, but with the pragmatic fortitude similar to that one had with the approach of a storm: there was nothing to do except get ready for it, close the shutters, get the animals into the barn. To do otherwise was foolish. Yes, he would rise tomorrow for the last time, eat his last meal, take his last breath, and that was all there was to it. It was as simple, as straightforward, as uncomplicated as that. There was even a kind of cold comfort in that certainty. No man lived forever. This was his time and to fight it was not only futile but foolish.

Since yesterday though, he'd felt a strange feeling rising in his chest. A raw burning in his lungs, as though he'd inhaled smoke. He had to concentrate hard to breathe or he'd start coughing. For some reason, he thought of the feeling as regret, a vague longing after something he couldn't even put his finger on. Yet what did he have to regret? Though still a young man, he'd been all over, seen things, done things, had had a bellyful of living. More than most men twice his age. Perhaps, he reasoned, anyone facing death felt that way. Even if he lived to be a hundred. Maybe it was the innate greediness of the human heart, always wanting more than it could ever possibly hold. Or perhaps it was the fact that he felt he'd come to a certain understanding about the world and about himself as well, but too late for it to be of any real use to him. Maybe if he had lived. Maybe . . . But to hell with it, he told himself. That was all in the past. Just let it go. Give the whole damn thing up. There was nothing to be done. You could think until hell froze over, and it wouldn't change a damn thing.

Daley returned to the cell then, accompanied by the guards. His eyes were strangely luminous, his pockmarked skin mottled. There was a high, burnished color to his cheeks and forehead, as on a man who had been sitting too close to a fire. It was obvious that he'd been crying and was embarrassed by it. He looked chastened and subdued, his shoulders hunched forward like a reprimanded schoolboy. And yet at the same time he appeared serene, his face emptied of fear. There was about him a calmness Halligan had not seen before.

"How'd it go?" Halligan asked his friend.

"Your turn, Jamy boy," was all he said, a foolish grin on his face. His expression reminded Halligan of that of the boys back in the orphanage, after they'd left the confessional. Relieved that they'd made it through somehow and feeling smug enough to taunt the others still in line.

"You told him I wasn't going to make confession?"

"Just go talk to him. You'll like him."

"You told him though, right?"

Daley only winked.

As Halligan entered the cell, he found the priest kneeling on the floor. He held a large silver cross with both hands, and he was praying silently, his back to the door. Despite the noisy racket of his chains on the stone floor, the priest continued, undisturbed by the noise. Halligan took a seat on the bunk and waited. Even in his vestments now, the man looked unpriest-like somehow, too small and frail, more like a student studying for the priesthood. An old-looking altar boy. His face was puffy and bruised, his right eye swollen, the skin taut and shiny beneath it. It looked as if he'd come out on the short end of a fight. There was about him, Halligan thought, something very sad. Why, you'd have thought he was the one bound for the gallows. Halligan decided there was no harm in just talking to the priest. He would be polite, make conversation, pass the time. But that was it. If he started in on all that other business, he would tell him not for him, thank you very much.

"Hello, James," the priest said to him finally.

"Good morning, Father."

The priest rose and sat beside him on the bunk. His surplice was dirty at the knees and threadbare. The large cross hung on a heavy silver chain around his slender neck, almost seeming to weigh his head down. As he spoke, he nervously fingered the cross with his thumb.

"How are you, James?"

"Not bad considering," he said, trying to make a joke. Cheverus didn't smile. "How's the eye, Father?"

"It hurts a little," he said, touching it.

"I'm sorry you got hurt on our account."

"It wasn't your fault. It was my own . . ." But he didn't finish the thought.

"I want to thank you for coming, Father," Halligan offered graciously.

"Your letter made quite a compelling case. You've obviously had some education."

"Aye. A bit. Your being here means a lot to Dom."

"He is a man of great faith."

"Indeed, he is. He's always praying. I've never seen anyone pray so much."

"It is good to have such faith at a time like this," the priest said. He looked over at Halligan, as if expecting a response. Halligan didn't say anything, though. "He speaks highly of you, too," Cheverus said. "He says you're like a brother to him."

Halligan nodded. "Dom's like a brother to me, too."

"You have no family in America, James?"

"No. No family a'tall."

"Is there someone you would want me to contact back home?"

He thought about it for a moment. Who would care to learn of his death? Of all the men he'd known or worked with, shared the road or a campfire with, fought with during those few desperate months during the Uprising, was there not even a single soul that would tip a pint in his memory? Or, of all the women he'd slept with, was there not even one who would shed a tear and recall Jamy Halligan with fondness or affection? Finally, he shook his head.

"I was an orphan, Father. After my mother died, I didn't have any folks."

"Who raised you?"

"The Franciscans took me in."

"Ah. So that's where you learned to read and write?"

"Yes, Father."

"Why did you leave Ireland?"

Halligan shrugged. He didn't see the point in telling this man his reasons. Yes, he was a priest and used to hearing the maggoty underbelly of a person's life. But Halligan's life was nobody's business but his own. Besides, the man wouldn't understand. How could he possibly know what it was to feel what he'd felt for a woman like Bridie. The touch of her skin, the smell and taste of her. The fact that they'd been lovers, that what they had done the Church considered a sin. He was a priest. And Halligan didn't want him giving him a lecture, telling him that it had been wrong, and not in the way that Halligan knew it to be wrong. The priest would want him to ask for forgiveness and he'd tell him to say ten Hail Marys and five Our Fathers. As if that would do any bloody good at all. So instead he replied, "Same as everybody, I suppose. Looking for a better life here," he said, a soft laugh escaping from him. The priest nodded sympathetically, as if he understood exactly why men left one place and came to another. Halligan looked down at the other's hands. They lay palm up on his lap, resting on the white surplice. Though small and delicately shaped, his hands were callused, the nails cracked and dirty, the fingers strangely gnarled for someone of his profession. He was a man, thought Halligan, who'd grown up in ease, who hadn't been accustomed to hard work, but who came to know it only later in life and then as a kind of penance.

"How long has yourself been here, Father?" Halligan asked.

"Ten years," he said.

Halligan saw the little priest get this faraway look in his brown eyes. He noticed now the small wrinkles around the mouth and the crow's feet at the corners of his eyes. They gave his childlike features an oddly haggard look. After a while he glanced over at Halligan and asked, "Are you quite certain there's no one you would wish me to write to?"

Again he shook his head.

"There must be somebody. A friend from back home. Somebody you knew at the orphanage perhaps."

"Nobody," he said again. He was a stubborn one, this priest. "There was a couple of lads I worked with, but I wouldn't know where they'd be now. I kind of moved around a lot."

"Is there nothing I can do for you?" the priest asked again.

"No, I don't think so, Father."

"I see," the priest said, his shoulders sagging in disappointment. "Perhaps then we ought to get started."

Halligan frowned. "Started, Father?"

"Your confession, James."

"Didn't Dom tell you?"

"Tell me what?"

"Begging your pardon, Father, but I've not made confession in years."

"All the more reason we should begin," he said, smiling, as if he'd made a joke.

"That's not what I meant. The truth is, I'm not much on church and all that. I've not been to Mass since I was a boy."

"But I thought . . . the letter spoke of confession?"

"Ah, that was Dominic's idea. I just wrote it for him. It's not that I'm not grateful for your coming. I am."

"You are Catholic, aren't you?"

"I was baptized Catholic. Or so they tell me."

"Then you are still a Catholic. The Franciscans must have taught you your catechism. The importance of confession."

"That they did," he said, nodding. "They tried to anyway. I just never took to it is all."

"Do you believe in God's love?"

Halligan shook his head. "I don't think He's all that interested in me to tell you the truth."

"But He is, James. He loves you very much."

"You don't know anything about me, Father. I mean the sort of person I am. Whether God could love me or not."

"I don't need to. He loves all His children. And His love means He forgives them their sins."

"I don't know much about forgiveness, but to my way of thinking there are some things beyond forgiveness."

"There is nothing beyond His compassion, my son. Nothing a man can do. You've committed sins, have you not, James?"

"Sure. What man hasn't?"

"Mortal sins. You know what they are?"

"Of course, Father," he said, an edge slipping into his voice. All this talk of sins and forgiveness only annoyed him. They didn't change a thing. Not a bloody thing.

"Then surely, you would want God's mercy."

"Seems kind of late for that." Then he added, "Sort of like closing the barn door after the cow is already out."

"It's never too late, James. No matter what you did before, no matter how terrible the offense, He would forgive you. God gave His only son for our sins, so that we may have eternal life. All you have to do is open your heart to His grace."

He'd heard all this before. He could remember Brother Padraig talking about God's grace. About mercy. About redemption. How God loved each one of us, even the worst man in the world. It was the same old line.

He hadn't bought it then, and he didn't buy it now. We were born alone and we died alone, and nothing we did in between would change that fact. And when your time was up, that was it. Whether we were good or bad, whether we repented our sins or not, we all of us ended up pretty much in the same sinking boat.

"I mean no disrespect Father, but you're wasting your time with me."

"Think of your immortal soul, James," the man exclaimed, his brown eyes burning with a fierce intensity. "While there is still time. You don't have to go to your grave with that terrible black mark upon it."

"Black mark, you say?"

"What you did. You can be forgiven. You can, James. It's never too late. Never."

The small priest was staring at him, his features drawn tight as a drum over the delicate bones of his face. He was sweating profusely, as if he had a fever. The sweat beaded on his forehead and slid down over his flushed cheeks. His dark eyes shone with the glow of some great expectation, or some great fear. Halligan could no longer look at him, so he closed his eyes. An image of Bridie came to him. She was standing there in the moonlight, up on Mount Eagle. Her dark eyes full of that same expectation, as he told her he would meet her in Cobh, and they would sail for America together. He wondered about the nature of forgiveness. Had she known he was lying even then, that he would betray her? Had she loved him enough to forgive him? No, he didn't think so. No one loved that much. Not even God could love another that much.

He opened his eyes but did not look over at the priest. He hung his head in his hands, staring down at the floor. "I think it is too late, Father. For me anyway."

"Not if you confess," Cheverus continued. "The Lord will forgive any-thing you've done. Anything at all. You need only ask Him and show true repentance for your sins."

"What I've done, nobody can forgive me for."

"You're wrong, James. His love is infinite. It depends only on your ask-ing Him for it."

He found the earlier rage returning. Now that burning in his chest was anger. It was like a smoldering piece of turf that had been fanned and suddenly burst into flame.

"I can only hope there's not a hell," he said, cruelly, as if trying to punish the priest for interfering. "Because if there is, I've got a first-class ticket for it, bought and paid for."

"No, James. You can be saved. Come," he said, extending his hand to him as he got down on his knees. "Let us pray together."

"No, Father," he said firmly, the anger rising up into his throat like bile. He couldn't even say why. He knew the priest was only trying to help him. But he didn't want his help. Or maybe he believed he was so far beyond help that the offer of it now merely teased him, like a thirsty man teased by the false lure of a mirage.

"James, please. Let me be of help to you."

"I said no. Now just leave it be, Father."

"There is nothing you could've done that He won't forgive. Even this."

"You don't know what you're talking about."

"He'll forgive anything. He can forgive this, too. Even this. Come. Pray with me, James." The priest tried to take hold of his hand, but he pulled violently away.

"No!" he cried. "I don't want any of your damn prayers! D'ye understand?"

"But how can I help you, my son?"

"You can't, Father. That's what I've been trying to tell you. I know you mean well. Dom says you're a decent man, and I believe him. But there's nothing you can say or do that's going to help me. So please, just leave me be."

Halligan fell silent. He sat there for a moment thinking about something the priest said. Even this? What did he mean by that? He looked over at Cheverus. Slowly, it dawned on him. He saw in the priest's eyes what he was really asking him.

"You're of a mind that we did it?" Halligan asked.

"It's not too late to receive God's mercy, my son."

"You do, don't you, Father? You think we killed that fellow."

"James, I beg of you. For the sake of your soul. Reconsider what you're doing."

"But we didn't do it, Father. We didn't."

"Confess and seek His forgiveness. Before it is too late."

"For God's sakes, Father, listen to what I'm telling you," Halligan cried. "We didn't kill the man. I swear we didn't."

The priest looked hard at him, as if for the first time. He squinted, his brown eyes those of a man looking into a sun that had just emerged from behind the clouds. The sudden light was almost too bright for him.

"But what of the money?" Cheverus asked. "I'm told they found the man's money on you."

Halligan wagged his head. He exhaled, trying to calm this growing anger in him.

"It was his, yes. That we did lie about," Halligan replied. "When they caught us and said we were being charged with murder, we didn't know what else to do. So we lied and said it was ours. But the truth was we found it lying on the ground, down near the river. Dom picked it up."

"You found it?"

"Aye."

"You didn't steal it?"

"No, we didn't steal it," he snapped. "His purse was lying there just off the road, and we picked it up. I don't know how it came to be there. Maybe in the fight it got thrown there. I can't say. We just picked it up. If we're guilty of anything, that'd be it. Nothing more than that. We never even met the man. Didn't know he was killed until the posse arrested us."

"I thought . . ."

"We told you in the letter we were innocent."

"But it spoke of your desire for salvation. I thought that's why you wanted me to come. So you could confess and receive absolution."

"Dom wanted to make confession. Not to this though. He's not a murderer. And neither am I. We didn't do this. I swear to you, Father."

Cheverus stared wide-eyed at him, his lips parted. His brought a hand up to his mouth. For several seconds he just stared at Halligan. "James," he said after a while, "you are telling me the truth," but it came out sounding like a question.

"Yes, Father. Why on earth would we lie now?" Halligan pleaded. "It doesn't matter so much to me whether you believe us or not. But it's important to Dom."

The priest shook his head. He took a breath, and when he exhaled, his shoulders sagged.

"You are telling the truth, aren't you?"

"I don't know who killed that fellow or why, or how his purse came to be lying there. I don't know any of that. All I know is we're innocent."

The priest closed his eyes. "*Cher Dieu dans le ciel!*" he said, as he folded his hands in prayer. He didn't say anything for several seconds. Finally, just above a whisper, he offered, "Forgive me, James. I have made a terrible mistake."

The little priest looked so pathetic, confused and lost, as if he had just learned there was no heaven after all. Halligan couldn't help feeling sorry for him. The anger had drained from him as quickly as it had come. He reached out and touched Cheverus's shoulder. "It's all right, Father," he offered at last.

"No, it's not all right. I thought . . ."

"There's a whole town out there thinks the same thing."

"But I should have had more faith in you."

"You hardly know me, Father. For all you know, I did do what they say."

"I know Dominic though. I should have known he wasn't capable of something like this. In your letter, you told me you were innocent. I should have believed you. Please, forgive me."

"Don't worry about it," Halligan said. "And I'm sorry for losing me temper, Father."

The priest nodded.

Halligan stood then, his chains rattling at the floor. "I suppose I'll be going now."

"Wait, James," Cheverus said, holding up his hand. "Stay a moment."

"I won't be wanting to make confession, Father."

"Yes, I understand. Perhaps we could just talk. I would like to get to know you a little, James."

"Why, Father? What's the point?"

"I don't know. I just would."

"I pretty much told you all there is to tell."

"Please," he said, patting the bunk with his hand. "As a kindness to me."

Halligan shrugged but sat down. What did he have to lose? Harmless chatter to pass the time. "I suppose I could cancel my other plans, Father," he said, smiling.

How wrong he had been, the priest thought. How terribly wrong. He, like everyone else, had doubted them, had believed them to be cold-blooded murderers. And he had looked upon their sentence, though perhaps harsh, as not altogether undeserved. He had come here, he knew, to save the souls of sinners, not of innocent men. Cheverus now believed this Halligan was telling the truth. In fact he knew it, knew it with a certainty in his heart he had felt about few things in life. He had heard enough final confessions to know when someone was telling the truth or not. He recognized in the man that frightening calm, the resigned look of someone drawing near to death, a look stripped of all pretense, pared of all necessity to dissemble or equivocate. Yes, they were innocent. That much was clear to him now. And their fate seemed almost unbearable, a monstrous travesty of justice. Innocent young men going to their doom and yet so placid about it all. How brave they were.

He had been wrong not only about them but about so many things, he realized now. Deceiving himself about whether he should return to France or not. Trying to convince himself it wasn't his *own* desire but God's will that he go back, that he was needed there. When in truth he knew in his heart God wanted him to stay here, to serve His Church in the new world. He saw it all so clearly now as he sat in this tiny jail cell so far away from France. Worst of all, he had been wrong about his own reasons for coming to the aid of these two men. He had told himself it was to perform this great service in God's name, to save their souls for His greater glory. But it wasn't for God, he knew now. And certainly not for the two of them. No, it had been for himself. He had wanted to do it for his own glory, his own vanity, his own egotism. That great deed his mother had predicted for him so many years ago, which he had failed at, would finally be his. And perhaps in helping to save the souls of these two men, hadn't he really also hoped to save his own? Wasn't *that* his real reason for coming? It was all so painfully clear to him now.

Dear God, he prayed. *Forgive me.*

He looked over at the condemned man, seated on the bunk. Of the two, he felt far worse about this Halligan. Dominic Daley had his faith, the love of his wife and family to see him through. Cheverus could pray with Daley, give him communion and spiritual comfort, help prepare him to meet his Maker. But what of this man, someone who didn't believe? Someone so cut off from his fellow man, from the solace of faith, from the grace of God. How could he help him? How could he ready him to climb the steps to the gallows tomorrow? He saw in the man's cool blue eyes such a terrible loneliness. Such solitude and remoteness. It was like gazing up into the heavens at night, the stars so distant they took your breath away. He would help him in any way he could.

"Do you miss your home, James?"

"Home?"

"Ireland."

"Oh. Some things, I suppose."

Unlike Daley, Halligan was harder to talk to, more reserved. He was obviously intelligent, articulate when he chose, but he was a man who was used to keeping things to himself. At first he answered most of Cheverus's questions in a few words. But the more they conversed, the more Halligan seemed to grow comfortable talking with him. He said he used to love the spring in Ireland. The lush valleys, the green hills covered with gorse and heather and bog cotton. Most of all, he missed tramping about.

"I loved walking the hills on a day like today," Halligan told him. "The sun in your face. 'Tis beautiful this time of year. Have you never been to Ireland, Father?"

"No," Cheverus admitted.

"A lovely place. You would like it."

"How old were you when your mother died, James?"

Halligan shrugged. "Three or four. I don't recollect much of her. I remember she had black hair and smooth pale skin. I want to say she was pretty, but the truth is I don't remember what she looked like."

"Where was she from?"

The man smiled wistfully. "I dunno. Never even knew where they buried her."

"It would have been nice to have a place to go to. A grave to visit."

Halligan tilted his head to one side and shrugged.

"Just a piece of ground is the way I see it, Father."

"My own mother died when I was a boy, too. But I was fortunate enough to know her. When she died, it was a great comfort to be able to visit her grave."

"I suppose for some it may be," the man responded, glancing quickly at him and then away.

Halligan fell silent, seemed to draw into himself again. Cheverus watched him rub the knuckles of one hand. They were raw, scabbed over, as if he'd been in a fight.

"We were very close, my mother and I," Cheverus continued, talking just to keep the silence at bay. "It was because of her that I went into the priesthood."

"You don't say?"

"Yes. She was a very devout woman. I used to accompany her to Mass each morning."

"Do you have brothers and sisters, Father?"

Cheverus nodded. "Yes. Two brothers and three sisters. I was the eldest."

"Not the tallest, I suppose," Halligan said playfully.

"No," he conceded with an awkward chuckle. "Fortunately they were all taller than I."

"Have you not seen them in all this time?"

"No. It has been almost fourteen years."

"You must miss them."

"I do very much." Then before he quite knew it, he blurted out, "I have been contemplating going home." He couldn't say why he had told this man, a complete stranger, such a thing. Then again, perhaps it was because he was a stranger. At the same time, he no longer knew if he would return home now. Why then did he say it? Was it just to acknowledge to himself that the opposite was true?

"Are ye now, Father?"

"Perhaps. But please don't tell Dominic. It might upset him to think I won't be here. I told him I would look in on Finola."

"Don't worry, Father. Your secret's safe with me," he said with a wink.

Feeling as if he had to justify his reasons though, he explained, "My old parish needs a priest. And my father is growing old."

"I understand," Halligan said.

"He'd like to see me again before he passes on to his reward."

Even as he said it though, the prospect of his leaving began to fade, to slip off into the hazy distance like a ship vanishing at the horizon. He felt saddened to think that he wouldn't see his father again in this life. That he couldn't fulfill the old man's wish. And yet if God willed that he stay here, then so be it.

Halligan nodded, then pursed his lips sympathetically. Cheverus thought perhaps he shouldn't have brought that up, about his father passing on. It was foolish to broach the subject of death to a man this close to his own. Then again, perhaps not. Perhaps it was exactly what he needed to talk to him about.

After a while he asked, "Are you prepared, James?"

"Prepared?" he said. "Oh. You mean about tomorrow." He knitted his brows in thought, as if considering this possibility for the first time. "As much as I'll ever be, I guess. But the way I figure it, we all got to die sometime or other. And at least it won't come sneaking up on me, not like it does with most."

Cheverus nodded. He had to admit the man did look oddly calm, self-possessed. He wondered how any man, but especially a young, healthy man who had his whole life in front of him, an innocent man, one dying for a crime he didn't commit—how could such a man be so sanguine about his own end? And yet he had seen it before, countless times—a child passing from yellow fever, a woman dying in labor, a young man whose chest had been crushed in a factory accident. The resignation in their faces. More than resignation—a certain peacefulness of spirit, a look almost of joy in their fading eyes. The heart fully disposed to the notion of its own end. He had always wondered about that. Being a religious man, he shouldn't have, but he did. The calm acceptance of death by others amazed him, humbled and shamed him, too. He, on the other hand, in his one real brush with death, had fought it tooth and nail, something he should have welcomed with open arms.

"Some men make their peace with death," he said to the prisoner.

"Is that so, Father?" he said, his tone not so much mocking as it was of cool skepticism.

"Yes. Near death some speak about a light. A light in the darkness. To many it is very soothing."

"I don't reckon there'll be any light for me," he said. He paused for a moment, then asked, "Have you never had any doubts, Father?"

"Doubts?"

"You know, about there being something after. After we're dead and gone, I mean."

"No, not about that. About myself perhaps. About whether I am worthy or not. But not about whether there is life everlasting."

"Can I speak frankly, Father?"

"Yes. Please do."

"I mean no disrespect. But it all just seemed like, I dunno, a fairy story to me."

"What does?"

"All of it," Halligan said, waving his manacled hands in the air in front of him. "The virgin birth and the rising up from the dead. All those miracles. The whole business. It just seemed like a child's story."

Cheverus didn't know how to respond.

"I know Dom believes," Halligan went on, "and if it helps get him through tomorrow, then I say good for him. But it's not me."

"You don't need it? Faith in something," Cheverus asked.

The prisoner looked over at him. He frowned, trying to find the right words. "It's not that so much, Father. It's more just that, it wasn't in my heart."

"Do you fear dying?"

"I reckon I do. A little. I mean, what man doesn't?" His eyes took on a distant look. "It's not fear so much that I'm feeling, Father. The truth is, I was pretty mad there for a while. A fellow takes something from you, you're angry. It made my blood boil to think they were going to rob me of my life, and I'd not done a thing. Why, I wanted . . ." he said, pausing, his hand clenching into a fist. "To kill someone. Aye, I did. If they were going to hang me for killing somebody, then I ought to give them what they wanted."

Cheverus nodded. "And now?

"I'm still a bit angry. But what's the use of it?" He opened his fist and let his hand fall against his thigh. "It won't change anything, right?"

"Yes. You must try to let it go, James," he advised. "It will poison your heart."

" 'Tis easier said than done though." Cheverus noticed the man's gaze seemed to turn inward, become the sightless stare of a blind man. "Can I ask you something, Father?"

"Of course."

"What was your reason for coming here?"

Cheverus felt the man's eyes weighing heavily on him. "I thought I could be of some help to you and Dominic."

"No, I meant to America. Why did you leave France?"

"I didn't have much choice actually. The Jacobins passed a law that priests who wouldn't sign the loyalty oath to the new government must leave the country or face imprisonment."

"Not much of a choice that. I heard they gave you priests a pretty rough time over there."

"Yes, it was very bad. Many were killed or imprisoned. Some, like myself, went into exile."

"Back home, too, they killed a good many priests after the Uprising. Some didn't have so much as a trial. The British just took 'em out and hanged 'em from the nearest tree. Others they tortured to get information on the names of rebels."

"How terrible."

"Aye. Ever hear of a Father Roche?"

"Yes, I have."

"He fought against the British. He led troops into battle. Later he tried to surrender. When he rode into Wexford to give himself up, the bastards—begging your pardon, Father—pulled him from his horse and threw him in jail. General Lake, the Butcher of Wexford, as he was called, had him hanged. Some Catholics said Father Roche was wrong to do it. A priest taking up arms. Killing. But for my money, he was a good man. He died fighting for his people."

Halligan looked over at him. There was something almost of a challenge to his stare. Cheverus was reminded of his conversation with Máirtin Kelly about moral questions, the nature of hatred.

"I could not kill another," Cheverus replied. "But that's something only one's conscience can answer."

"You never were in war, Father," he said.

"No, you're right. I wasn't."

"It's not wrong that a man—be he a priest or not—defend what's his. Or when he's being treated like a dog." Halligan rubbed his beard, then swallowed hard. "I killed a few men meself in the fighting. I had nothing against them. But they were the enemy. They were trying to kill me. I don't think what I did was wrong. The only thing I'd have wished for was to die then, fighting for something. Instead of now. Like this." He glanced around the cell, as if looking for a space through which he still might crawl to freedom.

"I understand," Cheverus said.

"Do you, Father?"

"Yes, I think so."

"We'd heard French troops were supposed to join us before Vinegar Hill. By the time they showed up, it was all but over."

"You should have known better than to place your trust in a Frenchman," Cheverus said with a smile.

Halligan chuckled. He stood and went to the window. Though he couldn't see out, he gazed up at the light that trickled in.

"You never married, James?"

"Me? No," the man scoffed.

"May I ask why not?"

"I moved around a lot. Never stayed long enough to settle down. I'm not the marrying sort. Not like Dom."

"Was there no one you ever loved?"

Halligan shrugged. With his back to Cheverus he said, "I had my share of . . . well, of women. I know what the Church says on that, Father. That it's a sin and all. But it never seemed that way to me. They were lonely and I was lonely, and we offered each other a bit of comfort. That's how I looked on it."

Cheverus nodded without making a comment.

Halligan stared straight ahead at the wall for several seconds. Then he turned around and leaned back against the stones. "There was this one girl," he said after a while.

"Yes."

"Bridie her name was. The daughter of a wealthy man I worked for. A Protestant," he offered, shaking his head. "Can you fancy that? I should have known better, I suppose."

"We can't always understand the ways of the heart."

"That's the God's truth, all right. Though before this I always kept my heart in check."

"What happened? With this . . ."

"Bridie," he answered for him. "I came here."

"She didn't want to come with you?"

"Actually, she did," Halligan said, scratching his beard. "It's a long story, Father."

"I have all the time in the world, my son."

"The thing is I don't," Halligan said, with a smirk. He paused for a moment, then added, "I thought this wasn't going to be a confession."

"It's not. We're just talking. As one man to another."

Halligan seemed lost in thought for a moment. "It's just that I never told anybody about her before."

"If you would rather not . . ."

"No, that's not it," Halligan replied, lifting his manacled hands, palms up. Then he let them drop to his thighs. The metal clanged. After a while he said, "You see, Father, I'd got her with child."

"Oh," Cheverus said, unconsciously raising his eyebrows. "And you did not want to marry her?"

"No. I couldn't, you see. Even if I wanted to, how was a fellow like me going to marry a girl like that, Father? Someone from money. A Protestant."

"So you left her and came here?"

"Worse. I lied to her. I told her I would meet her and we would sail together for America, and we'd get married here." He shook his head. "But it was just a lie. Truth is, I was afraid. Of what would happen to me if they caught us. There wasn't much I could do, Father. Besides, she wouldn't have been happy with someone like me."

"How do you know?"

"I just do. It wouldn't have worked. A girl like that, used to certain things. What could I give her?"

"Did you ever hear from her?"

"No. She wouldn't have known where I'd gone. She didn't even know my real name. I'd lied to her about it when I first met her."

"You never wrote to her?"

"I thought of it. I did. But I didn't know what to say. What was done was done. And like I said, she was better off without me." He chewed on his cracked lower lip for a moment. "Funny though, right before we were arrested I thought of writing to her. Asking her to come over. But it was too late by then."

"So you don't know what happened to her? Or the child."

"No."

"Have you considered writing to her now?"

"Huh!" he said with a bitter laugh. "And just what would I tell her? Sorry, I made a mistake. And oh, by the way, I'm going to hang. I don't think so."

"She would always wonder what became of you. Don't you think she deserves to know the truth?"

"It would sound like I was asking for her pity. I wouldn't want her pity. And anyway, after what I did, she'd probably think I deserved what I got. No, I don't imagine she'd be none too happy to get a letter from me now."

"Do you love her still?"

Halligan angled his head away, toward the bars of his cell. Then he turned back to face Cheverus. He lifted his hands in the air again, held them slightly apart, as if he were holding an invisible but heavy object. He seemed to look at the thing, to turn it over in his hands. Then, whatever he'd had in mind to do with the object, he seemed to change it, and let his hands slowly drop to his lap. "I don't know. Maybe. What difference does it make now?"

"Perhaps she should know of your feelings."

Halligan laughed softly. "I know it was a terrible thing I did. I know that, Father. I tried to fool myself into thinking I had no choice. That what I did was the best for her, too. But at the same time, if I had it to do all over again, I don't know as I'd do any different. I'd probably run again. See, that's the sort of fellow I am, Father."

Cheverus was going to say something, but the man took a deck of cards from his pocket and asked, "Do you play, Father?"

FOURTEEN

Later that morning, Cheverus left the jail and set out to meet Finola Daley as he had promised. He had decided to put on his cassock and to wear his cross. He was a priest, and he would dress as one. He didn't care who knew it. He told himself his life was in God's hands.

The day was already warm, the air rippling. Ocher dust, kicked up from all the traffic, hung thick in the air. It parched the throats of those who had to breathe it. Wagons and carriages cluttered the streets, and crowds of people milled about, all with the air of excitement and anticipation associated with a county fair. Not one but two stages from Boston had just pulled up in front of Pomeroy's Tavern, and passengers were getting off, ladies wearing India mull turbans and parasols held against the heat, men in fine top hats and silk cravats. Along Main, shopkeepers had put their merchandise out on display, and vendors pushing carts hawked their wares. One man sold cider from a barrel while a woman called out, "Pork pies for sale." In the center of town where the bonfire had burned down to a charred black skeleton, a fiddler played music to a small crowd. The whole thing reminded Cheverus of the feast-day processions back in Mayenne.

He walked briskly, trying not to make eye contact. Still, various taunts were hurled at him as he strode through the town.

"Look!" cried a woman seated in an elegant chaise. "A priest." She said it with the startled tone a person would if she had just spotted a camel walking down the street.

A bearded man in the crowd yelled, "Go back where you came from, papist."

"We don't want your kind here," called another.

He kept his head down and continued up Main Street. Marching toward him was a company of militia. He didn't look to see if the red-haired man was among them. When he reached the meetinghouse at the top of the hill, he saw a man standing on the steps, calling out to passersby. The man was dressed in a blue waistcoat, with a red silk stock about his neck and a tall beaver hat. He removed the hat with a dramatic flourish, exposing a bald, sweaty pate. Curious, Cheverus paused to listen for a moment.

"Now for public sale," he yelled in a loud theatrical voice, "a poem about the murder of Marcus Lyon." Then he began to recite part of it:

Since murder was the dreadful plan
Their dearest friends must silent lie,
For by the law of God and man,
The man that sheds man's blood shall die.

"Only a penny," he said, waving a piece of paper at Cheverus. Cheverus turned and hurried on.

The last line, he knew, was taken from Genesis: *Whoso sheddeth man's blood, by man shall his blood be shed.* An eye for an eye. Vengeance. And yet, this wasn't vengeance, he thought. At least not for the murder of a man. It was simply the anger of a people against two outsiders.

He followed the same road he'd taken the previous night, though now in the searing light of day it looked altogether different. He had gotten beyond the town proper and found himself surrounded by rolling pastureland and newly planted fields. The dust was less noticeable here. Sheep and cattle grazed beyond a stone wall. In the distance, greenish-blue hills unfurled like waves. He bore to the right when he came to the fork in the road and continued on. He was sweating profusely in the oppressive heat. The back of his cassock was wet clean through. He paused to take out his handkerchief and dab his face. Once again he caught the stench of the slaughterhouse. Now in the daylight he could see a long, low wooden building of rough-hewn logs. It was set back from the road, with a pen at one end to hold animals. Smoke, carrying the foul odor of rendered fat, floated from a chimney. Occasionally there came the plaintive lowing and bawling of animals. To the west of the shambles, the land fell sharply away to a swampy area surrounded by cattails and sycamores and swamp maples.

As he approached the Clark farmhouse, he saw Finola sitting under a large oak tree out near the road, her bag on the ground beside her. She was occupied with Michael and didn't see him right away. He watched her for a moment. Her head was uncovered, her reddish-blond hair falling loosely about her shoulders. She was playing a game with the child, clapping his hands with hers. Each time the child squealed with laughter, she threw her head back and laughed as well. She looked young and carefree, the sadness gone from her face. He'd never seen her appear so gay and easy. He imagined her sitting under a tree with her husband, eating a picnic lunch, watching their child play, laughing, touching each other, him singing to her. Death a thing as remote, as alien as the moon. He almost didn't want to interrupt this moment, it was so pure, so innocent. He thought of his own mother, recalled her reading to him beneath a willow tree beside the Mayenne River. *Someday, Jean, you will perform a great deed in His service.* It had taken him three thousand miles and all these many years, but he thought he knew finally what it was God wanted from him: to comfort this woman and her child, to help those two men in jail. That was what He intended for him to do. Everything in his life as a priest, all his training, all his prayers, even that black day fourteen years ago—all of it seemed merely preparation for this.

"Father," she said when she finally spied him standing there. "I didn't see . . ." But she stopped in mid-sentence when she caught sight of his eye. "Goodness. What happened to you?" She stood and went over to him. She fussed over him the way a mother would a child.

"It's nothing really," he said. "I fell."

"Looks terrible, it does. You ought to have a surgeon look at it."

He reached out and stroked the child's face. "Good morning, Michael," he said. The baby stared at him warily, uncertain about this man dressed all in black. In this light, Cheverus saw the father in the child's face, detected Dominic in every lineament of his son.

"Did you see me husband, Father?" she asked eagerly.

"Yes."

"Did he make confession?"

"He did."

"How did he seem to you?"

"At peace. He has placed himself in God's hands."

Finola Daley nodded, her face turning solemn again. "Forgive me, Father, for what I said last night. About God."

"He understands."

"Still, I didn't mean it," she added. "I know it's not His doing."

Cheverus nodded.

"Would you care to pray?" he asked.

"Why, yes, Father. I would."

They knelt together in the shade of the oak and prayed. On the blanket, the baby made soft clucking noises with his tongue. In the distance Cheverus could hear the plaintive bellowing of a steer.

Halligan wondered why he'd told the priest what he had. About getting her pregnant and leaving her. He hadn't meant to. He'd never told another soul. Unlike Dom, he didn't believe a man had the power to forgive another man's sins. So why had he told him then?

The air in the jail was growing warm and stale. Outside, the day was dragging its woolly self toward noon. Cicadas made their sharp whirring sound as if to wake the dead. It was then that Dowd appeared before their cell. "You got a visitor," he stated.

Standing out in the corridor behind him was the familiar figure of Francis Blake.

"Why, Mr. Blake?" Daley exclaimed, excited but also a little apprehensive at his sudden appearance.

"Hello, Dominic," Blake said, as he entered the cell. "And you James." He shook each of their hands in turn.

They made room for him to sit on one of the bunks. Blake took a moment to catch his breath. "Unseasonable weather we're having," he said, offering up a foolish grin. He removed a handkerchief and wiped his face, which was flushed, streaked with sweat and grime from his long ride. He wore high boots and a velvet-trimmed riding coat that was frayed about the sleeves. He rubbed his hands together, as if they were cold, but Halligan saw it was just nervousness with what he'd come to tell them. Finally, he took out his silver flask and took a sip, and then passed it around. Each of them took a tentative draught and handed it back to Blake, who took another one, a long drink.

"I've just come from Boston, gentlemen," he began, picking his words carefully as if each one had a sharp edge that might cut his tongue. He filled his cheeks with air and breathed out slowly. "Our appeal has been denied."

The cell grew very still. Blake glanced from one to the other, confirming with his gaze what he had just said. His blue eyes were filled with a terrible sadness.

Only then did Halligan realize some part of him had still been hoping the appeal would save them, that something would still come between him and the gallows. With this, though, all hope vanished. A part of him seemed to drop away. It was like the feeling he'd had when he was a lad and would jump from the limb of a tree, plunging earthward, his stomach suddenly falling away, everything draining out of him. That's what he felt now, this wild sense of freedom, a feeling beyond fear and despair. Just this strange lightness, as if he'd left his body.

"Which means what?" Daley asked, stubbornly persisting in denying what should have been obvious now.

"Christ, Dom," Halligan snapped. "Means they're gonna top us tomorrow."

Daley looked vacantly at Blake for corroboration. The lawyer pinched his mouth and nodded. "I'm afraid he's right, Dominic."

Daley shook his head. "Jaysus." He swallowed dryly. "So that's that then."

Blake touched the big Irishman's shoulder. "Yes, I'm afraid so. I'm sorry, gentlemen."

"Don't you worry, Mr. Blake," Daley said. "You done all you could."

"I just wish I could have done more."

"*Och.* You done a right fine job. You got nothing to be ashamed of. Ain't that right, Jamy?"

"Yes, Mr. Blake. We'd like to thank you for all your help."

Blake nodded soberly, his fleshy mouth sagging at the corners.

"Is there anything I can do for you? Anything you need?"

"I don't think so, Mr. Blake," Halligan said.

"I am sorry," he said again. "Here," he offered, taking out his silver flask and handing it to them. "You may keep it."

"Why, thank you, Mr. Blake," Daley replied.

The lawyer called for the turnkey then. While he was waiting, he shook their hands and said, "God be with you, gentlemen." He headed out the door, then stopped in the corridor and turned, seemed about to say something else, but finally he decided against it and left without another word.

When he was gone, Daley said, "He was a good skin."

"That he was," replied Halligan.

Daley sat musing for a moment. "Tomorrow, I want you to read that letter we wrote, Jamy boy."

"Aye," he said indifferently.

"No, I mean it. When we're standing up there on the gallows, I want you to read it. I want everybody to hear we're innocent."

"I will."

Daley glanced over at him. "Jamy?"

"Yes?"

"I just want you to know something," he said. "I'm right proud to call you me friend."

"Same goes for me, Dom."

"There's not a lad anywhere I'd rather have with me when we climb those steps tomorrow."

"I suppose I should thank you for that," he said with a smirk.

Daley returned the smile. "Do ye think we'll do all right tomorrow?"

"We'll do just fine."

"Funny, but I niver reckoned I'd go like this," Daley explained.

"Nor I."

"How did you think you'd die?"

"I dunno. I guess I never really pictured it."

Daley rubbed his face. "I thought I'd be an old man dying in me bed with a bunch of old women keening around me. And the men smoking their pipes and drinking their whiskey and telling tales about me."

"They'll talk about us, all right."

"Aye. That they will."

Daley fell silent. After a while he started to sing softly.

On the banks of the Roses,
My love and I sat down,
And I took out my violin
To play my love a tune . . .

Halligan closed his eyes. The song came to him as if from very far away. So it was final now, he thought. Well, so be it. At least there was no more pretending or hoping. That was all behind him. Now it was just the waiting. He felt so tired suddenly. If he let himself, he could have fallen sound asleep. Yet what was the point in sleeping? Now, with so little time left? With Blake's news, something had happened to him. A change of heart. Maybe it was the stone-hard irrefutability of death. Or maybe it was his talk with the priest. He couldn't say exactly. He no longer wanted to make his mind go blank, no longer wanted to forget, to avoid even what was unpleasant or painful. He wanted to use whatever little time remained to him. To be aware of each hour, each minute, each second. To savor what was left to him—the beating of his heart, the thoughts that swirled in his brain, even the fear that grew in his belly. Even that was precious now.

He wondered what she was doing. Right then. At that very moment. Was she riding her white charger Tristan, galloping along the high green hills overlooking the ocean, the salt breeze in her face, her raven hair sweeping back behind her? Or was she with her child, playing with him, taking the lad for a walk. He tried to imagine too what the boy would look like. It was always a boy he pictured, whenever he pictured the child. His child. Near to four years old, he'd be. Dark hair and those serious eyes of Bridie's. A good-looking lad, he had to be. What would she have called him? Certainly not James. No, not that. He tried to imagine the boy doing something, moving about, laughing. What his voice would sound like. But he couldn't. He saw just a still image of him, like a small likeness in a locket. Just like that single image he had of his mother. In this one, a dark-haired lad was standing before the Big House, looking down the long stone drive as if waiting for something. He wondered, too, what she would tell their son when he was old enough to understand. What would she say to the boy about his father? Would she tell him anything at all? Would she make up some lie to protect him? To protect herself? Or would she tell him that his father was a man she had once made the mistake of loving a long time ago, a bad man, someone who had lied to her and left them? Or would she tell the child how much his father had loved his mother and would have loved him, too, had he the chance? After all, a child should know that his father loved him.

The lines of Daley's song echoed in his head.

On the banks of the Roses,
My love and I sat down

He thought of that place in the woods beside the stream where Bridie had led him once on that hot summer's day. The stunning cold of the water, the dappled light through the treetops. The touch and smell and taste of Bridie.

Remember this, she had said. *Remember us, Jamy.*
I will.

Daley stopped singing, glanced over at him. "You all right, Jamy boy?"

"What?" he replied. "Oh. Just thinking."

He could still feel the frigid water on his skin, the cool sweetness of Bridie's mouth on his.

Cheverus returned to the jailhouse with Finola and the child. Before letting them in, one of the guards, a small man with pale pinkish eyes and a pronounced stutter, searched Finola's bag. He even checked the blanket she had wrapped around the baby. The child woke at this and began to cry.

"It's all right, love," Finola said, cooing softly to him. "We're gonna see your da."

When the guard made as if to search Finola's person, Cheverus objected. "Is that really necessary?"

"She might be c-c-carrying a weapon, sir," the guard said.

"I'll vouch for her."

"I have my orders."

"The attorney general is a personal friend of mine," he lied. "You can be assured he shall hear of this."

The man considered this for a moment. Finally, he shook his head and exclaimed, "Very well then. B-b-but we'll keep a sharp eye on you."

Dowd led them into the empty cell. "You can wait here, ma'am," he said obligingly.

"Thank you," Finola replied.

"May we have a candle, Mr. Dowd?" Cheverus asked. "Yes, and a chair if you wouldn't mind."

"Certainly."

After putting on the manacles, the guards escorted Daley out of the prisoners' cell and down the corridor to where Cheverus and Daley's wife and son waited.

"Dominic!" Finola cried. She turned to Cheverus and asked if he'd hold the child, which he did. Then the woman threw her arms around her husband's neck and kissed him hard on the mouth, her body pressing into his, not embarrassed in the least to do so in front of a priest or the pair of guards that stood leering out in the corridor. Cheverus had forgotten the disparity in their sizes. Finola barely came to the middle of her husband's chest. It had seemed so long ago that he had last seen them together: probably for the baby's christening last fall. To hug her in return, Daley had to lift his manacled hands over her head. He did this carefully so as not to hit her with the heavy iron chains, and then, effortlessly, gently, as if he were handling a fragile ornament he feared breaking, he lifted her off the ground. They stood like that for several seconds, content just to hold each other. Cheverus, who stood cradling the child, watched them silently. The scene touched him deeply. In fact he was more moved by the sight of the two than he had been by anything in a long, long time. There was a rare sacredness about their union. The sort he felt when he broke the host and ate of it.

"I've so missed you, Dom," she said after a while.

Daley set her down. He sucked in his mouth and wagged his shaggy head from side to side.

"What's the matter, love?" she asked.

"You should not of come," he replied.

"Why?" she asked, searching his eyes.

"You just shouldn't of is all."

"But I thought you'd want me here."

He shook his head again. Cheverus saw that he was struggling to hold his emotions in check. His eyes were already moist, glassy, focused on some distant thing no one else there could hope to see. The flesh between his brows was pinched, his jaws clenched tight.

"I did. I mean, I do. I wanted to see you and Michael more than anything in the world. It's just . . . I didn't want you to see me like this."

"Dominic, please. It's all right."

"No. I wanted you to remember me as I was. Not . . ." He held his arms apart, as wide as the manacles would allow him, in a gesture of supplication. He looked down at himself, this forlorn expression on his long unshaven face. "Like this."

"I had to come," Finola pleaded. "I couldn't stay away. Besides, it's only right you saw your son."

He swallowed with difficulty and glanced down at the baby in Cheverus's arms.

"Mr. Blake come," he explained, meeting Finola's gaze.

"What did he say?" she asked eagerly.

"Our appeal . . ." but his voice broke, and everything he'd been trying so hard to hold in spilled out in great heaving sobs. "Ah, Lord," he cried. His knees buckled and Finola had to help him sit down on the bunk. She sat beside him and held his large head against her breast as his sobs convulsed his body.

"There, there," she comforted, rocking him. " 'Tis all right, love."

When he'd quieted down a little, he managed to say, "Would you look at me now. Cryin' like a wee babe."

"Musha, Dom. It's all right."

"I love you more than anything, Finola," he said.

"And I you."

"Promise me you won't come tomorrow. I don't want you there. I don't want you to see me like that."

She nodded resignedly. As she stroked his head, she gazed over at Cheverus and her son. *Help him*, he remembered her telling him the night before, which seemed now like ages ago. After a while Dominic's sobs ceased altogether, and he wiped his eyes on the back of his hand. He took a deep breath and gazed upon his son.

"He's gettin' so big, ain't he now, Father?" Daley said.

"Yes, he is. Here, Dominic," Cheverus said, handing the baby over to him. The child stared uncertainly at the bearded stranger and began to fuss, looking for the familiar face of his mother.

"Why lookit that. The little fellow's scared of me."

"It's all so strange to him," Finola explained.

Dominic rocked him against his chest. He sang softly to Michael and the child eventually quieted down.

"More and more he favors you," Daley said to his wife.

"No. Everyone says he's the spitting image of you."

"Do you think so?"

"Aye. He's got your chin."

"Begob. The poor lad," he said, glancing at Cheverus and smiling.

Cheverus smiled back. They spoke for a while, of Daley's mother, of how the trees were in bloom along Hanover Street in Boston, and how she was making a quilt for Michael's bed, that is, when he was big enough to sleep alone. They spoke of home, of Ireland, their voices full of longing and regret. Cheverus waited patiently. He thought how she had told him she might go back home after this was over. Back to where her other child was buried. They chatted pleasantly for some time, and then, as if suddenly the reason for their being there dawned on them, they both fell silent and looked over at him.

"Would you like to receive communion now?"

Daley looked at his wife. "Please, Father. We would."

From his trunk in the corner of the cell, he took out his surplice and drew it on over his cassock. Then he put the stole about his neck. Over the single chair in the cell, he draped a white altar cloth he had brought for the occasion. Next he lit two candles, poured water into a small bowl to wash his hands, and placed the pyx with the sacrament on the makeshift altar. Daley and Finola sat there watching him. The child in her arms began to squirm and whimper softly. She bounced him and cooed to him, but his crying escalated.

"I think he's hungry, Father," Finola offered apologetically.

"Go ahead and feed him," Cheverus said. "I shall wait."

While she nursed the child, Cheverus knelt before the sacrament and prayed. *O Heavenly Father, make me Thy instrument of deliverance.* After Finola had finished feeding him, Cheverus began the sacramental prayer.

"Kneel," he intoned.

They did.

"*In nomine Patris, et Filii, et Spiritus Sancti,*" he began, making the sign of the cross. As Cheverus repeated the familiar words he had uttered so many times before, they felt different in his mouth now, strange and new and thrilling, as if he'd never before said them, as if he'd never entered into the holy mystery before that moment. He felt a pressure building within him, something pure and consecrated well up in his breast, surge into his throat, and finally make itself felt behind his eyes. The pressure pushed out the corners of his eyes, and tears ran silently down his cheeks, falling onto his surplice. It was a sensation he used to have when celebrating the Mass, but which he hadn't felt in a very long time. A sanctified feeling, one of great humility and profound holiness. It wasn't as if he were simply uttering words, but doing nothing less than speaking to God Himself. The terrible silence that had surrounded and isolated him for so long seemed to vanish. He could almost feel the warm breath of God on his face, just as he once had. As he said "*Panem coelestem accipiam, et nomen Domini invocabo,*" he was reminded of the first Mass he had ever said, on that long-ago Christmas after his ordination, at the midnight service in the great cathedral in Mayenne. When he had said the words of the Mass then, looking up at the figure of Christ before him, he had felt the comforting spirit of his mother beside him, just as she had been when they would kneel together in prayer. Now as he said, "*Agnus*

Dei, qui tollis peccata mundi, miserere nobis," he did feel God's forgiveness wash over him like cool, clear water. He felt anointed, cleansed. Then he held the host before him and said, *"Corpus Domini nostri Jesu Christi custodiat animam meam in vitam aeternam. Amen."* He placed it on the tongue of Daley, and then he did the same for Finola, who couldn't fold her hands in prayer because she held the baby. Finally, he blessed them.

When he had done all this, they stood and, as if he had just performed the sacrament of marriage instead of offering them communion, they kissed one another gently on the lips. They too were crying, softly, silently. He felt the love between them, a thing powerful and sacred, something consecrated by God Himself. And what he felt now for Finola Daley was pure and chaste, as a brother loves a sister. Nothing more. He would watch over her and help her, and see to it that their son was educated and provided for. He would remain here to see that this was done. Yes, he would.

"Dominic," Cheverus said to him. "I wish I could tell you why this terrible thing has happened. But I cannot. God's ways are beyond our capacity to understand. Yet He loves you, my son. Of that I am certain. And I am equally certain that this time tomorrow you shall be sitting on the right hand of the Lord. So do not fear death. It is not the end."

"I know, Father," he said, wiping his eyes and glancing at his wife.

Cheverus then called to Dowd and asked if he would permit the couple some time alone together. The turnkey said they could have a few minutes. Cheverus left them and made his way to the other cell, where he found Halligan sitting with his back to the wall, crosslegged. He was playing a game of solitaire, the cards spread out on his bunk.

"Do you mind some company, James?" he asked.

"Please, Father. Come in," Halligan said. "Now you look like a priest."

Cheverus took a seat on the bunk opposite him. Halligan appeared different somehow. Something about his eyes. They looked lighter, a pale watery blue, the color having faded from them. His shoulders sagged, and there was about him the look of a man having just come to the end of a long and tiresome journey.

"How is Dom holding up?" Halligan asked.

"He received communion. I think he is prepared. And you?"

Halligan turned up a card, put it on another. "As much as I'll ever be."

"Is there anything I can do for you, James?"

He shook his head.

"Are you sure you don't wish to make confession?"

"Thank you, Father. But I don't think so."

He thought of pressing the issue. Of talking once more of Halligan's soul, of the grave danger it was in. He wanted very much to help this man, someone who appeared so lost, so utterly alone. He had seen men, wicked men, lifelong sinners, thieves and rapists and murderers, have sudden revelations just before they died. They wished to receive communion, to have their sins absolved. But then again, he had seen others die silently, remorselessly, their hearts hardened, still others go to their grave cursing God with their last breath.

"That woman," Cheverus said after a while. "The one you left back in Ireland."

Halligan looked up from his cards. "I'm not sure why I even told you about her, Father."

"Sometimes it is good to talk to another. Especially at a time like this."

"It doesn't change anything. What I did. What I left her to face alone."

"No, you are right. But then again, maybe by talking about it, it changes you," Cheverus said.

"How?"

"In here," he said, touching his chest. "Who you are."

"*Och*, Father," Halligan scoffed. "Like they say, talk is cheap."

"Not if it comes from the heart."

"I'm the same fellow I always was. Like I told you before, if I had it to do all over again, I'd have run off and left her just the same."

"Maybe. Maybe not."

"I would. Believe me, I would," he said with a forced laugh. "I'm not a good man. I'm the sort of fellow that looks after his own neck. Always was. Though I won't get my neck out of this one," he said with a snort.

"Perhaps you have changed."

"I doubt it," he replied.

"The approach of death changes some people, James. I have seen it many times. You loved her very much, didn't you?"

Halligan set the cards down and looked at his hands. He looked at them as if they were things he had never before seen. Then he glanced over at the priest. "Maybe." Then, musing on it for a moment, he conceded, "Yes, I suppose I did."

"Perhaps you ought to write to her and tell her that."

He shook his head, glancing toward the small window where a narrow patch of blue sky seeped in. "I told you, Father. It's too late. She's probably already made a new life for herself and hearing from me now would only cause her pain. No, it's no good," he said, shaking his head.

Cheverus rubbed the cross that hung from his neck.

"You said you had never told anyone about what you did. About abandoning the woman and your son."

The words had their effect on Halligan. He seemed almost to flinch, as if his sin had been made word suddenly, for the first time spoken out loud like this.

"No, I didn't," he replied.

"Not even Dominic?"

"No," he replied. "Not even him."

"Why, James?"

"Why? I dunno," he said. He pondered that for a moment. "No, that's not true. I do know. I was ashamed. 'Twas a cowardly thing, a terrible thing I'd done, and I didn't want anybody to know."

"And yet you told me."

Halligan took a gulp of air. "It didn't seem to matter anymore who knew about it. Not where I was going."

"Still, you wanted someone to know your secret. You didn't want to go to your eternal rest without telling another soul."

He looked over at Cheverus and a thin smile of capitulation crossed his lips. He nodded slowly. A glassy stillness settled over them. Outside the jail somewhere, a young boy's voice could be heard calling. Though the actual words could not be made out, the tone was playful, light, a child enjoying a summer's day.

"You had asked me why I left France," Cheverus said at last. "And I told you that it was because of the Revolution. That's true. But I didn't tell you everything." He paused for a moment. "Like you, I have lived with a secret. A terrible secret. Something I have been too ashamed to tell anyone."

Halligan looked at him, waiting.

"I denied God," he explained. "I denied Him to save my own miserable neck."

That's how Cheverus began. How he started to tell the prisoner what he had not told anyone, what he had kept in his heart for fourteen years: about that September Sunday at the Convent of the Carmes and what happened later in the alley. He found it difficult at first, a physical pain in his throat and mouth, each word having to be yanked out of him like a surgeon pulling a rotted tooth. Once he got going though, a certain momentum seemed to take over, carrying him forward. After a while, he could not have stopped himself even if he wanted to. He told Halligan everything. How the sunlight fell on the garden that day and how brightly the whitewashed walls shone. How sweet the air smelled. He wanted to make this man, this confessor of his, see and feel everything that day, just as if he had been there. He wanted him to know all of it. And then he told of how the mob suddenly appeared. How the terrible slaughter started, and how quickly it progressed, overwhelming him, flaring up like a wildfire, immolating him. How it had paralyzed him at first and then, when he'd come finally to his senses, how he had run for his life, run madly, like a crazed animal, with the singleminded will to live. And at last, when he was caught in that alley and questioned, how he had denied—not once, but like Peter, *three* times—his Lord, his faith, all those martyrs who had died back at the convent garden. Simply to save his own neck. He told all of this to the prisoner, who sat across from him quietly listening.

When he had finished, he was surprised by how quickly and effortlessly it had slipped out of him, the way a soul departed the body of a dying person. There one moment, gone the next. Yet he couldn't really say he felt better or worse for having told it. He didn't know how he felt, except perhaps that he sensed a certain loosening in the muscles of his shoulders, a subtle lifting of the weight he'd carried on his chest for so long. And he didn't know exactly why he had told it now, to this man, someone he didn't know, someone who didn't even believe in God's forgiveness. Someone who would be dead in less than a day's time and take his secret with him.

"So you see," he said at last, "I, too, have done something which has shamed me."

"The way I see it, Father, you had no choice," Halligan replied.

"Ah, but I did. I could have chosen to die. Many others did."

"And what purpose would that have served?"

Cheverus thought for a moment. "I would have died a martyr's death. Loyal to my faith and to my God."

"But then you couldn't have been here to help Dom," he said. Then with a hint of a smile, he added, "Or me."

"Have I?" he asked. "Helped you?"

"You've listened to me, Father. That's something. Like you said, it's good to get some things off your chest."

Cheverus looked over at him and nodded.

"And besides, now you believe we're innocent."

"Yes, I believe you," Cheverus replied, taking a deep breath. "Forgive me for placing this burden on you now."

"It's no burden, Father. I'm glad you thought enough of me to tell me." They both fell silent for a few seconds. "Want to play?" Halligan asked, holding up the cards.

"If you would like," he said.

"You wouldn't happen to have any money on you, would you, Father?"

"No," he said. "I don't gamble." Then he saw the man was only joking. He smiled sheepishly.

They passed the time talking and playing cards.

PART IV

O what sad, what awful sight!
To see the two on the scaffold stand,
And just about to take their flight,
To unknown worlds by law's command.
  Too much for human sight to see,
  Inflicted in an other case:
Was it for crimes of less degree,
I'd curse the hangman to his face.

—ANONYMOUS, "AN ELEGY COMPOSED ON THE OCCASION OF
THE EXECUTION OF DOMINIC DALEY AND JAMES HALLIGAN"

At 3 o'clock, sentence was executed by Major General Mattoon, sheriff of the county. Notwithstanding their protestations of innocence, in which they persisted to the last, it is believed that of the 15,000 supposed to be present, scarcely one had a doubt of their guilt. Daley and Halligan were natives of Ireland. Daley was about 34 years of age; he left a wife, a mother, and a son in Boston. Halligan was about 27 years of age; and we believe had no connections in this country.

—MASSACHUSETTS SPY
WORCESTER, JUNE, 1806

A day remarkable for the execution of Dominic Daley and James Halligan . . . The criminals who were executed this day, in their last words, denied the crime, and declar'd their innocence in the most solemn manner, and forgave everyone, as they hoped for pardon themselves—poor men, they must have been guilty.

—JOURNAL OF MRS. MARY SHEPHERD

[The condemned] appeared to be sensible of their awful situation and to be impressed with a proper sense of religion. A Clergyman of the Roman Catholic persuasion, the Rev. Mr. Cheverus of Boston, attended them to the place of execution, and offered every consolation which could be administered to men about to be launched into eternity. Daley and Halligan both affirmed in the most solemn manner to the last moment that they were innocent.

—REPUBLICAN SPY, JUNE 8, 1806

FIFTEEN

The day of the execution broke with a fierce, searing light flowing over Mount Holyoke. Mists above the river and the low bottomlands quickly scattered, leaving a bluish, drowsy haze suspended over everything. By eight, a listless warmth already hung in the air. The drone of cicadas sounded along Main Street, and turkey buzzards rode the air thermals high overhead. It would be one of those sweltering summer days that drove cattle and dogs for shade.

Despite the hour, an enormous crowd lined the route the condemned would walk. Northampton had never seen a gathering this large, not even back in the days of Jonathan Edwards's great revival. There hadn't been a hanging for many years, so people had come in early to get a good view of the two Irishmen as they passed from the jail to the meeting-house where they would hear a funeral sermon delivered by Reverend Williams. Young boys had taken up positions in the great elm trees that lined Pleasant and Main streets. They sat there waiting, eager, obstreperous as magpies. One small boy who couldn't find an empty limb had taken his grandfather's old spyglass and climbed atop the courthouse to get a better view.

A half mile west of town, people had also begun to gather on Pancake Plain, a flat area which surrounded a small knoll called Gallows Hill. Chairs had been assembled there for the town's dignitaries, as well as for those who'd come from far away. Most of the merchants had closed their shops for business to be able to watch the spectacle, though a clever few had set up stalls in the street to take advantage of the large crowds. Because of the heat, a man peddling ices did a brisk business, as did the Osborne sisters, whose millinery shop sold ladies' hats and parasols and fans. They also sold a good many handkerchiefs, for it was said that no lady of any real modesty could watch a hanging and not be made sick to her stomach by the sight of it.

One man, the blacksmith Wallace, continued to work as if it were any ordinary day. The fire in his forge blazed and sweat ran down his sooty face. His hammer blows could be heard reverberating up and down the street. Yet even he would occasionally push his way through the crowds in front of his shop in anticipation of catching sight of the prisoners as they passed by. People parted to let a burly man wielding a hammer through.

Halligan woke groggy-headed from a dream of soft green light and the salty smell of ocean. For a moment before his head cleared, he thought he was waking in a green field after a night of hard drinking. He almost expected the sound of the ocean and of gulls squawking and wheeling overhead. But then he saw the dark stone walls and the iron bars, and he knew. Yes, he knew. *Well, today's the day, boyo,* he said to himself, with neither dread nor excitement, with a feeling closer simply to curiosity. He sat up, wiped his eyes. Daley was already on his knees praying.

"Mornin', Jamy boy," he said.

Halligan nodded a greeting.

They were served a special breakfast. Dowd brought them salt mutton and ham, potatoes and corncake and buttermilk, and a pot of very hot tea.

"Eat hearty, lads," Dowd said, as he passed them the trenchers of food. "It'll likely be a long day for you," he added.

The guards stood watching behind him. Halligan heard a mocking laugh from one of them.

"Your big day, paddies," said a burly militiaman with deep-set, rust-colored eyes.

"Mind your tongue," Dowd warned the man.

"It's all right, Mr. Dowd," said Daley. "Let 'im talk. I don't mind."

"Are you scared?" the man continued, smiling. "Can you feel the noose around your neck?"

Dowd turned on the man savagely. "There's no call for that. Don't you have any respect?"

"For them?" he said, snorting. "When you get to hell, paddy, tell the devil who sent you."

"I'll save a place for you," Halligan offered, winking at Daley.

"Do you want me to tell the sheriff?" the turnkey threatened the man. "If you don't shut your mouth, I'll tell him."

The man stared at Halligan, but didn't say anything more.

"Is there anything else I can get you lads?" Dowd asked solicitously.

"I don't think so," Daley said.

"Some paper and ink, sir, if you don't mind," Halligan requested.

When he returned, Dowd said, "Here you be."

"Thank you, Mr. Dowd," Halligan said.

"You've been decent fellows. Good luck and God be with you."

"Thanks for everything you done, sir," Daley said.

The man nodded and left.

After they had eaten, the guards placed the manacles on them and led them out. As they passed the cell where the priest had stayed, they saw it was empty. Daley glanced at Halligan, frowning. They were escorted to the paddock out behind the jail where they were allowed to wash at the water trough. A company of militia surrounded them. They were given soap and even permitted a razor to shave their long scraggly beards. The priest must have seen to that, Halligan thought. Daley hummed as he shaved, an odd nervous rattle in his throat. His long white limbs hung thin and slack from disuse. Without his beard Daley looked funny, big jawed, with that sharp hatchet face of his. Halligan felt a little strange without his own. Lighter. Almost airy. But also somehow naked, as if a mask had been removed from his face.

"Where do you think he's off to?" Daley asked.

Halligan knew he meant the priest. "Dunno."

Well before dawn, Cheverus had awoken. In the fine-grained darkness he looked slowly about himself, momentarily confused. Where was he?

Had he awoken in his parents' house back in Mayenne, were the snores he heard those of his brother Louis? Or was it his narrow room at the seminary? He lay in bed for some time, letting his thoughts settle. The dream hovered close by, a fly buzzing near his ear. In his mind's eye, he recalled the smells and sights and sounds of it, things grown so familiar to him. And yet, something about this one had been different. This time the clerics were not praying quietly. They were not praying at all. In this dream, as he had walked about the garden, he saw them lying there, so still, their cassocks and robes covered with gore, their severed limbs scattered about like so many leaves, their martyrs' blood already turning black and drawing flies in the heat. In this dream, he heard a low moan as of one near death. He followed the noise and found one priest still alive. It was, he recognized even in the dream, his friend, Father Landry. He lay mortally wounded, the light in his eyes fading. Cheverus knelt and cradled the dying priest's bloody head. Landry looked up at him and whispered, "Bless me, Father, for I have sinned." Yet when Cheverus tried to say the words of absolution, nothing came out of his mouth.

He rose in the darkness and prayed: *Give me courage, O Lord. Help me this day to lead them to Your everlasting glory. Even the one who doesn't believe. He is most in need of my help.* Then he dressed and left the cell.

He wandered about the town, thinking, praying, meditating. The morning was cool and the air still sweet with night smells. Few were out and about yet. A young girl lugging two pails of milk suspended from a yoke over her slight shoulders headed toward Main Street. A man carrying a lantern and a fishing pole walked down toward the river. Somewhere a calf made a deep bawling sound and a dog barked from an alley. Cheverus thought of the dream again, of the holy martyrs lying dead in the garden. He thought of the fact that he had not fled this time, that he had stayed behind to help. But he also thought that he had not been able to give his dying friend absolution. Why, he wondered. Why couldn't he bless him?

He continued to walk up and down the streets of the small town. As his head cleared, he considered what he would say for a sermon this day. Finally he decided on the First Epistle of John: *Whosoever hateth his brother is a murderer, and ye know that no murderer hath eternal life abiding in him.* And then he thought of the next verse, which had nothing to do with hatred and murder, everything to do with love and loyalty: *Hereby perceive we the love of God, because he laid down his life for us: and we ought to lay down our lives for the brethren.* Yes, he thought: *to lay down our lives for our brothers.* He would speak of the bitter fruit of hatred. Of how it tore men apart and kept them from loving their brothers as God intended. But more importantly, he would speak of the nature of divine love. How He loved us all, saint and sinner alike.

Without the whiskers, Jamy boy, you're not half-bad lookin'," Daley said, with a lopsided smile. "And how's about me?"

"You're still as homely as a pig's arse," Halligan said.

Daley feigned anger. "I ought to crack yer head, I should." Instead he struck him playfully on the shoulder.

As Halligan scrubbed himself, he glanced up at the soft blue sky, the few clouds scudding brilliantly toward the river. The sun blazed a reddish gold color. He thought of that old ditty: *Red sky at night, sailor's delight; red sky in morning, sailors take warning.* The ridge of mountains was a lazy, greenish-blue line, the trees fully leafed out, solid, impenetrable. Below, by the river, the newly planted fields and pastures glistened still with dew. It was all so lovely, so luscious and full and ripe, that the breath was pulled from his lungs as if by an invisible hand. Wasn't that the way of it though, he thought. Wasn't that always the way, a fellow values only what he can no longer have? He could feel his heart beating, chugging fiercely away in his chest. He bent over the trough and dunked his head beneath the water. He held it there for a while. Things slowed down. It was quiet suddenly. The only noise the distant beat of his heart. The world and his fate seemed momentarily to fade away. He thought of that time in the yard of the Maguire place, while he stood at the water trough on that frigid winter's day, what seemed like a lifetime ago now. The cold, stinging water on his skin. He could remember looking up, seeing her there in the window, framed almost, like a painting of some highborn lady. *Bridie,* he whispered into the water, bubbles floating up around his face. *Bridie.* Did he love her even then, he wondered. Could a person fall in love just like that, with one look? And was love a thing enduring, lasting beyond sight and touch, beyond time? Beyond the grave even?

He felt something prod him in the small of the back. It was the hard butt of a musket. "Just wonderin' what you're doing," said one of the guards, a stocky man.

After a while they were taken back inside the jail. Daley picked up his rosary, and Halligan slipped the two pieces of paper into his shirt. They were then brought to the priest's cell, where he was now kneeling in prayer. He rose when he saw them. He was dressed in the white surplice and stole. Around his neck hung the large silver cross.

"Good morning," he said, his face pale except for the bruise below his eye. It was a deep purplish-black, like a birthmark. He seemed oddly calm and self-possessed, Halligan thought.

"Good morning, Father," Daley replied. "I was wonderin' where you went."

"Just out for some air. Good morning, James."

"And you, Father," offered Halligan.

The priest made the sign of the cross before Daley, and then he turned to Halligan. Cheverus didn't insist, it was more just a courtesy. For his part, Halligan didn't want to show him disrespect, not in front of the guards. So Halligan said, "Please, Father." What did it matter, after all? What did any of it matter anymore? Just some words.

Smiling benevolently, the priest blessed him as well. Then Cheverus knelt, and Daley followed suit. Halligan didn't have much choice but to do the same. He folded his hands. It felt odd, doing that. He hadn't prayed in a very long time. In Latin, the priest said an Our Father and a Hail Mary. Then, in English, he said, "Holy Mary, Mother of God, pray for us sinners, now and at the hour of our death." Daley, holding his rosary, joined in, and they said the prayer over and over again, until the words lost their individual meaning and were like the whirring of insects or the rushing sound of water down a mountain stream. They stayed like that for a long time, kneeling in prayer. Halligan remained silent, though he moved his lips. He was reminded of his days with the Franciscans, praying during matins. The sound of the other orphans, the smell of incense, Father Padraig's gruff voice. He recalled how, when he was just a boy, he used to say prayers for his mother's soul.

After a while he heard movement behind him in the corridor, and turned to see the tall sheriff standing there. "It is time," Mattoon said, his voice subdued, in it neither kindness nor cruelty, just the tone of duty.

They stood.

"Are you ready, my sons?" Cheverus asked them.

They both nodded.

The guards led them out into the street. Though a large crowd had turned out for the trial, it was nothing compared to this. Halligan was amazed by the number of people he saw. They lined each side of the street a dozen deep, all the way up to Main. As soon as someone spotted the pair coming out of the jail, this great roar went forth from the crowd, like a gigantic belly rumbling out of hunger. People stirred and jockeyed to get a better look. They stood on tiptoe and craned their necks. A number had thought to bring crates or milking stools to stand on.

"Jaysus," Daley exclaimed in an undertone. "Would ye look at 'em all, Jamy boy."

"Bloody vultures," Halligan cursed.

Sheriff Mattoon, accompanied by several aides in full parade uniform, sat on horseback near the front of the entourage. The sheriff rode his large roan, the animal bobbing its head and prancing sideways nervously, snuffling and whinnying. Beside him was the young blond captain, who kept turning in his saddle to look anxiously at something toward the rear. This group was followed by a detachment of regular military, the Second Massachusetts Light Artillery. In addition to some twenty soldiers there were a horse-drawn six-pounder and a limber containing a caisson of ammunition, the cannon more for show than anything else. Next came the militia guards who took up positions in double rows on either side of the prisoners, muskets shouldered with bayonets already fixed. Bringing up the rear was a wagon in which two men sat, neither dressed in military uniform. Father Cheverus got in line in front of the prisoners. He held his silver cross in the air before him as if today were a feast day and this merely a procession through town. As Halligan stood there in the heat, the sweat trickling down between his shoulder blades, he happened to glance back at the wagon. In the bed he noticed a pair of narrow boxes made of gleaming, fresh-cut wood. *Coffins.* What need had they for coffins, he wondered. Perhaps they were to be buried after all. Maybe the priest had worked that out, like with the razors. Not that it mattered so much to him. Dead was dead. Still, he supposed it would be better to lie quietly in the ground than have his bones scattered about.

The blond captain pulled out his gleaming saber and gave the order to move forward. As soon as they started, Halligan heard an odd rapping noise. A drumbeat, a low, somber rhythm, almost like the heartbeat of a sleeping man: *doont, doont, da-doont.* A single militiaman at the very front of the procession banged on a drum. The noise vibrated in the air, raising the hair on the back of Halligan's neck. He knew what it was. He'd heard it back home. The British loved to play it before they topped some Irishman: the Death March.

As the retinue moved up the street, Halligan noticed that the large crowd this morning was strangely subdued. The spectators spoke, if at all, in hushed whispers which rose collectively like a breath. No one called out insults or threats as had happened for the trial. No one threw anything or in any way tried to impede the progress of the procession. There was about the crowd a formal, even reverential quality. It might have been the lulling, funereal sounds of the drummer or the increased military presence. It might have been simply the strange sight of the priest, dressed in his surplice and stole, holding the cross in the air before him. Few had probably seen a priest before.

Halligan felt the heat on the crown of his head. He would like to have had a hat. The sweat gathered at his hairline and rolled down his face. Along the way he spotted a watering trough, and wished he could have a drink. He licked his dry lips and swallowed. When the procession reached the meetinghouse at the top of the hill, it came to a sudden halt. Cheverus went on ahead. For two or three minutes they just waited there, motionless, wilting in the heat. Then Halligan saw what the matter was. The tall minister, Solomon Williams, stood blocking the doorway of the church, Bible in hand. He was conversing with Sheriff Mattoon and Cheverus. The pink-faced preacher, dressed all in black, towered over the tiny priest. He spoke heatedly, his face turning a deeper red, gesticulating with his hands, then pointing at the two Irishmen. At first the crowd's low rumbling noise drowned them out, but then things slowly quieted so that he was able to hear the confrontation between the two men of God.

"I have prepared their funeral sermon," the pastor said sternly to Father Cheverus.

"With all due respect," the priest countered, "I have come here today by their express wishes."

"But this is my church. Do you understand?"

"This is God's church, sir," Cheverus replied calmly but forcefully. He turned to look at them, then back at Williams. "The will of the dying is sacred. They have desired to have no one but myself, and I alone shall speak."

The minister remained standing there for another moment or two, his dark brows furrowed, his pinkish face burning with outrage that he would be challenged so openly, in his own town, his own church, by, of all people, a papist. Finally, though, he must have realized the little priest was not about to back down, for he threw his hands in the air and stepped out of the way so that they could pass into the church.

As Cheverus stood in the pulpit of the Protestant meetinghouse, he felt more nervous than he had been even for his first Mass. It was an enormous crowd, larger than he had ever spoken to before. People stood in the aisles and along the back. They had taken out the windows so those assembled in the street could hear what he said. Faces pressed in at every opening. Well-dressed men of means had seats up toward the front, and women sat beside them in their finery, fanning themselves. Toward his right he spied Finola Daley. She was holding her child in her arms. Her face was blanched, colorless, her large eyes shiny and lustrous as mother-of-pearl. Up front, seated on a pair of low stools set apart from the rest of the congregation, were the two Irishmen. The sheriff had, and only at Cheverus's insistence, removed their manacles, but he stood close by. Heads lowered, the condemned looked like the pathetic outcasts they were.

Cheverus took a deep breath, trying to quiet his nerves. His hands trembled, his heart fluttered wildly in his chest. Finally he cleared his throat. The noisy din of the crowd slowly subsided, but he waited a moment or two until there was complete silence before beginning.

"Orators," he said, his voice thin and quavering at first, "are usually flattered by having a numerous audience. But I am ashamed of the one now before me!"

An outraged sigh rose from the crowd. Some of the men frowned indignantly, a few muttering contemptuously under their breaths, while others looked on perplexed, waiting. One man could be heard to say, "Get on with it, priest."

Cheverus again reminded himself of Father Matignon's warning that he be careful, that he not do anything that could provoke sentiment against the Church, but he would speak his heart. Let them be angry. He no longer cared. He would tell the truth this day.

"Are there men," he continued, "to whom the death of their fellow beings is a spectacle of pleasure, an object of curiosity?" Then, staring at one finely dressed older woman on his left, he said, "But especially you women. What has induced you to come to this place? Is it to experience the painful emotions which this scene ought to inspire in every feeling heart? No," he said with disdain. "It is to behold the prisoners' anguish. To look upon it with tearless, eager, and longing eyes. I blush for you. Your eyes are full of murder!" He continued in this vein. A few of the women gave the priest haughty, defiant looks, but many seemed embarrassed. "If the suffering of others affords you pleasure, and the death of a man is entertainment for your curiosity, then I can no longer believe in your virtue." He glanced out over the gathering, his searing gaze falling on first one woman and then another and another. Each one in turn lowered her eyes.

"You forget your sex," Cheverus went on. "You are a dishonor and reproach to it."

He paused then, allowing the weight of his words to settle over the crowd. There was a shuffling of feet, at first only a few, then a few more, then dozens of women stood and made their way out of the church, their heads lowered in shame. Soon almost all got up and left, leaving behind only a handful of women, too brave or frightened or stubborn to leave.

Cheverus continued his sermon. He quoted the passage from John. He spoke of hatred, that of man for his brother. How it was a form of murder, worse in fact than an actual murder. Why? Because it denied God's love. Because it killed what God had intended for children: to love one's brother.

Finally, after he had spoken for a long time, he looked down at the two Irishmen seated before him.

"We must love and not hate our brothers." Then making eye contact with Halligan, he added, "We must forgive in order to be forgiven. And we must have the courage to ask for forgiveness."

When the priest had finished his sermon, the sheriff stepped forward and placed the irons back on the prisoners and led them outside into the street. It was early afternoon now, and the heat sat over everything like a heavy yellow stone, oppressive, palpable. Halligan was more thirsty than ever. He recalled the Irish words for "I'm thirsty" that Brother Padraig had taught him: *Ta tart orm.*

"Dominic," a woman's voice called. It was Finola Daley. She was standing just outside of the church, the baby in her arms. She tried to press forward to see her husband, but the guards at first kept her back. With a nod from the sheriff, she was permitted to go to him.

"Oh, Dominic," she said, hugging him with one arm as she held the baby with the other.

"I told you not to come."

"I know. But I had to see you one more time, love. I had to."

He nodded, then bent and leaned his head on her shoulder. She rubbed his back as tears fell from her cheeks. So softly that only Halligan could hear it, he said, "I love you."

"And I love you," she replied.

Then he kissed his son on the top of the head. "Goodbye, Michael. You'll tell him the truth, won't you?"

"Yes, of course."

"Don't follow us where we're going. Promise me."

"I won't," she said. "I promise."

"Goodbye, love."

"Goodbye, dear."

A guard then took the woman by the elbow and led her away. The entourage reformed, the drummer in front, followed by Sheriff Mattoon and his aides on horseback, then the company of artillery, next the militia surrounding the priest and the two prisoners, and finally the wagon with two workmen.

They began the long, slow march to the place of execution. Along the route, spectators fell in behind them, joining the procession. Once, as the line had gained a little rise in the road, Halligan chanced to look back over his shoulder. He was surprised to see that the line stretched out nearly a half mile behind them, wavering and undulating in the shimmering heat like some giant serpent.

Along the way Cheverus prayed with Daley, their heads down. Halligan remained silent. He didn't look at the countless faces that gawked at them as they passed. He looked straight ahead, at the road and the backs of the soldiers in front of him. His heart was beating faster now, and he knew it was fear. Yes, he was afraid. But more than that he was curious. Curious about it all. About death, about what would happen to him. Despite all his protestations to the contrary, he couldn't really imagine himself ceasing to exist. In a few minutes he would know the secret, that which poets and priests and wise men had written so much about. Or perhaps he would know nothing at all. Perhaps he would just be a part of the great black stillness that waited for everyone. As he walked along he fingered the two pieces of paper he carried inside his shirt. In his mind he sang the words of the song Daley had sung the previous day: *On the banks of the Roses, My love and I sat down* . . .

And then as they came around a bend in the road, the procession stopped for some reason. They looked up to see what the matter was. That's when he saw it, the small hill in the middle of a low-lying field used as pasture land. On the top of the hill sat the gallows, newly built, its bright yellow wood glistening like the fat of a freshly butchered sheep. He heard Daley utter a small cry deep in his throat, and he saw his head sink down upon his breast, as if none of this had been real to him until that moment.

"Mother o' God," Daley cried. The color had drained from his face, and his knees suddenly trembled and almost gave way. He staggered backwards. Halligan reached out and laid a hand on his shoulder to steady him.

"Easy, Dom," Halligan offered. "It's all right."

Daley turned to him, his blue-gray eyes in a terrible panic. "I'm scared, James. I fear I'll piss me pants."

"No," he assured him. "You'll do fine. I'll be right with you."

"I'm afraid."

"I know," Halligan said. "I am as well. Think of your daughter, Dom. You'll be with her in a bit."

Daley looked at him. This thought seemed to calm him a little.

"Aye," he said after a while. "Little Eva."

They continued waiting there for several minutes. Halligan could feel the sweat pouring down his face, burning the newly shaved skin. He was so thirsty. A dog, a scrawny black thing with white along its belly and throat, came running through the crowd. It scrambled into the procession, darting between the soldiers' legs. Sniffing first this one and that, as if looking for its master or simply for a handout. Some in the crowd laughed nervously at the appearance of the animal, its presence seeming to relieve the tension of the moment. Finally it came up to the prisoners. It sniffed Daley, and then moved on to Halligan. Halligan squatted, extending his hand to show it meant him no harm. The dog warily watched his hand, cowering a little, as if he'd been beaten. "Hello, fellow," he said. At last the animal allowed him to pet it. Its hair was coarse and tangled and knotted with burrs. Beneath his coat, Halligan could feel the thing's muscles quivering, the sharpness of its bones. The dog pressed in closer, smelling Halligan, sniffing about his pockets. Then he glanced up at the man with a look of expectation. "Sorry," he told the animal. "I've nothing to give you." The dog remained standing there for a moment, waiting, then it turned and bolted off into the crowd.

About then a young girl approached the group. She wore a white bonnet and a blue shortgown over a skirt of homespun. In one hand she carried a wooden bucket.

"For the prisoners," she said to one of the guards.

They allowed her to give them a drink.

She went up to Daley and ladled out some water and he bent and took a long draught. He thanked her, and then she did the same for Halligan. As he drank, he looked at the girl. She was young, no more than sixteen. She had pretty blue eyes and blond hair under her bonnet.

"Thank you, ma'am," he said. "You've been very kind."

"You're welcome, sir," she said.

Soon they were in motion again. The soldiers marched them to the very top of the hill. Though it wasn't a large hill, Halligan found himself winded by the time he reached the top. A large crowd already encircled the gallows and flowed on down to the bottom. Some sat in chairs placed here for the occasion, others in the shade of trees. As Halligan looked over them he saw a familiar face. It was the woman he had seen in court, the one who'd spat upon him. Lyon's mother. She was dressed in the same black dress and bonnet she'd worn to the trial. She looked pale and tired, wilting in the heat. An old and broken woman who had hoped this would somehow make her feel better.

The guards then stepped back so that Cheverus could say a few final words to them. He made the sign of the cross one last time and said a pater noster.

"May God bless you," he said when he was through.

"Be sure to give me wife the letters, Father." Daley sighed.

"I will."

"Father," Halligan said. The priest leaned toward him, so he could smell the incense and tallow odor of his robes. He took out his own letter, the one he'd written that morning, and he pressed it into the priest's hand. It was addressed to a Bridie Maguire of Dingle, Ireland. "Would you see to it that gets posted?"

"Yes, of course," Cheverus said.

"You were right, Father. She deserves to know the truth."

"I will pray for you, James. For your soul."

"Thank you, Father," he replied, and he meant it, too, though not in the way the priest believed.

Halligan thought of the priest's story. How he had denied God to save his neck. Hell, who wouldn't have done the same, to remain here under the lovely sky and warm sun? Still, he was a decent sort, and Halligan couldn't help feeling sorry for the man. He thought being a priest had to be a hard and lonely life. Then the guards stepped forward and took them firmly by the arms. "Thanks for everything, Father," Halligan called to the priest. "You take care of yourself now." Their gazes lingered on each other for a moment, before Cheverus nodded and turned away.

They were led up the gallows, the sheriff in front, followed by several guards carrying lengths of rope and two white, cloth hoods, the sort falconers placed on their birds. Sheriff Mattoon began by reading a statement about their sentences. About the murder of Marcus Lyon, and how they were to be hanged by the neck until dead, and that their bodies were to be dissected and anatomized. So the coffins were just for show, Halligan thought. While the sheriff spoke, he had a chance to glance around. He saw the rope holding up the platform on which they stood, and nearby an ax, its blade newly honed and glistening in the sun. Then the sheriff asked if the prisoners had any last words. Halligan said they did.

He removed the piece of paper from his shirt. He had written it, though Daley had added things he wanted to say, especially about his faith, his belief in God and all that. But otherwise it was all true what they'd put down on paper. He stepped forward, stared out over the enormous crowd. The buzzing of the spectators lessened, and then it became as still as the church had been right before the priest began to speak. They all wanted to hear what he had to say, this Irish murderer. They were hoping, he could see, for a confession, for a last-minute disclosure of their crime. In his ears and in his mouth, he could feel his heart beating, rapping wildly. His gaze happened to light on Mrs. Lyon, who stared up at him with a savage bitterness still in her weary old eyes. But it had been diluted now, perhaps by the sight of the two on the gallows. As he read, he looked directly at her.

These are the last dying words of Dominic Daley and James Halligan.
At this awful moment of appearing before the tribunal of the Almighty,
and knowing that telling a falsehood would be eternal perdition to our

poor souls, we solemnly declare we are perfectly innocent of the crime for which we suffer, or of any other murder or robbery, and never saw, to our knowledge, Marcus Lyon in our lives. And unaccountable as it may appear, the boy never saw one of us looking at him, nor either of us leading, driving, or riding a horse, and we never went off the high road. We blame no one, we forgive every one. We submit to our fate as being the will of the Almighty, and beg of Him to be merciful to us, through the merits of His divine son, our blessed Savior, Jesus Christ. Our sincere thanks to the Reverend Jean Cheverus, for his kind attention to us during our long confinement.

Sincerely, Dominic Daley and James Halligan.

Halligan handed the piece of paper to the sheriff.

"Would you kindly see that they put that in the papers, sir," he said. "Just as we wrote it."

The sheriff said that he would. Halligan glanced down one last time at the priest, who stood off to the side of the gallows, his hands folded in prayer. Between them passed a knowing look, the sort that passes between those who share a secret. He gave Cheverus a little nod and the priest returned the same. The guards then removed the manacles but bound their arms and legs snugly with lengths of rope. Next they placed the white hoods over their heads. The last thing Halligan saw, the last thing he would see of this world, was a dark bird wheeling across the blue sky, swooping downward, its glistening wings backswept. Then he felt the noose being placed over the hood and tightened about his neck.

"Jamy boy?" Daley said, his voice dry, near to cracking.

"Aye."

"Goodbye."

"Goodbye, Dom."

"You been a good and true friend, Jamy."

"As have you."

"See you in heaven."

Halligan thought of replying but didn't know what to say. Then he heard Daley praying, the sounds muffled by the hood.

A few awkward seconds of silence stretched out, when the world and its affairs seemed to move off somewhere, to grow silent and still and very distant. His heart now was beating so hard he thought it would burst. *Easy*, he told himself. *Take it easy, boyo. You're almost there. It's almost over.* He heard the sound of a magpie squawking not far off, and someone in the great crowd clearing his throat. Then he heard a swift *whooshing* sound followed by the shuddering smack of an ax blade striking wood, and the next thing Halligan knew, the solidness, the firmness of the palpable world melted beneath his feet and he was falling. It was as if he had jumped over the steep cliffs of Slea Head and was dropping into the sea far below. His bowels fell out of him, his head swirled and sparkled with a tingly light. Things sped up suddenly, rushed across his consciousness. There was a clattering, a terrible jumbled noise in his skull, followed by a raging fire that erupted in his eyes and ears, then spread to his throat and lungs. He was suddenly so thirsty. So damn thirsty. More thirsty than he'd be working cutting wheat on the hottest day in August. Oh, what he'd give for a pint of ale!

Then just as suddenly, everything abruptly slowed. He found himself in that quiet, cool place in the woods. Bridie was standing there in the middle of the water. He was afraid to enter it at first, the shocking cold of it, but she was smiling at him so sweetly, holding out a hand, beckoning him in. *Come*, she seemed to be saying. *Come love.* Finally, he stepped into the water. Its frigid cold seemed almost to burn the soles of his feet, and he shuddered violently, his entire body quaking. But then as he got used to the cold, it felt good, refreshing, the bottom soft and slick beneath his bare feet. Bridie put her arms around his neck and kissed him. Her lips were also wet and cool, and her body felt soft and pliant against him. Her hair smelled of apples, sweet, ripe apples. He bunched the soft black fullness in his hands and inhaled its aroma. He buried his nose in it. He cried out, "Bridie." But the damnedest thing—no sound came from his throat. Not a peep. He tried again but still nothing.

Then he could no longer see her and everything faded first to dull gray, and then to tan, and finally to a dingy whitish-yellow, the color of old sailcloth. Then there was nothing. Nothing at all. Just a dark silence.

. . .

The two bodies swung in the afternoon heat for upwards of an hour. Some of the large crowd remained, staring at the two hooded figures hanging limp and still. A few boys stayed to watch the rest of it from their perch in a nearby ash tree, but most of the spectators had had enough. They turned away, sated and chastened, and walked slowly back to town, to work or to their families, to their lives. Cheverus noticed, however, the change in them. They moved quietly, solemnly, with the almost reverential comportment of those having just received the sacrament. The scene they'd just witnessed had humbled them in some way. He liked to think it had been the final profession of their innocence, right there on the gallows. The utter sincerity of it. But he was not so sure. Perhaps it was just the heat.

Finally, two guards approached and cut the dead men down. They fell leadenly, limply, like bags of wet wool, their limbs spilling awkwardly on the ground. Cheverus had waited nearby, praying silently. He went up to them and knelt. When the hoods were removed, he saw that their eyes were bloodshot and staring vacantly toward the sky. They were as empty as eggshells from which birds had already flown away. He closed them gently. From Daley's hand he had to pry the beads loose. Then, though they were already quite dead, he performed conditional extreme unction, first for Daley and then for Halligan. Touching their foreheads with the oil he'd taken from the pocket of his robe and then saying the words: *Ego te absolvo ab omnibus censuris et peccatis* . . .

The two men from the wagon approached the gallows, lugging the coffins. Cheverus, though, wouldn't move out of the way until he had finished his ministrations. They stood looking on, annoyed at the inconvenience. It was hot, and they wanted to get out of the sun. Finally, when he was done, they picked up the bodies and tossed them unceremoniously into the coffins. Then they bore the coffins over to the wagon, climbed in.

"Pardon me," Cheverus said to them. "What will happen now?"

One man, a thin, pock-faced fellow, glanced down at Cheverus. "Why, we'll take 'em to the slaughterhouse," he explained. "They'll be cut up and rendered."

"What of their remains?" he asked hesitantly.

"What's left we'll toss out for the dogs."

Then he slapped the horse with the reins and headed off.

Cheverus was thankful they hadn't seemed to suffer, that the whole business ended quickly. Though Daley had struggled for several seconds, his body jerking, his head twitching terribly. He was glad that Finola hadn't been there to witness it. He prayed then that God would take them into His loving bosom. Even Halligan. *Especially* Halligan. *He is so alone. Lord.* Cheverus pleaded. *And yet he believes. I know he does. In his heart, Lord, he believes.*

As he began the long walk back to town, where he would meet Finola and give her her husband's effects—the rosary beads and letters—he thought of that peculiar noise just before the end. One of them—he couldn't say which, though he thought it might have been Halligan— had called out just before he hit the bottom of the rope. At the last possible moment before his neck was broken. One word. Cheverus couldn't say what it was, or if it was anything intelligible at all. Perhaps just a grunt as the air was squeezed from his lungs. Still, he wondered if at the very edge of mortality, before crossing over, he had asked for God's mercy. Cheverus prayed that he had.

Epilogue

Father Matignon's tomb lay facing the small chapel's front door. The red brick of the recently completed Gothic-style building, the second church in the Boston diocese, shone brightly in the June sunlight. A handful of white sandstone markers lay scattered haphazardly about, gleaming as a baby's first teeth. Yet aside from the modest chapel and the abbé's tomb, and perhaps a half dozen other stones, the cemetery was still mostly vacant. After all, the parish had only purchased the land three years before, when the city's board of health had finally granted permission for "a group of Christians known as Roman Catholics" to establish a cemetery of their own. Father Matignon's remains had been removed from their temporary resting place in the Old Granary burial grounds and interred here. It was Cheverus who had said his funeral Mass. Many of the city's dignitaries had come to pay their last respects, including old John Adams and Charles Bulfinch, even Caleb Strong, who would himself die the next year. All of the nearly sixteen hundred Irish of the parish had come. The crowd was so large it had spilled out of Holy Cross and onto Franklin Street. Even those who had once openly scorned Catholics made an appearance. They could no longer afford to ignore their growing numbers.

The epitaph on the abbé's tomb was from Ecclesiastes: *Beloved of God and men, whose memory is in benediction.* Cheverus had selected it for his dear friend. He thought of their conversation so many years ago. How Father Matignon had told him that Boston had become his home, and that it was here he wished to be buried. And so it had come to pass. Cheverus found it hard to believe that his mentor and closest friend had been gone three years already. He had founded the mission, had cast his bread upon the waters, but he had not lived to see it come back to him: for Catholics to have their own cemetery, a second church, their first American-born priest, Virgil Barber, ordained in Holy Cross, for the state to grant "papists" the right to hold public office in Massachusetts. How surprised he would have been to see such changes. How surprised, indeed.

Cheverus came here as often as he was able. He especially liked paying a visit on Sunday afternoons. He would make the long walk from Franklin, crossing over the South Boston Bridge to this isolated region once known as Dorchester Neck. He looked forward to it, as one would to meeting an old acquaintance he'd not seen in a while. While he felt his friend's absence each day as a physical ache, he found it comforting to say the rosary or to offer up a prayer, or simply to sit quietly, the way they had so often in life. South Boston was removed from the bustle of the city, and the cemetery was quiet and peaceful, situated on a grassy hill overlooking the harbor. Near the chapel rose a large chestnut tree which spread its limbs for shade. The place reminded him a little of his mother's gravesite back in Mayenne, not so much in its physical appearance as in the quietude and solace it offered. He would kneel on the grass and tidy up about the large white tombstone, perhaps lay some wildflowers he had picked along the way. He would reflect on their early years together, sometimes even speaking out loud. "Do you remember my first day?" he might ask with a rueful smile. And he would think back to the first moment he'd set foot in America a quarter century before: his legs still shaky after three long months at sea, wondering where he would find his new superior, how he would fare in this strange land. Or the many hardships the two had had to endure, which nonetheless seemed to lessen in severity in the hazy light of memory. Mostly he preferred to recall their pleasant evenings in the parlor, their games of chess and cards, reading by the fire. The soothing effect the abbé's voice had upon him.

When his visit was at an end, he would say simply, "Goodbye, old friend." He would rise to his feet with difficulty, the rheumatism making his bones ache painfully. He was getting on in years himself, and he had gained weight, which showed in his heavy jowls and in the thickness of his waist. His gait had slowed, and though he still preferred to walk on most of his rounds about the city, it was without the spring in his step he'd once had. His hair had thinned and turned completely white, and his face had become lined with wrinkles, so that now, in his fifties, he had at last given up his boyish looks and taken on a venerable appearance, which matched his office—he was, after all, Bishop Cheverus now. His brown eyes had remained just as sharp and lucid as ever, yet the vague look of melancholy that had always darkened them had altered into something else, something deeper, more profound. There was about them now the hardened look of acceptance, an unflappable resignation toward whatever the future might hold.

Though it was almost the start of summer, he would not be making the trip north to visit the Indians. He had been spending less and less time at the mission, having too many other duties requiring his attention here; and quite frankly, the journey had become too much for his frail health. He let that duty fall to one of his several younger assistants, Father Ryan or Father Byrne. And since his appointment as Bishop, he had been slowly relinquishing much of the day-to-day running of the parish to his vicar-general, Father William Taylor. Cheverus thought Father Taylor, an Irish priest, quite capable. A man of impressive erudition and learning. He was also somewhat stubborn, even at times overbearing. He often disputed with Cheverus about church matters and policy, even about Catholic dogma, so that Cheverus found himself muttering under his breath when he had left him. When he thought about it, Father Taylor was not so very different from himself in his younger days. Perhaps a little more headstrong. Yet the bishop was willing to overlook that, so long as the Irish finally had one of their own to offer them the sacraments.

He had come early today to have a moment alone before he was to meet them. The afternoon was one of those balmy late spring days, warmish but not unpleasantly so, the sky clear and wide and so blue it almost hurt the eye to look directly upon it. A light wind washed softly in off the harbor, rippling the surface and bringing the smell of salt and of spices from the ships at anchor. He could see several small boats, their white sails unfurled, dipping and canting, the light shimmering off the water like scattered diamonds. Across the habor he could see Beacon Hill and the Capitol's dome. As he was looking out, a blur of brilliant red swept across his field of vision and alighted in one of the chestnut tree's lower boughs. A cardinal. Fascinated, Cheverus watched it sitting there for a moment, a red stain on the leafy green. His heart thrilled at its sudden appearance. If he had been someone prone to accepting omens, this would have been one, though he could not have said what it presaged. In a moment though, the bird took to flight again and was gone. He was pleased with how the cemetery and the chapel had turned out. It was really quite lovely, he thought. If left up to him, he would, when his own time came, be very content to rest here, next to his old friend. But he had ceased to hope for things concerning himself. If the years had taught him anything, it was this: his life was not his own to do with as he pleased.

He made his way slowly over to the edge of the cemetery, near a spreading yew. There he gazed down at the two stone markers, side by side. One was for Rose Daley. She had died back in 1806, hardly a month after her son. The priest had been with her at the end. He'd given her the last rites in that small room that smelled of death. She lay peacefully, as implacable as some great stone. Just before she expired, her eyes took on a wild, incandescent look. She stared up at him, but didn't seem to see him. "Father!" she cried frantically, almost blindly reaching out for him. "Father!" He told her it was all right, that he was right there. "D'ye think I'll be seeing me boys in heaven?" He patted her hand and said she would. Then she slowly loosened her grip and let herself go, as if dropping off to sleep. As with Father Matignon, her remains had been removed here.

Next to Rose's was a second stone. It had been placed there just recently. The grass around it was only now beginning to cover the raw wound in the earth. Cheverus himself had paid for the stone. There were those in the parish who didn't want it. Who objected to including it among law-abiding souls. Others spoke of trouble when the Protestants found out. But times had changed during the past decade and a half. It was still difficult for Irish Catholics but not quite as bad as it had been. Many of Boston's Irish had the vote, and they were slowly becoming a political force to be reckoned with. Besides, Cheverus was a bishop now and wielded more than a little influence, not only within the diocese but among many of the city's elite. The little bishop had insisted, and in the end he had won out. He read the simple inscription: "In Memory of Dominic Daley and James Halligan."

As he looked at the stone he couldn't help thinking back to those times. The months leading up to the trial, all the troubles surrounding it. The bitterness and hatred and fear it had caused for so many. He recalled those few days he had spent with the men before their deaths. Innocent men who had died for no reason other than the fact that they were Irish Catholics. And yet in the wake of their deaths, he liked to think he had noted a change even then, a lessening of the enmity in which Catholics were held. Perhaps it was due to the bravery with which the two had faced their end, or with their declaration of innocence there on the gallows. Who could not believe their sincerity? Or perhaps it was simply the fact that people had had their revenge, their fill of blood, and they were sated—at least for a time.

He thought of the one named Halligan. Even now he recalled that last look the man had given him, seconds before he plunged to his death. An expression so disconsolate, so forsaken. How alone in the world he had seemed then. How utterly and completely alone. Cheverus hoped he had been of some comfort to him in his final hours, but he could not say for certain. Every man comes to his death in his own way. Yet each day he prayed to the Virgin on behalf of the man's soul, and at night before he went to bed, he beseeched God to forgive the man's sins, whatever they were. He knew only God could see into a man's heart, only He could know what lay there.

He thought too of the letter Halligan had written to that woman back in Ireland. The letter Cheverus had posted when he returned to Boston. He had never heard from her, though of course there was no reason that he should. Still, from time to time he couldn't help wondering what the man had said to her. And if she had finally come to forgive him and understand that he had loved her. Or were there, as Halligan himself had told him, some things beyond forgiveness? Cheverus's entire life had been based on that not being true.

"Father," a voice said softly behind him, interrupting his reverie.

He turned to see the woman and the boy beside her.

"Hello, Finola," he said. "And you, Michael."

He hugged Finola, then shook the hand of her son, who towered over him now. Michael was a tall, rawboned youth of fifteen, six-foot or better, already with a light beard on his sharp chin. He had his father's long face and broad shoulders, his mother's doe-like eyes and full mouth. Yet he had grown into a handsome boy nonetheless. Finola had hardly changed at all. She was as thin as ever. Though her orange-blond hair now had more gray in it, and there were hard wrinkles about her mouth, when she smiled, as she did now on seeing the priest, she looked as she always had, like a timid country girl unsure of herself.

"Hope you haven't been waiting long, Father," she said.

"No, not at all. How have you been, Finola?"

"Good," she replied, glancing down at the newer headstone. Finola crossed herself, and the sight made her mouth go hard and furrrowed. " 'Tis a lovely stone. Thank you, Father."

He nodded.

She had not remarried, nor had she talked again of returning home. Like Cheverus, she had stayed on in America, though as with him it had never truly felt like home. She had raised her son alone. Michael had attended the school Cheverus had started and could read and write, though he had dropped out at thirteen to work in order to help make ends meet. He was a good boy to his mother, never gave her any trouble. Except, that is, for the occasional fight he was in over some remark a boy had made about his father. Cheverus had heard all this in the confessional. He advised the boy not to pay them any mind, that it was better to turn the other cheek. Michael listened, nodded soberly, but continued to fight just the same. Secretly Cheverus took a kind of fatherly pride in him for such spirit, such loyalty. The priest had kept his word to Dominic Daley. He had looked after Finola and her son, helping them as much as he could. He had taken Michael under his wing. From time to time,

Cheverus would slip him a nickel to buy an apple, or see to it that he had a new pair of shoes, or have his mother and him for dinner at the rectory. When the child asked whether it was true what they said about his da, Cheverus would tell him only God knew the truth. But what he did know was that his father had been a good man who loved his wife and son very much.

"A lovely day, is it not, Father?" Finola said.

He agreed that it was. They stood quietly, awkwardly in the gleaming sunlight for a moment, looking down at the stones. Finally, the three knelt on the grass, and Cheverus led them in prayer.

Author's Note

While this is a work of fiction, the actual incident upon which it is based is real, as are most of the main characters—Father Cheverus, Dominic Daley and James Halligan, Father Matignon, Governor Caleb Strong, James Sullivan, and Francis Blake. In the service of fiction, however, I have taken many liberties with real characters and events and chronologies. By all accounts, Father Cheverus was a remarkably literate, gregarious, courageous, and dedicated man, one who almost singlehandedly turned the scorn of New England Yankees toward Catholics into respect and toleration, so much so that when he finally returned to France in 1823, he was universally admired and missed by all, Protestant and Catholic alike. Yet historical fiction resides in the dark crevices between what is known, flourishing in the hidden recesses of the undocumented heart. It is a fact that Father Cheverus was there at the Convent of the Carmes on that bloody Sunday, the first day of the September Massacres, and what would become known generally to history as the beginning of the French Terror; it is also a fact that he, along with some forty other clergymen, did somehow manage to escape the slaughter by climbing over the convent walls and running into the Paris streets. What happened as he fled from the bloodthirsty mobs hunting all priests that day in the city, as well as what private lifelong effect this may have had on such a sensitive and gentle man, is, finally, only conjecture.

Many years after the hanging of Daley and Halligan on that warm June day in Northampton, Massachusetts, a rumor began that a man, on his deathbed, had confessed to the killing. Some said it was the uncle of the boy who had been the eyewitness, Laertes Fuller. As with Sacco and Venzetti, another pair of immigrants who were put on trial more than a century later, there is little doubt that the politics and prejudices of the time were played out in the courtroom of the Daley-Halligan murder trial. In the following year, 1807, Attorney General James Sullivan ran again for governor as the Republican candidate, this time defeating the Federalist Caleb Strong. Two years after his prosecution of the Irishmen, Sullivan would die in office. And though Strong would later win back his seat, the zenith of the Federalists had passed forever, and the Republican star was on the rise. Father Cheverus decided to remain in Boston, not returning to his beloved France for another seventeen years. Two years later, he was made the first Bishop of Boston, and upon his return to France, a cardinal. In 1818, his dear friend and mentor, Father Matignon, died and was buried in Boston. Nearly a century and a half later, the despised Irish Catholics would become a political force, not only in Masschusetts but nationally as well with the election of John F. Kennedy. Yet it was not until 1984 that the governor of Massachusetts, Michael Dukakis, finally pardoned Dominic Daley and James Halligan for the murder of Marcus Lyon. Part of the official pardon is presented below.

The Commonwealth of Massachusetts
By His Excellency
MICHAEL S. DUKAKIS
Governor
A PROCLAMATION

WHEREAS: Dominic Daley and James Halligan were executed by hanging following their arrest, trial, and conviction for the murder of Marcus Lyon in the Town of Northampton in June, 1806; and

WHEREAS: Dominic Daley and James Halligan were Irish Catholic Immigrants who lived in the Commonwealth of Massachusetts; and

WHEREAS: The historical record shows that religious prejudice and ethnic intolerance played a significant role in their arrests and trial which resulted in the denial of their right to due process and a miscarriage of justice; and

WHEREAS: Legal counsel for Daley and Halligan were appointed by the court only two days prior to the beginning of their trial and had no opportunity to prepare a defense, or visit the murder site; and

WHEREAS: Not a word of testimony was offered in defense of Daley and Halligan and they were helpless to defend themselves because at that time defendants were not permitted to testify in their own defense; and

WHEREAS: The trial and execution of Dominic Daley and James Halligan are reminders that we must constantly guard against the intrusion of fear and prejudice in all judicial and government decisions, and to resolve to not allow the rights of any racial, ethnic, or religious group to be denied or infringed as a result of such prejudices.

NOW, THEREFORE, I MICHAEL S. DUKAKIS, GOVERNOR
OF THE COMMONWEALTH OF MASSACHUSETTS,
DO HEREBY PROCLAIM MARCH 18TH, 1984 AS

DOMINIC DALEY AND JAMES HALLIGAN
MEMORIAL DAY

On a small hill overlooking the town of Northampton, at the site where the men were hanged, sits a simple monument to the two men.

I would like to acknowledge a number of sources that were of invaluable help to me in the writing of this book. Foremost were Annabelle M. Melville's wonderful biography *Jean Lefebvre de Cheverus* as well as André J. M. Hamon's *Life of Cardinal Cheverus*. Extremely useful for nineteenth-century Irish culture and politics were *The Conversations at Curlow Creek* by David Malouf, *Famine* by Liam O'Flaherty, *The Silent People* by Walter Macken, and *The Diary of an Irish Countryman* by Cín Lae Amhlaoibh (trans. by Tomás de Bhaldraithe). For information about Federalist Boston and early Massachusetts, I am indebted to *Bulfinch's Boston, 1787–1817* by Harold and James Kirker; *The Book of Boston: The Federal Period* by Marjorie Drake Ross; *Boston's Immigrants* by Oscar Handling; and *Coaching Roads of Old New England* by George Francis Marlowe. For information about the French Revolution I relied on *The King's Trial: The French Revolution vs. Louis XVI* by David Jordan. I am also grateful to Mr. Joseph Trainor for his translation of passages from Saint-Armand's book *Marie Antoinette and the Downfall of the Royalty*, and I have used his interesting hypothesis that it was the revolutionary, Anacharsis Clootz, who led the *sansculottes* in their attack on the Convent of the Carmes. For information on early French missionaries in America I relied heavily on *Black Robe* by Brian Moore and *The Jesuit Relations and Allied Documents*, from which I used a quote in Chapter nine. For early execution practices in America, I found *Rites of Execution: Capital Punishment and the Transformation of American Culture, 1776–1865* by Louis P. Masur and *Until You Are Dead: The Book of Executions in America* by Frederick Drimmer especially useful. And more generally I would like to acknowledge the following: *The Northampton Book* by Daniel Aaron, Harold Faulkner, et al; *History of Northampton, Massachusetts* by James R. Trumball; and *The Look of Paradise: A Pictorial History of Northampton, Massachusetts* by Jacqueline Van Voris. For the politics of the period I found the following of particular interest: *Life of Theodore Sedgwick, Federalist* by Richard E. Welch, Jr.; *Life of James Sullivan* by Thomas C. Amory; and *A Memoir of Caleb Strong* by Henry Cabot Lodge.

I would also like to thank the American Antiquarian Society, the Boston Athenaeum, the Dubois Library of the University of Massachusetts, Elizabeth Marzuoli of the Massachusetts State Archives, the Massachusetts Historical Society, the Connecticut Valley Historical Museum, as well as Historic Northampton for their gracious help with research. Of particular assistance for research on the trial itself, I would like to thank Blaise Bisaillon of Forbes Library of Northampton for providing me with a copy of the unsigned pamphlet called *Proceedings on the Trial of Dominic Daley and James Halligan*, from which I quoted quite liberally in chapters six and eight. I would also like to acknowledge several works upon which I relied for information about the trial: "The Hanging of Daley and Halligan" by Richard C. Garvey; "Who Murdered Marcus Lyon?" by Andrienne G. Clark; "Anti-Catholic Prejudice in Early New England: The Daley-Halligan Murder Trial" by James M. Camposeo; and "The Murder Trial of Halligan and Daley—Northampton, Massachusetts, 1806" by the Honorable Robert Sullivan, himself a former Massachusetts Supreme Court Justice.

I owe a large debt of gratitude to the folks of the Eastern Frontier Society for providing me with a cabin and with the peace and quiet of the Maine woods to write a large portion of the novel. I would be remiss if I didn't acknowledge my deep debt of gratitude to Fairfield University for the generous financial support they provided me. A special thanks goes out to the staff of Fairfield's DiMenna-Nyselius Library for their unwavering help in locating many books and articles, and for providing me with a quiet space to work. I would personally like to offer a big thanks to Jonathan Hodge and John Cayer, who were able to locate rare books and articles for me, and to Sharon Sparkman for being such a friendly face in the morning. I also want to thank several other individuals at Fairfield: foremost among them, Father Charles Allen, S.J., for his helpful suggestions about Catholic rites and practices; Dr. Marie-Agnes Sourrieau for translating passages of French for me; and Carleigh Brower, my assistant, for her keen editorial eye. I would, of course, like to acknowledge a deep debt of gratitude to my editor at St. Martin's, Diane Reverand, who has shown more confidence in my career that I can ever hope to repay. Finally, as always, I would like to thank my agents, Nat Sobel and Judith Weber, for their insightful editorial help, their unfailing support, and their ongoing friendship.